D1453038

LEGACY

of

WAR

ED MAROHN

ISBN: 978-1-54396-871-2 (print)
ISBN: 978-1-54396-872-9 (ebook)

*Would the young men called to arms laugh
and joke and exchange hearty platitudes
in imitation of popular fiction, while they
waited to be mutilated by the stupidity and
arrogance of aged politicians?*

– *The Summer of Katya* by Trevanian

VIETNAM, NEAR CAM RANH BAY, JULY 1970

I almost killed him!

"Stand down," I ordered. *The helicopter blades sliced through the thick humid air over war-weary Vietnam at three thousand feet; the trademark whopping sound of the Huey UH-1 oppressed my ear drums as I pulled my .45-caliber pistol from its black leather holster. Its safety off, I pointed it at CIA Agent Todd Ramsey. He hesitated, alarming me. Seconds passed. Then, with dejection, he released his hold on the POW, dropping the North Vietnamese Army (NVA) lieutenant onto the Huey's vibrating floor. The POW slid himself over to his fellow countryman, a full NVA colonel. Both POWs stared at me, but the colonel's eyes acted as if he recognized me. His lips mouthed something I didn't understand.*

Unnerved, I returned my focus to the CIA agent who uttered an obscenity. The noise of the helicopter drowned out whatever he said. At that moment, the Huey UH-1 descended to fly nap-of-the-earth, trying to avoid being targeted by NVA machine guns in the thick jungle below. Ramsey stepped back from the open door through which he had attempted to toss the POW and sat back on his bench seat across from me, his supplicating hands free of any weapons, his .30-caliber carbine rifle at his feet. His distress seemed genuine, but I couldn't be certain.

He raised his head toward me, wearing a depressed look. "You fucked me over, Captain."

I felt the hairs on the back of my neck rise—I should have sensed hate, but instead I recognized his fear.

The Huey continued its flight to our destination, Cam Ranh Air Base. Vibrating, the helicopter agitated my thoughts. I hadn't expected my last two days in Nam to embroil me in saving two unarmed POWs as I headed to catch the freedom bird to the US tomorrow. After more than 365 days, my tour in the war had ended.

Suddenly, tracer rounds streaked toward our Huey. The pilot banked the helicopter sharply to the left, taking evasive action. The rounds flew by us. A foreboding came over me: being shot down, killed, on my last two days in-country. The common fear all short-timers had.

As the pilot straightened the Huey's flight path again, his voice came over my headset: "Are we OK back there?"

"Roger," I said as I glanced at Ramsey and then the South Vietnamese Army (ARVN) officer seated next to him. The ARVN officer's fearful eyes vacillated, unlike Ramsey, who had withdrawn into another place, ignoring the pilot's violent evasive action. The ARVN officer's face looked like a rat's. Then I recognized him: Colonel Loan!

Loan, the head of the Saigon Police, became my nemesis when I met him in Saigon some eleven months ago. He showed no recognition of me now in my dirty, sweat-and-blood-stained fatigues—I had just stood down my company after a month of combat with the NVA near the A Shau Valley. Loan was internationally famous during the Viet Cong's Tet Offensive in 1968, because a reporter photographed him shooting an unarmed Viet Cong on the streets of Saigon. The photo made worldwide headlines. This reprehensible killing by a pistol shot at point-blank range to the prisoner's head received no inquiry from the corrupt South Vietnamese government, and once again justice had been perverted.

And now I shared a helicopter with this immoral ARVN officer.

I turned toward the deflated CIA agent as I yelled over the din in the helicopter, "I'm following the Geneva Convention."

He gave me a worried look before he turned away. I couldn't tell if Ramsey's sweat-stained jungle fatigues were the result of the hot humid heat or his nervousness. Probably both. But I thought I could smell his fear. He looked down at his feet while perspiration formed tiny rivulets on his cheeks.

I relaxed my hold on my drawn .45-caliber pistol.

The two NVA POWs, hands still bound behind their backs, now sat upright on the floor of the copter, with the colonel still studying me. Why?

Suddenly the Huey's skids smashed into the top branches of a banyan tree. The helicopter hovered and swayed in place, caught in the tree limbs. And just as abruptly, the tree catapulted the Huey forward. My stomach churned and bile crept into my mouth. We stared at each other, ashen-faced. No one wanted to die today.

"Sorry, Captain. We're good now. Raising our altitude," the pilot spoke through my headset.

I acknowledged him as I noticed the broken tree branch and its leaves clinging to the skid on my right side. Moments later it fluttered away, disappearing toward the ground.

Keeping an eye on the CIA agent and the ARVN colonel, I spoke to the door gunner on my left, "Listen up."

The buck sergeant turned toward me. He looked nauseous.

"Until we land, you'll assist me in securing these two POWs. Understood?"

The gunner nodded, swallowing several times, and unholstered his .45-caliber pistol. He looked toward the CIA agent and the ARVN colonel, their backs to the wall that separated the pilots in their cockpit.

Again, the pilot's voice came over my headset, "Captain, we're descending into Cam Ranh. I've alerted the MPs." I had kept my mic open for him to monitor the goings-on.

"Roger that," I said.

When we touched down, the army MPs were waiting. They escorted the two NVA officers to a jeep. A CIA agent in clean, dark green jungle fatigues met Ramsey and Loan and guided them to another jeep. As the NVA colonel clambered into the MP jeep, he stared hard at Ramsey's disappearing back. His eyes projected hatred that went beyond today's event. I remember my last observation of Ramsey. He looked frightened, so much so that I shuddered slightly. I knew it wasn't fear of me, since my pistol had been holstered. What then? Had it to do with the NVA colonel? This damn Vietnam War, its dark and murderous jungles had penetrated to the depths of all our souls. Ramsey's fear seemed cancerous, infectious. His look of dread as he drove away forced unexplainable concern on me.

CHARLOTTE, NORTH CAROLINA, THURSDAY, DECEMBER 12, 2002

"John . . . finished for the day?" a voice asked.

Jerked from my reverie, I swiveled my chair from the large office window to face my associate, Dr. Sally Catton, standing in the open office doorway. I hadn't heard the door open.

"Sally! I'm sorry. Some recurring thoughts of the Vietnam War."

"Are you OK?" she asked.

I nodded, tired from my flashbacks of Ramsey. "I think I'll call it a day and come in early tomorrow," I said, seeing the time. The clock pointed to almost seven.

"Good. We have a full schedule, unusual for a Friday," she said, scowling at me. Sally functioned as my barometer for honesty. The slight scar on her chin, a result of an abusive husband she divorced years ago, flared. It showed as her badge for toughness, driving her to get her PhD in psychology, with a specialty in marriage conflict counseling. Besides being a great associate, she became my friend. "And you have that VA referral, the Vietnam War PTSD patient, for a session late tomorrow."

"Yes, at four o'clock?"

She nodded, then said, "I think you need to refer that patient. You shouldn't be dealing with possible triggers to your own nightmares of the war."

"I'll be OK, Sally. Really."

She shook her head, turned, and closed the door behind her. My mind retained the image of her petite five-foot-four body, a knee-length black wool skirt accenting her toned legs, and her long blonde hair cascading onto her shoulders.

Her blue eyes, intriguing even behind her wire-frame glasses, seemed to affect me more and more. Since my wife died three years ago, I had not been with any woman. Certainly, my loneliness impacted me, and Sally was an attractive forty-five-year-old. Still, she worked with me, having earned her PhD years after me at my alma mater, the University of North Carolina. An office romance wouldn't be correct, but why was I even thinking that way?

I stared at the closed office door and reflected on how we were both damaged. Despite our demons, we strived to do good for others. Her destroyed and violent marriage molded her feelings and moods, as my depression from the death of my wife, compounded by my war nightmares about the deaths of the men I commanded in Nam, controlled me.

My name is John Moore. I'm a psychologist, and even though I strive to help people with mental issues, I have avoided dealing with military vets—until now. Recently I have started reflecting back on the Vietnam War, some thirty years ago. War events keep popping into my head. I thought I had forgotten the killing fields and their ugliness. I served in that war as a US Army captain, an infantry company commander, fighting and killing the VC and NVA in the deadly jungles while leading my 110 soldiers. I wanted to ensure that, after completion of their tour, my troops returned safely to the States, affectionately known as "the World." But I didn't succeed. Some died. And I reflect often on the deaths of those young draftees, fighting by my side as AK-47 bullets whizzed over and into us, and as mortar shells exploded in our ranks.

I entered the US Army as a second lieutenant, commissioned through the ROTC program upon graduation from college. Gung ho, dedicated, and idealistic, I had the intention of making the military my career. I believed I had found a noble profession—sworn to uphold the Constitution and defend the US from all enemies, foreign or domestic. But after my tour in Vietnam and the completion of my ten years owed to Uncle Sam, I could no longer stomach the ineptness and the politics of the colonels and generals running the army, merely ticket-punching their careers on the backs of soldiers who died needlessly. Command and leadership became buzzwords, meaningless tripe that sounded good. Young company grade officers like me lived and died with our men on the ancient soil of Nam, under the jungle canopies. Men died for each other. Not for god or the flag or patriotism, but for fellow comrades in arms. No other reality existed.

Stifling my war depression for the moment, I tidied my desk and stood. My mind still clung to war memories as I exited the office building at 7:30 p.m., unusually late for me on a Thursday evening. I walked to my condo a few blocks away on North Tryon Street. My wife's death deepened my sadness; we were married for thirty-one years, after meeting in college and becoming sweethearts. After Katy died from cancer, I moved to a ten-story condo building in uptown Charlotte from our fifteen-year-old suburban house in Providence Hills. I hoped the constant urban noise, the city's vibrant hustle and bustle, and its game days at the Panthers' stadium and the Charlotte Bobcats' arena, would help me forget her death.

After three years of solitary confinement in my condo's rooms void of love and companionship, I still grappled with my anguish. My daily movements created echoes against the condo's walls, like a bat living in an empty cave, reflecting my self-pity, my loneliness.

Unlocking the door to my third-floor condo, I switched on the lights and stared at the functional two-bedroom apartment, bland with its beige walls and white baseboards. I cared little about decorating the place. No reason existed to do otherwise. A large Jacuzzi in the master bathroom alone stood out in the unexciting apartment. Basically, I relied on this place for sleeping, eating, and bathing. Only my clothes, books, PC, and a few other basic personal items moved with me to this furnished, modern condo. Even the kitchen came with dishes, utensils, pots, and pans.

My bedroom continued the starkness—no wall decorations, little personalization other than Katy's picture on the night table. She smiled at me from her framed photo, beaming and happy. Katy represented another life. Another time that was gone forever.

Work became everything, and I spent over sixty hours a week there. My career became my religion, my philosophy, and my sanity.

Not hungry, I prepared for bed.

$$\infty$$

I looked at Katy. She was cuddled next to me in bed. We had just finished making love, and she looked at me while I stroked her back as she leaned over me. We were whispering silly things, intimate talk between two people who loved each other. It dawned on me that Katy was alive after all. I had been dreaming this terrible nightmare of her death for years. We were still together. I was so happy that all of that was a bad dream and began touching her long black hair strewn over my bare chest, looking into her black eyes! Why weren't they green? Katy had green eyes and her hair should be blond!

I jolted awake; my sleep shirt wet. What did this dream mean? I looked at the radio alarm clock and saw it was five in the morning: I decided to get up and get ready for work. *Why all these crazy dreams?*

CHARLOTTE, FRIDAY, DECEMBER 13, 2002

"We murdered them . . ." Tom Reed said.

My hand froze; the pencil became deadweight as my notepad sagged onto my lap. I leaned toward my first Vietnam War client.

The vet's remarks had kick-started my own kaleidoscope of reflections of the war where fifty-eight thousand Americans died—some that I had commanded as a twenty-four-year-old army captain. The brutal firefights with the tough NVA were faded recollections, as were the names of those who died fighting beside me, permanently engraved on the black granite surface of the Vietnam War Memorial in DC. Nam still lived within me, like those jungle parasites that had invaded my body back then. Eventually the parasites had left, but the painful war memories had not.

"I . . ." Reed started again. "Look, Dr. Moore . . ."

Sweat formed on his forehead, and his right leg twitched. His lanky, six-foot frame sagged in the black leather club chair. A balding head bowed toward me. Seconds ticked before he slowly raised his head. His face, heavily lined from years of excessive drinking and drugs, formed the backdrop for his bloodshot eyes that searched the room, confused.

The silence continued as the small desk clock controlled the therapy session. A pungent odor permeated the office as Reed's deodorant continued to lose its battle; his underarm stains grew.

I served in the Vietnam War from 1969 to 1970 and now years later that war still haunted me. From his VA file, I knew Reed had served in Nam as an eighteen-year-old draftee—a teenager.

"I shot those villagers . . . their faces, their screams . . . but I was ordered." He shuddered.

The hum of rush hour traffic filtered in from the streets below, vehicles moving people on a Friday afternoon. The clock continued, pushing the minutes.

"I wake up sweating from these nightmares."

"It was war. But to kill civilians . . ." I said and tried not to shake my head over what were probably war crimes.

"We were told they were VC villagers," he blurted.

"How many did you kill?" I asked, thinking of the My Lai Massacre by an American infantry platoon and its cover up in 1968.

Tom Reed paused and rubbed his tearing eyes. He stared back hard.

I looked down at my notes: *December 13, 2002: First Session / Tom Reed, Vietnam Vet, PTSD, VA Referral: Depression: No suicidal behavior currently observed.* I jotted the newest input from Reed: *Killed innocent villagers!!* The pencil stopped.

Then Reed looked toward the large plate-glass window in my seventh-floor office in the Duke Building. The December day slowly turned to dusk, its darkness encroaching the lit desk lamp, forming shadows in the room.

He shook his head. "Maybe a hundred? I guess . . ."

"Who were the others?" I asked.

"The CIA agent who ordered me and a South Vietnamese colonel," Reed said. He once again rubbed his moist eyes. "They participated. We even killed the few South Vietnamese Army troops assigned."

Confused, I asked, "Why the ARVN troops?"

"To cover up what we did! I was assigned to temporary duty to the CIA and the Phoenix Program," he said, searching for his own rationality.

My body tightened. *The Phoenix Program!* My mind buzzed.

"This memory of the massacre . . . a probable cause of your recent nightmares?" I asked, trying to ignore my thoughts of the old CIA program.

"But why after over thirty years?" Reed asked.

"It's repression. The subconscious can bury traumatic experiences."

"God . . . PTSD . . ." His eyes dilated. "I shouldn't give a shit about this. They are part of the fucked-up war. Fucking slant eyes."

The racial hostility startled me, but I pressed, "To deal with the death of any human being in war is difficult. Soldiers dehumanized the Vietnamese, called them gooks—a coping mechanism during combat. We can work through this, but you did kill civilians."

His detached gaze seemed to close the topic. His bigotry and hatred remained. There could be more to his story, but I hesitated to dig deeper since his own mood had darkened. He seemed unready to continue.

"Do you feel remorse?" I asked, wanting him to accept responsibility for his actions.

He ignored the question and said, "After Nam, I drank, did drugs. My wife left me and took our baby daughter. Did jail time. My normal nightmares come and go—seeing the body bags, dead GIs. But this nightmare of the villagers . . . started about a month ago." His eyes seemed lifeless.

"What triggered these new nightmares?" I tried to work around his stonewalling.

"I . . ." He looked past me again and stopped talking.

"What you did violated the Geneva Convention," I said, deciding to bring sanity to the discussion. "The horrors of combat are real, but . . . we need to face our issues honestly to resolve them."

Reed turned toward me again and seemed to grasp what was said. He shifted in his chair. "How long does PTSD last?"

"It usually never leaves. Time and counseling help reduce the pain though. We just need to manage it."

Shaking his head, tears appearing, he reached for the tissue box on the small end table, pulled out a tissue, tore it. He glared at the tissue scraps in his hand and then violently wadded the paper into a ball and tossed it into the small wastebasket next to him.

I felt drained but repeated: "Tom, do you feel any remorse over killing the villagers?"

Reed sat there in silence, not answering, struggling. His post-traumatic stress disorder was real. This anxiety disorder based on events in combat had messed up his life. Combat is living with death, and the fear of dying and seeing brutal death is a growing cancer. Sadly for Reed, his past thirty years had been spent dealing with his key PTSD symptoms with heavy alcohol and drug use, destroying his marriage.

No answer came from him. I tried another path: "What caused you to think about these killings? Understanding that can help?" I waited, hoping the silence would crumble his defenses.

A couple of minutes passed and then he said, "I was at the Salisbury VA hospital last month for evaluation of Agent Orange poisoning. I saw him there, but I couldn't place him until I got home."

He stopped to take a deep breath, and it seemed as if he was mulling something over.

"Later at home I remembered. It was Todd Ramsey, the CIA agent who had ordered me to shoot the villagers."

He paused as he noticed my shocked look. But I nodded for him to continue, forcing myself from thoughts and emotions about Ramsey. He continued to talk while I tried to focus. My chest tightened.

"Anyway, when I called the VA over my new nightmares, they referred me to you. They were swamped this month."

I took a deep breath and said, "Tom, I read through your VA files. There was nothing in there about this event. Now I understand why you are struggling."

"Yeah, it just started . . ." he interrupted, and then paused.

Unknown to him as he talked, I was trying to suppress my flashbacks of the war—of the UH-1 Huey helicopter over the jungles of Vietnam in 1970, where I confronted CIA Agent Ramsey over attempting to kill two NVA POWs. Slowly, I pushed the memory aside and returned to Reed.

"Let's summarize. The Ramsey encounter triggered the new nightmares. Now you're experiencing more anxiety. Is that accurate?" I asked.

He sat back and wrapped his arms around himself, defensively shutting out the world. He seemed confused.

"Aw . . ." he murmured and again looked down into his lap.

It seemed we were stalled for today.

"OK, Tom, are we good to wrap up this session?" I looked at the clock as the hour and minute hands pointed to five. Next to it on the wall, my framed PhD in psychology stared back at me.

He nodded, but a quizzical look appeared on his face.

"In summation, we discussed the stressor for your current anxiety—the killing of unarmed villagers. Seeing the CIA agent, Ramsey, seems to be your trigger for the nightmares. Is this accurate?" I repeated, waiting for confirmation.

Silence! He took his eyes away from me and sat staring out the window again. I glanced at the clock then returned to looking at Tom Reed and waited—I had no other sessions today. His body sagged a little as he brought his hands to his lap. He tilted his head. He showed indecisiveness. He raised both hands to his face and rubbed the mixture of sweat and tears. The clock ticked past five. I sat and waited. His head turned toward the door and his escape.

He said softly, "I have to go." Slowly he stood up.

Confused, I said, "Remember to call if you need me." I handed my business card to him.

He towered over me as I remained in my chair. His hardened face formed a barrier as he pocketed the card.

I stood up, too spent to pull more out of Reed, and walked with him to the door.

"Any plans for Christmas?" I asked, worried about his depression tied to holiday loneliness.

He unwrapped his arms, picking up on my concern. "I'm spending the holidays with my daughter and her family."

Relieved, I opened my office door. "Again, I'm available." We shook hands and he departed. Pad in hand, I walked to my desk and sat down.

I added to my notes: *He is suppressing, using maladaptive defensive mechanisms to conceal issues over killing Vietnamese civilians.*

Closing the notepad, I sat in the partially lit, darkening room. Through my office window, Charlotte spread before me, a view I normally enjoyed in the evening. After all, I could see the Carolina Panthers' football stadium to my left, immersed in floodlights. However, this evening was different: Tom had unknowingly forced me back to the Vietnam War, to the one incident that connected me to Ramsey.

I picked up my old army desk nameplate. JOHN MOORE engraved into the face, all capitals, stared back at me. I massaged the oak wood like a talisman, stained dark from years of my fingers rubbing it, embedding skin oils and enriching the sheen of the wood. The silver captain bars, once set in the red felt square to the right of my name, had been replaced by the caduceus. My fingers continued to caress the nameplate as I thought of the war. It felt creepy that Tom Reed had unintentionally connected his past with Ramsey to my own memory of the agent.

"John . . .?"

I turned my head toward Sally, framed in the open doorway to my office. Nam faded.

"Sally," I mumbled.

"Are you OK?" she asked, walking toward me. Reaching my desk, she leaned against it and stared down at me.

I lowered my eyes to Tom Reed's therapy notes on my desk, unable to explain. Reed's killings, under Todd Ramsey's orders, and my encounter with the CIA agent were separate events. My recall of the helicopter event yesterday seemed to be a prologue to today's therapy session. Was this fate?

"John, I warned you," she said. "You should have never taken on that PTSD Vietnam Vet. Now you are remembering too much of Vietnam. Or as you say, Nam."

The slight scar on her chin drew my eyes.

She hated my silence and shook her head. Not about to leave me alone, she waited, pressuring me.

"Well, maybe Reed . . ." I dropped my eyes again. My stomach churned. I knew that I couldn't tell her everything.

"John, you are a good psychologist, but you are only human. I worried about you after your wife died . . . and now Vietnam flashbacks on top of her death. Don't do this. Trauma caused by a struggling combat vet is taboo for you."

"OK, OK!" I leaned back in my chair. "It was just one session with Reed. You know . . . the VA backlog. Maybe I should refer him to another psychologist."

"That would help," she affirmed.

I rubbed my eyes and nodded. The room had suddenly become tense.

"Do you need to talk?"

I pondered, but finally I said, "No, Sally, I'm OK."

She straightened herself, smoothed her skirt, and walked to the doorway. "Go home, John. It's late. Use the weekend to forget. But call me if you need that talk."

I frowned. "Thank you." I looked at my watch. It showed six thirty. For a Friday, it seemed late.

I then watched her petite body disappear down the hallway. Had I become more attracted to her?

Taking a deep breath, I closed Reed's folder and filed it in my desk drawer. The computer screen showed my pending email message to the VA hospital in Salisbury, confirming my inability to treat Tom Reed and referring him to several other psychologists that I knew. I clicked the send button. Ending it—sick of the war.

The unfinished paperwork stacked on my desk would have to wait until Monday. I stood up, stretched, left my office, and headed to my place.

As I neared my apartment, I knew I could not face staying alone this evening. I wanted noise and people tonight. I walked past my condo building and turned toward the Capital Grille on Tryon Street a few blocks away, where the more affluent Charlotteans eat, old and new money mixing. As I walked, I focused on ordering a good steak with a first-rate glass of wine and immersing into the Friday restaurant crowd. I needed to forget the CIA agent on that helicopter. And I had to erase Reed from my thoughts as well.

I walked through the open door and Charles Riebry, the restaurant manager, looked up from his reservation book. Nodding, he greeted me with the knowing smile reserved for one of his regulars: "Good evening, John. I can seat you at the bar immediately." His English still held a floral French accent. Physically, he reminded me of Claude Rains from the old movie *Casablanca*.

The waitress had just poured my first glass of wine when Charles returned and sat down. The corner booth gave enough privacy that allowed him to relax and talk.

"You look tired, John!" Charles said. "Something wrong?"

"I need this drink," I said and took a hearty swallow.

"The wine is on the house tonight then." He reached for the wine glass from the second table setting and poured it full. He lifted his in a toast and we clinked our glasses. Sitting back into the booth, he waited for me to talk.

"God, will I ever forget the Vietnam War?"

"I have the assistant manager at the desk. I am free to listen."

The handsome Frenchman made it easy for me to talk.

"Wars! Such tragedies. So many people die—mostly young men," he said.

"I have come to the realization that there is this dark side to humans, a willingness to kill," I said, staring at the wine glass.

"Yes," Charles said. He patiently waited for me to go on.

The waitress came to our table and whispered something to him. He stood up.

"John, I have some matters in the kitchen. When I return, we will talk more?" He reached for his glass and swallowed the remaining wine. He headed to the kitchen.

"OK, I should order," I said to Katrina, my smiling waitress. Her name tag welcomed me, and her cute face allowed for a pleasant distraction from today's session with Reed. I picked up her eastern European accent, which sounded similar to my dead mother's. She left to place my steak order as I thought of my mother, imprisoned by the Nazis, a slave laborer at a concentration camp in 1942.

〇〇

"So what concentration camp was she sent to?" Charles asked. He focused on me as he swallowed his wine. His nods pushed me to continue.

Between bites of food, lubricated excessively with good wine, I revealed my childhood.

"She went to a camp near Grajewo, Poland, after the Nazi SS arrested her in her hometown of Kiev, Ukraine. Not being Jewish saved her from extermination, but the Nazis still forced her to work at a German munitions plant near the concentration camp. Slave labor freed many Germans to fight.

"There she met a French Foreign Legion officer, also a slave laborer, arrested by the Vichy government, banished for his opposition to the Nazis' puppet government. Anyway, they became lovers. And I was conceived in early 1945, just before the war ended." I shrugged.

"Yes, the Vichy government betrayed France. So you were not born in the concentration camp?"

"No, as the Russian Army invaded Poland, driving the Germans back to the west, the camp was abandoned by the SS guards, which allowed many of the prisoners to escape and flee westward too. The Ukrainian prisoners feared the Russians more than the hated Germans who had imprisoned them. My mother and her lover became separated then.

"She made her way, carrying me, into Eastern Germany, where Russian soldiers gathered her with others around September of 1945 and scheduled her to be shipped back to the Ukraine or Russia. The war had ended in May, and Europe was smothered with refugees, displaced persons from the Eastern countries now occupied by the Soviet Union."

Charles studied me, full of questions. "First of all, we are both French, oui?"

"Well, yes, but I also have a Ukrainian blood line." I grinned.

"That is a minor point, my friend," he said, laughing. "But then how come you are not living in Ukraine or Russia?"

"As luck would have it, or maybe my fate, US Army medical personnel stopped the train my mother and other Ukrainians and Poles were on and pulled off all the pregnant women. So in a way, carrying me saved her from being forced to return to the Soviet Union's control. She ended up in an American army field hospital where I was born. Then eventually, while living in a displaced person camp in Germany, we were sponsored by the Baptist Church in the States to immigrate there."

"And then you became an American."

"Yes," I said.

"But you never knew your real father?"

"Never. In fact, my mother revealed this entire story to my wife when I served in Nam, with the promise not to tell me until I had returned from the war. I guess they worried that I would lose focus on staying alive," I said, grinning, feeling relaxed. "Thanks for listening. I feel better."

Charles poured the last of the wine from a newly opened third— or probably a fourth—bottle into our glasses. I studied the table; the empty wine bottles glinted from the lounge lights. The restaurant had closed for the evening, and final cleaning surrounded us.

Charles looked at his watch then put his hand on my shoulder. "It is midnight, John. But you must know that Vietnam is your past, your legacy. However, you need to focus on the future. Serving in the war, you have developed a connection to the land and people," he said. "However, now you need to get to bed. We'll talk more about our French bloodlines. But now we had too much wine and I need to finish closing. Do I need to call a taxi for you?"

"No, I can walk the few blocks to my condo. Goodnight, Charles. Thanks for listening." I stood up and felt the wine buzz kicking in, balancing myself with my right hand on the table. At the door we shook hands, and I eased out onto the street. Some nighttime revelers passed me, laughing off their night of drink.

I once again felt lonely and sorry for myself.

CHARLOTTE, SATURDAY, DECEMBER 14, 2002

Todd Ramsey looked perplexed, his face inches from mine as we stood on a helipad at Cam Ranh Air Base. Ten feet from us, our parked helicopter stood as a backdrop while the MPs hauled off the two NVA POWs.

"You don't know what you fucking did to me!"

He looked devastated. No hatred toward me, but instead a worried fear. I started to say . . .

"Country road, take me home . . ."

I sat up. The bed was disheveled around me. My brain, groggy and aching from the wine last night, struggled. I wiped my moist forehead before I turned to the radio alarm clock. Sharp bolts of pain shot through my neck. John Denver blared at me from the radio as I focused on the digital screen. Its red numbers displayed 6:00 a.m. Set to the normal schedule, the radio obediently woke me.

I jammed the radio off and tried to clear my head. I needed to get a grip about the war and forget that past. Ramsey existed as one part of the war for me, but like wet snow stuck to a wool coat, I couldn't shake him.

I stumbled out of bed. The pain in my head punished me for the three or more bottles of wine I'd shared with Charles last night. The last time I had a hangover was after Katy's funeral, the result of hunkering down in some small tavern outside of Charlotte and drinking myself senseless with scotch. The concerned bar owner had found me passed out in the small restroom and called a taxi to take me home. I'd never drunk excessively since—until last night.

Groggily, I headed to take a shower. Afterward, delaying getting dressed I put on my bathrobe. Then I took some aspirin and made a latte with three shots of espresso. In about an hour of sitting quietly in the dark, eyes shut, listening to Joan Baez CDs and sipping my latte, I started to feel human again.

Eventually I cooked a breakfast of eggs and bacon, then I settled into my lounge chair, coffee mug in one hand—my second latte. My eyes wandered. Dust motes floated lazily in the streams of light with the reverence found in a church cathedral on a bright Sunday. I hadn't been in church since my return from the war; the Vietnam killing fields created a distaste for organized religion.

I needed a distraction and reached for the book on the end table. John Updike's *Toward the End of Time* dealt with the strange character Ben Turnbull. As a psychologist I enjoyed analyzing Ben's depression and despair as he strives to deal with his mortality, ever dwindling at age sixty-six, a lonely man. I disliked Turnbull's chauvinism, but I had empathy for his depression and loneliness.

As I read, my mind wandered sporadically to Tom Reed. His revelations still bothered me. Finally putting the book down, I stood up and went into the kitchen and cleaned up the breakfast dishes, then headed to the bedroom to get dressed.

In my jeans, a red-and-white striped Rugby shirt, soft brown leather loafers, and dark blue socks, I walked out of the bedroom just as the phone rang. I went to the phone in the living room and scanned the caller ID: Rock Hill Police.

Confused, I answered the phone.

"Doctor Moore? This is Sergeant Wilson, Rock Hill Police. We've a suicide, and per the business card found in the apartment, we assume you were his psychologist. I'd like to talk to you to validate the suicide."

I felt my heart pounding, knowing. "May I ask the name of the person?"

"Sorry." He chuckled. "I suppose there is more than one nut, I mean patient, that you deal with. The name is Tom Reed."

I pulled the handset away and stared out the window. Had I misread his condition from yesterday's first therapy session, failing to diagnose him as suicidal? "It can't be," I said.

"Um—I'm sorry, but his identity has been verified. It's Tom Reed. I'm here at the scene now. . ."

"I'm sorry. I meant . . . could I see him?" I asked.

"Well, we could talk at the station, but hey . . . it could speed things up if you came here. You OK with a dead body? And I don't want you disrupting the scene while the ME and CIs investigate."

"I've seen death in Vietnam. Can you give me his address since I'm not in my office?" I took a deep breath and waited.

As he rattled off Reed's address, I jotted it on the notepad by the phone and said goodbye. I grabbed my car keys, locked the door, and took the elevator down to the building's parking garage, retrieving my Toyota Highlander.

Saturday morning traffic wasn't too bad, and I sped out of town on Interstate 77, heading south to Rock Hill, South Carolina, about twenty miles from Charlotte. Rock Hill had a high population of tire workers from the Continental Tire manufacturing facility in Charlotte.

I learned yesterday that Tom Reed worked for the tire company for about twenty years as a tire builder, controlling his drinking, starting to slowly change his life. Working in the plant and assembling tires seemed mundane and tedious to me, but for him it meant consistency, a positive in his life. The strenuous twelve-hour shifts kept his mind focused, tiring him, usually blocking war demons when he slept. His

PTSD probably would never be cured, but he at least had a better life than the turbulent years he experienced immediately after returning from Vietnam.

His VA file also told me about his small apartment in a forty-unit complex and that he enjoyed the quiet of a small town versus the growing Charlotte metropolis. He spent free time fishing on the nearby Catawba River, enjoying the outdoors and its isolation. Reed dated occasionally, but he had no serious connection, and for him that was OK. He was realistic enough to know he had issues that required his full attention.

Twenty minutes later I pulled into Reed's apartment complex parking lot, drawn by the flashing strobe lights of two Rock Hill police cruisers, askew, driver doors open, parked front to front, serving as barriers. I glimpsed the gray ME van parked by an entrance to the apartments.

Questions and concerns about Reed occupied my mind, but I was distracted as an approaching cop stopped me, right hand held high, palm facing me, his other hand languishing on the pistol holster strapped on the left side of his wide utility belt.

I introduced myself through the open car window, and he shouted my name to another policeman standing by the open door of the building next to the ME van. He nodded and checked off something on his clipboard. Instructed to leave the car parked where it was, I got out as the officer held the car door open for me. Young but serious looking in his starched tan uniform with razor creases on his pants, the cop then stepped behind me while nodding and pointing to his colleague with the clipboard. I walked the forty or so feet toward the clipboard officer.

"Apartment ten, down the hall to your right, sir," he said. He studied me for a second as I passed him, brawny like his partner. The muted light in the hallway seemed to harbor ill will, but I proceeded, looking at the apartment numbers to the left and right of me as I passed the closed doors. The hall resembled a dark tunnel with a light at the end. Sadness engulfed me as I walked forward looking for number ten. I felt the dark and dank of another place, another time: the tunnels of Cu Chi in Vietnam, where I had tried to save one of my tunnel rats—a short, young soldier, badly wounded from the exploding mine he'd tripped.

The memory hit me. I hesitated and stopped, confused, my feet frozen, chilled by a cool breeze passing by. Regaining my will, I forced myself to take the steps, heading for the open door on the far right, a guiding light emitting from the apartment, leading me to the death scene. In Nam, the light at the end of the tunnel meant safety as I pulled on the dying grunt behind me. Ironically, I again headed to death. Passing apartment nine, I turned toward the open door of number ten.

Standing in the living room by a small TV on an old-style foldable stand and talking into his cell phone stood an overweight man in a brown suit. I assumed this was Sergeant Wilson. He glanced at me and held up his hand, mouthed for me to wait. The heavyset Wilson stood shorter than my six feet. My full head of brown hair with some strands of gray countered his receding brown hairline—balding, in fact. I guessed him to be in his mid-forties, but his appearance made him look older. Cop life, with its stress, long hours, bad eating habits, booze, and little to no exercise, was taking its toll on him. While he talked, he ran his hand through his thinning hair.

Hanging up, he walked over to me and asked, "You Doctor Moore?"

"Yes. And you're Sergeant Wilson?" I offered my hand. He took it.

"The body is in the bedroom. He has a neighbor who goes fishing with him, and they'd planned to get out early this morning. He knocked on the door for several minutes and knew something was wrong. He got the super, and then they found the body on the bed. There weren't any signs of a break-in. The door was locked."

I followed the cop into the bedroom where the ME was closing his medical bag. He straightened up from the bed.

I looked at Reed, his body face up on the bed, still in boxer shorts and a T-shirt, chalky stuff around his mouth, his blankets and sheets tousled on the bed and the floor. His body looked very rigid, tense. His fists curled tightly.

"Doc, this is John Moore, the deceased's psychologist." Wilson pointed to me.

We shook hands. I asked, "Are you certain of suicide? Doctor..."

"It's Ted Mahone. Yes. The preliminary exam indicates suicide. There's a suicide note on the dresser and empty bottles for Lorazepam and Paroxetine tablets on the floor. The empty vodka bottle indicates he drank heavily while downing the pills. I will confirm during the autopsy how many he took, but the prescription bottles were dated a week ago, with each holding a ninety-pill count. Those amounts would have easily killed him. The white powder around his mouth also indicates he chewed some of the pills in addition to swallowing them. He definitely went overboard. Also, as his psychologist, you should read the note to verify his state of mind for me." He looked at Wilson, who nodded, then continued. "Of course, it goes into evidence."

"The note could help me understand," I said, directing myself to Wilson's quizzical look. "And Lorazepam is used to treat anxiety, while Paroxetine is used for treating depression, all of which Reed exhibited at our therapy session yesterday. And he shouldn't have taken alcohol with the pills. Dangerous combo. If he was in a suicidal mood, overdosing with Paroxetine alone could have done it."

Mahone nodded in agreement as we focused on the body. All the evidence pointed to Reed taking his own life.

"Interesting. You two are into these meds, I guess. Dr. Moore, go ahead and read the note, but don't touch anything else, as we need to verify fingerprints," Wilson said.

The ME said, "The autopsy should be completed by Monday evening."

I nodded as Wilson grunted and returned to his notepad.

While he wrote, he said, "It has to be suicide. Hey, I know how you feel, Dr. Moore. You missed one. Hell, I've made bad calls myself—let a bad kid go because he acted sincere, then later he gets picked up for robbery again. You can't win them all." Wilson smiled.

"Hey, Sergeant, I've found something in one of the kitchen drawers," a CI yelled from the kitchen.

I read the bagged suicide note quickly. The almost illegible scrawl stated: "I'm tired. Fucking shit won't go away. It don't mean a fucking thing. Goodbye, Vietnam." And it was signed, Tom Reed. I felt a chill down my back. The suicide became real; his use of slang from the war convinced me. GIs talked that way over there.

Wilson walked past me, and I followed him through the living room and into the kitchen. A CI wearing latex gloves held up airline tickets. "These are for December 16, this coming Monday, from Charlotte to Nashville. They were bought two weeks ago."

Wilson asked me, "Who was he going to see?"

"That would probably be his daughter. She lives in Nashville. Reed said he planned Christmas with her and her family. He didn't seem suicidal yesterday." I stood looking at the airline tickets held by the CI. Reed's suicide occurred last night, even though he had planned to travel to see his daughter. What the hell spooked him to end his life? I stared at Sergeant Wilson.

"C'mon, Doc. He probably snapped last night so all his future plans were meaningless."

Doctor Mahone came into the kitchen and said, "Wilson, we're ready to move the body, so I will talk to you gentlemen later." The ME walked out.

"Have you notified his daughter?" I asked, looking into Wilson's heavyset face.

He pulled the waist of his pants over his beer belly, tucking in his shirt and straightening his tie. "No, not yet. Do you have her phone number? That would help. Also, I take it he wasn't married?"

"I'm heading back to the office and will call you with the daughter's number. And no on the marriage—he is a divorcee."

Wilson gave me his business card. I shook his hand and walked out the door, retracing my steps to my car. Reed's suicide suddenly felt like the sixty-pound rucksack I carried on my back in Nam.

☙❧

It was almost noon when I arrived at my office. I lost my appetite over Reed's death and skipped lunch. Confused on how I missed his suicidal tendencies yesterday, I knew I had to research his files and background as a professional psychologist.

I unlocked the door to the reception area that was mostly used by a temp to file health insurance claims; Sally and I preferred answering our phones or allowing the voicemail system to fulfill such secretarial functions. There I found Sally, her blonde hair gathered in a ponytail sticking out the back of a baby blue UNC cap, dressed in a pink university sweatshirt and blue jeans, typing on the PC keyboard, her coffee cup on the desk.

She looked up and said, "Why aren't you home?"

I smiled. "Same question to you."

She pointed to the PC. "Insurance claims to complete—money is always good."

"What about our temp?" I asked.

"She won't be in this week. The holiday."

Nodding, I said, "I need to review some notes."

"What's wrong?" She turned to me, examining my serious mood.

"Tom Reed committed suicide last night."

She stood up and came over to me. "Oh, John, you can't beat yourself up over this. Something triggered the suicide. Nothing to do with you." Putting her hand on my shoulder, she asked, "Are you OK?"

"Not certain." I spied the full coffee pot through the open door to the little kitchenette. "Is that fresh coffee?"

Sally nodded. "I'll bring you a cup. Give me a minute."

I thanked her and went to my office and sat down at my desk. What had I missed in yesterday's session? The death scene, with the emptied bottles of antidepressant and anxiety prescriptions, and the empty booze bottle, conveyed a suicide. At my session, he showed no signs of suicide. Maybe Sergeant Wilson wanted to rush to close the case, which could cause him to overlook something at the apartment. The autopsy should resolve it in any case. And if it wasn't suicide, then what? Murder didn't make sense. Something pushed Reed to end his life.

Sally placed a cup of hot black coffee on my desk as I laid Reed's file in front of me. I had just finished a quick review of my notes, plus the separate thick file that the VA hospital had sent to me before my session.

"Thanks," I said. Sally pulled one of my session chairs to my desk and sat in it, studying me, not saying a word. Sally's psychoanalysis technique kicked in as she observed me and my emotions.

I flipped through the files again, found the personal information sheets, and locked onto the name Jane Phillips, the daughter, and her home phone number. I dialed Wilson's cell phone and gave him the number. He seemed busy, so the phone call was short.

To avoid missing key information, I again reviewed my notes and the evaluation forms used during the session on Friday. Reed's nightmares, his drinking and drug use, his dysfunctional relationships, and his depression had impacted his life. However, we had only one session together, and I would have needed more time with him to fully understand his condition. An hour passed reading and rereading the two files and talking with Sally as she read and analyzed the same files.

Several times she looked up from her reading and shook her head. By Saturday afternoon, Sally stood up.

"I see no red flags that you missed his suicide," she said, returning the notes to the folders.

"I can't find anything either," I said.

Still it nagged me. I was a professional. I should know when someone was suicidal. Was my personal vindication at stake?

"I didn't mention yesterday that part of my funk came from Reed mentioning a name. A CIA agent named Todd Ramsey. I met Ramsey under less than desirable circumstances in the war," I said.

"How does that matter?" Sally interjected.

"Reed said that Ramsey ordered him to execute a hundred Vietnamese villagers. Let's see . . . also, there was a South Vietnamese Army colonel who participated in the incident."

"So seeing Ramsey recently triggered his nightmares and his depression. That is plausible."

"Well guess what, I'm having bad dreams about Ramsey. This is haunting me. And was Reed's sighting of Ramsey in the VA hospital the real reason for him committing suicide?"

Sally looked at her watch and said, "John, I have to go see my parents—I promised to be there for dinner. But first I have some errands."

"Oh . . . hey, I'm sorry. Yes, please go. Crap, here I am holding you up."

"Why don't you join me?" she said.

"Thanks, but I'm bummed out."

She patted my hand. "Don't stew over this. Your notes make it obvious that you didn't miss the suicide. He had a relapse last night and failed to call you for help."

I frowned as she started to walk out of my office. Then she stopped and turned.

"You can't continue obsessing over this. I know you. We both have baggage in our past that impacts us individually. But we still function professionally."

"I know, Sally. I know . . ."

"Please listen, though. This is my tough love. You are focusing on what you think you did wrong with Tom Reed. What you need to look at is what drove Reed to kill himself. Get off your high horse about being the perfect psychologist. There is no such thing. The frigging mind is a mystery to all of us, no matter how long we study it." She almost glared at me.

"I . . ."

"I'll stay and skip going to my parents' function if you insist on sitting there and beating yourself up. But you need to get over it!"

The silence became intense as she waited. It seemed an eternity passed with her standing halfway between the office door and my desk. I wanted her to stay but couldn't ask her.

"You're right," I said.

"Well?" she said.

"I'll wrap up now," I said, shuffling and closing the files. "I have a phone call to make and then I am out of here. Please go on to dinner."

The Sally stare that I had accepted over the years continued. She bore into me with her blue eyes, looking for any falsehoods. A minute of added silence passed.

"Alright. You call me if you get into a funk again. Make your phone call and get out of this office," she said.

I nodded and reached for my desk phone, not looking directly into her eyes. She slowly turned to the door and walked out, not closing it behind her, as I dialed an old friend, one who had my back in Vietnam.

Jim Schaeffer answered his cell phone on the fifth ring. "John Moore, you bastard. Why do I have the honor of you calling me at home?"

"Because I can't live without you," I said. My banter sounded hollow to me.

"Hey, you shouldn't make fun of one who saved your ass in Nam."

"Yeah—I recall I saved your ass," I said. I felt a small smile coming on. Jim's hearty laugh could do that.

We had a friendship created in the war, formed when we first met in the Twenty-Fifth Infantry Division, serving near Cambodia. It further grew when we both served as company commanders in the 101st Airborne Division—he commanded B Company, First/501st Battalion, and I commanded C Company in the same battalion.

Currently we tried calling each other at least once a month. Before, after his return from Vietnam, some six months after me, we had talked weekly, sometimes daily, healing each other, ridding ourselves of the angst from the killing fields of Vietnam. At first the army hadn't recognized that many of the returned vets had post-traumatic stress disorder. Jim and I didn't have PTSD, but we had had our share of nightmares and night sweats those early years after Nam. We witnessed too many of our own soldiers die in battle; an awesome burden of being young company commanders that still nagged us some thirty years later.

"I need a favor," I said, refocusing on the reality of the present.

"You got it, as long as it doesn't involve getting too drunk like we used to. Kim would kill me." He laughed again. I shook my head.

Jim had married a Vietnamese woman whom he had met in the war. Kim was a lovely lady who had given Jim three boys, whom he adored and spoiled. He had served in the army for twenty-five years, retiring as a lieutenant colonel, burned out from the military bureaucracy. He used his retirement income to forge ahead and form a boutique security company, Schaeffer and Sons Inc. His past military career gave him connections to clients who needed bodyguards, like politicians and business executives—anywhere worldwide. I think he had over fifty employees, including his three sons, who were being groomed to run the company. Based in Washington, DC, he utilized the area's concentrated political network for his business.

I briefed him over the phone about Reed and his suicide.

"Look, I don't know where I'm going with this, but a name, Todd Ramsey, came up and I . . . just want to ease my concerns. I need to find out about Ramsey, a CIA agent, and whether he had a role in Reed's suicide."

Jim fell into his usual supportive role and promised some quick checking with the CIA on Ramsey and to pull any information on Tom Reed from the military records he could access.

"I'll call you as soon as I get some info. Are you coming to DC for Christmas with Kim and me? I don't know why, but she thinks you're a nice guy. You and I know better," he said and snorted a laugh.

"After being married to you, she knows she can only improve," I retorted. My chuckle eased some of my tension. "I guess it has been a while, and I'll try to see you guys for Christmas. Just need to work on getting a few open days."

"When I call back about your query, you tell me your flight schedule to come stay with us. It's a commitment, my friend. And make it for a couple of weeks." Jim hung up.

CHARLOTTE, MONDAY, DECEMBER 16, 2002

After a restless Sunday, working with clients on Monday eased my sour mood. While at my desk sipping from a mug of fresh hot coffee, Sally buzzed me on the intercom. "Jane Phillips is on line two for you. Do you want me to talk to her?"

Some of the hot brew spilled from my mouth, dribbling down the cup's side. I hastily set the coffee mug on my desk, watching the black liquid trickling slowly, partly drying on the cup's side, partly being absorbed on the coaster. Anxiously, I took a deep breath, trying to ease my tightness, and said, "No, I should handle it."

I pushed line two. "Hello, Mrs. Phillips. This is John Moore."

"Dr. Moore, the police called me Saturday night. Is it true that my dad killed himself?" she said.

I paused, trying to form the correct response, trying to be helpful. "Mrs. Phillips, I am sorry for your loss, but yes, it looks like suicide. I assume Sergeant Wilson explained."

"Yes, but what happened?" Her bluntness weighed on me.

"I wish I knew. They found him dead, and it looked like he took an overdose of his depression and anxiety meds. And there was a suicide note."

"I'm not surprised he killed himself, although I had hoped that he was getting on with life. Dad and I had finally reunited. And our son was so happy to finally have a grandfather. . . You see, Chuck, my husband, lost his parents before our son was born."

I listened, respecting her time to talk. She needed the release.

"But he was so uptight these last few days that I knew his PTSD was getting worse. I'd hoped him visiting us over Christmas would help, so my husband bought him tickets to fly out."

I stayed silent. She finally stopped talking, and failing to cover her mouthpiece, I heard her crying now. Finally, her silence crept into my office. I waited, allowing the seconds to tick forward. Then I said, "I know this is difficult, but you will recover from this."

"Thanks. I don't know. Look, Doctor . . ."

"Please call me John," I said.

"OK, John. I found his journal, which he left when he stayed with us on December 7. He has been to see me regularly. He needed family, I guess. The journal is confusing. Maybe sort of a diary?"

I knew the answer: a VA psychologist had told Reed to keep a journal to record nightmares and other PTSD issues to discuss during therapy. "Is it OK with you that I read the journal?" I asked. I thumped my fingers on the desk.

At that moment, Sally's voice intruded from the open office doorway, where she stood looking at me. "Sergeant Wilson is on line one."

I nodded, holding my hand up. Jane Phillips confirmed that she would send me the journal. I gave her the mailing address and we said our goodbyes. I hung up, wiping my moist palms on my pant legs.

Nodding to Sally as she left for her office and punching line one, I answered, "John Moore."

"Doctor Moore, this is Wilson. I've got the autopsy report."

"Thanks for calling me," I said. Sitting straighter, I tried to focus on Wilson's information.

"Well, here it is. I'll give you a quick summary. He died both suffocating on his own vomit and overdosing on his pills. He probably took all remaining antidepressants and anxiety pills, some of which didn't completely dissolve and lodged in his esophagus."

I imagined the pain and fear that Tom must have experienced. I shook my head.

"Anyway, the ME is saying suicide. There is no evidence for a homicide," he said.

I thought of something. "When I saw the body, his fists were clenched."

"Doc felt it was reflex. We can even explain the minor bruising on both wrists and both ankles; they're from his work at the tire plant. He wore heavy boots that rubbed his ankle and carried heavy rubber strips across his arms at his tire-building station."

Rubbing my eyes, I said, "Suicides normally happen quickly once the decision is made by the individual."

"I think he was determined. We also confirmed the high alcohol content in his blood. He was a mess. Was Reed right- or left-handed?" Wilson asked.

"A southpaw. Why?" I said.

"The note was written by a left-handed person. So, it was his handwriting in the note. Look, I got another call, but I knew you left his apartment out of sorts over this. But everything validates a suicide. He must have been totally depressed." Wilson hung up.

Putting my phone in the cradle, I stood. My office window now framed an uptown Charlotte with a dark midmorning winter haze creeping through the streets, its perceived coldness causing me to shiver, even within my heated office. Why did Reed kill himself?

The knock on my door directed me to my watch: It was my 11:00 a.m. session.

CHARLOTTE, TUESDAY, DECEMBER 17, 2002

By late Tuesday afternoon, Jane Phillips's UPS overnight package stared at me. I had completed my sessions and was prepared to open the parcel containing Reed's journal. I hesitated. Reed had killed himself, so what was the point of this? Why did I want to continue exploring Reed? As Sally had said—it wasn't about me.

Hesitantly, I opened the package and pulled out Tom's notebook—a typical college-ruled, spiral-bound notebook with a shiny black front and back cover. As I flipped through the first ten pages, scanning his scrawling penmanship, I found very little that gave me new insight on Tom Reed or his killing of innocent villagers. He rambled about his work, about his better relationship with his daughter, about his grandson.

It was the eleventh page that got my attention. The second and final paragraph gave a possible trigger for Tom's death: *December 6: I saw him today. After all these years, it was Ramsey. I recognized him immediately. He stood in the hall at Salisbury VA. He looked past me and continued walking by me. I thought he hadn't recognized me. When I turned to check him out again as he turned the corner, he glanced back at me. I know he recognized me. He still scares me. And why was he there?*

Then memories of the village near My Son came back, and the horror I committed. Other things are still vague in my head—about the ancient tribe in Nam, but my mind just has this blank. I don't want to remember!

This confirmed that Reed's mind had repressed a very harrowing event that occurred in Nam. Running into Ramsey brought the trauma back—the horror of killing civilians. I now felt that his connection with Ramsey was the real story: the sinister, violent things that he had done with and for Ramsey. Did the killing of so many villagers finally cause anxiety overload for him on Friday night—enough to kill himself? The answer seemed to be yes.

I sat at the desk realizing that in our Friday session, I had helped create a crack to his repressed memory, allowing it to flood out later, overwhelming him, and I wasn't there to help him. I rubbed my tired eyes, attempting to remove the sadness that I now felt. In trying to heal him, did I help him commit suicide?

But something bothered me. Why did he lie to me on Friday, December 13? He said he didn't remember Ramsey in the hall at the VA until he got to Rock Hill, just before our session. His own notes in the journals contradicted that by stating he had immediately recognized the CIA agent in the VA hospital.

I had to know more about Reed and Ramsey. This would help me understand the awful pain Reed felt that forced him to commit suicide. I had one way to find out, and that would be to go to Washington, DC, and use Schaeffer's connections. It would be better to have a face-to-face with Jim and avoid the phone. I picked up the desk phone and dialed him at his office and invited myself to visit him at his home.

"Hey, I'm glad you are coming early, but plan on staying for Christmas. Your room is reserved for you, buddy."

"I think that will work. And I need to get my questions answered . . . to help me deal with it emotionally. I'm afraid I opened a Pandora's box that Reed couldn't cope with," I said.

"I'm still waiting for all the info on Ramsey and Reed. Hope to have it when you get here," Jim responded.

"Good. I'll call you when I arrive tomorrow. I'm staying at a hotel for the first night because my flight will get in late." I hung up after Jim agreed.

I called US Airways and booked Wednesday's 10:00 p.m. flight to Washington Dulles International Airport. I had client sessions tomorrow to handle first. Glancing at the clock, I saw that it was past five. I turned off the lights to my office and headed to Sally's office, hoping she was still here. Her door stood open and she sat writing at her desk.

As she looked up, I blurted, "Would you handle the few sessions I have for Thursday through Christmas? I have to fly out to DC tomorrow night."

We hadn't talked much about Reed's death since Saturday. She sat back and sighed.

"John, are you getting involved with something that isn't your concern?"

I paused. "Jim Schaeffer invited me to spend Christmas with him and Kim." I didn't explain that Jim was gathering information for me as well. I hated the lie.

"Hmmm," she murmured.

Sally was a good friend as well as my associate, in ways replacing my dead wife by giving me brutal honesty when I needed it. Sometimes she knew me better than I knew myself. She suspected there was more.

This time I shook my head. "OK, I did ask Jim to gather some information for me to help me understand why Reed would kill himself."

Sally stood up, turning away from me toward her office window overlooking the streets of Charlotte. Talking to the window, she said, "Just be careful. I'll cover your sessions but keep me informed on what the hell you're doing. You owe me for the worry you cause."

"Thanks, Sally."

With her back to me, she waved me away. Her bowed head worried me. I looked down, then turned away and walked out of the office.

I thought Sally turned to look as I departed. Somehow that felt good.

℘ℴ

I had finished packing for my flight Wednesday night and now had to decide what to do about dinner. It was almost seven.

The doorbell rang. When I opened the door, Sally stood there with a plastic bag of food from the Thai restaurant we occasionally use for working lunches at the office.

"I thought you would need some food and maybe company. You seemed a little out of it at the office," Sally said, stepping into my condo.

She looked exceptionally enticing, wearing a flirty, silky skirt, countering her business look at the office. She turned to me and noticed my stare.

"Want me to set this food in the kitchen?"

"Aw . . . yes, please," I said.

An hour later, we had finished eating and I was stuffed but happy, due to the wine, the meal, and her presence. We laughed about some of our silly experiences with our clients. We laughed to just laugh—her presence became cathartic.

Maybe it was the wine, maybe it was her sitting next to me, maybe it was my loneliness, but I suddenly leaned into her and kissed her, gently at first. With no resistance from her, I put my arms around her as she did the same, and we became meshed as one.

℘ℴ

I heard her dressing as I woke up. It was almost five on Wednesday morning.

She smiled at me as I eyed her beautiful, partially nude body. "I need to get home and shower and get a change of clothes for work."

"Stay, please. We could do breakfast."

"Next time, John. And you should know, last night was special."

"So, there is a chance for us together?" I said, a big grin on my face.

"You think?" Finally dressed, she leaned over and gave me a long kiss. We clung briefly, but she had the willpower and released me. "I'll have coffee and rolls waiting for you at the office. Now get ready."

As Sally disappeared from my bedroom and headed to the condo's front door, I lay back down. What a gorgeous evening last night had turned into. Our lovemaking was more than I could have expected. It seemed we both needed each other. *Damn, I should cancel the DC trip,* I thought. What was the point of going now? Sally had changed things in my life.

WASHINGTON, DC, THURSDAY, DECEMBER 19, 2002

By seven that morning, I sat in the Courtyard Hotel's restaurant. After a breakfast of two eggs over easy with two strips of crisp bacon, I relaxed with my second cup of coffee. I would have favored a Denny's, but I was not up to driving around to find one. My room had been waiting for me when I arrived in Washington, DC, past midnight and, after quickly putting on sleep shorts and T-shirt, I brushed my teeth and plopped into bed to catch five hours of sleep. I never enjoyed traveling on business, and this whole trip had the same feel: I used to consult for human relations with Fortune 500s. They had me jetting all over the world to help implement psychological evaluations in their hiring practices. The hotel beds now were better than in the earlier years of my travel, but they were still hotel beds.

Sipping my coffee nervously, I looked at my small list of phone calls to make. The first one was to Sally. She knew I had committed to stay over the holidays with Jim Schaeffer and was good with that. But she wanted me to drop my inquiries about Reed. I stated I would once Schaeffer briefed me, but deep down something pulled me to continue to investigate.

Handling my cell phone on the restaurant table, I had waited for a decent time to call. I dialed Sally's office number and she answered on the first ring. "Hello, John." Her cool tone came through.

"Are my sessions going to be OK?" I asked.

"Yes. I'm ready," she said.

I tried to think of something funny to say, but her seriousness stopped me as she said, "Just finish whatever you're doing and get back to Charlotte. You are playing with issues that don't concern you."

"Well . . . here are my plans. I need to see someone besides Jim who can shed some information about a war program involving Reed in Nam."

A subdued Sally replied, "Yes?" There was more silence. "Well at least you're being honest now."

I felt dejected by her tone, so I didn't mention Ramsey to her. Sally could be tenacious and stubborn and now, after our night together, upset with being relegated to a secondary role. She cared for me.

"Look, Tuesday night was unbelievable for me, and I want this to go somewhere with us if you will let it." I paused and then said, "I'll call you tonight."

"I'll be home," she answered, a nicer tone emitted over the phone. "Just be careful, because I do care." She hung up. The silence on the other end caused me to reflect again on why I was doing this trip. I again second-guessed my coming to DC. What could I really do? In the end, Reed's death impacted only his daughter and grandson. I felt unsure.

Next week was Christmas, which left me a short window of time to learn anything. I needed to finish this in the next few days. Throwing my uncertainty aside, I picked up my cell phone.

My planned next call resulted from an idea I had while flying to DC last night. During Reed's session, the CIA's Phoenix Program came up, and it gave me direction: I would pursue this further with Edwin C. King, a political science professor at Georgetown. I met him at an academic seminar on psychological manipulation of politics and government. He had been one of the speakers, and we had talked several times by phone since the seminar to get a reality check on the polarization of American politics. We both felt the ultra-extremes—right and left were counterproductive, the no-compromise mentality drew a line in the sand: my way or the highway.

The waitress poured me another cup of coffee as I dialed. I mouthed my thanks to her as she left the bill. I knew Edwin King taught mostly in the afternoon, so there was a good chance of catching him in the morning.

He answered with his professorial, educated voice—pleasing to the ear. "Hello, Professor King speaking."

"Professor King, this is John Moore."

"John, how are you? Good to hear from you. Are we going to discuss the politicians who avoided the Vietnam draft?"

"No, not today," I said. His remark reminded me of the first young soldier to die in my arms—an eighteen-year-old black American, a draftee with no political clout to avoid the draft.

"OK, John. But we do have a wealth of war hawks who never served. Maybe we should call them chicken hawks," he answered, gleefully.

"I'm not calling about these zealots, Professor. I need some solid information about the Phoenix Program during the Vietnam War."

"Well my dear boy, I have done some research on that program. When do you want to discuss it?"

"Today, hopefully, since I'm here in DC," I said, looking at my watch, which showed eight o'clock.

"You're in luck. I have the whole day free. I'm finished with my classes for the semester and am just grading final exams in the office. Why don't you swing by? I think you know how to find me. We can start, do a nice lunch and then work the rest of the afternoon. Lots of material John, all of which makes me sad on how the politicians mismanaged the war."

I confirmed, hung up, checked out of the hotel, and headed for the exit to get my car rental, a black S60 Volvo. I planned on staying with Schaeffer tonight. If Sally wanted me back sooner, then I pondered on skipping the Christmas stay with Jim.

As I walked to the parking lot, my memories of Vietnam emerged again; the Phoenix Program was indeed a sad remembrance. Ramsey had been a part of that program when he tried to kill the unarmed POW NVA officer in front of me. The murder I prevented that day. Now Reed's death pushed me back into the quagmire of the Vietnam past, a swamp full of leeches sucking on my current life.

Shaking off the recollections, I made my last call before pulling out in my rental. Schaeffer didn't answer his cell, so I left a voicemail message confirming that I was in town and would be there this evening for dinner and to stay at his place.

 exo

The seminar where I first met Professor King had been held on the Georgetown University campus, so with a little finger-pointing from students still roaming the campus prior to Christmas break, I located the offices of the Political Science Department, leaving my rental in visitor parking. Professor King's office, situated on the second floor, seemed deserted when I walked into the small reception area. Peering to my left and through the open door of the first office, I saw him at his desk reading a book, his feet resting on his cluttered desktop. He put down the book as soon as he noticed me, lowered his feet, and moved agilely around his desk. For an overweight sixty-five-year-old, his movements impressed me. He grasped my right hand with both of his.

"John, it's good to see you. It has been a while. A year?"

"At least. Thanks for seeing me." I returned his smile.

"On the contrary, I love research, and you just whetted my appetite. Why are you digging into this?" His bushy gray beard, the matching unruly thick hair piled on his round head, and his short, plump body all conveyed the stereotype of a college professor enjoying tenure.

I waited to answer him as he offered me one of the two chairs in front of his desk, while he returned to his, sinking heavily into the old-fashioned wooden desk chair; its swivel base squeaked in protest to his weight. I noticed the book he had been reading: *The Pentagon Papers.*

"I thought I would reread this book. Good stuff on how our government blundered along in the conduct of the war," he replied to my inquiring look. "Again, why the Phoenix Program?"

"My knowledge is limited. I remember being briefed about it when I served in Vietnam, mostly in reference to neutralizing the peasants who were communists. I knew the CIA operated it. I even had a serious confrontation with one of the agents in the program, but I had a different mission: to fight the North Vietnamese Army while trying to keep my men alive. Now I have questions related to one of my former patients who committed suicide."

Professor King looked at me. "Sorry to hear about the suicide. Seems to be a growing problem not only with military vets, but also active-duty personnel. Well, let's get started. I have tons of notes and reference books. So let me give you a quick overview and then we can go into the details. OK?"

I nodded in agreement.

"Now, let's see where to start . . . ah, here we are." He pulled a file from the foot-high stack of files and magazines on his desk, threatening to collapse, adding chaos to the war zone he called his desktop. He had his own system for locating material.

"Yes . . . indeed, here we are. In 1967, the CIA dreamed up a program to eliminate the communist cells in South Vietnam, naming it the Phoenix Program. The phoenix, or *phung hoang* in Vietnamese, has its roots in many cultures, based on ancient mythology of a bird. Per legend, it resembles a colorful feathered eagle that had lived for five hundred years. The lore told how the phoenix burned itself to death on a pyre and then resurrected itself. A rebirth."

I knew that the phoenix represented a sacred symbol used in celebrating Tet, the Vietnamese New Year. "And from its ashes another phoenix arose, becoming a symbol of death and resurrection. This is Taoism. The Yin and Yang for the Vietnamese," I said.

He grinned at me, nodding. "I'm impressed, John. In Chinese cosmology, the Yin is the female, where the Yang complements as the male. Both are needed for harmony of life on Earth. If one part is missing, there is disharmony, an incompleteness in life." Professor King leaned back after his explanation.

"I can see the CIA planners choosing the phoenix symbol to represent the killing of the communists to ultimately resurrect from their ashes, so to speak, Vietnamese who are loyal to the South Vietnamese government and are anti-communists," I said.

"It's a very loose application by the CIA, but certainly a more appealing symbol than some of the other creatures used mythically in Chinese or Vietnamese lore, such as the turtle or the goat."

"So what were the actual details of the American plan?" I asked, wanting to get to the crux of the matter, unlike the professor, who enjoyed the lecture and its building-block approach to teaching.

"The CIA and selected American military advisors worked jointly with the South Vietnamese officials, mostly the intelligence services, which had the duty of preventing or destroying the communist cells and cadre that had infiltrated the villages and the countryside. As you know from your own tour, corruption was rampant in the South Vietnamese government. Its intelligence services had competing factions and individuals manipulating each other for power, for money or gold. Graft ran amok, and these South Vietnamese, and possibly some Americans, saw the new funding source for the Phoenix Program as another way to make money off the backs of the peasants." Professor King frowned at me.

At that moment, a young woman walked in carrying a deli bag and three sodas on a cardboard tray. I looked at my watch—it was noon.

"Perfect timing, Marcie. I am hungry," the professor said.

"There was no line," she said. "Students are abandoning campus for Christmas."

"May I introduce Marcie Malcolm, my student assistant? Marcie, this is John Moore. John . . . well, this is Marcie. What have we got for food, my dear?"

"I decided healthy, and we have turkey hoagies loaded with vegies."

The professor had discarded the idea of going out to lunch.

He said, "I didn't want to interrupt this meeting by going to a restaurant. This is exciting stuff, John!"

We paused to break out the food. The professor didn't wait for us as he chomped down, chewing with gusto, thoroughly enjoying his sandwich.

Marcie, a thin, young woman with black hair tied in a bun, peered at me from behind her librarian glasses and then said to both of us, "My research for my thesis on various forms of corruption in world governments, past and present, found that anti-war Americans called the Phoenix Program a mass murder operation."

I looked at her quizzically.

She anticipated me. "Professor King already briefed me on your meeting, so I'm not a mind reader." She giggled.

"I'm sorry, John. I should have told you Marcie was helping us today." He smiled at me, enjoying his passion for research and his tendency to forget those around him in the process.

I turned to Marcie. "Welcome. Maybe we can get Professor King to slow down a little for us average humans." She laughed, and I sensed that behind her staid librarian disguise existed an attractive young woman.

King, now refreshed with his first bites of food, jumped in again. "This is the key. The program was riddled with corruption, inefficiency, and severe abuses. The task was to neutralize the structure of the Viet Cong in the villages and the rural countryside, and to stop supplies, food, asylum, money, and recruits for the Viet Cong. If the

CIA program could destroy this support, then in theory the communists would wither away, and thus help win the war."

Again King chomped into his hoagie like a bulldog devouring table food before his owner discovered the theft, noisily enjoying the flavor, eyes flashing satisfaction with the food, burping as he slurped his drink. Marcie looked at me apologetically while I grinned, knowing the professor's eating habits.

"So now you had all these South Vietnamese intelligence agents, police, and soldiers going into the villages, trying to destroy the cells built up by the communists. They were even assigned quotas—head count, in other words, which was a serious mistake by the planners because of the corruption in the South Vietnamese government. Quotas created abuses, and innocent Vietnamese were arrested to achieve the allocated goals and monetary rewards."

Marcie quickly added, "Some data reveals that 70 percent of the captured VC suspects were able to bribe the South Vietnamese for their freedom. Figures vary, but Colby, the CIA executive who headed Phoenix, claimed in 1971 that twenty-eight thousand Viet Cong had been captured, another twenty thousand killed, and seventeen thousand repatriated to the South. Thousands died in captivity, tortured by the South Vietnamese in the notorious Saigon prisons. Records of others have never been found. Individuals lost forever."

"You understand now, John, why I said this is a sad part of American history. To fund such a program, which seems rational on the surface, then to allow our South Vietnamese allies to exploit it for personal riches and power, just shames our involvement."

"Yes," I said. "The war became an American mess. It was fought with our vast resources but no clear understanding of the people and their culture. We could have saved all those American soldiers if we had." I thought again of the names on the Vietnam Wall Memorial in DC; many were young draftees sent to die in the war like chum, bait for communists in a conflict that engulfed five American presidents.

"The village heads, or elders, were given monthly quotas, which often resulted in innocent peasants being imprisoned or killed to further bulk up the numbers. Also, it was used to remove personal political enemies. Maybe the idea was that if you kill enough people, you eventually kill some bad guys as well." King paused and stared out the window of his office, absently brushing breadcrumbs from his pink tie, finally shaking his head.

I thought of a question: "Were any of the Americans, CIA or military, legally charged with murder or extortion?"

"The tragedy is that there were observed abuses committed by some Americans, yet the military chain of command buried the reports due to insufficient evidence or to protect careers. There were episodes where prisoners of war were thrown out of helicopters by South Vietnamese military personnel. No doubt that some Americans assigned to the Phoenix Program did the same. I would offer this, John. Some of the American participants became damaged goods."

"You mean psychologically?"

"Yes, exactly. Some suffered from PTSD with such experiences. But you would know this as a psychologist. Now, you have to ask yourself: Were the bad Americans bad when they got to Vietnam, or did they become bad after serving? I'm sorry, John, but the military archives that I have searched offer no input on corrupt Americans. They always point to some 'bad' South Vietnamese. And just think how a mentally stressed CIA agent or army officer could manipulate the 'direct order' bit. Threatening punishment by court-martial if a young American draftee hesitated to follow orders, say for argument's sake, to shoot a Vietnamese civilian. These PTSD souls struggled, and by having someone else do the dirty work, they helped justify themselves."

Unknowingly, he probably had described Ramsey's use of Reed in the war, but I didn't want to involve the professor in my speculation about the ex-CIA agent. There could be associated danger. After the revelation about his encounter with Ramsey, Tom Reed's suicide had made me cautious, not knowing what role Ramsey really played in all of this. I didn't want to expose those helping me.

My watch showed the day had gone by fairly fast and it was now close to three-thirty. I would have to leave soon, but first I needed my hunch addressed. I asked King, "Would the CIA resort to a cover-up if linked to past killings of unarmed villagers?"

"That's a difficult question, John. I suppose yes because of the damage it could do to the agency and careers, not to mention possible prison time. A question you should ask: If an agent killed illegally in Vietnam, what would prevent him from doing the same during peacetime? Power is a heady thing, and power can corrupt one's perception of the law. The Vietnam War, where everyone had weapons and killing was 24-7, strained the morals and ethics of some Americans, causing some to completely disregard them.

"Look at Lieutenant Calley and the My Lai massacre. His lack of leadership allowed his platoon to run amuck, killing innocent villagers and committing rape. Not a bright example for the American military. The army helicopter pilots who flew in and stopped the carnage deserve great accolades for decency!

"Whereas Calley lost control and failed as an army officer, some CIA agents would have more propensities to take matters into their hands, knowing exactly what they were doing and not giving a second thought to their illegal actions. They would have felt omnipotent and that the end justified the means. But I still go with the theory that some of the bad eggs turned bad after their own anxiety and trauma invaded them. PTSD is a severe illness."

"Thanks, Professor . . . and Marcie. I need to go. I have another appointment in Alexandria. You've been very helpful. As soon as I can, I'll fill you in on why I'm asking these questions."

"John, just a word of caution. If these CIA agents are still around, they may not like you bringing up these events. Be very careful. I appreciate your concern about our safety, but I want to help you any way I can. Just let me know what you need."

Nodding, I got up and shook hands with King and Marcie, thanking them both. Departing from the office, I sensed that Reed's suicide had been long overdue. I just didn't have enough sessions with him to understand that. The killing of villagers and noncombatants violated decency as well as the Geneva Convention. Such illegal acts could get a soldier court-martialed and sent to the stockades. Reed killed himself for the horrendous acts he committed. His actions had been so brutal that even with his racist soul and cold heart, he could no longer bear it. These events that his mind had repressed for over thirty years finally drove him to suicide. Seeing Ramsey must have triggered Reed's recall. They committed the war crimes together, and the more I explored, the more questions I needed answered.

☙❧

Walking to my rental car, I pondered, what did it all mean? I hoped meeting with Jim Schaeffer tonight would give me more information on Reed and maybe on Ramsey.

Jim lived in Alexandria, Virginia, some ten miles from Georgetown University, and dinner at his house was set for seven. As four o'clock approached, I decided that I had time to find a local coffee shop, have an espresso, and call into the office. Afterward I would leisurely drive over to Jim's. I checked the voicemail he had left me during my meeting with Professor King; Jim confirmed he would be at his house any time after five, as he got home from the office then. I retrieved my car from visitor parking and drove away.

Being a Starbucks junkie, I drove onto M Street NW and found one. With Starbucks's Wi-Fi service, I could do some more research on the Phoenix Program with my laptop. I parked in a lot nearby and hoofed over to the Starbucks, ready for my espresso fix and access to my emails. I also would have time to check in with Sally.

While waiting for my grande nonfat latte, I pulled out my laptop and thought about Sally. It felt good to know there was a chance for us.

"Grande nonfat latte for John," the barista yelled. I got up from my table where my laptop waited for the Wi-Fi connection and took my drink.

"Thanks," I said.

"Let me know if that tastes OK," the young lady said, beaming like we were old friends—a perk of getting coffee at Starbucks. I sipped my drink, nodded my approval, and headed back to my little table.

The emails finally came up. Sally had sent me a summary of her sessions with my clients. She would still be doing psychotherapy until six, so I couldn't bother her and instead emailed her my thanks for covering my workload. Deep down I really wanted to talk to her, but it would have to wait.

On the internet I searched for any more information about the Phoenix Program. The only additional details came from congressional hearings on the program after the war. They took no action.

I pulled out my notepad and jotted bullet points on the Phoenix Program gleaned from the various links: *labeled a CIA assassination campaign by critics; claims of human-rights atrocities and violations by the CIA, allied organizations, and US military intelligence; US congressional hearings showed abuses occurred; corrupt Vietnamese abused the program to remove personal enemies, falsely calling them VC—allowing their execution; Phung Hoang (Phoenix) chiefs were often incompetent bureaucrats, enriching themselves; monthly neutralization quotas were used, which only increased false arrests; often bribes were paid by the NLF to release their own.*

I remembered that the NLF stood for National Liberation Front—shortened to Viet Cong—the communistic political and guerrilla warfare structure in South Vietnam.

I also wrote the time period of the program in the Vietnam War: 1967 to 1972. I served there when it was operational. More facts surfaced and I added to my notes: *81,740 NLF members were neutralized, with 26,369 killed.* The final tally was larger than Professor King's data, although figures had to be scrutinized; US and South Vietnamese troops often inflated body counts. I suspected the opposite occurred in the Phoenix Program, which likely downplayed those actually killed since innocent civilians were murdered under the American program. We, the good guys, had crossed the line by not controlling the program, condoning by silence any travesty and allowing the blight on American morality.

Closing down my computer, I repacked it in the briefcase and went to the counter to order another latte. I still had some time to kill, so I decided to just sip and relax, enjoying the memory of the night that Sally spent with me. After fifteen minutes, with my to-go cup and briefcase in hand, I walked out of the Starbucks and headed for the car. After clasping my seat belt, I started the drive to Jim's home, figuring that even with the heavy DC traffic, I would get there before six.

ALEXANDRIA, THURSDAY,
DECEMBER 19, 2002

In rush hour traffic on Interstate 395, I thought about Jim Schaeffer. We met in Nam and became close friends, serving as captains in the 101st Airborne Division in the northern most operational area of South Vietnam, designated the I Corps. We both commanded infantry companies in the same battalion, often working in the same combat operations, which focused heavily on repulsing the NVA crossing the demilitarized zone, familiarly called the DMZ, dividing North Vietnam and South Vietnam.

The dangerous A Shau Valley and its environs became our home. We lived and fought in the steamy jungle and on the plateaus, enmeshed in the pungent smells of the jungle decay, feeling the grit meld with our unwashed bodies, enduring the heavy humid air, hearing the forest creatures in their domain, and seeing death regularly—friends and foes grotesquely molded in their final poses. When I left at the end of my tour, Jim extended for another six months of combat near the DMZ. In that time frame, he met Kim at the Phu Bai airbase officers' club, fell in love, and eventually married her within days of his scheduled return to the US. It was a bureaucratic nightmare working with the US Army as well as the South Vietnamese government's archaic system, but Jim's tenacity prevailed. She had to stay in Vietnam for a few months before getting her documents cleared, but Kim eventually joined him in the States.

As couples, we often got together after she arrived in the States. My wife, Katy, helped Kim acclimate to America, and they became good friends. Because I left the army after completing my six-year obligation as a regular army officer, while Jim's military career took them all over the world, we drifted apart, staying in touch only with Christmas cards. Once Jim left the military, however, we managed to reclaim our friendship, and they were at my wife's funeral, providing the strong shoulders that I needed.

Making decent time, I pulled into Jim's townhouse driveway just before six. As I got out, I thought I noticed movement within a black Ford Taurus parked on the street, fifty feet from Jim's driveway; its tinted windows prevented me from seeing inside. I was looking at the car when Jim's front door swung open, flooding me with light.

He stood framed by the front doorway, greeting me with a broad smile. Ignoring the Taurus, I headed to the door. We hugged. Our respect for each other developed into a bond that would go to the grave.

"Come in, old man! God, you look fit," he said, escorting me with his right arm around my shoulders and his left hand tousling my thick brown but gray-streaked hair. Jim's townhouse was a colonial, three stories high, with a driveway leading into his attached garage at the base of the unit. It was a homey place, yet meticulously decorated with a blend of American and oriental designs. Kim stood in the foyer with her arms outstretched. We hugged and kissed. Kim, unlike Jim, was fit and trim; her dark hair was streaked with gray, adding to her Eurasian beauty. Her father, a French Army captain during the French Indochina War in the 1954, had a brief affair with her mother, a young waitress at a bar in Saigon. Kim's delicate facial features and the mystery of Far East Asia had drawn Jim. Her petite five-foot-two frame completed the beautiful package.

Jim on the other hand had added forty pounds to his six-foot body because of his long work hours, extensive business travel often spent entertaining customers with food, and lack of regular exercise.

His lean, muscular body of Vietnam had disappeared, conceding to the good life and the cost of earning it. Some baldness showed through his gray hair, making him look more like a scholar than a business executive. He was happy with his life, having overcome his war demons from Nam.

"John, a drink?"

"Just red wine," I said.

Kim said, "I'm so happy to have you in our home again. We miss you terribly." She patted me on my shoulders as she stood in her high heels, wearing black slacks and a green blouse. Seeing them together made me ache, knowing I wouldn't experience my lovely wife hugging me again. The pain of her loss appeared within me too often.

Jim handed me a glass of Merlot.

"And what are you drinking, Jim?" I said.

"Aw, I have fallen into the habit of Grey Goose vodka martinis with two olives." He picked up his drink from the coffee table.

"Cheers to our dear friend," Kim said. She raised her wine glass, clinked my glass, then Jim's. After the toast, Jim hugged his wife, planting a kiss on her cheek; the gaiety added to my loneliness over Katy's loss. Being surrounded by good friends helped marginally. And the possibility of a relationship with Sally Catton felt right, but no certainty existed with that. Being cautious seemed to be my mantra.

"John, I have book club tonight, so we must eat dinner soon, and then I will leave you two men to discuss your business," Kim said.

"Oh, I'm sorry. We should catch up tomorrow." I took another sip of wine.

"Don't encourage her, John." Jim finished his martini and laughed.

Kim lightly slugged him on his right shoulder. "You should always respect the wife. It is the Vietnamese way," she said, winking at me. Jim winced.

"Yeah, well, once Kim is at her book club, I'm calling the local strip club to come over here and party. What do you think, John?"

Before I could answer, Kim laughed and said, "Poor Jim, he doesn't even know where a strip joint is. And if you do find one, please ensure the house is as clean as I am leaving it."

"On that note, I think we should eat, and then we can talk business," Jim said.

∾

After dinner, Kim kissed me goodbye and paused, looking into my eyes. She slowly stroked my arm.

"You will be OK. Just be happy for the lovely years you had with her. Her spirit is with you. Our ancestors watch over us," she whispered as her eyes misted. "John, you cannot live alone forever. I knew Katy, and she would have wanted you to be happy. This loneliness is not you. You need to start dating."

"Thanks, Kim." My eyes felt moist, and my bravado had taken a step back, shaken by Kim's sincerity, her kindness. I struggled with my many emotions, but I sensed a positive for my life: the beginning relations with Sally. It seemed to relax me.

As Kim shut the front door, I looked at Jim quizzically. "Oh, don't worry; she parked her car on the street so that you had the driveway. She's OK. Let's go into my den. I've got cognac ready."

I followed him into his small lair. "That was a good dinner, Jim. I forgot what a great cook Kim is."

"Yeah, Kim's meals are . . . well, an exquisite blend—oriental and French cuisine. I just enjoy."

He pointed me to a lounge chair by his small desk as he parked his heavy body in his swivel chair. Rotating to face me, he poured two glasses of cognac.

"OK, what I'm about to tell you has to be between us for now. My source is in the CIA and a business friend. He should be trustworthy."

"OK," I said, glancing at my watch. It was after seven. "Wait a moment though—I need to check in with Sally."

"Tell me, have you . . . you know . . . gotten involved?"

"Well," I said, worried that I had assumed too much with her. "She's my associate—a great psychologist."

The deflection didn't fool Jim. He winked knowingly and raised his hands in mock surrender as I dialed the office number on my cell, thinking Sally was still there.

The office phone rang the normal three times before I got the answering machine: "This is the office of Doctor John Moore and Doctor Sally Catton; our office hours are . . ." I punched code number two, Sally's message box. "At the sound of the beep, please leave your message."

"Sally, this is John. I'm running late, but I am at Jim's house and will be staying here. I know you have to be bushed after a full day of sessions, so I'll call you tomorrow. I was thinking maybe I should come back before Christmas. That is, if you want? OK, aw . . . goodnight." I turned off the cell, closed it, and placed it in my suit pocket. I wanted to say that I missed her, but something told me to not push, to be patient.

"You should be dating her. Not a healthy life you have, you know." Jim smiled to counter my shaking head.

I leaned back in the club chair. "Jim, I think there's something but it's still too early to broadcast. I will keep you up to speed. Let's just focus on Reed first. I got the official verdict from the Rock Hill Police, and Reed committed suicide."

"John, I'm sorry. Shit, I know how you care about your patients. Maybe what I'm about to tell you will answer things."

As Jim finished his remark, the doorbell rang. Jim smiled mischievously and said, "Just in time. Wait here." He rose and headed into the living room toward the front door. My curiosity piqued as I sipped the cognac, looking around the den.

Shortly, Jim came back into the den with a man in tow. "John, I want you to meet James Woodruff, assistant director of the CIA. He knows a little about you."

I rose and shook his hand. His smile disarmed me, my surprise showing. Why was he here?

Woodruff's blue eyes were penetrating, a stare probably developed from many years of being an agent for the US. He was about fifty years old, but he looked older, due to the agency and its demands. I could imagine the headaches that came with being a CIA assistant director with little time for anything else. His gray-and-brown streaked hair was thinly combed over his head, delaying the bald look. His slouch disguised his five feet and eleven inches of height. Woodruff's wrinkled cheeks and tired eyes took away from his expensively tailored navy-blue suit. The black diagonal bars on his deep red rep tie completed his look of power. He turned to Jim and accepted the glass of cognac, then returned to probing me with his eyes while claiming the chair opposite me. Uneasiness crept within me.

The caffeine from my espressos earlier had worn off, bringing fatigue.

Jim started. "OK, here goes. I will let James interrupt when he feels the need. Todd Ramsey was a CIA agent in the war and got bounced out of the agency after fifteen years of service. The reason: He had a very severe case of PTSD."

"Why didn't the agency get help for him?" I looked at Woodruff.

"We tried, but his mood swings worked against any healing and thus made him too unpredictable for any assignments. He got a decent buyout to return to civilian life," Woodruff answered.

"So is he the reason for my patient's suicide?" I continued.

"Aw . . ." Woodruff hesitated. "Probably indirectly. But then again, we can only speculate."

"OK, as a psychologist, I can buy that Ramsey triggered Tom Reed's depression . . ."

"Look, John—may I call you by your first name?"

I nodded.

"I know you're familiar with the Phoenix Program," he stated.

I nodded again, not surprised. *They probably know about today's meeting with Professor King*, I thought.

"His handler in the American Embassy in Saigon during the war years verified to me a report that came across his desk in 1970. It was from a South Vietnamese Army captain who charged that Ramsey violated Geneva Convention rules by tossing a Viet Cong POW out of a helicopter. Later there were unproven reports of him executing over one hundred villagers who were noncombatants, west of Da Nang. His US Army assistant, SPEC 4 Tom Reed, served with him during those same periods. All these reports were buried."

"No investigation?"

"Look, I am not making excuses, but the CIA certainly couldn't allow such accusations to come out."

Jim and I glanced at each other. The corruption in that war never ceased to dismay me. Why did we lose so many Americans on the battlefield fighting the NVA while CIA agents destroyed the rule of law, tarnishing the noble but misinformed mission of helping the South Vietnamese stay independent?

I said, "Yeah, and probably that ARVN captain who had the guts to write the report disappeared—killed or sent to a South Vietnamese prison. One of the few ethical South Vietnamese officers. Remember our two assholes, the two psychotic ARVN colonels we encountered in Nam? That night in Saigon." I looked over to Jim.

"Colonels Hung and Loan," Jim said.

"Yes, those two," Woodruff said.

Shocked, I leaned forward in my chair toward the CIA man. "How the hell do you know about those two goons?"

"Suffice it to say that Ramsey, Reed, Colonel Hung, and Colonel Loan knew each other very well. Ramsey and Reed probably sold their souls to those two psychopaths—Hung and Loan. In return, they became mental cases with PTSD. And we know about your encounter with Ramsey, when you saved the lives of the two POWs onboard the Huey," Woodruff said

"This is a bad dream. What don't you know about me?" I said and sat back.

Ignoring my question, Woodruff seemed eager to finish the narrative. "In April 1975, with the US Embassy evacuation as NVA tanks entered the outskirts of Saigon, Ramsey returned to the US. Then he went on special cold war assignments in Europe, particularly in West Germany and the Netherlands. He became the go-to guy for interrogating suspects seen as threats to the US. But his bosses noticed his mental breakdowns and had to keep moving him to less-demanding jobs, and eventually out of the company."

"So he finally gets booted for suffering from PTSD. And no one helped him." I finished my cognac and held it out for a refill.

Jim poured the amber gold into my glass.

"The breaking point occurred over a prisoner going insane while Ramsey interrogated him. It went very bad—Ramsey lost control," Woodruff said and offered his empty glass to Jim for a refill.

I shifted in my seat and stared out the only window in the den, overlooking an alley. My eyes returned to the room. "Then what happened?"

"He became a contract employee for the CIA, continuing the same dirty stuff."

I took another sip of the cognac, shaking my head.

Jim looked hard at me and said, "The two had an ugly secret they shared. Maybe what they did in Nam came back to Reed when he saw Ramsey. A PTSD-damaged vet like Reed could certainly kill himself. You and I know many Nam vets committed suicide upon return to the States."

"There could be something else between Reed and Ramsey besides the PTSD," I said.

"That's plausible," Woodruff said.

Jim and I looked at Woodruff.

Woodruff suddenly stood up and focused on me. "I am requesting we meet in a couple of days. I will have a better briefing for you to explain all this. When Jim contacted me, it raised concerns but also some solutions. I can't say more until I get the plans finalized, so to speak. I didn't want to do anything until I talked to you. This all could work."

"What could work?" I said. My concern must have shown.

"James, John is staying at my house through Christmas. Let's plan on meeting here tomorrow."

"Agreed." Woodruff extended his hand to me as I stood. We shook. Then he quickly walked out, saying, "I can find my way out."

"What the hell, Jim," I said. "What crap are you getting me in to?"

"I don't know, old buddy, but I trust James, and I think he will help clear up the mystery for you." Jim lifted the bottle and asked, "Another one?"

"Hmmm." I rubbed my tired eyes and then picked up my glass of cognac, finishing the remains in one swallow, the burning sensation jolting me. "No, I better not. And I was hoping to return to Charlotte tomorrow to see Sally."

"Reed killed himself because of what he did," Jim said. "I suggest you stay here and return to Charlotte after Christmas. You need the thorough briefing from Woodruff."

We stood in silence.

"Do you have a gun?" Jim said, studying me.

I focused on Jim. My .45-caliber pistol stayed in a drawer in my condo, a replica of the one I used in the war. I was an expert shooter with it.

"Yeah, my .45, why?"

"Precaution. Just to be safe. Please keep it handy when you get back to Charlotte."

Feeling uneasy, I said, "This is a strange conversation."

Jim shrugged. He looked worn. I could tell the conversation had drawn him back to Nam. We stood up.

"Leave the glasses. Now, let me take you to your room."

Jim was silent as he escorted me to the guest bedroom. "You know your way around. Extra towels are on the bed. It is late, and I need some shuteye too. Kim is running late, so we will see you for breakfast." He closed the door behind me as I told him goodnight.

I glanced at the digital clock on the nightstand. It showed midnight. I decided to call Sally even though it was late. I turned on my cell phone and speed dialed her cell number.

After six rings she finally answered. Her sleepy voice said, "Rather late."

"I hoped to catch you at the office earlier today. And now before you went to bed. I'm sorry."

"That's OK. I suppose you are struggling with what we started. Is it hard to include me in your schedule?"

"Sally, that's not fair. I planned on getting a return flight tomorrow. Just so I can be with you," I said.

There was a long pause and then Sally said, "I like that. Maybe you do care about me."

"Of course I do. I think we started something good. Anyway, I feel that way."

"OK, handsome. Call me tomorrow on your return times. I will plan a nice dinner at my house if your flight schedule works. And I do expect you to stay over." She giggled. "Boy I am bold tonight."

"I will be there, Sally. I am slightly drunk from Jim's cognac, so I better get some sleep. Miss you," I said. The words came out easily, surprising me.

"I miss you too, John. Goodnight."

I wanted—needed—to make this work, and deep down, I knew I desired her in my life. I would not hang around DC over Christmas as the CIA had requested.

ALEXANDRIA, FRIDAY, DECEMBER 20, 2002

Kim, Jim, and I had just finished an early breakfast at which I had argued with Jim that I needed to get back to Charlotte today. Upset, he kept insisting that Woodruff expected me to hang around for at least a few days. Just then, Reed's daughter called me on my cell, so I retreated into the living room to answer the call and avoid arguing with Jim.

"Hi, Jane," I said, noticing that Jim had picked up his cell phone. His waving hand conveyed frustration with whomever he was talking to.

"Hi, look, I'm here in the apartment at Rock Hill going through Dad's stuff," Jane said. "I want to get done and get home by tonight. Most of his stuff is going to charity. Did you get the journal?"

"Yes, and thanks for sending it. I want to hold onto it for a while if that's OK?"

"Keep it. It will only remind me of his death. For your information, I'm cremating him. The funeral home will send me the urn later. Don't think badly of me, but I'm not doing any type of service. It's time we moved on, and I can't handle all this anymore."

"No judgment . . . do what you feel is good for you. Are you OK? I'm hoping to fly back to Charlotte late today. Do you need to meet me in Charlotte before you return?"

"No, that's fine, I'm just about done getting everything arranged in boxes and then will get them to the Goodwill drop off. With luck, I can catch the evening flight back to Nashville," Jane said.

"That makes good sense," I said.

"One thing . . . I did find some more of his journal notes here in his apartment. I want you to have them and will drop them off at your office today." Her silence kicked in.

". . . That's fine." I wanted to say something, but the silence took over. Reed's whole life would be summarized simply as ashes in an urn, his personal stuff given away. Reed had evolved into a memory now.

Jane broke the silence. "I don't think I can ever forgive him for killing himself. He left a mess for me to clean. It's so like him."

"Jane, he had mental issues . . ."

"That's all well and good, John. But he failed my mother and me in the end. But thanks for trying to help him and now me."

We hung up. Tom Reed's daughter couldn't be blamed for being upset with her dead dad.

ℰℐℴ

Placing the cell phone in my suit pocket, I returned to the kitchen. Still on his cell, Jim seemed frustrated as well as angry. I noticed Kim gave him space by focusing on cleaning the breakfast dishes. Something seemed wrong. Still, I needed to call US Airways for a flight out today and began dialing the number, all the while studying Jim.

He finally hung up, deep in thought; he took a minute before pocketing his phone and heading to the living room.

Something forced me to follow him as I waited for the airline rep. Ignoring that I had a phone call in progress, he said, "Sorry to do this to you, John, but that was Woodruff. You need to hang around for a day or two, at least."

With disbelief, I hung up on the airline. "Why?" I asked. "I promised Sally I would fly back today."

"I know, I know. Shit, I feel like I am reporting to my old battalion commander."

"You didn't answer me, Jim." The anger showed on my face.

"For national security reasons. He will explain when he comes over tomorrow morning. I'm sorry, buddy. I don't know where the fuck this is going."

"Shit," I said and sat down on the sofa. "National security? What bull is this? And tomorrow is Saturday, which is weird, since he said he wanted to meet today."

"Something came up. You and I are good soldiers. We need to hear him out."

"Crap. What do I say to Sally?"

"Tell her that you are stuck here for a few days because the CIA wants to discuss Reed's suicide. Leave it at that. In the meantime, you will be spoiled here with more home cooking. Not all that bad." Jim's sheepish smile did little to soften my anger. "You better call her," he said as he went into the kitchen to talk with Kim.

It was close to noon, and I hoped Sally had finished with her sessions as I dialed her office phone.

She answered on the second ring. "You're not coming back today. Are you?"

"How do you know these things?" I said, trying to lighten the mood.

"Just tell me why. If you have a good reason, then I have a solution for you to get out of the doghouse."

I felt relieved. "The CIA needs to discuss Reed's death with me. Something about national security that I don't really buy, but Jim convinced me that this is serious, so I should stay over one or two extra nights."

"God. You are making it hard for me to be in a relationship with you."

"But I would pout, and you don't want that. I want you, but I am stuck with Reed's suicide for now." Jim looked at me from the kitchen doorway. His empathy showed. "You were right, I should have just accepted the death and moved on. My nosing around must have hit a raw nerve somewhere. I am so sorry to do this to you . . ." My disappointment boiled.

"Well, John, that's being honest. And since you are beating yourself up, which is good, my solution is whenever you get done with DC, hopefully by Christmas at the latest, you come out to my folks' place on the Outer Banks to spend what is left of the holiday with me. I am driving to the Outer Banks this Sunday since we have closed the office until January 6. No clients. No sessions."

Her tone seemed upbeat, happy. I grasped the solution without hesitation: "Yes, I will be there, and hopefully by . . ."

"No, don't tell me a day. Just wait until your CIA friends are done. And you need to spend some time with Jim and Kim. They are your closest friends. Christmas Day arrival works for me. But you will have to share my bedroom." She laughed.

"I can't wait," I said.

"OK then. I need to get ready for the rest of the sessions today. Call me later. Kisses."

I sat back, relieved. Jim came over, a little nervous, worried about what he may have done to my budding romance.

I smiled at him and said, "It will work. She wants me to come to the Outer Banks by Christmas Day. I just need to get all this CIA bullshit done."

"How about that," Jim said, his big grin dominating the living room. "She is good for you. Oh, I called into the office. My sons are covering the business, so what say you and I tie one on. It is a holiday after all. I make great martinis. Right, Kim?"

Kim came in and sat down next to me on the sofa while Jim hovered over me. "Yes, but also please say you will stay for Christmas with us."

"Yes, but I have an important date with Sally on Christmas Day, so I will leave later that day. OK?"

Happily, she clapped her hands. "Jim, you better make the drinks for you two. I am going food shopping for holiday meals." She kissed me on the cheek and then Jim, grabbed her purse on the foyer table, and disappeared out the front door.

"Well, buddy, it's time you and I get in a happy mood." Jim marched to his bar, rubbing his hands, delighted that things had worked out.

I nodded, relaxed as I hadn't been in days, knowing that Sally and I would be OK despite my delays to see her.

Jim returned with two martinis. "Hey, why change now," he said, noticing my raised eyebrows. "We drowned a lot of demons with booze in Nam. Now we can reminisce about that fucked-up war."

"We seem stuck in a time warp. Always talking about Vietnam," I replied. "After Woodruff's discussion yesterday, I keep thinking of Saigon with Colonels Loan and Hung."

"How the hell could I forget them? Now they're back in our lives," Jim said, dropping next to me on the sofa.

Jim's living room felt good and safe, but Saigon in 1969 did not.

SAIGON, AUGUST 1969

Saigon, the Paris of the Orient, absorbed us with its streets crammed with vehicles: cars, bicycles, mopeds, motorbikes, and military trucks. People scurried in every direction, on sidewalks and through the vehicle traffic. Allied military presence existed throughout the turmoil. US Army and ARVN MPs roamed the streets, ignored by the general Vietnamese population except for the vendors and beggars. Many of the American soldiers, sailors, and airmen, watched by the MPs, sought diversions from the war: bars, willing girls, hookers, or massage parlors with prostitutes. The largest city in Vietnam melded millions of various ethnic backgrounds. The Vietnamese represented the largest segment, but the Chinese population, concentrated in the Cholon district of Saigon, embodied the largest retail and wholesale market region with a bountiful black market. The Colonial French had helped make Saigon a vibrant, international city. The sights, sounds, and smells were unlike anywhere else in the world, and former French colonists still reminisced nostalgically as if it were Paris in Indochina.

Our jeep driver soon found Tu Do Street, which traversed the heart of the red-light district through which we drove, passing the various shops and massage parlors. We were enthralled with the hubbub and flow of people. Throughout the side streets, the black market appeared, stands loaded with US military supplies, everything from uniforms to OD cans of insect repellent—something we lacked constantly in the field. Leaving the red-light district, we spotted the Continental Hotel. We pulled up to the main entrance; Captain Jim Schaeffer and I jumped out with our duffle bags, M-16s, and field gear in hand.

Our driver drove off with instructions to pick us up tomorrow at noon to catch our flight north from Ben Hoa Airport. Our new assignments as company commanders with the 101st Airborne Division awaited us. With our .45-caliber pistols holstered under our fatigue shirts, we watched the jeep disappear in the traffic. Saigon represented danger, not unlike the jungle. The Viet Cong, disguised as civilians in small hit teams, often attacked the city, bombing crowded restaurants, wounding or killing Americans, ARVNs, and civilians. By wearing our holstered .45s, we felt a degree of safety.

The crowded hotel lobby revealed war correspondents and American and South Vietnamese military officers. We had planned to stay at the Rex Hotel nearby on Nguyen Hue Boulevard, but we knew that the US brass held daily press briefings there, called the "Five O'Clock Follies." Having strutting colonels and generals giving us the once-over quickly killed any inclination to stay there. On the other hand, the Continental Hotel appealed to us company grade officers and war correspondents. Unfortunately, the effects of war still confronted us, with begging amputees on the sidewalks by the hotel's entrance, all wounded former ARVN soldiers. South Vietnamese President Thieu cared little about these poor soldiers who had sacrificed much for their country. Schaeffer and I checked in at the reception desk, agreeing to shower and then meet at the Continental Shelf, the veranda lounge of the hotel that overlooked Tu Do Street. I looked forward to having drinks and relaxing with the sights and sounds of Saigon around the hotel.

The hot water sprayed over my body, washing loose the red clay soil that invaded my skin, a part of me over the past months of field operations with the Twenty-Fifth Infantry Division at Dau Tieng and the Michelin Rubber Plantation. The shower pummeled me for thirty minutes before I relented and got dressed to meet Schaeffer at the Shelf. Armed with my holstered pistol on a web belt under a clean jungle fatigue shirt that matched my clean pants, I pulled on my polished jungle boots, courtesy of housekeeping, and made my way to the lounge.

I found Jim waiting for me, seated at a table on the veranda with two cold 333 Beers, called ba ba ba. His gaze stayed riveted to the flow of people and vehicles below, a mesmerizing street scene of a vibrant city surrounded by war. I sat down.

He grunted a greeting. "I ordered the beers. The local Vietnamese beer is much better than the Millers we got in the field," Jim said while still concentrating on the traffic and the scurrying people.

I nodded and took a swig from the bottle. The 333 Beer tasted good. My watch said 1830 hours, prompting us to discuss dinner. We didn't notice the civilian, dressed in a khaki safari outfit with shirt pockets everywhere, approach us. He stopped by me and patiently waited. I turned to him and recognized the French reporter who had joined me during a firefight near the Michelin Rubber Plantation. He had a heartthrob look: He was tall, with olive-toned skin, curly black hair, a Gallic nose, and a smile that captured women's hearts. In his left hand he held what appeared to be a gin and tonic.

"Hello, Captain Moore," said Jacques de Mont.

ॐ

"Well, I'll be damned. You did find me," I said as I stood and shook his hand and introduced him to Jim.

"As promised. After reporting on your unit's combat with the VC at the Plantation, I learned of your new assignment to the 101st Airborne Division as a company commander. There is heavy fighting up there near the DMZ and the A Shau Valley. Be careful, my friend! The NVA are brutal soldiers. The Screaming Eagles are losing company grade officers at a high rate. They will be lucky to have you."

"Thanks. Jim is also taking a company command. Please sit down."

"Merci." He sat down across from us. "And good luck to you too Captain Schaeffer."

As Jim nodded, De Mont put his drink down. He lit a cigarette and offered one to us. I shook my head while Jim instead pulled a cigar out of his breast pocket, bit off the end, lit it, and sucked on it, exhaling a puff of smoke.

"Jim, Jacques de Mont is the reporter I met when I helicoptered in to take over command of the company that got ambushed. The acting CO, a first lieutenant, got killed."

"Shit, that was a bloody mess. We just returned from the Cambodia border operations and missed all that fun you had, John," Schaeffer said, puffing on his cigar.

Jacques began exhaling smoke from his mouth. I watched, fascinated by the cloud of smoke, which he immediately sucked into his nostrils in two thick columns, moments later exhaling the smoke from his mouth, forming two smoke rings. Jim took his cigar in his fingers and stared at the feat, openmouthed. De Mont looked back at us, confused by the attention.

"Captain Moore, I had an interesting talk with one of the retired French officers who fought at Dien Bien Phu in '53 and '54. I am researching for my book about Vietnam."

"OK?" I leaned back in the chair. The beer had relaxed me. De Mont pulled out his field steno pad and flipped some pages before finally stopping, pausing, and reading silently for a minute. I recognized the dark stains on the steno pad's cover; the blood came from the dying soldier next to me during the ambush. De Mont had tried to help me administer first aid while the unit's medic lay a few yards from us, dead from a bullet in his head.

De Mont looked up and said, "The French Foreign Legion lieutenant colonel examined the photos I took of you taking command of the ambushed unit that day by the Michelin Rubber Plantation. He studied the photo of you calling in artillery, while you had that wounded soldier next to you. He seemed shocked. I was too . . . you both bear such a close resemblance to each other. He spent a long time looking at it.

"But there is more, of course. This lieutenant colonel, a Roger Mongin, was captured when the French were defeated at Dien Bien Phu in 1954."

"Hey, that's heavy stuff," Jim said. He was intrigued. Fifteen years before Jim and I had entered the war, the NVA had beaten a modern European army.

I looked at Jacques and asked, "We look alike?"

"I had only a day to spend with him on my way to Paris to finish the edits on my book about Vietnam. My wife was giving birth to our third child, and I was rushing, of course. He seemed very curious about the picture, but he wouldn't talk more about it."

"Well, we probably look alike because I have some French blood, among other blood lines." I chuckled. "Look, we're just getting ready to go to dinner and we should be leaving." I stood up. "You should join us, Jacques."

Jim swallowed his last beer and jumped up. He seemed confused.

I looked at Jim while Jacques hesitated to speak. "Jim, I think Jacques is speculating about my real father. I really don't want to get sidetracked— not now. I need to focus on staying alive and returning home to my wife!

"Look, I never knew my real father and I was adopted, so this might make a good story for your paper, Le Monde, but simply put, my biological father died after World War II. My mother met him in the Grajewo Nazi concentration camp. He died; we presume after the Nazis abandoned the camp. I know nothing about him. She went to great lengths to prevent me from ever knowing. No, I don't believe for a minute that this Roger Mongin is my real father."

"Hell," Jim said. "Maybe you should check this out." He caught my dark look. "OK, then," he said, "guess we should change the subject and go eat."

De Mont swallowed the last of his gin and tonic and signaled the waiter for the bill. "Let me pay as my compliments for your dangerous duty in Vietnam, and now you are heading north to do more combat. N'est ce-pas?"

Nodding to de Mont, I asked, "Will the Rex be crowded with brass?"

"It will not be bad at this time. The Five O'Clock Follies are over by now."

"Yeah, the fucking Five O'Clock Follies," scoffed Jim.

"These briefings have become a show rather than valuable war updates. To get the truth, I talk to regular combat officers like you." De Mont took another drag of his cigarette.

We were ready to leave, but de Mont obviously had more to say.

De Mont stood and continued: "When General Westmoreland first took command, he inflated the success of the US troops using the body count of the dead VC and NVA. Then he deployed the marines as bait at Khe Sanh in 1968, to draw the NVA into battle. The NVA used that battle to conceal their main plans: the Tet Offensive—when the VC and NVA attacked over one hundred cities throughout South Vietnam. Again, these briefings are for political show, to keep getting American troops and funding here. It's manipulated information to tell the world that the Americans and South Vietnamese are winning."

What he said bothered me, but I had no counter reply. I had never dug into the basis for the war, accepting the official version from the army and our political leaders—mostly old men who would never serve—that we were fighting communists to preserve democracy for the world. Being a career army officer meant duty and country with no questions asked.

De Mont took a deep breath and continued. "That is why reporters call these briefings 'the Follies.' Whatever the generals say, we try to validate the information. Many of your top brass are more concerned about ticket-punching their military careers."

"The NVA soldiers are tough and dedicated. Some haven't seen their families for years while fighting the French and now us. I'm not certain if we are fighting communism or nationalism anymore," I said.

"Oui, but your political leaders focus on the Domino Theory and that communism will spread unless they fight here and now."

Jim butted in. "The Puking Buzzards up north will stop them. Hell, they will have John and me fighting there soon." His beer buzz had taken over.

De Mont looked confused, so I said, "That's one of the many nick-names for the 101st Airborne Division. The Screaming Eagles is normally used." I turned to Jim. "You are confusing Jacques. Keep focused."

"OK, Dai uy. Oh Captain, my Captain." Jim rocked on his heels and smiled like a mischievous little kid.

De Mont smiled at the Vietnamese term for "captain."

"We need to go to dinner." I grabbed Schaeffer around the shoulders, pulling him to the lounge exit.

De Mont closed his notepad. "I thank you gentlemen for your insights."

I nodded and pushed Schaeffer closer to the exit while de Mont threw some bills on the table and followed us. The evening breeze on the open veranda made the humidity feel less muggy. I turned to de Mont. "Are you joining us at the Rex Hotel restaurant?"

"Thank you, but I need to finish my dispatches. I will stay in contact as I will be reassigned to cover I Corps, which is where your 101st Airborne Division is located. John, I still have a gut feeling about this French officer and . . . but . . . well, we will see."

I paused at the lounge entrance, still confused and not grasping de Mont's angle about me resembling some retired French lieutenant colo-nel. My mother had never revealed my biological father or provided me his name. I just knew he was French and that they met in the same Nazi concentration camp as slave laborers to the Third Reich during World War II. I felt no curiosity since he had never existed in my life.

As the three of us departed the lounge together, de Mont said, "You will enjoy the walk to the Rex Hotel, a few blocks southwest from here. The Rooftop Garden Restaurant is highly rated. Please use my name with the French chef—he knows me. He will prepare you a tasty meal."

We said our goodbyes again and parted company. After a fast walk through the congested center of Saigon, we arrived at the Rex and immediately made our way to the restaurant. We were quickly seated at a table with a view of Saigon below and its hectic throngs on the streets. I ate slowly, savoring the morsels, while Schaeffer, overpowered by the fantastic aroma, dug in like he hadn't eaten for days. We enjoyed pho (rice noodle soup) and cha gio (spring rolls), followed by the main course of bo tung xeo (sliced grilled beef) and com nieu (rice in a clay pot). And of course we had more of the 333 Beer.

De Mont was correct—the food was excellent. The chef had taken it upon himself to treat us to traditional Vietnamese dishes accented with European flavorings. As Jim babbled, induced by alcohol, I observed the various American senior military officers in their fresh-pressed khakis enjoying their dinners, some accompanied by attractive USO girls.

Jim turned to me and winked. "Rank has its privileges, old buddy."

I turned to my left to see where Jim had been staring. A giggling, young, round eye woman, the slang used for Americans and Europeans, caressed an American colonel's forearm. Our attention had been captured. The colonel had a slight paunch in his tight, pressed khakis. His greedy smile confirmed our thoughts: The young woman would be going back to his air-conditioned trailer for the night. I noticed the wedding band on his left hand.

Returning my gaze to one of the windows facing the west and the darkened jungle and Mekong Delta region, I saw distant tracer rounds— ours in yellow, the enemy's in red. It annoyed me the colonel lived a life of luxury while young draftees were dying in the damp and muddy Mekong Delta, fighting Charlie, the slang for the VC and NVA. This rear area officer was going to get laid in a soft bed while death made its rounds among the less fortunate young Americans in the jungle.

"John, I think I'm going to explore the nightlife of Saigon. You should join me." Jim was horny after scoping the colonel and his young thing.

"You go ahead, Jim. You're single. Enjoy. Besides, I'm looking forward to the hotel bed with clean sheets. Just be careful, and don't get married to a lovely Vietnamese woman."

"No . . . no marriage for me, just some fun." Jim grinned.

"Hello, Captain Moore!" A familiar and menacing voice sent a chill down my back. My discussion with Jim had been harshly interrupted.

Schaeffer and I turned around and looked up into the face of Colonel Hung, who stared down at me. His revolting smile tightened my stomach. Next to Hung stood another ARVN colonel, thin and slightly taller than Hung, with a scowl on his rodent face.

We started to get up from the table, but Hung said, "Please, please, stay seated. May we join you and your friend?" His voice mellowed.

I shrugged and extended my arm, pointing to the two empty chairs across from us. Jim, with his sense for danger, bristled and set his bottle of beer on the table. I felt Schaeffer's tension—he was sitting erect and coiled like a tiger, a predator ready to attack. His beer buzz seemed to have evaporated. I put my right hand on Jim's left forearm, signaling for him to cool it and leave the .45 alone. But Schaeffer stared at the two ARVN colonels, looking for any excuse to shoot them. His hatred for corrupt ARVNs came from seeing Americans die while some ARVNs enriched their lives. The ARVN officers sat down. Both laid their swagger sticks on the table in front of them. Out of my periphery, I saw that Jim had pulled his .45 pistol from his holster and placed it in his lap.

"May I introduce my brother-in-law, Colonel Loan, commander of the Saigon Police?"

The tension thickened like the humidity outside the air-conditioned restaurant. Both ARVNs looked at me sinisterly while Jim kept glaring, his unseen pistol at the ready.

"My pleasure to meet you, Colonel Loan," I said.

"Well, Captain, we had a chance to track you down. We understand you are going north to the 101st Airborne to fight our NVA countrymen." Loan sat with a smirk as Hung spoke.

I nodded in frustration, knowing they could pull strings as allies to access US troop deployment details, a fact I didn't relish. Individual and unit movements were deemed classified, and my intuition told me they communicated such information to the VC when it was beneficial for them.

"You seem to know a great deal. Why do I have the pleasure of your company tonight, Colonel?" I said sarcastically.

Loan interjected, pointing his finger at me. "Your attitude toward a senior allied officer is not appropriate! Remember you are our guests in Vietnam."

Jim's face hardened as I said, "Colonels, I'm enjoying dinner here and have no desire to show any disrespect. Is there something we can do for you?"

"Yes, yes, of course there is!" Colonel Hung said, eager to calm the situation as well. He epitomized the desk jockey, unlike his brother-in-law, who was a killer. "Your report of the ambush at the rubber plantation is delaying reparation funds to me for land that I own there. I would like you to modify the report so as to expedite the payments from your government and, of course, before you go up north. After all, you called in the artillery and destroyed the rubber trees on my acreage within the No Fire Zone of the Michelin Plantation. If you get killed up north, issues with the payments could go unresolved."

Jim blurted loudly to the whole table, "Do you mean the ambush where my friend here lost nine killed?" He leaned forward, daring them to make a move. "According to the rules of engagement, if the enemy attack American or South Vietnamese units from a No Fire Zone, the commander on the spot can dictate return fire of any sort."

Several diners stopped eating and turned toward our table—most of them senior-ranking US officers.

"Jim, let me handle this," I said, again patting his arm, feeling like I had a killer dog leashed at my side.

"I will only speak to Captain Moore!" Hung glared at me, emboldened by Loan's presence. "Change the report tonight. Put the VC outside

the Plantation. That is an order from a superior allied officer." Colonel Hung began to pick up his swagger stick, shaking with anger, trying to hide his fear.

"Like hell he will," said Jim. He stood up and stared down at the two ARVNs, who jerked into action and slid their chairs back, looking around the restaurant for support. Jim held his drawn .45 to his side, pointed to the floor, barely visible. I had never seen him this angry. The occupants at the other tables stared in disbelief. The romantic couple stopped their light petting; the American colonel's eyes showed fear.

I raised my hands, palms facing the ARVNs, and gestured for calmness. "I'm sorry for my friend's outburst. We have had a long day and maybe too many beers. I will not change my report—it's the truth. The VC fired on us from the rubber plantation—a No Fire Zone. They violated the rules and I called in artillery fire, as the commander on the ground, to save American lives. The previous commander was killed, and I flew in to take command, which is something you should be considering with your personal and greedy request. You can talk to my superiors if you wish." I stood up next to Jim. "And now, excuse us."

Hung blurted something in Vietnamese to his brother-in-law. They both stood up. Loan pointed his fisted right hand at me, unfolded his index finger, and moved his middle finger as if he had pulled a trigger on a pistol, the thumb coming down like a pistol hammer. His rodent face grinned, his black eyes looking through me. And just as quickly, Hung and Loan turned and walked out of the room. I then definitely knew Loan as a killer.

Schaeffer and I stared at their backs as they exited the restaurant. Jim still seethed. Nervous, I pondered what had happened, concerned for both of us. We had just pissed off two powerful and corrupt South Vietnamese officers. I wondered if this would get to some American senior officer and I would be dragged onto the carpet with an ass chewing or a written reprimand with ruinous impact on my career. I didn't understand why Hung hadn't gotten the reparation dollars. The American military command bent over backward to embrace the South Vietnamese, buying their support in the war against communism with a lenient reparation payment system. South Vietnamese President Thieu ran a feudal system, surrounded by greed, intent on becoming rich, even on the backs of the poor Vietnamese population. As long as the Americans supported this nepotism, they were sinking in the morass with them while young American troops died in the process.

Jim startled me from my reverie. "What the hell was that all about?"

"Yes, Captains, what was that all about?" Now the American Colonel stood by our table, his drunken conquest for the night draped around his left arm, giggling and eyeing Jim, flirting with him as well.

Horny, Jim returned her smile, turned to the officer, and said, "What the f—"

I grabbed Jim's left arm, pinching him to shut him up. "Sir, those two ARVNs confused us with someone else, and I'm afraid the misunderstanding irritated both sides. Rest assured there's nothing else. We're all good."

Relieved, the colonel, showing off for his bimbo, said, "Well, see to it that there aren't any repercussions, Captain. Those ARVN officers are fine gentlemen and our allies. They deserve the best treatment from us." He swayed briefly as he attempted to stand straighter, trying to impress his pending lay, who still smiled at Jim—the officer too drunk to notice.

His corpulent face revolted me, but I swallowed my pride. "No, sir, we're good. Thanks for your concern and help." It was pathetic but politically necessary BS, and I heard Jim snicker under his breath.

"Well, goodnight. You two enjoy the evening." He turned while the woman kept giggling and whispering to him as well as glancing back at Jim, mouthing something to him.

Jim turned. "What the fuck? Why suck up to that poor excuse of an officer? That SOB would have been dead in minutes in a combat line unit."

"Yeah, and so would have half his unit because he's not a leader. Also, you're drunk, and I just saved your ass and your career, so shut the fuck up around the brass, will you?"

Jim finally smiled. "OK, OK . . . I know. I could have gotten into some serious shit with my mouth." Then he changed the subject as quickly as the weather changes during monsoon season. "Did you see her? She wants me, man. That fat-ass colonel will only pass out on her. What a waste of good puss."

"Christ, Jim, anger and horniness, what a combo. Don't forget you're not in the boonies. You can't just shoot ARVNs or American colonels. Get a hold of yourself."

"I'm sorry, John. I can't see paying those two ARVN assholes a penny."

"Neither can I. That dickhead ARVN colonel doesn't care about the loss of American lives. He just wants American dollars since he has small acreage overlapping the Michelin Rubber Plantation. The same acreage I took fire from."

"That sucks. The fucking corrupt bastard." Jim looked at the entrance of the restaurant, as if he wished the two officers would return. He wanted the physical confrontation. "Those assholes almost ruined a good dinner," he said.

"Let's get out of here. You do the red-light district, and I'm going back to the hotel to write to my wife and go to sleep. This is way too much excitement for one night."

Jim looked at me and said, "I don't know. Maybe I should go back to the hotel with you."

"Jim, go have fun. I'll be OK."

He nodded, concerned though as we walked out of the restaurant.

Standing at the entrance of the Rex Hotel, I said, "Let's meet for a late breakfast at the hotel before departing for Ben Hoa."

"OK. But lock your room." Jim hailed a taxi for his night on the town as a young bachelor.

I turned and began walking to the Continental Hotel to clear my head from a hell of an evening.

I looked at the street signs to orient myself. The Rex stood at the corner of Le Loi and Nguyen Hue, and I had to go northeast to the Continental Hotel on Tu Do Street. I crossed Nguyen Hue with Lam Son Square on my left, knowing I only had a few blocks to the hotel. As I *negotiated the busy night traffic around Lam Son Square, I felt uneasy, as if I was being watched. I stopped on the corner of the square and looked around again. In addition to the Vietnamese scurrying around, I saw two American MPs on patrol approach me. One was a tall, burly black staff sergeant who greeted me with a salute that I returned as they passed and turned right at the corner along Lam Son Square. The staff sergeant's partner, a buck sergeant, shorter and stocky, resembled an Italian American from New York. They were busy eyeing Vietnamese women as I scanned the crowd; I still sensed someone watching me.*

Suddenly I saw them. Across Le Loi Street facing me, three Vietnamese wearing white tropical shirts over their black slacks, concealing any possible weapons, talking and gesturing toward me. Now I had no doubt. The one in the center looked to be five foot eight, tall for a Vietnamese. His two shorter buddies on either side deferred to him for instructions; he had to be their leader. He started to cross the street with his two followers in tow. They focused on me as they swaggered in my direction, not concerned about stalking an American. They had to be Loan's undercover police agents—thugs under official sanction. The hustling Vietnamese pedestrians cleared a path for them as they walked toward me. I turned to continue on Le Loi Street and then saw a fourth person, same attire, walking directly toward me. They had me blocked from the Continental. I looked around and couldn't find the MPs who had passed earlier; however, I knew the direction they had taken.

I changed direction to walk along the square and catch up with the MPs, hoping to have them escort me to the hotel. Moving quickly, I kept glancing behind. Only two followed now: the tall one and a shorter Vietnamese. Then I saw the third one paralleling me across the street of the square. I couldn't see the fourth one and knew that I had made a mistake. I should have returned to the Rex when I first spotted them and then taken a taxi to the Continental Hotel. These guys had me cut off, and I still didn't see the two MPs.

Walking faster, glancing back again to see what they were doing, I collided with an old man sweeping the sidewalk in front of his shop of silk scarves and clothes. The collision caused a melee as the crowd of people swerved or stopped, some yelling as I bent over to help the old, toothless Vietnamese who blurted, "GI, you dinki duo." He didn't need to call me nuts; I felt it.

"I'm sorry, Papa son," I said and pulled him up. Leaving him standing, I hurriedly walked away.

My new plan focused on getting me to the next street and cutting over toward the Continental, but ahead of me, the fourth one stood. His brash smile sent chills down my back. They had me boxed in. I stopped. My adrenalin surged as I weighed the options for my next move. They had maneuvered me into a trap, but they were still forty feet away; I had room to get away.

I turned around again and headed back to where I had collided with the old man. My revised plan meant a diagonal dash across Lam Son Square for the Rex Hotel—my only hope now. The two following me from behind became confused, seeing me reverse toward them. They stopped, hesitantly, and prepared to hold their ground. A voice stopped me. "You hurry in here, GI," said the old man I had knocked down earlier.

My other choices had disappeared. Being trapped by Loan's agents, with no MPs in sight, I ducked through the entrance of the Vietnamese's silk clothing shop—my instincts told me to trust this frail man. The old man's thin but strong arms pulled me toward the back of the shop.

A rear door appeared. Opening it, he said, "You hurry. Go this way to Tu Do Street. Maybe find American MPs. Go now." He shoved me through the door and closed it before I could say thanks. My nerves were frayed. The men chasing me obviously had carte blanche to do anything to me. If they killed me, Hung and Loan could claim the reparation payments without me being an obstacle.

My eyes adjusted to the dark alley littered with rotting fish and produce, creating a bracing stench; its pungency cleared my head. I continued to move. The gloomy alley pointed in the correct direction to merge onto Tu Do Street. I drew the .45 and chambered a round. Hearing voices on the other side of the door, I jogged toward the end of the alley, relieved that I had escaped Loan's agents. After going twenty feet, I heard the *door behind me slam open and two of the thugs rushed through yelling in Vietnamese.*

I kept running but I didn't see the crate in the dark alley and stumbled over it, falling, sliding a few feet on the dirty pavement through the trash, losing my grip on my .45 and hearing its metallic clatter as it disappeared into the darkness. I jumped up, slightly shaken, and saw that escape down the alleyway had been blocked by the third agent outlined by the streetlights. He must have come around the block to close the trap. The two behind me had slowed to a walk; their arrogance pissed me off. I didn't see the fourth agent anywhere. The three converged on me: The tall one stepped closer with a knife in his hand, while the other two stayed fifteen feet behind him with their knives drawn, forming a semi-circle and closing the trap around me. They planned to kill me.

In seconds I mentally prepared for hand-to-hand combat taught me at Ranger School. The tall Vietnamese stood about five feet from me when I feinted with my eyes to my left, his right. He took the bait and stabbed his knife to his right, anticipating my fleeing in that direction. Countering quickly, I stepped to my right. Both my hands grabbed the opponent's right wrist and arm thrusting by me, and I turned, shoving my back into him. The momentum and the push up from my legs lifted the attacker up and over me. The Vietnamese sailed to the pavement, slamming to the concrete on his back as I simultaneously twisted his right wrist until it snapped. The man screamed, and his broken wrist caused the release of his knife, clanking onto the pavement. My momentum carried my knees into his chest, collapsing his lungs. Without hesitation, my right fist slammed into his neck, crushing his windpipe.

His screaming stopped; rasping, gurgling, and suffocating, he knew he would die in minutes. Quickly, I spun to face the other two as I scooped up the dying man's knife and stood now in a crouch. The advantage of surprise shifted to me but for a short time, fleeting by the second. I eyed the remaining two assailants, frozen momentarily and shocked by their leader's demise. I couldn't retreat to the shop's back door because the two effectively blocked me. Slowly and cautiously, the two men regained some composure and closed in on me. Unbuckling my web pistol belt, I wrapped it around my left hand and arm, hoping to parry their knife thrusts with it.

With the captured knife in my right hand, thrust slightly forward, I waited for their attack, knowing that I had bettered my chances of survival. Suddenly a blurred shadow appeared, accompanied by a sickening, crunching thud as the attacker on my right collapsed, his cracked skull spattering blood on his companion. As the now lone assailant jerked back, seeing his buddy collapse, a baton smashed across his face; his nose exploded with a gush of blood as he dropped, joining his downed comrades on the alley floor.

A voice from the dark kept repeating, "You OK, Captain?" The black MP staff sergeant appeared with his hand out for the knife in my grip. "I don't think you need that anymore, sir. Talk to me . . ."

My mind in a trance and my back to a building, I stood frozen, my hand releasing the knife to the MP. The alley's normal stench reappeared, but now with a new smell: the coppery tang of blood seeping from the downed assailants. I knew they were dead.

"Sir say something. Are you in shock?" The Italian American MP buck sergeant stared, shining his flashlight into my eyes. I slowly took a deep breath, realizing I had escaped death. I shuddered, feeling a chill. Seeing the two Americans next to me, I finally relaxed. My dry mouth wouldn't move; both MPs nodded as they stepped in to support me.

"You'll be OK now. You had a close call. Percy, look in the gooks' pockets and see what IDs they have."

The buck sergeant startled me with his harsh response. "Fuck you, Charles. You, black bastard. Don't use Percy. I hate that name." He smiled, bent down, and went through the pockets of the three bodies. "Son of a bitch, these fuckers belong to Colonel Loan—his special agents of the Saigon Police. Fuckers are definitely dead."

"I guess we just killed three VC." Charles pulled out a black-and-white checkered scarf and kneeled over the tall one that I had killed. He tied the scarf around the neck. "There—a fucking dead VC. Percy, you keep their IDs. We'll trash them at the base."

"Shit, Captain, how did you piss off Loan?" Percy asked while nodding in response to Charles.

Unwrapping my pistol belt from my hand and arm, I slowly explained about Colonels Hung and Loan and their confrontation with me over the reparation money for the No Fire Zone.

Both MPs nodded their heads. Percy found my dropped .45, wiped off some rotting vegetables, and returned it to me. "Looks like it's not damaged. You should work the slide to make sure."

I pulled out the magazine from the handle and jerked the slide back, ejecting the chambered round. Charles caught it in midair.

"Nice catch," I said.

Chuckling, Percy turned to his partner. "Charles, you crushed the skulls of the last two—your baton is deadly."

"That's a fact—the stick can be lethal," the black sergeant said. "Percy, you escort this fine young officer to his billets while I will call my man at ARVN MPs. He's looking to make his quota of dead VCs. This will make him happy. Also, we won't have any questions about their deaths. I mean, we can't go around admitting we killed Loan's people."

"Won't there be . . . issues?" I asked.

"Nah, not with this crooked regime. How do you think these Saigon agents get away with murder and extortion? If the citizens don't cooperate, they're labeled VC and their asses are hauled off to prison. Loan tortures the shit out of anyone who is in his way. Even if they're not VC. Some great allies we have, huh?"

"That's why they weren't concerned about going after me on the streets? They would have blamed my death on VC?"

"You got it, Captain," Percy said.

I looked down at the three dead men again, and at the moment I felt little remorse for killing the tall Vietnamese. Raising my eyes from the grisly scene at my feet, I asked, "How did you find me here?"

"The shop owner ran us down and told us about an American captain in danger from police agents. The local Vietnamese hate these

SOBs. Ya know, the extortion, the intimidation. You owe him the thanks. He led us back to his shop and we took over from there."

"I'm John Moore," I said, extending my hand, taking another deep breath.

"Charles Smith at your service, sir. And my sidekick is Percy Barone, better known as Leftie. He hates me using his birth name, Percy. Claims it's a fag name—but I still do, just to piss him off."

"You know, Charles, you're one sorry fucker. If I didn't like you, I would have fragged your ass long ago," Sergeant Barone said, smiling at his own warped sense of humor.

My memory kicked in. "There was a fourth guy working with these three."

"He's in the shop. Must have sneaked in after the old man chased us down. His sons took care of him. We better go. Percy will get you back safely." Charles put his hand on my shoulder, guiding me.

We turned and headed to the shop's rear door. As we entered, the old man greeted us, a relieved smile on his face. "You OK, GI?" he asked, bowing slightly to me.

"Yes. Thank you." I returned the bow, pulled out my wallet, looking for piastres to give him.

He stopped me, placing his hand on mine, shaking his head. "No, no money, it OK."

I was spent and didn't argue. The old man smiled again, pointed to a small stairway leading to the second floor, and led us upstairs.

We entered a large room, barely lit, with several single-size mattresses on the floor. An old woman squatted by a small charcoal burner, heating a pot of tea. Behind her were two muscular young men. In the far corner, the fourth thug was trussed up, hands and feet bound with OD nylon rope, mouth gagged with a dirty rag. He was unconscious and his bruises explained it.

Smith whispered something to the old man, who nodded and pointed to the two younger men.

Barone leaned into me and said, "Those are his sons. They'll get rid of that gook for us."

"But . . ." I started to object.

"No other way, sir. He's a dead man. It's them or him. I think they prefer him dead," Barone said.

The old woman poured several cups of tea. She offered me the first cup. Bowing, I thanked her and took the tea; it was hot, fragrant, and soothing. I needed it. My two American companions helped themselves; they were obviously regulars of the old man's shop.

Barone finally said, "We need to get you out of here so Charles can deal with this mess."

I handed the cup back to the old lady and bowed to her again. Her smile exposed her bad teeth, darkened by years of chewing betel nuts, a common habit of villagers in the countryside. The peasants worked hard eking out a living, and to make it bearable they chewed the nut, a psychoactive substance that produced an energy boost through its natural alkaloids, which released adrenaline. But it also badly stained the teeth.

Shaking the old man's hand again, I hurried downstairs to the front entrance where Barone waited. He had already hailed a taxi.

The taxi took us to the Continental Hotel. My feelings over the incident were still in chaos as I sat in the back seat next to Barone.

Barone asked, "Are you sure you're not Italian?"

"No. Why?"

"Well, you fought like a street hood from Jersey. Did good!"

"Thanks, but I don't want to get in that situation again."

"Aw, shit, all in a day of war in Nam. You'll be OK. Listen, as you heard, I go by the nickname Leftie rather than Percy. Shit, I hate the name Percy. I don't know what my mom was thinking when she named me. Charles's the only one that can use that fucking name."

"Why do you let him?"

"*Ya see, we're good friends and have survived these streets. Fucking Saigon is dangerous. It's our bonding.*"

"*Yeah, I can see that,*" I said.

The hotel appeared and the driver pulled over to the curb by the lobby entrance. As I got out and paid the driver, Barone asked, "*What are your plans tomorrow?*"

"*I'm catching a flight with another officer to Phu Bui. We'll leave the hotel no later than noon after a late breakfast.*"

"*My black buddy and I will be here to cover you. We'll probably be drinking coffee on the veranda—just to be sure you get off safely. OK?*"

"*Thanks.*"

"*Just keep your door locked and the .45 near you tonight. And don't acknowledge us tomorrow—we'll be watching, though. Also don't tell anyone of this. The less who know, the better.*"

I nodded at our necessary conspiracy. We shook hands through the taxi's open rear window. Barone and the taxi drove off. The ordeal had ended.

I made it to the room after checking the lobby and the hallways. My watch said 2200 hours. Exhausted, I entered my room and locked the door. I also butted the desk chair against it. I stripped and threw myself onto the bed, placing my .45 under the pillow with its safety on and a round chambered. Thoughts of the fight rampaged in my mind as I drifted off to sleep.

Later I woke up nauseous, my stomach aching. Getting out of bed, I saw that my watch showed midnight. I wiped my moist forehead and rushed to the bathroom. Stuffing my head into the toilet bowl, I vomited. I had killed a human being with my hands.

ⓍⓍ

Suffering from a hangover, Schaeffer dozed in the web seat across from me in the C-130 as it began to taxi on the Ben Hoa Airport runway, preparing for takeoff and headed for Phu Bui.

At our late breakfast, Jim told me of his night with a prostitute while I acted captivated by his erotic tale. Even his hangover didn't curtail his storytelling.

While he talked, I tried to rationalize what I had done. My self-defense justified the killing, but the thug's death gnawed at me. I had already killed in combat. But this seemed different. I hoped my transfer to I Corps would take me away from the intrigue and corruption associated with Hung and Loan.

Schaeffer never noticed Sergeants Smith and Barone on the veranda drinking coffee, reading the Stars and Stripes newspaper, occasionally glancing our way with disinterest. As agreed, I didn't acknowledge them.

The aircraft's engines revved louder as it lumbered down the runway, gaining speed and finally taking off. I smiled at Schaeffer's sleeping form as the aircraft rose above the ground. Soon we both would be commanding infantry companies, and I knew that my killing would continue.

ⓍⓍ

I couldn't sleep due to the noisy, vibrating air force cargo plane, and I resorted to looking out my porthole at the gorgeous country below. The manicured and flooded rice paddies glimmered in the sun, blending with the forests and jungles. We flew over 500-pound bomb craters created by air force B-52 bombing runs, the ground pock-marked with craters full of turquoise-colored water, filled quickly with the water-saturated soil after the bombs exploded. However, some craters looked less appealing; water, mud, and dead bodies mixed, creating pools of brownish red.

Over the Central Highlands, I enjoyed a splendid aerial view of isolated Montagnard villages plugged into the forests, blending with the foliage and mountainous terrain.

"I'm glad we have sister companies to command in the same battalion," Jim said, stretching and yawning awake.

I gazed at Jim and said, "The high attrition of captains certainly helped us get commands."

The C-130 hit a pocket of air turbulence, lifting us off of the web seats and interrupting the discussion. The pilots were flying at top air speed to get to Phu Bui before it got too late. ETA at Phu Bui was 2100 hours—a long day for the two of us due to multiple stops, dropping off troops and supplies along the way.

"Yeah," Jim said. He stopped staring out the porthole, the evening darkness obscuring the scenery below.

The C-130 shook again. A storm started outside, and we saw the rain streaks across the portholes. In the mountainous region of I Corps near Phu Bui, the temperatures fluctuated from high humid heat in the day to cold in the evening, sometimes leaving frost in the early morning hours. It rained almost daily in the afternoon, influenced by the China Sea only miles away.

The I Corps area included the DMZ and the infamous A Shau Valley with its Ho Chi Minh Trail, the supply route for the NVA, entering South Vietnam from the North. The 101st Airborne, with its huge airmobile composition of helicopters, had the unending mission of fighting the NVA around the A Shau Valley and the DMZ. I didn't realize that night, while the aircraft bucked the turbulent air streams, that my new home for the remainder of my tour would be in or near the A Shau Valley.

ALEXANDRIA, SATURDAY, DECEMBER 21, 2002

Jim and I had just finished a light breakfast and sat on the couch in misery, trying to deal with our hangovers from last night, the war stories flowing as we drank. I struggled with the bright sunlight and ignored Jim's hurt feelings while Kim banged some pots and pans in the kitchen, ensuring we knew that we had little sympathy from her.

"I'm still pissed at you for not telling me about the fight with Colonel Loan's goons in Saigon. Why would you wait until now? I thought we had each other's backs," he said.

"Jim, I'm sorry, but at the time I worried about keeping both of us safe from any repercussions of those deaths. The less I said about it, the safer. I also wanted to protect the two MPs who really saved me."

He shook his head as he stood up to answer the doorbell. I closed my tired eyes, trying to ignore the new noise of the persistent door-bell chime.

As the visitors entered, I recognized them as Vietnamese; my year in war embedded their ethnicity in me. They were both about five foot four in height, with thin bodies and neatly cut hair with sidewalls. One looked in his thirties, almost boyish—a trait I found common among most adult males in Nam. His thick black hair glistened. The other man showed older; his white sidewalls and the gray mixed into his dark hair betrayed him to be in his fifties. Both wore expensive dark suits, although my mind flashed back to the older man wearing the OD fatigues of the NVA. He looked familiar.

My hangover made it difficult to stand while Kim rushed to greet the two at the front door, speaking her native Vietnamese. The older man entered the living room and politely bowed to me, while the youthful one stayed back a few feet scanning the room, barely acknowledging my presence. I noticed the slight bulge on the left side of his suit. I wondered what type of pistol he carried, but he looked as if he could deal with physical danger without it.

Kim, knowing Jim and I were out of it, invited both men to sit in the matching sofa chairs across from us. In my periphery, I caught the movement of the younger Vietnamese as he moved back to the front door and leaned against it, guarding it. He said something to Kim in Vietnamese, and she nodded. His stern face revealed nothing. I felt that any sudden movement by Jim or me meant a threat; the younger man obviously protected his older associate. Returning my attention to the older gentleman, I waited.

"Mr. Moore forgive my intrusion, but Mr. Woodruff recommended that I visit you as soon as possible," the older one said.

I raised my eyes, confused by him knowing my name.

As he settled into his chair, I checked him out. We seemed the same age, but unlike me, he still maintained a military bearing. I felt déjà vu, knowing I had seen him somewhere. The old, small scar on his left cheek had the look of a bayonet wound; he had been in combat.

"How do you know me . . . ?" I asked.

"I felt I could not wait any longer to finally meet you again." His attempt at smiling seemed genuine, but I remained cautious.

"Would you like tea or espresso, Colonel?" Kim asked him as she brought my latte to me. She gently placed two aspirin in my palm.

I murmured, "Thanks." I gratefully looked into her face. Her beautiful smile assured me that she would be taking care of me today. Jim, however, seemed to be in the doghouse.

Keeping his eyes on me, the older man said, "Yes, please, an espresso. You are a very gracious host, Kim." He followed that with a burst of Vietnamese.

She smiled in response, said a few more words in Vietnamese, and returned to the kitchen. Jim still nursed his cup of coffee. I hoped I didn't look as hungover as he did. But then, Jim always took things to extremes.

I whispered to Jim, "You look like hell."

"Thanks, buddy," he grunted. "You don't look so hot yourself."

"I'm confused. You said, 'to meet me again,'" I said to the older Vietnamese.

He ignored the question and leaned in toward me, offering his hand. We shook.

"I am Colonel Zang, the military attaché of the Socialist Republic of Vietnam at the embassy here in Washington, DC."

I released his hand, still trying to understand all this.

"Mr. Moore, you may not remember me, but I was a young NVA lieutenant, aide to Colonel Tin during the American Indochina War, when circumstances forced us together."

I had been correct about him being in combat. I searched my memory. During the war I had encountered all sorts of Vietnamese: Montagnards, peasants, South Vietnamese military, and of course the enemy—the VC and NVA. Since he was close to my age and part of the Socialist Republic of Vietnam, he must have confronted me on the battlefield. Zang's rank and aged eyes expressed a maturity and wisdom from years of war. Dressed in a black, slim-fitted, European-style suit, white shirt, and a bold gold tie, he conveyed authority.

"I'm sorry, Colonel, I can't place you," I said.

Zang nodded and continued to talk. "When I was assigned to the United States for embassy duty two years ago, I attempted to locate you. I am afraid I was misinformed that you were dead . . . I apologize for being . . . complacent . . . and accepted your death without further investigation."

"Moore is a common name. But I am still confused on why you wanted to find me," I said after another sip of latte.

He paused as Kim brought him his espresso. She placed it on the table by him.

"First, *how* is easier to explain. Your friend Mr. Schaeffer had made inquiries to the CIA about Todd Ramsey. Mr. Schaeffer was discreet using his personal contact, but Mr. Ramsey's name is red-flagged by my government because of the war crimes he committed while operating the Phoenix Program. Inadvertently, your name came into play."

"Hm. I take it that the CIA is cooperating with you as well?"

"Yes, they are, Mr. Moore." Zang beamed a confident smile, still holding his secret.

I sat back, waiting for the rest of the story. Reed's death seemed to be bringing up much from the past.

"Now, as to *why*. My ancestors, my family, and I are in your debt. I hope what I tell you now will allow you to remember. I was a prisoner of war on an American helicopter with you. I believe you were returning to Cam Ranh Bay from the jungles near the A Shau Valley. I memorized your name that day from the name tag sewn on your fatigues."

He paused as he looked into my eyes, waiting for my recall. Slight wetness appeared in his eyes.

"I placed it into my mind." He then sounded out my name as if he was reading it from that sewn-on tag: "MOORE." Another pause. "You saved my life!"

Silence took over the room as I sat looking at Zang. Everyone looked at me, waiting for the next bit of drama. I now remembered: it was the same daydream I had days ago before I met with Reed in therapy, in which Ramsey had been an integral part.

I didn't know Zang by name in the war, but I now recalled a scrawny, beaten-up NVA lieutenant, dressed in green cotton fatigues and spattered with dirt and blood, his left cheek crusted in dried blood from a bayonet slash; the wound was new then. I glanced at his cheek and saw scar tissue hiding some of the deep cut.

Ramsey had tried to toss Zang out of the Huey at three thousand feet to force cooperation from the other POW, a full NVA infantry colonel. Or so I thought. But I had stopped the CIA agent from killing the young POW.

I broke the silence and said, "I'm happy that you survived the war, Colonel. And I'm sorry that I didn't recognize you. It's been a long time. Unfortunately, unethical actions were conducted by both our countries. I take it that Tin is the name of your colonel onboard the Huey that day."

"Yes. And you acted honorably as a soldier," Zang said, bowing his head slightly toward me.

When he raised his head, he couldn't hide the moisture welling up in his eyes. Then, suddenly, catching me off guard, he reached over, offering his hand again. I smiled and returned his handshake. He shook my hand vigorously; his strong grip thrust me back to another time when NVA and American soldiers killed each other:

The evening monsoon hit hard, hurling rain in a strong, unrelenting downpour; rivulets formed throughout the landing zone, the LZ. My men, wet and tired, struggled in the mud in their firing positions. Their gaunt faces and bloodshot eyes tormented me as they fought both nature and the North Vietnamese pouring in from the surrounding dark forest of bamboo and palms. Visibility dropped in the darkening evening. Bullets sang—the familiar pop, pop, pop of the enemy's AK-47 rifles countered by the sharp metallic chatter of American M-16s. Both sides shot blindly in the dark hoping to hit their enemy. Another one of my men fell wounded. I shot my .45-caliber pistol, emptying the magazine at the enemy, a group in firing stances approaching me. They fell dead except for one lone survivor, an NVA officer, who stood alone among his dead comrades, a ghostly appearance out of the mist. Suddenly he rushed me, his pistol waving, yelling for others to follow—none were left. We collided and grappled; my pistol knocked out of my hand. I seized his wrist, holding him as I flipped him over me facedown into the mud. I heard a snap. Not releasing him, I dropped to my knees as he struggled to stand. I pulled out my bayonet and sliced down into his back, behind his heart. I turned to see my men still slugging over the wet terrain from one fighting position to another. Then I stared at the dead NVA's hand, broken at the wrist, fingers splayed, still held firm in my hand.

I stared at Zang's hand, my right thumb digging into his wrist. I looked up to see his grimace.

Kim, seated by Jim now, asked, "John, are you alright?"

I released his hand and dropped my hand to my lap. A trickle of sweat found its way down my back. I bowed my head as nausea swept my stomach. We should be paying tribute to each other as past enemies in an unneeded war, countries now at peace with each other. Instead we wearily stared at each other. The silence lasted for what seemed minutes.

"I . . . yes, we are OK," I said to Kim. Zang rubbing his wrist shook his head to his bodyguard, who I noticed had stepped toward us. The young man slowly returned to his post at the front door. Zang and I were like tired boxers returning to our corners, looking bewildered. I felt sick. I felt my hangover fighting me.

"I'm sorry, Colonel Zang . . . some . . . past memory . . ." I said, looking away from him.

The silence became unbearable as I sat, embarrassed. Zang made the peace overture.

"Mr. Moore, I understand. My own flashbacks of killing in the war still haunts me. You must feel the same."

"So long ago, wasn't it?" I said, fighting the memories that still held me. I took a deep breath to slow myself down as I waited for more, knowing I had intimately killed one of his fellow NVA officers. Yet we were not different—we both had killed, and we both carried the emotional baggage of that war.

"Yes. We paid dearly for our countries." He tried a weak smile, concerned.

"Again, I'm sorry about the grip . . ."

"Please forget it. I wish to pass on a message of gratitude from Colonel Tin, who thanks you for saving this unworthy aide's life as well as his. He is over eighty years old but still has strong influence with our party and our government in an advisory capacity. He is anxious to talk to you—in Hanoi."

"Hanoi!"

Zang looked slightly confused at my response, but he proceeded.

"Before we discuss Hanoi. . . Briefly, my government wishes to close the wounds from the war and help the aging relatives of the war dead have some peace. The CIA's Phoenix Program killed many Viet Cong freedom fighters—many thousands. There were also many innocent civilians killed or tortured by South Vietnamese officials and Americans such as this Ramsey. We know that Mr. Ramsey is responsible for the killing of over one hundred civilians from the village of Giang in the My Son area. This does not include the unknown number of prisoners of war that he killed—all actions violated the Geneva Convention."

"Giang is in the Central Highlands?" I asked.

Zang smiled slightly, his youthfulness as the young lieutenant sitting on the floor of that Huey showed behind the face lined with the wrinkles of an older man from a war some thirty years ago. His face continued to push me back to my grief over my men who died in combat.

"You do not disappoint me about your knowledge of Vietnam," he said, bringing me back. "Ramsey and a corrupt South Vietnamese Army officer—Colonel Loan—and also the American soldier, Reed, targeted the village on a false mission to destroy the VC cell that operated in the area."

"Loan was on the helicopter with us," I said.

Jim looked at me. "The same guy who ordered the thugs to attack you in Saigon in 1969?" he said.

Zang gave us a curious look.

"Last night I told Jim Schaeffer about my first entanglement with Colonel Loan in Saigon, which almost cost me my life due to his agents who pursued me in an alley in 1969."

"So you should know that as head of the National Police, he shot a captured and unarmed Viet Cong in the head while on the streets of Saigon during the Tet Offensive in 1968. The international press photo taken of him doing the shooting went worldwide," Zang said.

I nodded. "Yes, that would be the same Loan. But Reed wasn't on the helicopter with Ramsey, Loan, and us that day. Can you confirm that Reed was with Loan and Ramsey at the killing of the villagers?"

"He was," Zang said.

While Colonel Zang talked, my brain again sought the past about the South Vietnamese Army Colonel Loan and the other South Vietnamese Army officer—Colonel Hung—who confronted me because of my decision to call artillery into the No Fire Zone of the Michelin Rubber Plantation.

Then we sat in silence for several minutes, neither one of us willing to talk first.

"Mr. Moore, since we can share the past now, I wish to honor you in the present. Would you return to Vietnam to meet with my Colonel Tin?"

"Why? You already thanked me for Colonel Tin."

He seemed to be forming an answer. I sensed he floundered on how to say what he wanted.

"It would honor the Socialist Republic of Vietnam for you to visit us. I know now your wife has been dead three years, so maybe it is time for you to return to the country that has been the cause of your war memories and pain."

I frowned. "I'm not certain that will help. It may cause me more pain."

"Then for justice and your duty. What I tell you has to remain a secret," he said.

I nodded. My eyes struggled to focus from the alcohol buzz of last night. Suddenly I felt tired. The episode with Zang, Tin, Ramsey, and Loan on the Huey helicopter occurred a matter of days before I was due to out-process back to the States. The more than 365 days leading up to it, with all the horrors of war, had already tarnished my soul.

"Colonel Loan is an enemy of the state, and yet he managed to escape to America in 1975 as our glorious army entered Saigon. He was helped to flee out of the city by helicopter, as we now know, by CIA Agent Ramsey."

I raised my hands. "I'm not surprised," I said.

Jim and Kim listened intently, their eyes on me. For once, Schaeffer had little to say.

"My mission is to return Loan to our country for trial and imprisonment," Zang said. His tone was quiet yet forceful.

"The CIA is helping?"

"Unofficially," he answered.

"But how do I figure into this?" I asked, trying to read his body language. He remained sitting upright, studying me stoically. "If he is to stand trial, how do you get him back to Vietnam? I assume he would be a US citizen now." I took another deep breath, trying to remove the fog surrounding my brain.

"We will. That is all I can say. But we need your help, at minimum to be a witness against him based on the helicopter incident."

"Zang, I'm not certain," I said. "I feel you have something else planned."

I looked around the room. What had I accomplished coming to DC? Reed was dead. Nothing could change that. Ramsey—well, what did I really know about him? My brief encounter with him in Nam, even as violent as it was, still left him a vague memory after all these years. So why was he in my life again, years after Nam?

⚬✕⚬

After a light lunch that Kim made, we finished our talks. We all agreed that Zang and Woodruff would return together on Sunday to brief me more. I still planned on leaving DC on Christmas Day. As soon as Colonel Zang and his bodyguard departed, I told Kim and Jim I needed a nap and left them sitting in the living room. Jim continued to look like hell.

Taking my cell phone out, I sat on the bed and checked for messages. Sally had called while I got drunk last night. It pleased me that she had tried to reach me.

"Hello?" she answered after a few rings.

"It's John. OK to talk?" I asked, anxious like a teenager.

"Yes, I'm packing for the Outer Banks and leaving early tomorrow morning."

"Ah ... well look, I promise to drive down early on Christmas Day."

Sally seemed to hesitate. "You better," she finally said.

"Sally, I'm growing attached to you, you know." I hoped she would confirm the same.

She chuckled. "Just get back here. And get this Reed episode out of your system while you are in DC. Remember, you did not cause his suicide."

"I like that you care." I shook my head. What was next for us?

"I do care about you, but again, Reed killed himself over PTSD-related trauma—no matter what or who caused the triggering catalyst."

"OK, I agree. It's nice to hear your voice," I said, feeling something that I hadn't dare approach before.

There was silence and then Sally said, "You're not listening to anything I'm saying, are you?"

"Well . . . yes . . . It's just so nice to hear your voice."

"Have you been drinking?" she responded.

"Last night with Jim. I miss you."

She paused. "And I miss you too. Now hurry back to me on Christmas. Oh, before I forget, Jane Phillips came by late yesterday and dropped off some notes left by Tom Reed. Thinking you'd want them sooner rather than later, I scanned and emailed them to you."

"Yes, that's great. Maybe this will help me understand the CIA's involvement," I said. "I will call you later. Goodbye, Sally."

"Goodbye, John."

I felt comfortable about the two of us as I stretched out on the bed, closing my eyes, welcoming the nap.

☙

How had I survived the twelve-year-old scotch and martinis last night? I shook my head. I promised myself no more heavy drinking with Jim, not without Kim to run interference. I leaned back on the sofa and finally looked at the sheets of the scanned documents that Sally had emailed me before my nap. Jim had let me use his printer to make copies while he puttered in the kitchen. I hoped he held up on the booze until after dinner, which would be in another hour, at six.

My eyes searched the copies. I froze at the first sheet—a copy of a handwritten note with Todd Ramsey's name and a phone number. On a separate page, a copy of the Rock Hill Police evidence tag stated that the note was folded in with the airline tickets. Now I definitely knew: Reed had lied in our session and in his journal writings. He had talked to Ramsey at the VA hospital and exchanged phone numbers. Was this his only encounter since the end of the war?

Running into Ramsey triggered Reed's anxiety and forced him to seek the VA for counseling and got me instead for the Friday session last week. I now knew they shared the traumatic event of killing one hundred villagers. I glanced at the sheet with Ramsey's phone number again, pondering on whether to call him; I set it beside me on the sofa.

Next, I checked the other two sheets, which I had never seen before. There were puzzling lists in no particular order on both pages. Reed had jotted down places, names, or maybe events that popped into his mind, trying to retrieve items for his therapy. It proved Reed had knowledge of Giang, My Son, and the hundred killed villagers. More damning, it associated Tom Reed with the killings at Giang, along with Ramsey and Colonel Loan. I brushed my hand through my hair. Why did Reed participate in the killings?

Rereading the first page, I studied all the items; his sloppy handwriting slowed me somewhat:

My Son/Cham/Montagnards

Giang village/100 killed/VC?

Gold/Cham artifacts/Ramsey

Phoenix/Da Nang/Marble Mtn

The hundred villagers had become Reed's misery, but the other notations, such as the gold, the artifacts, and Montagnards, needed more clarity. Why were they not fighting the war like me? Some of the places, like Marble Mountain near Da Nang, I recognized instantly. Marines battled around that huge formation controlled by the VC in their catacombs in the mountain. From these caves, the enemy safely observed the marine base around Da Nang, directing mortar rounds onto the compound.

The Cham people reference confused me. Why would a young army grunt just out of high school have any knowledge of this ancient tribe of Vietnam's Central Highlands? Could Reed have been more cerebral than I thought? But I knew better. Also, Colonel Zang confirmed that the hundred killed were Vietnamese civilians, not VC. And even if they were Viet Cong, they were executed while unarmed.

I flipped to the next page to find more notes catalogued:

Grove of Banyan trees/caves/hill

My Son/Village elder/Giang

What had Reed tried to say? The lists must be tied to explaining the issues compounding his life days before he had his session with me. He created a puzzle for me to solve.

Jim walked in wearing jeans and a blue sweater. His evening dress code, I guessed. He grinned at me and handed me a martini. "Dinner will soon be ready. You need this drink."

I shook my head, resigned to the inevitable. I took the glass as Kim yelled from the kitchen, "Just one drink. No more. You two are pushing it. I want to see my guys normal, not the walking dead."

Jim winked at me. We both laughed.

ALEXANDRIA, EVENING, DECEMBER 21, 2002

Woodruff stood in Jim's living room. "I thought I would update you both in person before I get home."

"So, what is happening now?" Jim asked.

I stood next to Jim. The dinner that Kim prepared had me in good spirits. But now that could change.

"Ramsey lives in a cape cod off Casco Bay at Cape Elizabeth near Portland, Maine. Years back, he told me he loves the view, especially at night—the aesthetic reason he bought there. His key reason to buy the house came from his ability to monitor an approaching car from the mainland on the single road leading to his house on the peninsula. Surrounded by the Atlantic Ocean, it also provides observation for any approaching boats," Woodruff said as he took the scotch that Jim offered and sat down on the couch.

"Are you saying that Ramsey is there now?" I asked.

"Ramsey and Loan both are," Woodruff said. "We have them under surveillance and my men are concealed to avoid any attention."

"But you don't know," Jim said. "Ramsey is not a dummy. Even if he has PTSD."

"Of course, there is no certainty on our surveillance being unobserved. That is a risk we take. I wish we had the place bugged to hear their conversations."

"What are they doing together, I wonder," I said. "They don't live together?"

"No, Loan is probably selling coke to Ramsey. We know he has a habit." Woodruff took a sip of his drink and leaned back, relaxed.

"No further action by you?" I asked Woodruff.

"No. We just wait and hopefully draw them to Vietnam. Their activity does suggest something is going to happen soon."

Woodruff's cell phone buzzed. He clicked it to answer. "Hello," he said.

Jim and I focused on Woodruff as he quietly listened to the caller.

Finally, he clicked off, saying goodbye. "Loan just left Ramsey's house. We are tailing him, but we assume he is headed back to his place in Boston."

"You are cavalier about them. Hope your plan with the Vietnamese works," I said. I hoped my bemused statement would convince Woodruff that I wouldn't go to Vietnam.

"I wish I could tell every little bit of information, but please understand you have the broad strokes, the big picture. You need to consider that in your final decision. We need you to go."

"I'm sorry, James, but I think this whole project is far from clear to me, and too involved for an untrained person like me. That is why I am not in favor of going."

Woodruff sat on the couch and stared at me. Minutes went by and then he stood. "Fine, but we have another meeting to go into this more, which I have to reschedule from tomorrow to Monday. I need more time to get ready."

Jim said, "James, that's good... We'll see you Monday. I know that John will keep his mind open."

I nodded.

Woodruff headed to the door and said, "See you Monday, then."

ALEXANDRIA, SUNDAY, DECEMBER 22, 2002

After Woodruff told us that our next meeting was moved from Sunday to Monday morning, I decided to quit worrying and get a decent night's sleep. Having nursed one martini the whole evening, I felt better and went to bed early Saturday night.

At Sunday breakfast, I noticed that Jim had a buoyant mood as well—thanks to Kim regulating the drinking. As we finished eating, Jim's sons showed up and the morning got away from us as we talked and laughed.

Seeing Jim's family on this quiet Sunday made for a relaxed day, but my concerns over tomorrow's 10:00 a.m. meeting with Woodruff seemed to show.

"I feel the same," Jim said. "It feels as if we are being manipulated. On the other hand, you are spending the Christmas holiday with us. So that is a good thing."

"Yes, but this pitch by the CIA and Colonel Zang is confusing, and it all seems ambiguous."

"Well, let's see what they have tomorrow."

"I'm telling you now that I'm not going to Vietnam for whatever reason they give. I think I trust Zang more than the CIA. There is something missing in Woodruff's explanations."

Jim nodded and sat down with two martinis, handing me one of them. "Kim said we can have one before dinner," Jim said, a big grin on his face. "And it is your call on going back to Nam. I'm here to support you, buddy."

"To tomorrow and whatever it brings," I said, clinking Jim's glass.

"Did you call Sally?" Jim asked.

"No, she's driving today and left me a message on my cell to call on Monday or Tuesday. She will be busy with her folks getting ready for Christmas."

Jim grunted. "You know, this beats the hell out of the jungles of Vietnam," he said.

I took a small sip of my martini and nodded.

ALEXANDRIA, MONDAY, DECEMBER 23, 2002

Most men don't have close male friends since their lives are dominated by work, a competitive world especially where climbing the corporate ladder prevents closeness. Jim and I had the war as a bonding factor, as well as relying on each other for survival, allowing our friendship to grow stronger ever since, even with long gaps between seeing each other. It was a given that one of us would be there for the other. I still believed that about us.

And we unconsciously demonstrated our unique bond sitting on the sofa together, Jim next to me on my right. Opposite us James Woodruff comfortably sat in the plush club chair. Colonel Lin Zang of the Socialist Republic of Vietnam sat to Woodruff's right and directly opposite me in the other chair.

Zang and Woodruff arrived within minutes of each other after 10:00 a.m. All four of us were in business suits, white shirts, and conservatively patterned rep ties. Military habits of being in the correct uniform for an occasion were hard to break. It looked like a corporate business meeting. Jim felt it important to play the part, and I agreed.

I checked Jim. Even though he was polite, he harbored ill thoughts of the war and fighting the NVA. Having a former NVA officer again in his home and drinking a glass of his beer seemed strange.

My eyes turned to Zang. His uneasiness showed, more so than I experienced with him last Saturday in this same living room. Zang looked tired but still maintained his sense of power, fit and lean, dressed in a slim-fitted black suit and a bold, bright red tie with gray diagonals. The bayonet scar on his left cheek still served to identify him.

"OK, we should start this meeting," Jim said. He spoke low and without enthusiasm, performing an obligation. "I again vouch for John Moore, who served in Vietnam as a combat officer, as I did. His Top Secret security clearance as an army officer is on file. More importantly, he is my closest friend. My wife is out of the house, so we are just the four of us in the house with Colonel Zang's security man outside."

I glanced at Jim. This meeting had risen to another level compared to the previous meetings with Zang and Woodruff.

Woodruff nodded. Zang followed by bowing his head. His eyes were still on me.

I had to interrupt. "Jim . . . I'm confused."

"I apologize, John," Jim said, "but I was asked to keep the content of this meeting a secret."

I waited for the next bombshell.

"And John has his passport with him, and I believe, Colonel Zang, that you will facilitate the visa for him if this goes as planned." Jim's tone approached a monotone. His normal vivaciousness had disappeared. There had been pressure put on him.

Zang nodded. "Mr. Schaeffer, I will have them delivered to your house tomorrow night."

"But . . ." I paused, sensing my lack of control.

"John, trust me. As a precaution and to save time, give the Colonel your passport just in case you go."

If it had not been Jim, I would have refused. But Jim I trusted, and to support him and his business relation with the CIA, I pulled out my passport and handed it to Zang. "This doesn't mean I'm going," I said.

Zang gave a nod. "My associate whom you met Saturday is in the car with a camera and will take your photo before we leave here."

"Jim, I think you need to explain what is going on!" I looked at him, irritated.

Jim patted my arm. "Soon enough, John. And I'm sorry for being so secretive." Jim's stress showed. I didn't like it.

The ensuing silence dominated as I sat looking at Zang, waiting for the next bit of drama. He was no longer the scrawny, beaten-up NVA lieutenant, dressed in green cotton fatigues, spattered with dirt and blood, but a full colonel who had clout with the CIA.

I shot another look at Jim and then Woodruff. "I'm sorry, but I'm still waiting for an answer on why you think I'm going to Vietnam!" It was on them. "And as far as I know, I'm not going."

Woodruff said, "We need you to hear us out." He had just ordered me. Everyone recognized it.

My stomach churned acid, and I felt a burning sensation in my throat as he began.

"John, I'm being somewhat repetitive here, but we know about the threats and attack against you in Saigon by Colonels Loan and Hung during the war. Loan escaped to the US during the fall of Saigon with Ramsey's help. If captured, the NVA would have executed him for his part in killing captured Viet Cong prisoners. Some he only tortured for information. He freed some from Saigon jails after bribes were paid. Ramsey worked with Loan and participated in the interrogations, using electrical charges from batteries, ancient torture racks, and the infamous tiger cages. Also, as you may know, Colonel Hung never escaped the NVA take over, and he is still in prison in Hanoi, Vietnam."

"To buy his freedom, Hung has agreed to help us to lure Loan back to Vietnam," Colonel Zang interjected. As he talked, his military

posture stood out in contrast to Woodruff's slouch. Was the last statement on Hung the truth or contrived for my benefit.

"He has provided information on Ramsey and Loan and communicated with Loan over the past year. He claims he has no knowledge
of the murdered villagers near My Son, the ancient site of the Champa
civilization. He may be telling the truth. It seems from our own inves-
tigations the villagers were killed to prevent the secret of stolen gold
from being exposed. Ramsey and Loan executed them. And Specialist
Fourth Class Reed participated, as he himself told you during therapy
with you last Friday, on December 13. Mr. Schaeffer had conveyed this
to us while he researched your request for information."

I sensed that Zang was waiting for me to say something.

"Did I promise you anything from our last meeting here?" I asked,
looking at Zang. My mind struggled to recall the whole event, knowing
that I had a hangover that day.

"That you might be a witness against Loan," Zang answered.
"However, I know you were distressed with drink." He finally smiled.

"Let me reserve the final answer until after this meeting. Does
this still mean you don't have Loan in custody?" I asked, staring at
Woodruff, knowing the answer.

"No," Woodruff said, leaning toward my direction. "I repeat that
Loan is a US citizen now, and the CIA has no authority to arrest him.
And Ramsey, an American, is more than a serious embarrassment
for the company because of his involvement in these war crimes. The
Socialist Republic of Vietnam wants to capture and arrest Loan for his
war crimes. We at the CIA want Ramsey to also end up in Vietnam—it
would be the best solution.

"And speaking of Colonel Loan, Ramsey had protected him for
years and pulled strings to get him US citizenship. That is the sticky
part. If we have him arrested by the FBI in the US, then we will need
to follow due process of the law to protect him as a US citizen. Loan
should never have been issued American citizenship because of his
war crimes. However, if he is captured in South East Asia, then the

Vietnamese government can ignore all that since they never revoked his Vietnamese citizenship."

I digested this information and pondered what it meant for me.

Jim jumped in. "Is Loan out of country yet?"

"We're not sure. We know he lives in the Boston area, and we're trying to locate him now since he hasn't returned to his apartment. However, we'll not stop him from leaving the US as part of this plan we are forming here. We hope, based on Hung's communication with Loan over the last year, that Loan has been spooked to return to Indochina with Ramsey and retrieve the gold," Woodruff said and leaned back in his chair. A worried look appeared on his face. His baggy cheeks added to his aging look. "Colonel Zang is more intimately informed about Hung manipulating Loan to return to Vietnam."

"What about Ramsey? If he is a war criminal, why doesn't the US punish him for war crimes?" I asked.

"The CIA doesn't need more bad publicity over Vietnam. It could turn into a political storm if we handled it in the US. By having ignored Ramsey's crimes all these years, we look inept. It would be a mess for the CIA. And please understand, people higher than me allowed this to happen. Also, and I caution you to keep this a secret, Ramsey has some damaging files on a key CIA official. He needs to be stopped, but it's too messy for it to happen in the US."

"This stuff sounds like a spy novel," I retorted. "Who is this key official?"

"I can't tell you."

I glared at Woodruff. "Again, why do you want me to go on this mission?"

"Because you had Reed in therapy, and he later killed himself. Your queries through Jim about Reed and Ramsey after Reed's suicide triggered red flags first at the CIA, and then with the Vietnamese. Ramsey has some contacts who could have told him about your inquiry. It may have exposed you to danger. On the other hand, this created a unique opportunity for us and the government of Vietnam to lure

Loan back without us getting directly involved. We hope that the main assumption by Ramsey and Loan is that Reed told you about more than just the massacre—that he also told you about the stolen moneys and gold, hidden somewhere in Vietnam.

"We have joined forces to erase both our problems. We want to help Vietnam get Loan back. In exchange for that happening, they will return the favor and make Ramsey disappear."

I felt uneasy. "Are you saying that the plan to get Loan and Ramsey back to Vietnam is based on them assuming that I, among others, now know about their hidden gold?" I asked, rubbing my eyes. "This is a wild card at best."

Colonel Zang suddenly stood up. He looked at me. My body tightened and leaned forward to stand, but I felt Jim's strong grip on my right forearm.

"Yes, Captain Moore, that is so. You saved my life and you are an honorable soldier. But remember my price for fighting in this war was significant—I lost my father in the war at Hue during the Tet Offensive.

"Then, my mother's sister, a noncombatant, died during the bombing of Hanoi by the American Air Force. She lived a simple life. She and the others deserve some justice. We should punish our own war criminals," he said.

He turned away from me and bowed his head to Jim. "I apologize for being emotional. If I can get Loan, and to do so I must help the CIA with this Ramsey, then I will do so. Colonel Tin demands it to be so since he lost loved ones in the war as well." Zang finally sat down.

Jim said, "We're all old soldiers, including James Woodruff, who served in the navy. There is no apology needed." He looked at me, trying to say something. I sensed he wanted me to relent.

Zang bowed his head to me, and for a brief moment I saw respect and friendship coming from him. "I do owe you my eternal loyalty for saving my life. You honor me as a comrade in arms."

I nodded to him.

Woodruff shook his head. I sensed his push for a resolution. "We need to come to some kind of agreement, John."

"Which is what? I go to Vietnam to be a witness for a nonscheduled trial of an uncaptured war criminal, all the while I'm to be used as bait to help lure these bad guys back to Vietnam? I sense a weakness in your plan." Forcing myself to stand, I walked around the living room, trying to burn off my confusion and tension.

Woodruff said, "Look, we monitored Loan's cell phone through NSA, and he is preparing to depart Boston soon with reserved tickets for South East Asia—Cambodia specifically—departing January 1. Colonel Zang plans to have Loan arrested as soon as he lands in Phnom Penh."

Looking at Zang, I asked, "If—and that is a big if—if I go to Vietnam, what are the details?"

"Captain Moore, you will arrive in Hanoi soon after your Christmas Day to help interrogate former Colonel Hung. You met Hung in the war, and he has specifically requested you in order to share specific information. Quite honestly, he does not trust our government, but you, he finds you very ethical. Your presence could move Hung to reveal the final information about the gold, which we plan to continue to use to draw Loan and Ramsey."

"I don't know why Hung would say that about me. We only met twice, under adverse conditions, and it was so long ago," I said. My anxiety grew—just like Reed during his session, Woodruff and Zang were not telling me the complete story.

I continued looking at both Zang and Woodruff. "Since you know about my confrontation with Loan and Hung in Saigon, and the subsequent attempt on my life by the four goons who belonged to Loan, it's hard for me to believe that Hung wants to be my friend now."

Both Zang and Woodruff nodded.

"You forget an essential element, Mr. Moore. Both Colonel Tin and I insist on your help," Zang said.

"Why?"

"You have proven yourself in battle. And are trustworthy," Zang asserted. "And since Hung requested you, we now know we can, once and for all, get the truth from him through you."

An American, a US lackey, siding with the Socialist Republic of Vietnam against a corrupt ARVN officer would help nullify past South Vietnamese influence and work toward unification. That part I got. But something still seemed unsaid.

Apparently reading my mind, Colonel Zang explained that Loan and Hung had been accused of accumulating wealth in the war while working in the South Vietnamese regimes: money from bribes under the Phoenix Program to avoid arrest and prison, torture, or death; money from selling stolen supplies from the US Military on the black market; and money skimmed from the reparation monies paid by the US government for war damages. There were rumors of another incident—the stealing of priceless Champa artifacts at My Son. The location of those missing Champa artifacts remained a mystery.

Woodruff stared at me. "How can we not try to remedy such corruption by these former South Vietnamese officers?"

His piousness seemed staged. I didn't offer my input. Jim and I had served in the boonies trying to survive with our men, unaware of such exploitation. The various corrupt South Vietnamese regimes only had to claim they were fighting for democracy to receive billions in US aid. And it didn't help that unethical and unmonitored CIA agents roamed with corrupt ARVNs.

Woodruff slid back into his chair and crossed his arms, sensing my thoughts, my disdain.

"Jim and I were exposed to Hung's greed," I said. "However, now that I think of it, Loan was undoubtedly worse than Hung—Hung was just a follower."

I couldn't believe that I had encountered each of these ARVN officers twice: Hung at Dau Tieng Fire Support Base after the ambush at the Michelin Rubber Plantation, and then the Hotel Rex's restaurant in Saigon; Loan also in the restaurant with Hung, and then on that tense helicopter ride to Camh Ranh Bay with the NVA POWs—Zang and Tin.

Woodruff sat up, combed his hair with his fingers, and said, "John, based on Colonel Zang's input, we suspect that Loan and Hung may have accumulated over 13 million US dollars from all these illegal activities mentioned. We believe that Ramsey had a key part in this. He probably abused the US reparation payments program and also funneled military supplies into the black market. Loan and Hung needed Ramsey to get them and their moneys out of Vietnam."

As the morning approached noon, we speculated that Loan and Ramsey converted the moneys and material into gold ingots. By 1973, knowing the war would end due to US and North Vietnam negotiations, they would have hidden the gold to return for it later. Woodruff had researched and guessed that the Chinese in the Cholon district of Saigon could have smelted 400 troy ounce bars. Thirteen million dollars would have equaled 895 bars of gold at 1970 US dollar prices of thirty-seven dollars per ounce.

"I see you guys are trying to do the math on the 895 bars, each at 400 troy ounces with today's value of $300 per ounce. We estimate $110 million. Not a bad thirty-year investment hidden somewhere in Vietnam," Woodruff said, settling further in his chair.

"How do we know Ramsey didn't recover the gold already?" Jim asked.

"We don't, but the peace accord in 1973 pulled all US troops out and left Ramsey with no safe access to the countryside, being exposed to the VC and NVA units on offense throughout the area. Moving the gold out of the country from 1973 and after would have been impossible, as the NVA destroyed ARVN unit after ARVN unit from the DMZ to the south. Ramsey was reassigned to the US after he and the remaining Americans were evacuated from the US Embassy on April 1975 as Saigon fell to NVA troops. He would have had no chance to return safely to Vietnam. We assume he waited for things to stabilize in Vietnam.

"He got Loan out of Saigon on the last helicopters. Hung on the other hand had been captured by the NVA on the outskirts of Saigon, abandoned by Ramsey," Woodruff said.

"Why couldn't Hung have taken the gold before he was captured?" Jim asked.

"Good question. We don't know if he even knew where the gold had been hidden. Loan is a sneaky bastard," Zang said. "That is the reason Mr. Moore needs to meet with Hung and find the truth. He is dying of cancer, so there is a very short window of opportunity for this discussion to happen."

It became clear that Ramsey must have bided his time, waiting for the right year to get the gold. He couldn't get into Vietnam earlier without risking capture. Even in 1997, when the US and Vietnam resumed formalized diplomatic relations, it would have been risky for him. Then there's the logistical nightmare of moving 895 bars of gold. Each gold bar weighs twenty-seven pounds. That means 24,165 pounds, or twelve tons. How does an American move that much bulk in Vietnam, logistically, without being noticed? Still we speculated; the gold could have been found by others by now.

"Where is Ramsey, since you can't find Loan?" Jim asked, sitting up and leaning toward Woodruff.

"The FBI observing his house on Cape Elizabeth confirmed his departure for the Portland, Maine, airport yesterday, with final destination to Hong Kong. They followed with orders to not stop him. We want him out of the country."

"Could Hung's willingness to cooperate by sending misleading messages is working on Ramsey and Loan?" I asked, looking at Zang.

Woodruff said, "Ramsey has to act fast to recover the gold, based on Hung's phony messages that others know of the hidden gold. Ramsey would be getting this info from Loan, who somehow stays in touch with Hung and others in Vietnam."

"What if Hung doesn't really know more than he is telling?" I asked.

"Colonel Tin believes Hung is being truthful at this time. Hung's request to see Mr. Moore has impressed my former commander," Zang said. "And Hung wishes to get out of prison to die at home."

"Lot of assumptions to the project," Jim said. "I have concerns." He looked around the room, shaking his head.

Ignoring the statement, Woodruff focused on me and said, "We assume that Hung knows something, enough to guess where the gold is or who else to pursue for information. His ace in the hole is you, John. He agreed to share everything he knows with you. He has cooperated with the Socialist Republic of Vietnam by passing on false info to Loan to trigger all this sudden planning activity and actions by Ramsey to hurry and recover the gold. The main problem we have is knowing where in Vietnam will they arrive. Hung can provide clues to where."

"Why me?" I asked, mumbling more to myself, worried about what Jim had gotten me into.

Woodruff spoke again. "John, the Vietnamese won't allow CIA agents to set foot in the country outside the US Embassy. It is a delicate matter for the Vietnamese Communist Party, even though we have a trade treaty and diplomatic relations now. Colonel Zang and Colonel Tin have identified you as friendly to their country and the only one they will trust. They want US help in this matter, but only through your involvement. The short of it is Colonel Tin personally requested you."

"One other question. Why do we need the location of this gold if Colonel Zang says Loan will be arrested in Cambodia once he arrives?" My scowl must have been evident.

"Because we also want Ramsey to be caught. The buried or hidden gold is our trap. We have to assume they are taking different paths to Vietnam. Besides, Loan is clever, and he may not go to Cambodia, or he may have friends there who can help him avoid the Vietnamese secret police," Woodruff stated with intoned authority that should not be questioned.

I sat back and shook my head. Where would this end?

ೲ

After eating a take-out lunch in the dining room, we were back in the living room. We used the time to socialize, hoping the afternoon would resolve any issues. Zang's bodyguard took my visa picture. I went along with all of this. Deep down, I knew I would not go to Vietnam. No sooner did we settle into our previous seating arrangement, then Woodruff excused himself to take a call. We waited for his return.

Woodruff confirmed the earlier news: "Ramsey arrived in Hong Kong—flew there Sunday, as I said before. He also has an open roundtrip ticket to Saigon."

"Looks like your plan is working," I said. "What about Loan?"

"No update."

The afternoon sun filtered into the room, and I sought it for its winter warmth and bright light, giving my low mood a pick-up.

It must have been the hour for incoming phone calls; my cell rang. I struggled up from the low sofa and walked into Jim's den, answering the phone. "Hello."

"Doctor Moore, this is Sergeant Wilson over at Rock Hill."

"Hi . . . why are you calling?"

"As I promised to keep you informed, I wanted to tell you that there was an Asian male, about sixty, who visited Tom Reed's apartment the day of his suicide. The property manager just thought to call us about it over the weekend. Thought you might know who this was."

"No, I don't know him. What does this mean?"

"I have no idea. Doesn't really matter, though—the case is officially closed as a suicide," he said. "I appreciated your concern about his death. I thought I owed you any updates. Maybe if you knew this guy, he may have explained why Reed killed himself."

I waited. What could I say?

"So it is done. Next time we should do lunch or coffee," I said. He agreed, and then the dial tone took over before I could say goodbye. Wilson had finished

I shook my head. Was this Asian guy Loan?

I returned to the living room and explained the call. Woodruff acted uneasy about the news but deflected to summarizing our many hours together today.

"First, we allow Loan to return to Vietnam. John Moore will be the catalyst for this action as he returns to Vietnam to meet with Hung to pinpoint the location of the hidden gold. Once the location is known, Vietnamese national police will wait to capture both Loan, if he escapes Zang's agents in Cambodia, and Ramsey in Vietnam. This is the primary plan.

"The earlier option of trying to capture and arrest Loan in Cambodia or elsewhere has a less than 30 percent chance, but it is a small possibility. Mr. Moore's services are needed to ensure the primary plan happens. He will be dealing with retired Colonel Tin, who has personally requested him, and Hung, who also requested him. Both refuse any other Americans."

"Wow, I am a celebrity," I said. My sarcasm didn't go well, by the look Woodruff gave me.

Zang looked at me, confused.

Woodruff continued and said, "We are allowing Ramsey to return to Vietnam. The CIA has not interfered in Ramsey's trip to Hong Kong. He will be watched until he flies to Vietnam or Cambodia. You should understand that the false message Hung had delivered to Loan in the US is that he learned where the gold is hidden. Hung threatened that if Loan and Ramsey did not recover it and agree to a three-way split that included him, he would use the information to barter his way out of prison with the Socialist Republic of Vietnam. Obviously, this worked, since Ramsey is in Hong Kong now. Loan and Ramsey also know that Hung has cancer and wishes to spend his remaining days with his relatives in Tay Ninh. His share of the gold or money would help his family."

I listened to this update, but I felt that Reed's suicide needed a review. "If the Asian man at Reed's apartment was Loan, don't you suspect murder rather than suicide?" I asked, disturbed that Reed may have been killed.

"John, it's possible, and we will look into this, but we have to be careful with keeping our plan a secret," Woodruff responded.

"So, Reed is another Nam casualty in all this?" I felt stunned.

"Possibly, for the good of the nation. To be honest, damage control is essential."

"This is crap." I turned to Jim. He shrugged but looked disgusted.

Zang asked, "May we count on you to help?" The duplicity seemed unimportant to him. He had orders from his former boss, Tin, and as a soldier, Zang would carry them out. No questions. Duty and country came first.

"I'm sorry, but I can't do this," I said. "I have no experience with this type of operation."

"Dr. Moore, you are truly needed," Zang interrupted.

"Colonel Zang, let's give Mr. Moore twenty-four hours before he gives us a final answer," Woodruff interjected. "Will you at least do that, John?"

"OK, I'll give you my answer by tomorrow," I said, buying time to be away from these two.

Evening had arrived when Zang said, "We would be honored for your help."

Woodruff said, "So you know, the CIA will contract you with pay to do the psychological interrogation of Hung and to be a witness at Loan's trial. That is your official job. You will not be affiliated with the CIA, however."

"So that is my cover," I said.

"And our National Police and secret services will be with you for security and protection," said Zang.

Woodruff looked at Zang and then me. "John, you will have no other American over there to deal with except me by cell or messages. You know what Ramsey looks like. Also, you understand his psyche." Reaching into his briefcase on the floor, he pulled out photographs. He passed sets of four different three-by-five, black-and-white mug shots out to each of us. I examined them: Ramsey's CIA employee file photo, dated 1967; Ramsey's CIA photo in Vietnam, 1970; Ramsey's CIA photo in Germany and Holland, 1978; and a CIA surveillance photo of him, 1990.

I easily recognized his face. He looked like a man pretending to be a soldier, with an arrogant, Napoleonic smirk; power-hungry eyes, almost feral; and short dark hair in a buzz cut. But his face didn't show the fear that I had noticed on that helicopter so many years ago. I had dealt with many psychopaths in my therapy sessions. They had no reservations about committing evil acts, and instead justified them with sane arguments, believing their own rubbish. Yet Ramsey's fear that day still haunted me. Why did he show such dread? Looking at the other photos, I saw that no matter how he aged, I would be able to pick him out of a crowd. His early photos had evilness. Yet his later pictures showed a distraught face full of emotional pain. He had PTSD! Was his deteriorated mental health due to the trauma caused by the killings in the war?

I looked up from the photos and noticed Woodruff staring at me. I knew now he was also a profiler: We both recognized Ramsey as damaged, and I understood now how I could be suited for this assignment.

James Woodruff smiled and said, "You now see why we need you. You know Ramsey better than anyone we have, and since the CIA can't operate in Vietnam, you'll be invaluable to helping the Vietnamese locate him and arrest him—and help him disappear." Woodruff's probing eyes showed no levity.

"Christ, you guys want me to interrogate Hung, you want me to help convict Loan during a trial, and now you want me to assist in capturing and causing Ramsey to disappear," I said, waving my arms.

"How crazy is this? And for god's sake, Ramsey is an American citizen. You can't just kill him."

Woodruff leaned away and picked up his open briefcase, slamming it shut. He stood. "We have to."

That shocked me. Remorse came over me even though I disliked Reed, Ramsey, and Loan for killing the Vietnamese villagers.

I remembered the copies of Reed's journal that Sally had emailed me. I retrieved them from my suit pocket. Zang and Woodruff could provide some insight. I gave the sheets to Zang, explaining the source.

Zang studied the two pages with the columns of words describing places, events, or things. "Certainly these are clues to the gold, and no doubt Loan will head directly from Cambodia to try and avoid us. Ramsey must rendezvous with Loan, and then we can capture him too." He smiled at Woodruff, who stood looking over Zang's shoulder reading the same pages.

I sighed. My strained eyes returned to Woodruff. "OK, give me the twenty-four hours to decide on my answer."

"OK. FYI, we believe Ramsey and Loan will try to enter Vietnam before the Tet holiday, the Vietnamese Lunar New Year, which for the upcoming year goes from February 1 to the third. The days and weeks before and after Tet will be congested with Vietnamese relatives coming from all over the countryside and other countries, jamming the roads, the railways, and the airports, heading to their villages and ancestral homes. Ramsey will use that chaos to blend in with the mass of people traveling into Vietnam." Woodruff stopped.

Zang added, "This is a very important holiday for the Vietnamese, and the influx of people will make it difficult for us to locate Loan or Ramsey. We will need you there weeks before to ensure we have time to act on information about Loan and Ramsey from Hung."

It sounded like I would be busy if I went.

"Based on your findings from Hung and your recommendations, we will also issue alerts at the airports and seaports with instructions on how to identify Ramsey and hopefully to arrest him." Zang looked to Woodruff and received a headshake that confirmed their agreement over Ramsey.

I stood up. I looked at the rest of them, then stared out the window, watching the Sunday night's darkness outside.

Woodruff suddenly acted defeated and said, "We hope to have you on board after Christmas. As indicated earlier, Colonel Zang will prepare your visa for Vietnam, just in case you accept the mission."

"Yes. We will endorse it for at least one year, and as a special guest of our government."

"Also, since you had a top-secret CRYPTO clearance from your nuclear surety duties, we'll be able to quickly reinstate you for access to our NSA codes and telecommunication equipment," Woodruff said, a slight pleading look on his face.

Zang stood, shook my hand, bowed, and then exited the front door. He took the copy of Reed's notes without asking. My copies of the scans were still in my briefcase. Woodruff tagged along behind Zang.

"See you both tomorrow at the party," Woodruff said. The door closed behind him.

"We're having a party?"

Jim glanced at me and nodded his head. "John, they were invited to the party weeks ago. Remember, my business depends on contacts like these two."

"Well, just so you know—I'm not going to Vietnam."

Kim walked through the front door and hugged me, planting a tender kiss on my left cheek. "You look tired, John," she said. "And Jim, talk about your rude visitors who I passed coming in."

"Well. They were frustrated. But I agree with John. Why should he take on this mission? Anyway, it's time for a late afternoon cocktail. I think we both need one after this intense meeting," Jim said and headed for his bar to mix drinks. "Grey Goose martinis or eighteen-year-old Bowmore Scotch . . . or both?" His eyes twinkled.

ALEXANDRIA, DECEMBER 24, 2002

It was Tuesday evening at Jim's house, and dinner had evolved into a party. Jim went all out to be the perfect host and to network for his company. Kim cooked a delicious Vietnamese dinner especially for Colonel Zang and his wife and three children, who now surrounded me, eyeing me as the guy who saved Zang's life. My cheeks were flushed, partially from embarrassment, partially from the third or fourth glass of wine, and partially from frustration of not being able to speak Vietnamese, with my back to the living room wall, unable to escape. I wanted to call Sally, but it had gotten late; I leaned against the wall annoyed with myself for letting the time slip away. Sally was too important to forget; I needed to refocus on her, or I would revert to my former self—not what I wanted. Hopefully she would be glad to hear my plan to leave Jim's tomorrow morning, on Christmas Day, and then drive to the Outer Banks.

As Zang's family finally left me to mix with the others, I observed Kim performing her duties. She had long ago graciously accepted Zang despite the memories of war that affected them both from being on different sides. Her stoicism matched what I had observed of both the North and South Vietnamese when I served in Nam. Kim and Zang accepted the war deaths, painfully, but strived to continue living honorably, for the future and in honor of their ancestors.

With Kim handling her role to perfection, Jim started to loosen up. Still, Jim and I had one main hang-up: seeing all this as black and white—the enemy versus us. Time healed much, but we still had emotional fragments embedded from the war, like pieces of artillery shells. I admired the religious philosophies that Vietnam had adopted over the centuries, and I knew we should forgive and get on with life. In a way, I had. But our dead soldiers still lingered in the darkness of our minds, and thus our defenses against our former enemies weren't completely down. Jim walked around, enjoying his drinks, becoming less reserved with the guests. When he got to Kim, his boys, or me, then it was all love and bluster, heavily boozed.

Just as Jim finished telling me a dirty joke, Zang pulled me aside and gave me my passport with the Vietnamese visa. It weighed heavily in my suit coat pocket, where I placed it. Meeting Zang's family made it difficult to refuse to take on the operation, but I held firm to my convictions. The ethics of the operation bothered me, in that eliminating Ramsey by the hands of the Vietnamese would be payback for the CIA manipulating the delivery of Loan to them.

I glanced at my watch, smiling at the young Vietnamese man who returned to me. He was one of Zang's sons. Facing me, he explained the Vietnamese Tet celebration in perfect English, filling in some information that I had forgotten from when I served there. As midnight approached, my fuzziness grew.

James Woodruff came over, just as the Zang's son went to look for his mother. He held two glasses of wine. He nodded to the empty glass beside me. I accepted the fresh one. "How are you doing?" he asked.

"Oh, I guess OK," I said.

"Are you ready to commit?" he asked.

"I think you know I won't be going," I responded.

He shook his head. "We'll try to make it happen without you. But you do know Colonel Tin's promise to help us with Ramsey may go nowhere without you there." His cell phone buzzed. "Excuse me," he said and headed to a quiet part of the house.

I set my full wine glass down and retreated to the upstairs guest bedroom, saying goodnight to Jim and Kim. I'd had my fill. In my room, I tried calling Sally but got her voice mail. I left her a message saying that I would drive from DC tomorrow and hoped to be at the Outer Banks by late afternoon, depending on highway traffic. Earlier I had extended my car rental agreement for the drive down.

OUTER BANKS, NORTH CAROLINA, DECEMBER 25, 2002

I left DC later than I wanted on Wednesday, fighting traffic as I exited the metro area at four o'clock. Woodruff and Colonel Zang were disappointed that I had said no to the project, as they called it. Expecting a change of heart, Woodruff insisted that I call him tomorrow. An optimist, he held hope that I would agree in the end. Rather than argue, I acquiesced to calling him after Christmas Day. It would be easier than another face-to-face confrontation. I tired of the whole discussion and didn't understand what part of "no" they couldn't comprehend.

The morning started with Zang and Woodruff on the phone, once again telling me how I could help the Vietnamese get Loan. However, Woodruff's desire for Ramsey's capture by the Vietnamese convinced me that he had not told me everything. And I didn't want to lure an American to Vietnam and captivity at best, extermination at worst.

I had placed a call to Sally early in the morning and she understood my delay; I explained the whole meeting with Woodruff and Zang. Her words were warm and accepting and encouraged me to hurry and get to the Outer Banks. She said she missed me, and I sensed I was becoming a new man through her. "Please drive carefully, but hurry," Sally said as we clicked off from that phone call.

It felt good, exciting, as I impatiently drove my Volvo rental, glad to finally not be involved with the CIA, knowing that I would do everything possible to make it work for us.

☙❧

Once I cleared the DC beltway, I decided I would make better time by taking Interstate 95 and then hopping on to 64 toward Norfolk, then dropping down into the Outer Banks. On a whim, I tried to call Sally again as I drove out of DC but had no luck and left a message on her cell phone: "Hey Sally, just getting out of DC now, and I will be there."

It had to be a hectic day for her with little time to check her messages. I figured that with traffic and night driving conditions, I would arrive in less than six hours, around ten o'clock, much later than I had planned.

☙❧

A little after ten, I drove into the Outer Banks area, following my Google Maps direction printout to the beach house. I became concerned, since Sally had not returned any of my voice messages. I hoped she wasn't mad at me for digging into Reed's suicide. Finding the house off the main road just north of the Village of Duck, I pulled into the driveway. The house looked dark except for the shining porch lights and the solar-powered perimeter lights along the crushed seashell driveway. I got out of my car, crunching the shells as I walked toward the steps to the front door. The ocean sounds, waves rushing onto the beach, propelled a calm feeling through the night, although from where I parked, I couldn't see the ocean nor beach on the other side of the house. I anticipated the days ahead lounging on the veranda, facing the beach. Reaching the door by climbing the dozen or so steps, I rang the doorbell. The night was clear but windy, and I continued listening to

133

the waves on the other side, rolling, whispering through the sand and seashells. No one was home.

Just then, as if planned, a police cruiser drove into the driveway, its sides marked with the North Carolina Highway Patrol logo. The trooper stopped the car and got out, a flashlight in his left hand while his right rested over his holstered pistol. "Good evening, are you John Moore?" he asked.

"Yes, I'm Moore. Is anything wrong?" I became concerned.

"I'm afraid there is." He dropped his right hand from his holster and walked up the steps to me. "May I see some ID?"

I pulled out my wallet and handed him my driver's license. "What's going on?" I asked.

His flashlight reflected off my license as he scanned my identity. "Mr. DuPee Catton is in the hospital. Sally Catton was too overwhelmed to return your messages and asked us to relay the info to you." He examined my driver's license once more. "OK, Mr. Moore," he said as he handed my ID back to me.

"God, did he have a heart attack?" I asked as I struggled placing my wallet back into my pants pocket.

"No, but just as bad, he was shot while driving with his daughter today. I think he's in critical condition."

As the full impact of the officer's words hit me, my chest tightened, fighting for air. I stood stunned, not understanding why this happened to Sally's father, a man I had met only a few times but who reflected well in life as a good husband and father. The trooper's words finally penetrated the dark fog in my head.

"Sir are you OK?" he asked.

I could barely focus on the trooper. I blurted, "I better go see them." I started down the stairs. Realizing I needed directions, I turned and asked, "Where?"

"You'll have to go to the Elizabeth City Hospital. Drive across the bridge and go thirty miles. It's the major hospital in the area." He stared at me, evaluating me while I walked to the rental.

Regaining some of my sanity, I stopped by my car and yelled, "How did he get shot? I don't understand all of this."

"A drive-by shooting."

He observed my even more confused expression.

"No motive that we know of. We're doing a manhunt now."

I nodded, got in the car, and started it. I drove onto the road and observed the trooper talking into the mic attached to his shirt collar. He was rather tall and fit, sharp in his uniform—the perfect poster child for the state police. His image faded as I concentrated on driving. Making my way back to Highway 158 toward Elizabeth City, I sped along analyzing what had happened, dreading the implication that Ramsey had been behind this. Could that bullet have been meant for me? I suppose Ramsey could have found out I was going to be here. Hell, he had to have some access to contacts in the CIA or the NSA. Could they have monitored my cell phone calls? The shooter could have assumed Sally's father was me since he was my height and build, especially if Sally was with him. I slammed my fist on the steering wheel; this had to be my fault. My delay getting here could have saved my life, but possibly cost Sally's father his.

Forty minutes later, I screeched to a stop by the ER entrance at the Elizabeth City Hospital. Leaving the car illegally parked, I rushed through the entrance and was directed to the recovery floor lounge where family members waited. Getting out of the elevator, I turned right and hurried to the waiting area, following the directional signs until I spotted a distressed group of people with Sally, who was consoling her mother with arms wrapped around her. Seeing me, Sally raised her hand for me to stop. She said something to her mother and the other relatives and then she stormed to me.

"Sally, I . . ."

Not saying anything, crying, she motioned for me to follow her. We passed the elevator that I had used and ended up at the emergency exit door, another thirty feet down the hall, around a corner and not visible to her relatives. Slamming it open, she stepped through to the landing and turned toward me. "Damn it, how the hell did this happen?" she yelled.

Frustrated, I just stood for seconds before I reached out my arms to her.

She pulled away from me. At a loss, I offered my hankie. Wiping her tears with it, she blurted, "I thought you were done with Reed? And I got involved with you because I cared about you, worried about you—this goddamn thing with Reed could cost my dad his life. You're a selfish bastard for not stopping when you said you had."

Stunned, destroyed by her scathing words, I struggled to reply. If this was tied to Ramsey, then I deserved the blame for pursuing answers to Reed's death while unknowingly endangering Sally's family. I nervously asked, "Sally, will your dad make it?"

Her voice exhausted from crying, she replied while her eyes avoided me. "The doctors will know soon." Sally gave my handkerchief back. "But it looks bad. I need to get back to Mom and the rest of the family. Dad's being shot is on you. You just couldn't let it go."

I grasped for words, but her fury froze me.

She started to walk away but stopped and turned. Looking at me again, her beautiful eyes hurt, betrayed by me, she said, "It would be better if you go back to Charlotte and forget the holidays with me. You're obviously not safe here, and neither is my family. Just go. If my dad dies, I'm quitting the firm. And there is no us—I could never forgive you. What we started—well, that was a mistake."

I grabbed her as she turned her back to me. Talking to the back of her head, I pleaded, "Sally, I will end this, I promise. And you'll be safe. But I don't want to lose you. Please . . ."

She shook her head, pulled way, and flung her arms in disbelief, then continued walking to the waiting area and her family. I followed her around the corner and stopped, watching Sally sit down by her mother. She refused to look back at me, bewildered and fearful. I felt dejected that her anger wouldn't allow me to explain or to offer any help.

If this was Ramsey's doing, he had just forced me to do something I didn't want. I remembered seeing a pay phone by the elevator and went to it. Using my credit card, I dialed James Woodruff at his home phone number. He answered immediately. *Does this guy have any other life?* I thought. We talked for ten minutes as I explained what happened and what I sensed needed to be done. After he agreed to my few requests, I committed to Vietnam. The date to be decided by him. He gave me instructions on where to meet him in about an hour. Despite my turbulent mind, I recognized that his authority stood high in the agency's hierarchy.

Hanging up, I started to walk back to the recovery lounge, but Sally and her family had disappeared. That felt ominous since they were probably summoned by the doctors. Struggling with dread, I turned and walked back to the elevator. As I prepared to enter and descend within its sterile womb, I heard a voice.

"John, are you OK?" Sally's mother, Mary Catton, asked, holding a cup of vending machine coffee in her right hand.

Startled, I turned and said, "No, not a good day. I'm sorry about Mr. Catton."

"I have to believe he will survive. He is stubborn as a mule. You know the southern heritage and all. The doctor will see us soon to explain DuPee's condition. I told the family to get something to eat or drink in the cafeteria." She tried to smile but I saw her sad face—her bravado did little to overcome the budding tears. "Did you and Sally have a nice talk?" She changed the topic, concerned. "She's really head over feet about you, you know."

"I . . . Can you tell her . . . " I said.

"John, why not tell her yourself? You are staying at the beach house, aren't you?"

"No . . . not now . . . just tell her I have strong feelings for her. I'm probably falling in love with her," I said and turned into the open elevator. The doors closed off Mrs. Catton's face and her voice, saying, "John . . .?"

I descended to the main floor and the ER entrance. My rental hadn't been towed, still parked where I had left it. I got in, drove to an empty parking spot several hundred feet away, put the car in park, turned off the headlights, and surrounded by the night's darkness, I connected my laptop to the hospital's Wi-Fi and searched the internet to find directions to the Elizabeth City Coast Guard Air Station. I had an hour to find it before Woodruff landed. I wrote the directions on my notepad and shut off the laptop.

Just as I put the Volvo in drive, I glanced back at the hospital. Sally stood in the ER entrance; her face concealed by the shadows created by the entrance's lights.

I hesitated, torn between returning to her or proceeding with avenging the shooting of her father. Hate-filled revenge won the moment and I stepped on the car's accelerator. Her image grew smaller as I drove from the hospital. I promised to protect Sally, but my emotions still roiled. I now knew she would not be in my future. Depressed, I avoided looking back in my rearview mirror. Ramsey and Loan had to be eliminated, and I had to focus completely on that. I had agreed to do a dangerous, hateful thing, purely out of love.

ELIZABETH CITY COAST GUARD AIR STATION, LATE CHRISTMAS DAY

The directional signs easily guided me to the base, which overlooked the inlet to Albemarle Sound south of the city. A US Coast Guard ensign waited for me at the air station's guard shack as I drove up. "Welcome on base, Mr. Moore. We've been expecting you."

"Thank you," I said, impressed by the recognition, but also with the military complex that spread out before me. In the distance, a C-130 Hercules taxied along the tarmac, preparing for takeoff, its powerful engines reverberating toward me. Scattered along the runway were landing pads with various Coast Guard rescue helicopters. The air station hummed with noisy activity even at this time of night, performing the Coast Guard's unique functions: saving lives on the high seas and securing our coastal borders.

"ETA on Mr. Woodruff is about forty minutes. I'll take you to the VIP lounge to wait. We have fresh hot coffee. Just park your car over to the right, sir."

Once I parked the rental, I took my briefcase and my carry on, leaving nothing behind, and followed him to his government vehicle for the short ride to the airfield lounge. From the time I had talked by phone to Woodruff, I sensed that much had been initiated. The ensign excused himself to his duty office in the same building, allowing me my own time as I drank the coffee he had provided. I smiled. Recall of army mess hall coffee flashed as I sipped the strong bitter brew. Time stood still, maintaining the acquired taste from my years of active duty.

After writing my business instructions for the firm, addressed to Sally, on a legal pad, I dozed off in the comfortable lounge chair, tired from the long drive from DC and from the devastating meeting with Sally. What the hell had I gotten into?

ᏔᏃ

"Sir, the plane is taxiing to us now," the ensign said, nudging me awake. I looked at my watch; it was just past midnight.

"Thanks," I replied and followed him out to the airplane parking area, just as a nondescript Lear Jet rushed toward us from the landing strip, its twin engines winding down as it stopped abruptly, fifty feet from me and the ensign. The ramp came down and the ensign escorted me to the aircraft, indicating for me to climb on board. I took my carry on from him, shook his hand, and thanked him.

Woodruff, wearing a pink golf shirt and black slacks, greeted me at the top of the ramp. "John, give the Ensign your rental's car keys."

As I handed them to the officer, Woodruff yelled over the jet engines' piercing noise, "Ensign, thanks for escorting Mr. Moore. Please secure the rental car. I'll have an agent pick it up."

"Yes, sir," the ensign said, saluting Woodruff, holding the keys in his left hand.

"Well, John, when you decide something, you certainly don't mess around. Come on board, the flight to DC will be less than an hour and we have a lot to discuss."

As I strapped into a cushy seat, Woodruff plopped into his seat, facing me across a small mahogany table, while a fellow agent, I assumed, brought us bottled water and cups of coffee, then sat nearby, observing me. The plane quickly taxied to the runway and within minutes ascended into the dark sky,

James Woodruff pulled out a sheet of paper and handed it to me. "Please read this and see if this works. I think it's solid."

I grasped the sheet of paper and read: *Press Release: On the morning of December 25, at the Outer Banks, North Carolina, a Charlotte psychologist was seriously injured by a random drive-by shooting. Accompanied by his associate, he was driving in the Village of Duck at the time of the event. He was taken to the Elizabeth City Hospital. Doctors stated that he sustained brain damage, and during the operation to remove the bullet, the patient died. Any witnesses to the crime should contact the local police. The name of the victim is being withheld until next of kin are notified.* The rest had a general description of a possible Asian suspect in the shooting.

"When will it hit the papers?" I asked.

"It'll be in all the morning newspapers in Eastern North Carolina and Southern Virginia." Woodruff turned to his man, handed him the press release, and nodded the go-ahead. The agent got up and walked to the cockpit. "We'll continue to stonewall the release of the name." Woodruff paused. "This should convince the hit man that he accomplished his task. You have something for me?"

"Yes." I handed him a large manila envelope that I had secured from the Coast Guard officer. "Please deliver this to Dr. Sally Catton at the beach house. It's my apology for endangering her and her family—especially her dad. I also gave her full authority to run the firm in my absence, with a power of attorney—which I hope you will get notarized for me. I assume the US marshals you assigned to protect her, and her parents will be there soon?"

"Don't worry, John, everything is handled. I'll ensure Sally gets the packet. I'll explain everything to her but will avoid compromising information that may endanger you in Vietnam. Leave everything to me."

"I guess I don't have much choice."

Woodruff's furrowed brow deepened as he ignored my remark. "I'll need your condo keys and car keys. We'll arrange to get your car from the Charlotte airport parking to your condo garage. I will need the parking ticket too."

I passed him all the items.

"You can get clothes and stuff for the trip while you are at Jim's house. Remember the basics: good comfortable shoes and a pair of hikers. Also Colonel Zang will provide access to gear and weapons when you are in Vietnam."

"I think I know what clothes to take. Can't believe I'm going back to Nam after all this time. But weapons—why?"

"A precaution while you are there," he said. "They, the Vietnamese, want you to be secure."

I thought for a moment. "I want to take my .45 pistol then. It's in my condo, locked up. Can you arrange that? I'm skilled with it."

"I'll have an agent pick it up. Where is it?"

"In the top drawer of my only nightstand in the bedroom."

"Good. I'll clear this with Colonel Zang. He can send it under diplomatic pouch ahead of you. It will be waiting for you in Hanoi."

"So when do I depart?"

"First we need to update your shots, such as Hep A and B. I'll have a year's worth of malaria pills sent over to Jim's. I already told him that you're committed, and he said that you're staying with him while you prep for the trip. You still have your passport with the Vietnamese visa?"

I pulled it out of my right inside suit pocket. "All set. I think I'm current on most shots since I travelled to India and China for business consulting two years ago."

"Are your shot records at the condo?"

"Yes. In the desk drawer of my little office."

"We'll get those with your .45-caliber pistol. I'll verify all your immunizations. The danger to you, besides the bad guys, will be exposure to mosquitoes and other crap while you're in the bush. But then, you know that."

"I guess I'm as ready as I can be."

"It's a hell of a commitment. Zang was elated when I called him and couldn't wait to call Colonel Tin to set things in motion. Jim Schaeffer is reluctant—worries about you going." Woodruff paused. "By tomorrow, call me with your bank account number so I can get your monthly contract payments deposited. I'll also deposit money for you to cover travel expenses. Arrange for Jim to pay your bills—credit card bills, utilities, cable, phone—so you will always be current. This keeps the CIA out of it and will help verify that you are dead. Also, turn off your cell phone and give it to me. Dead men don't make calls."

I nodded as I handed my cell phone over, but then asked, "You didn't want to discuss who shot Mr. Catton when I called you earlier tonight. I think we are secure now?"

"OK, it was probably Colonel Loan. We are trying to find him, but he must have fled the country. Ramsey probably ordered the hit, though."

"Did you have any idea this would happen?"

"John, we are as surprised as you. That is why it is more important than ever to have you get over to Vietnam. They both must feel that all loose ends tied to Reed have been taken care of. You going to Vietnam will catch them off guard since they believe you are dead now."

"How did they know I was spending Christmas at the Outer Banks?" I asked. My stare bored into Woodruff.

"Tonight, we were able to trace Loan's phone activity at the Boston Airport Hilton Hotel, on Monday, December 23. He listened to the office recording by Doctor Catton reaffirming that both of you would be out for the holidays and would return on January 6, 2003. Doctor Sally Catton left an emergency phone number to call. He obviously logged onto the web and determined the location for area code 252. It pinpointed the Outer Banks area in North Carolina—specifically the

Catton's beach house. We assume he left the Boston Airport Hilton and flew to Norfolk, Virginia, then drove to the Outer Banks."

"Why the hell didn't you know about this earlier, or where to locate him?" I asked, my frustration showing.

"He was good at hiding his whereabouts. I'm sorry we couldn't find him before this happened." Woodruff shook his head; the bags under his eyes seemed deeper than before. His voice intoned total exasperation.

I couldn't stop looking for clarifications. "Did Sally describe the guy as Asian, short, with a very thin face?" I asked.

"Yes. She had a good look at him before he shot her dad, just as he pulled up beside them at a stoplight. He sped off in blue-colored Chevy," Woodruff said.

"So it was definitely Loan?" I said.

Woodruff nodded then averted his eyes.

"Shit, so Ramsey is in Hong Kong, Colonel Hung is in a reeducation prison in Hanoi, and Tom Reed is dead. And Loan is probably on board a flight headed to Cambodia?"

Woodruff settled back and attempted to read some papers in his lap. His defenses had kicked in. His silence answered all.

Still I persisted. "You knew this was going to happen." I took a sip of coffee.

"No, we didn't. We know now after the fact, that's all I'm saying. Christ, John, it's simple as that." His anger showed.

I lolled my head back into the headrest of the executive-style seating and closed my eyes; I wouldn't get anything more from him. So there it was, if I believed Woodruff: Ramsey had orchestrated the hit on me, and endangered Sally and her dad by mistake. It confirmed my need to protect her by helping the Vietnamese capture Loan and ensure Ramsey ended up in the hands of the Vietnamese. My destiny had been set.

"How is Sally's dad?" I asked. It seemed we had forgotten the most important event tonight.

Startled, Woodruff sat up, staring at me quizzically. His silence became ominous. "John, I thought you knew . . . Mr. Catton died shortly after you called me from the hospital."

The shock hit me like a sucker punch. Nausea swept my stomach. "No . . . it can't be . . ." I mumbled as my head tilted back, my closed eyes. Anger welled in me. I finally glared at Woodruff and said, "Why the fuck didn't you say something earlier?"

He sat silent and stoic. Did he see my hate, my anguish?

"Again, I thought that was why you decided to go to Vietnam. Look, John, we need to move along—we can't undo this. . . We assumed you knew."

Woodruff's assistant leaned to him and said something. They nodded together.

"John, you will be travelling under your own name. We feel you are safe doing that. Moore is a common enough name, even if they get access to the flight manifests, which I doubt. There is no time to create a false identity for you. And again, we believe it's not necessary.

"We're almost to DC. I'll personally drop you off at Jim's. Rest up, and we'll meet later today and get everything worked out for your trip," Woodruff said.

Overwhelmed, I felt too tired to continue. My emotions over Sally's dad tore at me. I watched in a blur as Woodruff continued to instruct his man.

The man finally went to the back of the aircraft, returned with an aluminum briefcase, and gave it to me. "I'm Paul Tanner," he said.

He extended his right hand and we shook. Paul Tanner seemed forty and represented a younger version of Woodruff, with a balding hairline, a face and body showing the wear and tear of the job, but not as overweight. He glanced at Woodruff, still seated across the table from me, who nodded, then focused on me. My mind still couldn't grasp Catton's death as I stared at the case.

"Your standing orders are to contact James first." I raised my head to look at Tanner. "Should that fail, call me. In the briefcase there is an agency Palm phone together with detailed communication instructions with codes and passwords. There is also a critical contact list with phone numbers and a portable satellite telephone with GPS and the power pack. The lid is a flat plate antenna, which negates the need for a parabolic antenna. With the satellite link, you'll be able to communicate with us from anywhere in Vietnam, including the jungles or mountains, because NSA satellites are in space over twenty-two thousand miles high. Use the Palm phone mostly for emails unless it's an emergency. Both James and my phone numbers are already loaded on the Palm phone and the satellite phone, ready for speed dial." He had me sign a document for the equipment then patted me on the shoulder, recognizing my bewildered stare. The seat belt sign flashed, and accompanying warning chimes sounded for our descent into DC. Tanner stepped to a nearby seat and strapped himself in.

Woodruff added, "Are you OK?"

I had no more words for him and simply nodded.

Continuing to ignore my foul mood, he explained that the case weighed twenty-six pounds, measured eighteen inches by fourteen inches, and was five inches thick so it would fit into a back pack. The satellite phone was in digital mode, and calls would be digitally encrypted using NSA codes, which was more efficient than analog transmissions.

He stopped talking and focused on the jet's descent as I closed my eyes, wondering what I would face in the days ahead. Woodruff and Zang hadn't been completely truthful with me. They had manipulated me, but I had no choice now—I had committed to moving forward. I would avenge the death of Sally's dad.

ALEXANDRIA, DECEMBER 26, 2002

Tired, I had finished my second cup coffee when Jim, sitting across from me at his kitchen table, answered his cell phone. My watch showed 7:00 a.m. I slept only a few hours after I arrived at Jim's house early this morning, dropped off by Agent Tanner. A slight change by Woodruff, who knew he had done enough damage and needed some escape from me. Jim switched to speaker mode and I recognized Woodruff's voice: "Loan left the Norfolk Airport Holiday Inn by the shuttle to the air terminal this morning. He read the *Elizabeth Daily* newspaper story on the shooting and killing of a psychologist from Charlotte. Loan smiled as he read the article."

"Why didn't you arrest him for murder?" I asked.

Ignoring the question, Woodruff responded, his tone reserved. "My agent boarded the shuttle bus after him and followed him off the bus at the terminal. He confirmed that Loan boarded the flight to Washington Dulles Airport with a connection to LA and the final destination to Phnom Penh."

"Hell, why didn't your guy detain him?" I said, exasperated, mad.

"We can't legally detain a US citizen, and we are assuming he did the shooting. We have no proof. In any case, he is falling into the trap, allowing the Vietnamese to deal with him. Besides, he's on board the flight to DC. It took off five minutes ago. We'll watch and ensure he continues to LA and Cambodia."

"Christ," I said. I looked at Jim, who shook his head in bewilderment.

"OK, John, you keep preparing for Vietnam," Woodruff instructed, curtly.

"James, it's very risky what you're doing. Endangering John," Jim said, looking at me with concern.

"Shit, it all worked out, OK. Colonel Tin wants Moore in Vietnam, and we had to oblige—all for the good of our two nations. We need to secure the Socialist Republic of Vietnam as a buffer ally against China in the Far East. And Tin wants Loan for war crimes, and we are obliging. They can capture the fucker in Phnom Penh.

"And I don't fucking believe for a minute that Moore is in danger. And shit, there probably won't be a trial. Once Loan is captured, the Vietnamese agents will kill him, I assume. There's something afoot, but I can't put my finger on it. Tin is shrewd—I met him last year on that security pact negotiation. Tin needs Moore for something. But I don't know what that is."

I glared at the kitchen table as Woodruff hung up, confirming our meeting for tomorrow, the twenty-seventh.

ॐ

Once again, Jim and Kim did the gracious hosts bit, putting me up and consoling my bad mood. I wanted to call Sally, but I couldn't. I was officially dead, so I wouldn't endanger her any further. Besides, I knew it was over. She would not talk to me ever again. Stuck with self-pity for a holiday companion, I had to move forward.

Jim got me another coffee as we sat in his kitchen. He reflected on my sour attitude. "Come on, man. When this is over, you'll get her back."

"No, I don't believe Sally will ever accept me back. DuPee Catton is dead thanks to me." I took a sip of coffee. "Sally won't forgive that."

"For now, clear your head and focus on this trip. I still worry about the whole goddamn thing, but you are a good soldier, so do your best with the mission. Everything else is secondary at this point."

"You're right." I sat staring at my cup. "Nothing else matters but my revenge and the mission—right?" My sarcasm showed.

"That's right—just like in Nam. The mission is all," Jim retorted, allying with me. "Any idea when you fly to Nam for this bullshit?"

"No, I suppose we'll find out tomorrow when Woodruff comes over. Glad you can put up with these people dictating meetings, in your home no less."

"It's OK, John. I want to be by your side; I don't completely trust the CIA despite the business they give my firm. I trust Zang more. Ain't that a kick—our former enemy I trust more than Woodruff?" He took a deep swallow of his coffee.

"I don't understand Woodruff. He's hiding something. Maybe it's per Zang's instructions?" I mused and took another sip of coffee. "Remember, he mentioned that Ramsey had some embarrassing files on someone."

"Yeah, he did."

"And he refused to reveal the name or what that was all about," I said.

"Who knows? Anyway, watch yourself over there. You certain you don't want me to tag along?"

"No. Woodruff made it clear that the communist officials only wanted me—no other Americans. And I can't endanger you too."

"Well then, we'll get drunk later today. You're stuck here, so make the best of it." Kim placed some breakfast rolls on the table. Her presence helped calm me.

"Just enjoy, John, you'll be busy soon enough," she said.

I smiled weakly, my mind churning over the upcoming trip. Thinking about Sally, I hoped that after Woodruff briefed her and gave her my documents, the keys to my condo and my car, she would willingly run the firm in my absence and keep an eye on my apartment. Deep down I knew it was over between us and that she would do as the CIA asked, but nothing more.

Despite Jim sharing his home, I felt alone. Would I ever feel a woman's love again? I wondered. My life became more complicated as danger faced me upon my return to the country where I killed. Would I kill again in its dark jungles?

SOUTH EAST ASIA, JANUARY 1, 2003

Sitting in business class on China Air, I glanced out at the night sky as the big bird winged its way from LAX via Taipei to Hanoi and the Socialist Republic of Vietnam. I was reading *Flashbacks: On Returning to Vietnam* by Morley Safer of *60 Minutes* fame and his own description of returning to Nam after the war. His writing impacted me with lucidity: Safer felt that everyone who served in the war had his own conflicting truths and memories that tied us to that country and that time. As a Vietnam War correspondent, Safer had been drawn back to that place. And now I headed back as well. Nam was a part of me, like the blood flowing in my body. I realized that now, after all these years. Somehow, I knew that I would take my feelings and pain to the grave without complete cleansing of mind and soul. The war became an unforgiving partner the day I landed in Saigon so many years ago, forever a part of me.

Putting the book on my seat tray, I reflected on my final instructions from Woodruff as he and Tanner escorted me through security to the departure gate for my flight to LAX. Woodruff also updated me about his meeting with Sally at her Outer Banks house on the weekend following Christmas. Sally swore to keep my trip a secret and would manage the firm. Woodruff felt that she showed some concern, but she didn't ask about me. It confirmed to me that we were finished.

I closed my eyes and thought of the hectic activity of the last few days, snowballing on its own. The closer the aircraft drew to Vietnam, the more my memories of the war came back. Could I emotionally survive this return? I had very little confidence of that.

Ramsey had to be damaged goods from the war, probably with PTSD. He too headed back to Nam, where all his war demons were born. How would this end for him—imprisoned or killed by former NVA officers, as Woodruff expected? Would it be the same for Colonel Loan?

Woodruff worried about Ramsey's CIA connection and what information or files he held that could be used to tarnish and bring down someone at the CIA. Who was this person? And then there was Loan, who would not be wanted back in the US ever again. The Vietnamese agreed to do the dirty work for Woodruff and make Loan disappear once he was captured in-country, but then they wanted him in a bad way. And I had to avenge the shooting of DuPee Catton by assisting in the capture of Ramsey and Loan. Catton didn't deserve that death.

⊘⊗⊘

From my window of the descending Vietnam Airlines Airbus A321, I looked down at the city of Hanoi, partially covered by gray winter clouds. Three hours earlier, at 5:30 a.m. on January 1, I had landed in Taipei, Taiwan, after a fourteen-hour flight from Los Angeles. The two-hour and fifteen-minute flight from Taipei was reminiscent of a flight I took thirty-plus years ago. My destination at that time was Saigon and Ben Hoa Airfield, Vietnam, as I flew from Tokyo.

In 1969, I was a young US Army captain on board a chartered United Airlines jet dropping from thirty thousand feet with a full plane carrying 167 US Army personnel in sweat-stained khakis, exhausted from the long, twenty-one-hour, multistop flight from the States, from Oakland to Anchorage, Anchorage to Guam, Guam to Tokyo, and finally Tokyo to Saigon. Our apprehension about going to war showed in our disheveled appearance and the smell of perspiration. When we finally landed with a hard bump and quickly taxied to the open-air bunker terminal at Ben Hoa, it was midnight on June 1, 1969, and we were welcomed by the pungent smells of Southeast Asia's hot humid air.

Now, on January 1, 2003, I returned to Vietnam as a civilian, descending into Hanoi's Noi Bai Airport at 9:00 a.m., dressed in my dark blue business suit, sitting among mostly Vietnamese who were returning home for Tet celebrations, outnumbering me and the few Australians and French onboard. Vietnam had developed into an inexpensive tourist attraction for Europeans, mostly French, Germans, and Austrians, but especially the Aussies, due to Australia's close proximity. Modern Vietnam thrived on tourism and needed the steady influx of visitors to help support the economy. Even American tourists were welcome, despite the devastation that the US inflicted during the American Indochina War.

Just like thirty years ago, my armpits were wet and my hands clammy as we made the final approach to Hanoi. The mission to capture Loan and Ramsey would be as dangerous as my combat in that war, and I began to have second thoughts about my return to this country where I had left so many dead—both Americans and North Vietnamese—their blood now absorbed in the reddish clay soil.

As Vietnam drew closer, I began daydreaming of Saigon in 1969 and the meeting with the French reporter who told me I could be related to Roger Mongin, a French colonel who fought at Dien Ben Phu during the French Indochina War in 1954. No one except my wife knew that my mother, while I served in Nam, had confirmed that Mongin was my biological father. She had given Katy letters and photos explaining the romantic affair that conceived me. Katy promised to share those items with me after I returned from war. Both of them were concerned that I would lose focus on surviving the war otherwise.

It seemed my legacy stemmed from World War II and its concentration camps, where Mongin and my mother were imprisoned as slave laborers; to my birth at the end of the war in a US Army field hospital;

to the French Indochina War, where my real father, a French Foreign Legion airborne captain, was defeated and captured at Dien Ben Phu; to the American Vietnam War, where I served as a US Army captain, also airborne qualified. That legacy drove me to locate him in 1976, to confront him about abandoning my mother—and me! To look him in his eyes to understand his betrayal of my mother.

TROYES, FRANCE, JULY 1976

Assigned to duties as US Army NATO liaison for the Netherlands Army, I arrived in Paris two days early in July 1976, to attend a five-day NATO conference. My family quarters in 't Harde, Holland, were scheduled to be ready in a month, when Katy would arrive from the US. Since I currently lived in Bachelor Officer Quarters (BOQ) or hotels, I used the two days before the conference to go to Troyes, France, to see my father's birthplace and maybe even meet him, if he still lived.

My mother had told the truth to Katy, who was sworn to keep it from me until I returned from Nam: I had been conceived out of wedlock toward the end of World War II. My real father, Roger Mongin, was an officer in the French Foreign Legion who had been imprisoned by the Vichy government in the same Polish concentration camp in which my mother had been incarcerated. She loved him deeply, but when the Nazis abandoned the concentration camps as the Russian Army approached, they became separated. Her heart had been broken that he never looked for her, and the shame of being an unwed mother forced her to accept another life once she immigrated to the United States. So, the French reporter in Saigon, Jacques de Mont, had been correct. Not only did I resemble the French colonel that he wrote a book about, but he was indeed my father.

Arriving by train, I checked into a hotel near the Café de Troyes. Afterward, in my army dress greens, I walked to the café, where the young French hostess seemed pleased to wait on an American—maybe her first—and guided me to a window table.

Soon the café's sixty-year-old proprietor came over. "And monsieur, what wine do you wish?" He paused and stared at me, intrigued.

I finished looking at the wine list and said, "A Beaujolais, please."

"Oui, I will bring you my best." He continued to stare, remaining confused, standing by the table, uncertain of what to say.

I assumed he wanted my order. "OK. And I'll have the petit filet with green beans for dinner. Maybe an espresso afterward," I said, giving a smile that startled him further.

He retreated, glancing back several times. Shortly, a woman came out of the kitchen with him. They both stared at me and whispered to each other. Then they disappeared into the kitchen. My waitress, all smiles, soon served my dinner.

I ate with relish; their French cooking certainly didn't disappoint. After finishing, I skipped the espresso for another glass of wine and intentionally laid my copy of de Mont's book, La Mort de Indochina Française, *in front of me, facedown. The title expressing* Death of French Indochina *certainly had direct bearing on me serving in that war. If the French participation in Vietnam had been successful, then there would have been no American Indochina War.*

The photo of Colonel Mongin on the back of the dust cover stared at me and the proprietor when he appeared once more. I used the picture to question him on whether Colonel Mongin had morning espresso and croissants at the café every morning, as the book stated.

"Oui, monsieur. He is a part of this place, as are the tables." He smiled, pleased that someone asked about the town's celebrity.

He wanted to ask me something, but I continued to sip my wine as I browsed the book, intentionally avoiding further talk. He left the bill on the small tray as he returned to the kitchen, struggling with his thoughts.

I paid my bill with francs, stood up, and departed for my hotel before the owner could return.

⚬⚬⚬

The next morning, I stood by the corner newsstand across from the Café de Troyes, browsing the English edition of the Herald Tribune *and watching as an old hunched man with a cane walked to an outside table at the café. He gingerly eased himself into a chair and waited. Soon an attractive waitress appeared with a cup of espresso and a basket of pastries. I heard them talk, the French language flowing melodiously, enchanting me. The waitress patted the old man on his head, and he reciprocated by placing his hand on her hip, an old man's flirtations. She casually removed his hand, playfully scolding him, and returned inside.*

I watched, glancing between the newspaper and the old man. My dead mother's old photo of Roger Mongin, held on top of the daily newspaper, matched him.

"Monsieur, do you wish the paper?" asked a voice from behind.

Startled from my reverie, I nodded, reached into the back pocket of my military trousers, and pulled out my wallet. I found some francs and paid the proprietor, who gave a thorough once-over of my dress green uniform and garrison cap with the airborne patch. He examined the rows of ribbons, focusing on one award.

"Monsieur, I recognize the Vietnamese Cross of Gallantry—my father served in French Indochina in the 50s."

"We seem to have a war legacy, you and me, with Indochina," I said.

Confused, he still nodded. "Oui . . . I am thirty and have no memory of him. I was born while he served and died. C'est la vie." He shrugged and returned to another customer waiting to pay, not fully grasping my legacy comment.

I returned to staring at the seated Mongin; finally, I took several steps to the curb and toward the café. A truck suddenly careened by, halting me abruptly and momentarily blocking my view. When the truck, spewing a cloud of diesel smoke passed, I saw Mongin stand up. I stepped off the curb but stopped in the gutter, now undecided, watching the old man slowly walk, relying heavily on the cane, bent over, probably headed home. As he reached the corner, he slowly turned and looked at me. We stared at each other for what seemed an eternity, neither of us moving, our eyes locked. I sensed recognition in his eyes. Slowly the old man switched his cane from his right to his left hand. He gradually raised his right hand to a salute and waited.

In those moments, memories of my youth flashed in my mind, a kaleidoscope of images: my mother dying from cancer after a lonely life, still pining for Roger Mongin, the lover who abandoned her; my alcoholic stepfather, who gave me my legal name and the chance for American citizenship, and the miserable life he created for me; the father I never knew, now standing across the street, who abandoned me as well, leaving me a legacy, disjointed and cruel—perpetuated by years of war in Europe and Indochina, its killing and inhumanity. He had provided the seed for my birth, but others made me who I am.

Finally grasping what to do, I stepped backward onto the curb. Turning, I walked away from Mongin in the morning sun, leaving the darkness of my past behind. I cared little about this man Mongin, a total stranger to me. I never returned his salute.

☙❧

The pilot's voice blaring through the speaker system woke me from my reverie, forcing French Foreign Legion Colonel Mongin to return to my subconscious. We were descending on final approach to Hanoi.

NOI BAI AIRPORT, THE SOCIALIST REPUBLIC OF VIETNAM, JANUARY 1, 2003

Colonel Zang had told me that National Police Agent Hieu would meet me at the Hanoi Airport. Assuming that he would be waiting for me outside with my name placard after I cleared immigration and retrieved my luggage, I walked off the jet and headed down the ramp to the main terminal, looking for the baggage and customs direction signs. I carried the CIA aluminum briefcase in my left hand.

Wearing faded blue jeans and a black sweater, over which she wore a leather bombardier jacket, stood an attractive Vietnamese woman, who looked at me from her position by the gate check-in counter. About forty years old, she had lustrous black hair tied into a ponytail and a firm five-foot-five figure with slightly larger breasts than are typical for Vietnamese women. Her brown skin complemented her already beautiful face, and her black eyes were enticing, mysterious with the seductiveness of a French woman. I assumed she was Eurasian.

I tried to divert my eyes from her, trying to be polite and not gawk at her attractiveness. I smiled as she continued staring in my direction, which forced me to look behind to see who she waited for; I couldn't tell with the large crowd of Vietnamese following me.

She approached, blocking me from proceeding further into the terminal. "Mr. Moore, I am Agent Hieu. Welcome to Hanoi." She bowed slightly and then offered her hand.

Surprised, I extended my hand. "Thank you. It is nice of you to greet me here at the plane." Her handshake reflected her business manner and seriousness—no smile, no warm greeting.

"Our retired and senior Communist Party member Colonel Bui Tin instructed me to extend a greeting to you. As our government's special guest, you are to be given full courtesy."

"OK," I said in awe, staring into her beautiful face. Her expression cracked no emotion; her coolness permeated me.

Beckoning me to follow her, she turned and quickly began walking toward the exit signs. Over her shoulder, she crisply stated, "Your luggage will be loaded in the car. First, we process you in the VIP area. Please follow quickly."

I hustled to stay with her. Her muscular legs stretched her tight jeans as she strode ahead of me, her ponytail swinging, beckoning me—a very good-looking woman to follow. Minutes later, we went through an unmarked door, walked through a narrow hallway, and finally entered a large office occupied by customs agents and police officers, a mix of men and women. She led me to an unoccupied desk and motioned for me to sit down. As I eased into my chair, she plopped her body into a chair across from me.

"May I have your passport?"

After I handed it to her, she flipped through to the Socialist Republic of Vietnam visa glued in my passport and began completing a form on top of the desk. A Vietnamese man came over, gave me a stern look, turned to Hieu, and spoke to her, his Vietnamese drawing me further back into my time of war. He kept his left hand behind him, out of my sight. She responded with quick but polite responses, as if he were her senior. As they talked to each other, I noticed that Hieu's jacket barely covered the nine-millimeter pistol in a shoulder holster under her left arm. The gentleman talking to her wore a tailored black suit, his unbuttoned jacket also revealing a holstered nine-mil pistol under his left arm. My mind, trying to adjust from the jet lag of flying across various time zones and the international dateline, had sensory overload from the agents, customs officials, and weapons. My head felt stuffed with cotton, absorbing the sounds around me, dulling me, blocking and muffling my thinking.

"This is Major Han, my supervisor," Hieu said to me.

I stood up and offered my right hand, giving a slight bow in return to his.

"Welcome to the Socialist Republic of Vietnam, Mr. Moore," he said. Instead of shaking my hand, his left came from behind his back and placed a .45-caliber pistol in my extended right hand; it was my pistol from the States.

I took it wearily, and the room's noise suddenly stopped, with everyone staring at me and my .45-caliber pistol. Ignoring the room's distractions, Agent Hieu stood up and reached over the narrow desk, her hair inches from my face, her head bowed toward the desk drawer to my left. Opening it, she pulled out a leather shoulder holster with the communist red star embossed on the exterior. Straightening up, she took my pistol from me, put it in the holster, and glancing at my upper body several times, adjusted the shoulder straps before finally holding it up for me.

"Please remove your suit jacket, and I will fit you. I hope this is your pistol?"

I nodded. Holding my jacket, I allowed her to strap on the holster and adjust it to fit under my left arm. It seemed like everybody here was right-handed. Major Han nodded, content that matters were being handled. He walked away, disappearing through another door.

Hieu looked at me with serious eyes and then said, "Please, this weapon is only for, as you say, self-defense. Since I will be with you all the time, there should be no need to use it. Here is the official authority for you to carry the weapon." She handed me the form she had completed, already pre-signed. She reached into her purse and gave me three loaded magazines; the ones I had in Charlotte, which Woodruff retrieved along with my pistol over a week ago. She looked relieved when I took the magazines and placed them in my aluminum briefcase rather than loading my pistol.

"You are knowledgeable on this pistol?" she asked.

"Yes." I didn't explain my past expert status during the war nor my killing NVA soldiers in battle.

"It is per Colonel Tin that you have the authority to carry this weapon. Again, please comply with my instructions on its use."

Her cell phone rang. Chattering in the quick-paced Vietnamese that once was so familiar to me, she gave sharp commands. Clicking off her cell, she unemotionally said, "We are ready, Mr. Moore. The car and luggage are waiting. We will take you to the Hotel Nikko Hanoi, where you will want to rest and refresh yourself. Tomorrow I will meet you at 0700 hours for breakfast at the hotel, and then we will go to see Colonel Bui Tin. He is most anxious to meet you again."

"I wonder," I mumbled.

She ignored it. "Yes, that will be discussed tomorrow. Come." She stood up and retraced Major Han's steps through the door. I followed.

HANOI, JANUARY 1, 2003

The ride from the airport to downtown Hanoi progressed at a fast-paced thirty minutes, barely avoiding mopeds, motorcycles, cars, and scurrying pedestrians. Traffic lights were obeyed but pushed to the limit by all drivers. The ten million people that crowded into Hanoi and the environs all seemed to be in front, back, and to the sides of our black government Mercedes, its official tags earning it some respect from the walking, rushing, or driving masses. The gray winter sky mixed with the air pollution over the crowded city, blocking the blue sky and the sun. A slight drizzle made the late morning chilly and dreary but didn't slow the population in pursuit of its normal workday. As we sped down one street after another, I spied little shops crammed along the streets and sidewalks with entrepreneurs selling food, household goods, and clothes, always bartering with their customers. The activity blurred by as we continued the drive to the hotel.

"Mr. Moore, for your information, I am married and have three sons. They wish to go to America and attend a university there, but they are still young, and we can afford only Hanoi University, which I attended," Hieu said. "Is this your first time visiting Hanoi?"

"Yes, for Hanoi . . . but I served during the war in South Vietnam, quite close to the former demilitarized zone, the DMZ." She nodded her acknowledgement of me being here in the war. Silence ensued, probably from the surfaced pain of the war that affected both of us. On the airplane, I had pondered how the Vietnamese would react to me, a former enemy soldier who indirectly or directly had been instrumental in the deaths of some of their countrymen.

Sitting in the front seat, Hieu occasionally glanced at me with piercing eyes as I slouched in the back seat, forcing myself to stay awake. There was little friendship or warmth between us at the moment.

Finally, she offered a token of peace. "You will find that many of my generation have not totally accepted the end of the war and the losses to our families. My father died in the war. He fought and defeated the French at Dien Bien Phu, and then fought you Americans in Quang Tri Province, just below the old demilitarized zone. You served in the same area—I believe you called it I Corps."

I decided not to respond, since she had obviously read my military records.

Silence lasted a few minutes and then she said, "My mother and older brothers seldom saw my father as he spent over seven years in the South, fighting Americans and the South Vietnamese."

"I'm so sorry for his death," I said. I meant it.

My sincerity seemed to catch her off guard. She hesitated and nodded to me but continued to study me with her side-glances. The war wasted so many lives, but I alone could not alleviate all the pain, no matter what I said.

We finally pulled into the hotel turnaround. As a doorman grabbed my luggage, Hieu escorted me to the front desk, where my electronic room key waited for me. I only had to sign the registration form, already typed, complete with my home address and Vietnamese contact information; I noticed Agent Hieu's name listed on the form, her name highlighted in yellow. Isolation crept in as I knew that my life for the time being belonged to the Vietnamese, and Hieu in particular.

With a bellman in tow, Hieu escorted me to the elevator. She stopped there and said, "Please rest from the jet lag. We will be very busy from now on. For Colonel Tin, a suit will be very good."

I smiled at her guidance. She ignored it. "OK, tomorrow I will be waiting for you in the lobby for breakfast," I confirmed.

"Yes, tomorrow. And do not be concerned—you are well-watched for safety purposes."

She disappeared as I entered the elevator. The bellman, smiling at me, said in English, "Welcome to Hotel Nikko."

"Thank you," I said, wondering how many police agents were watching me. The swaying elevator rocked me, slowly wearing down my resolve to stay awake.

ೲ

I devoured a delicious but light room service lunch: a French baguette, crusty and fresh, filled with a tuna salad, accompanied by a beer. Then I collapsed onto the bed, the dark dreary day contributing to my drowsiness from the long flight. After I woke some four hours later, I showered and put on clean clothes: a pair of jeans and a sweater. I began to feel human again; international travel wears out the mind and body.

I walked over to my room's window and stared at the street scene below me, absorbing the noise and activity of a large city winding down as the evening light slowly descended into the dark of night. The traffic I observed from my twelfth-floor room continued to stay busy, and the noise rose up to me as people conducted their lives below. During the war, the US had bombed targets in North Vietnam, specifically Hanoi and the nearby major port, Hai Pong. In the end it did not win the war for us; bombing can't destroy an agrarian nation with little industrial base. The North Vietnamese burrowed into homemade bomb shelters, moved any industry into the surrounding countryside, and relocated their power plants. The Chinese and Russians provided military aid with supplies crossing over from the China border, something we couldn't stop without drawing the Chinese or Russians into the war. The US could never destroy North Vietnam's fighting ability.

After I returned from Nam, I eventually studied the war, trying to decipher why I fought there. The US used over fourteen million tons of bombs in the Vietnam War, twenty times as much as the bombing in the Korean War, and seven times as much as used in World War II. Over seventy million liters of toxic chemicals were dropped all over Vietnam, which included forty-four million liters of the famous Agent Orange defoliant, toxic and cancer-causing. My own combat operations were in two of the heaviest Agent Orange drop zones: south near Cu Chi in the Mekong Delta, and north near the DMZ and the A Shau Valley, in which existed the road network for supplying the North Vietnamese, famously labeled as the Ho Chi Minh Trail. This series of trails, roads, and bridges from China through North Vietnam into Laos, Cambodia, and South Vietnam fed the military needs of a war-weary country. We tried to destroy the supply network with B-52 bombings, artillery, and combat assaults, but within twenty-four hours, civilian laborers known as coolies would repair the roads or bridges and the supplies continued.

Now I was in Hanoi as a friend of the government. The past thirty-three years hadn't faded my memory of the dying soldiers from both sides. I shook my head as I gazed out my room's window. Ideologies and religions constantly stirred the pot of human emotions, negating rationality, promoting biases and wars and death.

It was time to check in on the message board to see if Woodruff had any instructions for me. The internet message board served as our agreed-upon method to exchange normal communication in short coded phrases. Only in an emergency could I use the CIA satellite telephone to reach Woodruff. My Palm phone was basically to be used for the internet access. Despite all the preparations for this mission, I served as a free spirit, developing plans as I went based on information from my new contacts in Vietnam. Zang had not offered a better plan for catching Loan or Ramsey; it depended on Hieu, Colonel Tin, and me to solve the riddle, starting with my interrogation of Hung. I still wondered if this even made any sense, but then again, Hung had asked for me personally.

I clicked onto the message board looking for any message for Puking Buzzard, my code name. Woodruff was Rex I, and Tanner, his assistant, was Rex II. One message existed: *Call on S phone.*

Before going to my satellite phone, I typed in the required message to Rex I: *Arrived safe and sound. Starting vacation tomorrow. Love, Puking Buzzard.*

As long as I signed off with "love," Woodruff would know everything was normal and that I wasn't in danger. Leave off "love" and Woodruff would try to come to my rescue—indirectly, of course. He couldn't risk clandestine CIA operations in Vietnam.

Basically, I had been inserted, isolated, in a foreign country, prohibited from dealing with the US Embassy but working for the CIA. How did I agree to this?

Turning off the Palm phone, I returned it to the CIA briefcase and pulled out the fully charged satellite phone, all the while thinking about eating dinner in the hotel's restaurant tonight and exploring more of the French influence on Vietnamese cuisine.

I calculated the time difference from 5:58 p.m., as shown on my watch. Hanoi would be ahead of DC by twelve hours, which meant I would wake Woodruff at 5:58 a.m. on December 31, 2002. That appealed to me, so I dialed. The phone rang for about a minute, then Tanner's voice came on: "Are you there, John?"

"Yes. Surprised that Woodruff didn't answer. I just sent message via the internet board of my safe arrival. Why do you need to talk?"

"Wanted to convey my thanks for you being there."

I held the phone, smiling at his words, which I didn't completely believe.

"John, did you hear me?"

"Yes . . . I heard you. Anything else?" What could I say?

Tanner's pause seemed to last forever. "As part of your mission, it's also essential that you retrieve Ramsey's files."

Confused, I said, "How am I supposed to do that?"

"We assume he will have them with him. If so, we can't afford for those embarrassing files to leak out. It will impact someone here . . . very severely."

"Again, you won't tell me who this person is?"

"No. I can't." He hung up.

I sat for some time pondering this whole operation. I had zero clue on how to find Ramsey or Loan, let alone any mysterious files that Woodruff wanted back. This whole trip began to overwhelm me.

While I played at being an undercover agent, the woman I cared about would be submerged in total, excruciating grief over her dead father. I had accepted that his death had to be on me, and that Sally could never forgive me. I felt my hate, a desire to kill, to avenge her. I lay back on the bed, too upset to eat. After several hours of tossing and turning, still dressed, I fell asleep, disgusted that I had caused the death of another, again. And that somehow, I would comply with Woodruff's request to retrieve the files.

OUTSIDE OF HANOI, JANUARY 2, 2003

As Hieu accompanied me, continuously glancing at me, we entered the house; I reflected on my exhaustion from the long flight and the anxiety about my upcoming role in Nam. We said little at breakfast in the hotel, both of us deep in thoughts. She had to think the worst of me, the ugly American syndrome. Brushing off my melancholy, I gave a weak smile to Colonel Tin.

Retired, in his late eighties, and showing a resiliency common to the Vietnamese, Colonel Tin greeted us in the small living room of his two-story, cement-and-stone house located on the outskirts of Hanoi, the Vietnamese version of suburbia. Tin's pink house resembled a small villa on a very tiny plot of land bordered on the south by a drainage canal, with rice paddies on the north and west. The house faced east, toward the main highway to Hanoi; similar houses ran parallel or adjacent to his along the same road. Tin had no verdant landscape or elaborate gardens on his property, just bare dirt and a few neatly maintained trees and bushes enclosed by a five-foot stone wall. Growing food for the populace dictated that the fertile farmlands were not wasted for building huge homes or elaborate landscaped properties.

With our driver waiting outside in the car parked on the narrow driveway, Hieu and I sat down in the living room. A young woman offered us hot tea served in small porcelain cups. As she stared at me,

Tin introduced her as one of his great-granddaughters. Eventually, she bowed and returned to the back of the house.

Left alone and seated near Tin with our holstered pistols—a gesture of his trust, no doubt—Hieu and I listened reverently to an old man recount his tale of entering the military service of the Viet Minh led by Ho Chi Minh in 1950 and ending his service in 1980, five years after the fall of Saigon. It astonished me that he had served in war for almost twenty-five years: first against the French, participating in the famous defeat of the French at Dien Bien Phu, then against the United States and its South Vietnamese allies. His stark white hair gave him a noble dignity and accented his piercing dark eyes, which were constantly focused on me as he talked. His five-foot-four height was slightly stooped, but the wrinkles on his face still accentuated a rugged handsomeness.

"Mr. Moore, when you fought us, I had the pleasure of encountering you twice."

"I'm not certain I remember more than once," I said, my interest piqued.

"Ah, yes. There was, of course, the helicopter situation in which you saved my young lieutenant, now Colonel Zang, and me as well. For that I owe you my gratitude. During the Tet ceremonies this year, we will honor your name with our ancestors for your noble, kind deed." He smiled and continued. "I have many relatives, many grandchildren, aunts, uncles, and of course, my wife and my four sons. You helped preserve our familial line. It will be a great event for us since you are also here. I would be honored for you to celebrate here with us. Agent Hieu will ensure the arrangements for that."

Hieu, still as serious as when I first met her at the airport, spoke respectfully to Tin. I heard the name Loan, Ramsey, and Hung in her discourse. He responded kindly, as if she were his own daughter and not a police agent. She turned to me. "The Tet is February 1 through the third, but as I explained, you and I may be busy looking for Loan and the American, Ramsey. We may not be available. We will see."

More tea was brought, this time by an old but elegant woman whom Tin introduced as his wife. She bashfully bowed to me and studied me, showing both respect and a motherly kindness. Taking a long time serving the tea, she finally departed to the back of the house, as the granddaughter did earlier, still sneaking glances at me. I wondered how many more people were scattered in this house, curious to see me, the former American officer who had met the colonel in the war. I heard children's voices as they played behind the house. As I sipped the strong tea, or *tra*, I reflected on how my Katy loved her teas. My addiction to coffee began after her death—another change of life.

"I apologize for shifting from subject to subject, but you would not have known the second time we encountered each other. You were in the strategic hamlet of Mai Loc Village when I attacked with my regiment. You commanded C Company of the 101st Airborne, and your frontal assault surprised us and threw us back. Afterward, I reviewed the order of battle intelligence and remembered your name listed as the commander. It was your strong counterattack that threw us into a quagmire, which eventually led to my capture, along with my young aide, Zang, several weeks later." He took a sip of tea, looking through me into that past battle. "And you know the rest when you bordered that helicopter for your return to America and found us onboard as POWs. I was not only shocked to see your name tag on your jungle fatigues, but even more so by your actions to stop Agent Ramsey from killing Zang and me."

Impressed, my mind swept back to that battle. I had developed a defense plan upon being airlifted in with my company two days prior to the NVA attack. It relied on friendly Montagnard warriors to serve as recon and reserve troops for quick response to fill any gaps that the ARVNs would create if they panicked and retreated. These aborigines were ruthless fighters who hated the Vietnamese and loved the Americans, and they would do anything to help us in the war. We, in turn, provided medical support and food supplies for their loyalty.

We were almost overrun by the tenacious and fierce NVA soldiers, but in the end, we held our ground with the support of the

Montagnards, the remnants of the ARVN companies forced to fight or die, and the air force's tactical air fighters. Tin's troops fought long and hard but had reached exhaustion. I finally ordered a counterattack with all my platoons on line, forcing the NVA retreat.

"Because of that day, I seem to have been drawn to following you," I said, showing a weak smile.

Tin's inquisitive eyes drew me to explain.

"I knew you had escaped from the POW stockade. And in 1975, during language training at the Foreign Service Institute in Washington, DC, in preparation for my assignment to NATO in the Netherlands, I learned of the final chapter in your almost thirty years of war. The TVs and newspapers were abuzz with the collapse of Saigon as the US Embassy started evacuation while marines secured the building's roof for American helicopters to airlift the fortunate few. Blocks away in Saigon, on April 30, 1975, I think, the South Vietnamese government fell when you rode on a T-34 Russian/Chinese-made tank onto the Presidential Palace grounds. As the senior NVA officer, you accepted the surrender from General Duong Van Minh, representing the defeated South Vietnam, while President Thieu, America's chosen head, fled to Taiwan."

I sat back, pondering why I shared my knowledge of him. I noticed Tin's inward focus. He had returned to those last few days of the war.

Agent Hieu must have been puzzled as we talked, but she undoubtedly felt our emotions. We lapsed into silence as Tin and I sat, studying each other, reflecting on the war, its pain, the loss of so many comrades-in-arms, and the guilt of living while others died. The moment became spiritual as we honored each other and our dead.

Finally, Tin stood and, using his cane, walked to a small window overlooking the rice paddies that butted against his small property. He gestured for us to stand by him, brushing something from his eyes.

"Mr. Moore, I am glad you came. My country needs your help to capture Loan in case our agents in Cambodia fail. There are some powerful men in our Communist Party who oppose any further trade agreements with your country. With you, an American, helping us with the capture of Colonel Loan, we hope to reduce that opposition. It is politics but also a healing process for our people. I have already summarized your noble actions on that fateful helicopter ride to the leadership of the party. Your support and help in this will help further economic growth with your nation."

"I see," I said. But did I really? DuPee Catton's death gnawed at me.

"When you interrogate Colonel Hung, who is in a reeducation prison, please discover more about Loan's entry into Vietnam. In turn, our government is willing to consider giving Hung his freedom for his remaining worthless years of life."

"I will try, but I just don't know how this will help."

"Nevertheless, you have agreed to try," Tin said. "I want Loan captured."

I hesitated at his command. "Yes, of course. We help you with Loan, and you in turn will provide payback to the CIA by capturing Ramsey." I wanted his acknowledgement.

His eyes avoided me. He smiled, trying to deflect. His façade held, but I sensed he hid something. "Of course, there is no guarantee that Ramsey will survive." His eyes locked with mine, a deadly look, telling me much.

And just as quickly, he changed direction. "You must know I picked Hieu especially for this mission, as she is modern Vietnamese and has tempered any hatred for Americans, unlike some of my older comrades. You can trust her. She is strong and very intelligent. The two of you, with any support you need from me, will be the key to the mission. Start with Hung in prison. He is a traitor to Vietnam and a liar, but you will have no problem obtaining the truth from him. Your dossier as a psychologist is impressive. Colonel Zang has researched your career very extensively. Our reeducation process is just weak brainwashing, and good liars can escape telling the truth." Tin reached and squashed a small mosquito buzzing on the window glass. "So many of my comrades died of malaria in the war." He pulled out his handkerchief and wiped away the dead remains.

"I was told that Loan and Ramsey's reason for returning to Vietnam was due to hidden moneys and Champa artifacts," I said, probing for more truth.

Tin paused as a pained expression appeared on his wrinkled face. "I feel the recovery of stolen gold and Champa artifacts is not realistic. As you would say in America, it is a pipe dream. If that occurs, so be it.

"And as for your American, Ramsey, I do not relish being used by your CIA. They should clean up their own messes. However, if we capture Ramsey with Loan, then we will see. We made a devil's bargain with the CIA for Loan. Ramsey's capture is the price for getting Loan. There are times we need to be pragmatic.

"Our goal is to capture Loan. You and Hieu start with Hung, then all else should fall into place," he said, turning to me. "Hung is old and broken, but he trusts no one, except you. I honored his request to have you here." He put his left hand on my shoulder and stared up into my face. "Thank you for saving my life." His sincerity enveloped me.

I felt some goodness in this man, but I also sensed that he'd held back the complete truth. On the other hand, he had sacrificed much to unite his country as a soldier. Maybe his war secrets should stay hidden.

"You and Hieu will make your plans accordingly. Just remember, the gold or artifacts are a trap, like a spider web, to lure Loan and Ramsey back to this country. I am confident in your abilities. You are an honorable man, and I sense something in you that makes you perfect for this mission. In our Eastern culture, this task is nothing more than a puzzle or riddle to solve.

"You two represent different cultures and thinking processes: one from the West, one from the East. You should work as partners, the Yin and Yang, to be successful."

"We should go. It is a long drive to see Hung," Hieu said, motivated by Tin's speech. Unlike Tin, she showed little emotion; her stern face conveyed her focus on the job at hand.

"Ah, Hieu, please stay for a little lunch with an old man who admires your dedication to our new nation. You are like a daughter to me—so beautiful and yet so intelligent. You are so much like me when I was young, dedicated to the cause. And please, Mr. Moore, you will enjoy my wife's cooking. She also wishes to honor the American who saved her husband's life."

LANG DA, NORTHWEST OF HANOI, JANUARY 2, 2003

The former ARVN colonel stared at me, a frail reminder of the heady times in Vietnam in the late 60s and early 70s, when he acted like a god, deciding life and death for those who opposed him, a true military despot. Hung, no longer a corpulent, privileged government official, sat across us at the scarred table, an emaciated, broken old man. His eyes darted between Hieu and me. Despite his appearance, I sensed a shrewdness in him still. His distressed and wrinkled face did not hide this.

Major Han yelled harshly at Hung, making him cower. Han turned left to me, where I sat between him and Hieu; the three of us faced the seated Hung.

"Please ask any questions you wish. I believe Hung has the proper attention," Han said.

It was almost two in the afternoon, and I was sluggish from the big lunch at Colonel Tin's. Forcing my mind to focus on the urgency of my mission, I said, "Do you remember me from Dau Tieng and Saigon in the war?"

Hung looked at me, furtively glancing at Han and Hieu. Finally, in fairly decent English, he said, "Yes, I . . . do . . . Captain." He struggled over some words, in contrast to Hieu's fluency. I also perceived sincerity in him, which confused me.

"Why did you ask to see me?"

"I trust you. And I want revenge for my betrayal."

"Betrayal?" I said.

"Yes, I helped Loan and Ramsey before the war ended. They were to ensure my escape to America. As you see," he looked around, "I have been in prison all this time."

I smiled. "Deals made among thieves. So how do you envision my helping?"

"Oh, you are already doing that," he smiled back.

I sat back, caught off guard, pondering how he might manipulate me.

Suddenly, Major Han stood and screamed at him as he hit the table with a wooden baton that had mysteriously appeared. The loud whack shattered the silence of the bleak interrogation room; I jerked back into my chair, my ears ringing. Hung's body collapsed in his chair, slightly shaken. The years since the fall of Saigon had not been good to him, having spent all that time in communist reeducation camps and prisons. But his greed got him here. He served as a soldier in name only; he was more of a common crook.

I waited as Han sat down, pleased with himself. Hieu shook her head slightly but said nothing. The secluded prison in Lang Da now only held a select few prisoners, a far cry from the thousands incarcerated here in the late 70s. Still, the atmosphere demoralized me, and Han's outburst added to my disgust. His arrogance also seemed to annoy Hieu.

I leaned back in my creaking wooden chair and let my open suit jacket reveal the pistol strapped to me, a show of power. Hung registered all that as he sat with both hands and feet shackled to rings in the cement floor. But he didn't seem all that intimidated by Major Han. I wondered why.

As we talked, the interrogation revolved around the culture divide between us, the West versus the Far East. I had experienced this Vietnamese mentality during the war, the thinking process. Hung seemed to be weighing all his options on what he wished to share with me, the American he had requested because he didn't trust his fellow Vietnamese.

I interjected, "Colonel Hung, your ancestors need you free before you die, living with your family. Don't disappoint them. These men, Loan and Ramsey, are not part of you. You owe them nothing." I sat back, using the silence to allow him to think.

The smell of urine from past interrogations permeated the air around us. My mood soured more as the meeting continued, leaving me exhausted and with a headache. My vision blurred as I stood to stretch, trying to grunt my way through the session with Hung.

Hung lifted his dejected head and made a contorted attempt at a smile.

"Well, are you ready to talk to me?" I asked curtly. I felt like crap. This trip was an ordeal for me, not knowing how it would all end. I sat down again.

"I will tell you what I know. I wish to see my family and live out my life in my ancestral village." The cough that followed didn't sound healthy; his cancer had to be eating away at him. What struck me was his will to live; I had expected him to still be a coward, but his incarceration had made him a survivor, and he'd grown stronger in the process.

Hung said that Ramsey had been preparing to return to Vietnam ever since normalized relations with America had been negotiated in 1997. Hung admitted to a prison network that sneaked in newspapers and letters that kept him posted on happenings outside, and he had grown more infuriated over how Loan had abandoned him. He knew Ramsey would need Loan to sneak into the country to retrieve the gold. He helped plant the seed by a letter to Loan in early 2002, stressing the need to retrieve the hidden gold and to get Hung his share, as promised in 1975.

"I am surprised you believe they would honor the request to share the gold with you. After all, you are locked up here," I said.

"Believe me, I expect no gold. I wish only revenge by luring Ramsey and Loan back to Vietnam—to be captured. Their capture will free me from this hellhole."

Hung admitted he met Tom Reed on some of the Phoenix operations. Reed and Ramsey complemented each other in killing, something Hung said he had no stomach for.

"During the war, Loan told me how the young American soldier Reed and Agent Ramsey loved killing. He wished he could recruit that type for his use," Hung said, bending at the waist, coughing again.

It disappointed me that the evidence continued to build against Reed. I really didn't know Reed's true character after all.

Then Hung jumped back to the gold. He explained that he thought the gold and artifacts were near My Son, the ancient ruins of the Champa kingdom, based on what took place in Da Nang in January 1973, when Hung had an unexpected visit from Loan and Ramsey. Loan had asked Hung to assign two APCs (armored personnel carriers) and a Rome Plow bulldozer with a tractor-trailer rig to haul it. Ramsey said little, staying in the background as Loan requisitioned the equipment. Hung never saw the vehicles again nor their drivers, and he wrote off the loss due to combat with the NVA or VC in the area. Then Loan transferred to Saigon weeks after the disappearance of the men and equipment. Later Hung reconnected with Loan, but he was told to be patient and to wait for the right moment to leave Vietnam as a rich man. Loan gave no explanation about what happened to the equipment or personnel, but he swore that he would handle everything.

Hung recalled the chaotic events of April 1975 that changed everything: Loan's evacuation from Saigon as the advancing NVA and VC entered the city's outskirts; Hung's failure to contact Ramsey prior to the evacuation of the US Embassy; and Hung's capture in the basement radio room of the Presidential Palace, still trying to contact the Americans to help him.

I leaned toward Hung. "Tell me what you know about the gold."

Hung looked around. He studied his aging reflection in the mirror to his right. "I know very little. I assume it is near My Son."

"Colonel Hung, you can drop your act. I have no time for games." My throbbing headache continued. I needed to get out of this dark, dank, urine-soaked hellhole. In addition, a putrid body order permeated the room—from the hundreds, even thousands, of South Vietnamese prisoners who had passed through this compound over the last thirty years. I didn't need to guess what occurred here. Hung's face told me enough about the beatings and torture.

Hung looked at me for a moment. His seemed at peace with himself. A single light bulb hung over the table; its conical beam framed the aged Hung. His wrinkles, his shallow pallor appeared to have grown as the minutes ticked by. I looked at Hieu in the shadows to my side, observing us both. Her veneer prevented me from reading her. Did she approve or not?

Knowing I had reached my own limit, I said, "Here is my problem. We want Loan and Ramsey. I assume they will go to where the gold is. So, I need to know exactly where they would go. If you help me, I will help you."

Hung stared down to the table top, looking for a life preserver like a sailor lost at sea. "I . . . know there were almost eight hundred gold bars. Where? I was never told. I swear this. There is one man who may know for certain. He is a survivor from village where I think Loan, Ramsey, and Reed killed everyone."

"Who is he? And where can we find him?"

"His name is Quan. I know he came to Da Nang, maybe when he was twelve years old, in 1975, and because he has Cham ancestry, he now works at the Da Nang Museum of Cham Sculpture. That is all I know about the gold. Please believe me."

I didn't, not completely.

Hieu stood up to stretch. It had been a long interrogation. "You will have to remain here in prison until we confirm your information," she said.

Hung looked down, resigned.

Hieu nodded to Major Han and me. "We take short break?"

I got up and said to Hung, "Please dig further into your memories while we are gone."

The three of us walked out of the room, leaving the shriveled and defeated old man to contemplate his miserable existence. Two arrogant guards passed us, going back into the room. I noticed one had a baton that he twirled, a smirk embedded on his face.

⸺

Hieu, Han, and I sat in a small isolated and windowless office near the interrogation rooms, drinking tea. Han said to me, "Hung is a traitorous capitalist pig, and if he was not needed, I would have told him to rot in prison." His English impressed me. These Vietnamese agents were well trained.

"Look, I don't like Hung. After all, he tried to kill me in Saigon during the war. But we need to give him hope in order to gain as much information as we can. Anyway, we have to return to ask more questions." I sat back, looking to Hieu for support and taking another sip of hot tea. The clock on the wall showed 3:35 p.m.

It had been a long day. I was rubbing my eyes regularly. The caffeine in the tea did nothing for me. A good, strong espresso would have been better.

"Mr. Moore is correct. We need to keep Hung cooperating to accomplish our mission," Hieu said.

Han grunted, acknowledging the rationality of this. He then said, "What is the best plan for now?"

I said, "No further physical abuse. And no harsh threats. He could say anything to stay alive. He's been tortured enough. I want to win his loyalty. If he feels he can trust Hieu or me, then we will gain more information. That means that you, Major Han, should not be in the room. Agent Hieu should be with me, however."

"No. That is not going to happen," Han said, glaring at me, knowing I did not share his bullying technique in the interrogation room.

"Major, he fears you. Yet his psychological defenses are strong. I want to tear them down with trust and honesty."

"No," Han said, then turned and poured more tea for himself.

"Well, look we all know what Hung told us in there collaborates what Colonel Zang told me about the gold. We are close to obtaining the critical piece needed to locate the place that will draw Ramsey and Loan," I said, resigning myself to Han's denial.

I shrugged and looked to Hieu. Her face reflected no emotion. She continued to look at me, all the while thinking. She stood and motioned Han toward a corner of the room. Furiously, he also stood and followed her. They jabbered for close to ten minutes. His anger dominated her calming tone, yet she wore him down. He pointed a finger at her as he lectured her. She bowed in agreement. Then he slammed his mug on the table and left the room.

"Major Han finally agrees," she said. Her stoic face expressed little.

"Thank you, Agent Hieu," I said, noting a brief twinkle in her eyes. She walked to the door leading into Hung's interrogation room.

She pointed her head toward the door. "Shall we?"

○X○

"Yes . . . " Hung's English flowed now. "Loan told me that he and Ramsey would smuggle the gold out of Vietnam before the fall of the South. We all knew that our troops could not stop the NVA without US military support and . . . "

I nodded for him to continue as I glanced at the peeling paint on the wall behind him. The room's musty and acrid odor still attacked us—a virtual swamp of anguished souls.

"This was about March 1973. I was told that CIA Agent Ramsey was at the US Embassy and would help Loan and me get out of the country. I was assured by Loan. We would divide the gold equally after we escaped from Vietnam. I trusted my brother-in-law. We were to escape with CIA support." Hung stopped and waited.

"How do you know that Ramsey had not already removed the gold?" I asked.

"Maybe weeks before Saigon fell in 1975, Loan told me, when I just transferred again to Saigon from Da Nang, that he and Ramsey hid the gold together in early 1973 but could not go to the buried spot because the NVA and VC controlled the area."

Obviously, Ramsey had not expected South Vietnam to collapse so fast, nor had he prepared for the gold to be shipped out.

Hung continued: "Ramsey fled with the American Embassy personnel in April 1975 . . . and took Loan with him. I tried contacting Ramsey but had no success. Then eventually I was captured by the NVA as they entered Saigon."

I now felt that Ramsey and Loan were the only ones left who knew where the gold had been hidden. They fled to return another day and retrieve the treasure.

Hieu glared at Hung and said in English, "It is not your money. You robbed your people and even your American allies. If you ever want to feel the free air, you will tell us everything, or else you can rot here until you die."

He was not used to a woman browbeating him, and his self-worth had diminished. In the rural areas where the villagers struggled to eke out a living in the rice paddies, men and women worked side by side, contributing jointly, a relationship of equality. For Hung, who had developed hubris in his corrupt life, a brutal confrontation by a woman shook him. He looked to me, maybe assuming the friendlier American would be supportive.

Finally, he said, "I am dying, and I wish to live out my life in peace with my family. The gold . . . it is probably gone. I never found it myself. But I tell the truth . . . I used the gold story to lure Loan back to Vietnam. And Ramsey too, as Colonel Tin wished me to do."

"I'm confused. Colonel Tin wants Ramsey back in Vietnam?" This countered Tin's laissez-faire attitude about Ramsey when we spoke earlier today.

Hung nodded. "But do not ask me why. I don't know. If you capture Loan and Ramsey, Colonel Tin will free me to die quietly." He looked at his folded hands, tears showing. "I want revenge as well and have helped Colonel Tin in order to achieve it."

"OK, then tell me where you expect them to enter Vietnam," I said as I pulled a copy of Reed's journal entries from my suit pocket and a folded map of Vietnam. I unfolded it and placed it in front of me on the table, continually staring at Hung. I pulled out my pen and waited. He looked at me, resigned.

☙ॐ☙

I held my copy of Reed's journal entries, all shared with Hieu and Major Han. "Let's look at what we now know." I stood and went to the old chalkboard hanging skewed on the wall in the little office we had been using at the prison. Major Han had rejoined Hieu and me after Hung had been returned to his cell. He sat stiffly watching my briefing. The lighting in the room shone marginally better than in the interrogation room. Taking the broken piece of white chalk, I wrote the following:

The key players—where are they now:

Ramsey (Hong Kong). Based on airline ticket manifest

Loan (Phnom Penh). Based on airline ticket manifest

CIA estimates: Ramsey comes to Vietnam before Tet Holiday (Feb. 1–3)

Maybe in late January? The 27th?

How: By air: Ho Chi Minh City (Saigon)? Da Nang? Both TOO RISKY

By land to Vietnam: Cambodia to Laos by vehicle—illegal border crossing. But per Hung, this would be the way!!!!

I underlined the land route bullet point. "This is the one—the one that Hung said Loan and Ramsey would use." Then I thought a moment. "Oh, there's another option, but it's not realistic."

I wrote on the board: *By sea: 1,000 miles of coastline. Too much logistical planning.*

Major Han sat up and waved his arms in disgust. "You, Mr. Moore, former captain in US Army, come here and lecture us on our job. We are quite capable to do it. Americans are all the same!"

"I'm sorry. I didn't mean to imply anything," I said. My isolation grew with his animosity.

"Yes, yes," he snarled. Standing up, he walked to me and stopped a few feet away, facing me. I smelled his acrid breath. "We have Loan under observation in a hotel in Phnom Penh and will kidnap him by tomorrow night. So . . . what is this waste of time you scribble on the board?" He glared while pointing to the blackboard.

"What if Loan escapes your agents?" I said and backed up a step.

"Bah, what garbage you preach to us. Americans think of all the answers. You destroyed many lives here in the war. Created many orphans. To be exact, I am an orphan because of your B-52 bombers." He turned and threw loud, harsh-sounding Vietnamese at Hieu.

I admired her composure as she stood up and gave back in kind. I had lost my rudimentary understanding of Vietnamese—my thirty-year absence had seen to that—and could only guess at what was being said. Han was technically her boss, yet I felt that Colonel Tin's authority and power had been passed on to Hieu. She seemed to show it as she shouted back at Han, who raised his arms and stormed out of the office. I waited.

"Please continue, Mr. Moore. He will work with us," she said as she returned to her seat, facing me.

I twisted my neck, working out the new tension, and rubbed my forehead again. "Look, I'm not trying to cause issues. Tell me what you want from me."

"Please continue," she said and pointed to the chalkboard.

"Well . . . " I hesitated. "Do you have any aspirin?"

She pulled her shoulder bag to her and reached inside. Taking out and opening a small bottle, she found two white tablets and gave them to me. She poured water from a pitcher on the table into my empty tea mug.

"Thank you," I said and downed the pills and water.

She nodded. In that brief respite I felt I liked her as a person. True, she was cool toward me—the American—but I understood after what the US did to her country. Her Eurasian bloodline didn't overcome her Vietnamese, but enhanced it in subtle ways, taking her striking looks to a unique level, as if a renowned artist had sculptured her face. She looked stunning and close to perfect in the dim light of that office. I had avoided concentrating on her because of her aloofness, of her seeming hate for Americans, but her argument with Han changed that. I continued to look, forgetting my manners, captivated by the mysterious flavor of her charms. Her ponytail heightened her appeal, making her look younger than her forty-some years. Her black eyes bore into me, revealing nothing of her thoughts; I worried about what she could see inside me. It became a regal look that made me think of her as a princess in ancient Vietnam, ruling over her subjects, demanding and getting complete loyalty and devotion. Still mesmerized with her eyes,

I focused on her meticulously shaped eyebrows, almost pencil lines, and then her mascara-highlighted eyelashes.

She was pure woman, yet by the strength she exuded, like a lioness protecting her pride, I felt she could be deadly. Everything about her conveyed control, every move seemed planned. I wondered what sort of man she had deemed to marry, to bear her children. He had to be like a god to qualify for her devotion, to share her bed.

"Captain Moore, will you continue?" Her strong voice returned me to matters at hand.

"Ah." I slowly turned to the chalkboard, my mind still fantasizing about this unique woman, wondering how I got off track. "I think these are the key points as summarized by Hung." I wrote furiously, focusing on the task.

1. *Gold near My Son, per Hung*

2. *Land route: Cambodia-Laos-Vietnam per Hung*

3. *Ramsey will still go to gold if Loan is captured*

4. *Cham native (Quan) working at Da Nang museum— possibly knows where the gold is hidden*

5. *What transportation to recover and haul gold?*

6. *Return by land, travel back to Laos or to Cambodia?*

Reed's journal pages served as the basis for our planning. The latest information provided by Hung coincided with the words written by Reed, giving us some hope that there was truth to this hidden gold, which would lure Loan and Ramsey to be captured by Vietnamese police agents.

Hieu, after reviewing the pages, stood and went to a filing cabinet, pulling out larger maps of Laos, Cambodia, and Vietnam. She spread them out on the table. As I sat down, she plotted the villages near My Son: Dai Lanh and Giang.

She let out a deep breath as she said, "If the gold is near My Son and the villages of Dai Lanh or Giang, then Ramsey, with proper vehicles, could transport the recovered gold along Highway 14 to the Laos border near village of D Cong, cross over, and drive to Pakxe, Laos, where there is an airport that can accommodate large transport aircraft. It is approximately 480 kilometers one way from Giang or Dai Lanh to Pakxe."

Looking over her shoulder, I smelled the delicate fragrance of her perfume. It momentarily distracted me.

Catching myself again, I studied the map's legend and did a quick conversion. That equaled about 320 miles. Depending on the condition of the roads and trails, it could take six to ten hours to drive.

"If we assume a full day to drive to Vietnam, then Ramsey has to allow at least one full day to load the gold, and then a third day for the return to Laos. And we are assuming that he can find the hidden spot quickly. It's been many years, and landmarks disappear with vegetation growth—well, you know all that."

Hieu nodded. "We must develop a realistic timeline for their arrival and be in the area of My Son before. If we can discover the hiding spot, we can wait for them there. However, this is only necessary should our people fail on Loan. If they succeed, Loan can give the exact location once he is captured tomorrow."

"If he is captured," I said.

She looked up at me. The coolness, maybe an arrogance of knowing the right answers while others floundered, had returned. "I agree—we need a contingency plan." She folded the maps.

"I will call Colonel Tin after I secure airline tickets. Today is January 2, so we should plan on going to Da Nang by tomorrow to talk to the Cham native working at the museum." She looked at me and pulled out her phone.

"Yes, that makes sense," I said. Trying to add some value, I pulled out the latest photograph of Ramsey and handed it to her. "It may come in handy."

Hieu had been placed on hold while arranging the flight from Hanoi to Da Nang, so she took the photo. She studied it until the other party came back on.

Hieu seemed excited as she hung up the phone. "I arranged a 4x4 vehicle for us in Da Nang. These roads can be difficult, and if the two of them use old trails, we will be able to pursue. Mr. Moore, I hope you have some type of hiking shoes for the My Son area."

"I am prepared, Hieu. The suit I am wearing is the only one I brought. The rest of my clothes are jeans and safari shirts."

"Good—we begin then." She then dialed Colonel Tin.

I turned and busied myself with collecting my CIA case. Hieu would be a good partner; I felt secure with her. The shrewd Colonel Tin had planned it well.

HANOI, JANUARY 2, 2003

As her driver steered back to Hanoi, I noticed Hieu had not used my first name so far.

When asked, she said, "Seniority and rank are important in dealing with many of the officials in our country. It is better to follow this custom as we are working together. In Vietnam, the last name comes first, followed by the middle name and then the first name." I recalled this tradition from when I served here, thus I would be addressing her by her last name, Hieu.

Sitting in the back seat, I absorbed the panorama of Hanoi's approaching city limits as Hieu stayed busy on her cell phone, orchestrating our travel for tomorrow. Farmers hauled produce, chickens, and even pigs into the city on their little motorbikes for evening shoppers, preparing for the morning market as well. One mini motorbike passed at a congested street intersection balancing six cages full of chickens stacked and tied down behind the driver, towering over him as he zoomed in between vehicles and pedestrians. It amazed me how adroitly he avoided collisions with others. Other motorbikes carried loads of small bushes, reed baskets, clay pots, or dishes.

With Tet celebrations approaching, Kumquat trees were everywhere; these small, three-foot trees, planted in large pots, were also hauled on bikes, cars, and motorbikes. The trees represented three generations of ancestors, selected to ensure that all family periods were represented: ripe fruit for adults, unripe fruit for children, and buds for babies.

As we approached the Hotel Nikko Hanoi and pulled into the driveway, bellmen rushing to greet cars delivering hotel guests, Hieu clicked off her cell phone and said, "I invite you to meet my family for dinner tonight."

That startled me. "OK . . . " I said, "but only if you have the time. I know you have much to do."

"No, we fly to Da Dang tomorrow at 1300 hours. So, time is OK."

"Good, then," I said. I looked at my watch. It was past seven-thirty, or 1930 hours.

"I will walk over and get you at 2030 hours. My apartment is four blocks away. You can freshen up." She nodded toward the bellman opening my door.

ⱺⱺⱺ

In my hotel room, I took a quick shower then changed into clean underwear and shirt, and then put on my suit. The stuffy and humid prison had taken its toll on my clothes.

I was not fond of wearing the pistol, but I had been cautioned to have it on me, so I strapped the holstered pistol back over my shirt. I tightened my tie with a Windsor knot and waited for the telephone to announce Hieu.

A few minutes later she called from the lobby phone, and I took the elevator down to meet her. She had changed into the traditional, beautiful *ao dai*, the classic trouser and slit tunic. I admired Vietnamese women in this attire. On her, it accented her beauty even more. A striking light blue in color, Hieu's *ao dai* changed her from the serious, efficient government agent to a delicate woman. Her black shiny hair hung long over her shoulders, encompassing her face.

"Mr. Moore, are you ready for Vietnamese dinner?"

"Yes, and may I compliment you on how nice you look?"

She paused and studied me with her dark eyes, nodded, and then turned away, hiding any emotions, no different from the professional, driven police agent I had worked with the last two days. On the other hand, I had settled on her acceptance of me as an ally—not a former enemy. As we walked out the door, she strode by my side. I don't think I had seen her smile yet.

"The last Vietnamese dinner I had was in a Montagnard village in 1969. I ate fish, rice, and *nuoc mom*," I said.

"Oh, the smelly fish sauce! Do you like?" She gave a slight nod, not revealing much of her thinking on the matter.

"Actually, it is tasty, but the smell . . . " I said. "But the worst had to be the Montagnards strong rice wine that they brewed and expected visitors to their tiny villages to drink. I think that drink can destroy the brain."

She nodded again and continued to study the street as we walked the four blocks toward her apartment. Further conversation dried up at that point. I followed her example and walked in silence. Near her apartment building, an old woman in black silk pajamas passed us with a *gong ganh* astride her shoulder, a wooden pole with hanging baskets at each end loaded with produce and packs of rice. Even at this hour, under the streetlights, peasants were moving food and other items to their open-door shops.

"Mr. Moore, you may be disappointed with dinner or our small apartment tonight. I know Americans live in big houses, but we have to accept the limited space here in Hanoi."

"Why would I be disappointed?" I felt stereotyped for being an American.

She ignored me and took longer strides toward the apartment building.

Reaching the lobby door, she turned to me and said, "Remember, you will have to carry your pistol regularly here—as an American, you are not completely safe—too many feelings from the war."

The words sent a slight chill down my spine.

HANOI, JANUARY 3, 2003

The next morning, I woke at six and decided to do an hour workout in the hotel's fitness center. After forty minutes on the treadmill at a sharp incline and mid-speed, I sweated like a plow horse on a hot, humid day. I switched to the weight machines to tone up my muscles. I needed to return to my yoga routine, but not today. As I worked out, I thought about dinner last night.

Hieu's husband, a professor of mathematics at Hanoi University, greeted me politely and with a big smile. He questioned me about my profession, as well as about professorships at American colleges. US politics were also peppered into the conversation. He knew a great deal about the US, more than I did about Vietnam. He had prepared dinner and revealed that he did this often since Hieu's job often meant long and irregular hours, but he respected her career, the money, and the class status of working for the socialist government.

Their three boys, still in grade school, talked to me, trying out school English, but they were mostly mesmerized by the tall American in their small apartment. After they became used to me, they reverted to eating and talking among themselves, glancing occasionally at me. Dinner was *bun thit nuong*, thinly sliced and grilled pork over noodles and vegetables, with hot tea and a rice wine, *ruou nep*, thick and sticky on the tongue, and strongly alcoholic. I enjoyed the family event, using chopsticks rather than the utensils that were placed on the table for me. That met approval by Hieu's husband.

Watching Hieu, who became a gracious host, serving everyone, ensuring our wine glasses were full, made me think of Katy and now Sally, who I had lost as well. Being eight thousand miles from home and lonely, working with a woman who probably thought Americans were barbarians, added to my down mood. Hieu didn't like the wine and stayed with Huda Beer, a Vietnamese brew. She relaxed among her family—her boys' antics even made her smile. Still, when she looked at me, her stone face returned. Her babysitting me the last two days probably didn't jive with her high level of responsibility within the National Police ranks.

After dinner, the boys cornered me and pumped me about cowboys and Indians. They had seen old John Wayne westerns, and for them that was the basis for the US. I'm afraid I didn't help matters by telling them stories about how Indians scalped people. They listened intently, their imaginations running wild.

By midnight we all decided it was time to call it a night, and Hieu, acting as my security, accompanied me down the stairs from her apartment to the street and looked for a cab.

"It's OK. I need the fresh air, and I can see the hotel. Only four blocks, you know. And thank you for the nice dinner."

She stood looking around, trying to decide. The night air chilled me, and I started to walk away from her.

"I will walk with you," she said.

"No, don't bother yourself," I said and wondered if she noticed my aloofness. "See you tomorrow. And again, thanks for the evening." I left her there, probably glaring, but certainly not smiling.

൙

At ten, I was waiting for Hieu in the lobby dressed in jeans, a yellow sweater, and my black leather jacket, wearing my harnessed pistol underneath. Hieu appraised me coldly as she entered the lobby while her driver and car waited for us. She wore jeans, a blue sweater, and a black leather jacket, her long black hair bunched into a ponytail under a light blue New York Yankees baseball cap. The slight bulge under her left arm conveyed she had her weapon as well.

"Did you sleep well?" she asked. Without waiting for my response, she gave me a black Yankees baseball cap. "This will help with protection from the sun and also help our agents identify us in Da Nang."

I smiled and said, "Thanks." I put the cap on, grinning to myself, knowing that it wouldn't be hard to find me, a tall, white American. A round eye. "Thank you again for letting me share your dinner. You have a nice family."

"You are kind, but we have much to do today, so let us go to the airport." Hieu maintained her professional mode, focused on the job, organized, and constantly thinking. "You have checked out already and left unnecessary clothes to hold for your return?"

"Yes. I left my suit and other extras with the front desk."

Hieu nodded and walked past the door held open by the bellman. I followed her long strides to the car for the drive to Hanoi's Noi Bai Airport and our flight to Da Nang. As we walked, I swallowed my daily pill followed by a mouthful of water from my water bottle. Prior to leaving the States, I had started taking the one-a-day Malarone pill for protection against malaria, reminiscent of the daily ritual for all US soldiers during the war. Hieu watched me swallow the pill; I decided she had no such protection and made a mental note to share my meds with her once we arrived in Da Nang. I wondered if she trusted me enough to take the pills.

DA NANG, JANUARY 3, 2003

At Hanoi's airport, we processed through security without delay, escorted by police agents, our weapons checked and placed in a special container onboard. I enjoyed the VIP treatment, avoiding lines and skipping the mundane process of checking in and getting seat assignments.

Hieu insisted that I take the aisle seat while she sat next to me by the window on the Vietnam Airlines Airbus A321. She took advantage of the hour-and-fifteen-minute flight to brief me on Tet, which is a movable date depending on the start of the lunar year. Her tone indicated pride in the country's customs.

The year 2003 started on February 1. There are four sacred mythological creatures revered by the Vietnamese during Tet: the turtle, the unicorn, the phoenix, and the dragon. All four are celebrated at home, during festivals, and in parades. Hieu reminded me that the phoenix legend was used by the CIA to name their extermination program of the communist cells in the South Vietnamese countryside. When she talked of that program, I noticed the sadness on her face. I avoided that topic for now.

The Vietnamese take the Tet celebration seriously and spend enormous sums for the holiday, in many cases going into debt. It is important that the family and all living generations are seen as prosperous in order to secure a good life going forward. The first-footing, or the first official guest invited to appear at the home, is carefully selected to be distinguished, if possible, with wealth, no divorces, and no family deaths within the year, all to ensure good luck and prosperity for the inviting family. The parents' homes, usually located in the villages and smaller towns, become the focal point for family members who come from all over Vietnam and other countries, leaving the big cities, shutting down commercial activity for three days. Many people start traveling to their childhood homes days or weeks before the main dates, effectively making the holiday much longer than three days. As Hieu explained, we would become entangled in all the travel congestion the closer February 1 approached.

"Also, Tet is considered everyone's birthday. We do not celebrate individual birthdays in Vietnam, but during Tet, everyone adds another year to their age."

"You make a great tour guide," I said.

"Hopefully we can finish this business soon and I will be your tour guide for Hanoi and the rest of Northern Vietnam. Colonel Tin insists on it. It is a wonderful country." Hieu looked at me, her pride showing.

Did I notice an inkling of friendliness?

"I'd like that." The silence ensued again.

"This mission is a priority, however," she said.

"Agreed," I said and looked away.

ФХ⊙

On our final approach to Da Nang airport, I noticed the almost forty-year-old concrete bunkered hangers used by the US Air Force during the Vietnam War—now used by my former enemy. Da Nang had been mortared regularly, thanks to the VC observers hidden in nearby Marble Mountain, which overlooked the city and the base.

The abandoned concrete jet hangers had in effect become historical monuments of the war.

We landed on time, and as we exited the terminal, a driver with a Mercedes SUV waited for us. Hieu chattered with the driver, a Da Nang police agent. He finally gave her the keys and went to a black Fiat parked nearby, got in the passenger side, and departed with his driver.

"We are ready. The vehicle is prepared with two AK-47s in the weapons case in the back seat, two field packs with energy bars and extra bottles of water, and good topographical maps of the My Son area, including nearby villages and the Laotian border."

She explained that to ensure my security, we had adjoining hotel rooms at the Palm Garden Resort in Hoi An. The new beach resort would serve as our base of operations. The Da Nang office of the National Police had already contacted the man we needed to meet at the Cham museum.

"His name, as we know, is Quan, and he expects us, although I imagine he will be very nervous. Police agents in our country tend to frighten people," she said without any qualms.

"So do the police in the US," I said.

She seemed to decipher my statement. Then she asked, "Do you know how to use the AK-47 rifle?"

"Unfortunately, I do." Saddened, I avoided explaining my use of the NVA automatic rifle during the Vietnam War, dropped by its owner as he died at my feet, killed by the last round of my .45-caliber pistol. I was forced to pick up his AK-47 and shoot it in bursts at the remaining NVA charging into our landing zone. That was the day I lost my RTO, my radiotelephone operator, killed by an exploding enemy mortar round just as we jumped from the Huey's skid pads onto the ground. His deadly gut wound ended his young life at nineteen. The scene of mangled bodies—Americans and NVA embracing each other in their death grips, their last efforts to survive, and their failure—still haunted me.

Hieu stared at me, trying to comprehend my darkened mood, not knowing that I had gone back in time. But she didn't pursue the matter.

I loaded our baggage into the rear of the Mercedes while she started up the SUV. There was an FM field radio mounted on the front dash for secure communication with her people. As we drove out of the airport parking lot, I felt déjà vu from over thirty years ago, when I had climbed into an army jeep in Long Binh, carrying my M16 rifle and .45-caliber pistol, wearing a flak vest and helmet, joining a convoy to head in-country and to war.

Da Nang is part of former South Vietnam, and even in the winter months it's humid. The wet, warm air took me back to those initial days at Long Bien, near Saigon, and I recalled observing the first body bags filled with dead Americans, the human cost of war, waiting to be processed.

Hieu drove as my thoughts of war burst in small flashes of the events and battles, and those endless faces of my dead men. I didn't talk about the war, yet she sensed the reason for my fugue and waited me out. As I looked out the window at the passing panorama, she sporadically examined me with her dark and penetrating eyes, saying nothing.

We had decided to meet with Quan in Da Nang before going to our hotel in Hoa An, located south of Da Nang with close access to the highway to My Son. Hieu drove into Da Nang, asking me to help look for 01 Trung Nu Vuong Street. I had the Da Nang city map spread out on my lap and helped as much as a stranger could. We were both new to the city. I had only been to the now-defunct US airbase during the war, passing through on my way to Phu Bai and the 101st Airborne Division, whereas Hieu had never been this far south of Hanoi in her whole life.

By mid-afternoon, we pulled up to the Da Nang Museum of Cham Sculpture and, having official police tags, parked by the entrance, ignoring the no parking signs. Within minutes we found our man. In 1973, Quan fled his village of Giang, over forty miles away, or sixty kilometers in metric terms, when he lost his father at age twelve. He appeared about forty, with a face lined with wrinkles from a stressful life spent living in war since the day he was born. He didn't resemble the typical Vietnamese, and Hieu explained to me, between interpreting Quan's answers, that he was part of the Cham bloodline, heavily influenced by descendants from India. As a different race, the Chams fought the Vietnamese for control of Vietnam from 200 to 1471 AD, establishing the Kingdom of Champa in the Central Highlands. About 1471 the Vietnamese defeated the Champa Kingdom and reduced it to a territory, eventually forcing the surviving members of the royal family and some of its subjects to flee to Cambodia in 1720, leaving the remaining Cham people to fend for themselves.

The frail Quan didn't resemble the Cham warriors of the 1400s, who dared to oppose the Vietnamese; he acted nervous as Hieu interrogated him. He claimed that his father, who was the village elder, and the other adult male villagers had been forced by ARVN soldiers and two Americans to march southwest from the village of Giang. None returned. As the eldest son, Quan took his younger brother, sisters, and mother to hide that first night in the nearby bamboo forest, as his father had instructed him to do whenever ARVNs showed up in the area. The area was VC-controlled, and the village had been previously brutally attacked by operatives of the Phoenix Program. He still remembered the name of the program used to eliminate any communists in the villages.

The next day, there was still no sign of the villagers who had been taken away. Quan then carefully followed the tracks of the two APCs and the big dozer, as he called the Rome plow. He walked in the brush and jungle to avoid being seen, paralleling the imprints in the ground formed by the armored vehicles' metal tracks. About eight kilometers (five miles) southwest of the village, he saw that the tracks stopped at the jungle overgrown with large banyan trees, sacred and lucky to both the Cham and Vietnamese. It was very quiet, and he carefully approached where the tracks entered the heavily wooded area but saw that much brush and dirt had been piled to cover the trail. Frightened, he continued to explore the area and, less than a kilometer from a grove of banyan trees near the trail, he found the mass grave where some hundred villagers were buried, including his father. He wept over the spot for hours, not understanding why his father was killed.

As I heard the story through Hieu, I sensed inconsistencies, but not knowing the area, I listened without interjecting my questions.

A week later, he left home to work in Da Nang to raise money for his struggling mother and his siblings. He saved the family by bringing them to the city; he never returned to the village of Giang. I looked at Hieu and knew this would change as she barked some orders at Quan while he bowed, acknowledging his obedience to police authority. Hieu took charge, not sugarcoating her authority.

"He is very willing to accompany us to Giang to help us search for the hidden APCs, which the government wants returned," she said to me, a conspiracy in the making, not knowing how much English Quan understood and not exposing our real mission. "He will be brought to us in Hoi An tomorrow by agents from the Da Nang office."

ᕮᘏᕽ

After checking into the hotel, an upscale resort overlooking the South China Sea and its beautiful beaches, we met at the pool area to cool off and refresh ourselves before dinner. Hieu pleasantly shocked me when I arrived at the pool to see her in the striking beige bikini, she had bought in the resort's gift shop, enjoying the perks of the trip, waiting for me while I bought swim shorts in the same shop. She acted bemused when I showed up in multicolored, Hawaiian floral swim trunks, which reached below my knees. They were the only ones in the shop that fit me. She dove into the pool and started swimming laps.

"You look great," I said, talking to myself as she continued swimming. I sat down on the edge of the pool and watched her stroke through the water.

Completing her laps, Hieu swam over to me and pulled herself up to sit on the edge of the pool by me, dangling her feet in the water, mirroring the slow movement of my feet. "You are different from my perception of Americans."

I shrugged, not knowing how to answer. I studied her tight and firm body, well-toned, graceful, and solid, with no fat, proof of her dedication to regular workouts. In a tight situation with bad guys, she could no doubt handle herself very well.

She stood up looking at me. Her wet body glistened in the setting sun, the beige bikini almost blending with her skin, giving an illusion of nudity. "I am going to my room to change for dinner. At 1900 hours?"

"OK. I'm taking a few laps and then I'll change." I watched her walk away, following her sensuous sway, tantalizing in her bikini, feeling a twinge of guilt for watching. I quickly dove into the refreshing pool.

GIANG AREA, JANUARY 4, 2003

Last night at dinner, Hieu had again mesmerized me with her feminin-ity. Dressed in black tailored slacks, short heels, and a white blouse, with her hair brushed out, falling around her face and onto her shoulders, she appeared as mysterious as the Orient. Our meal wasn't totally unpleas-ant, despite Hieu's reserved manner. We simply talked shop, becoming more in tune, knowing that a strong partnership had to develop.

Hieu's intelligence and her status as a daughter of an NVA officer gave her opportunities that kids of South Vietnamese parentage could not get, at least not for three generations—the penalty for opposing the North Vietnamese. Recruited to join the National Police after gradu-ating from Hanoi University, she rose through the ranks in her twenty years with the organization. She held the title of senior field agent, and very few outranked her. Major Han, normally her supervisor, had been circumvented by Colonel Tin for this assignment. Shrewdly, Hieu kept Han in the loop, however.

"Have you ever killed anyone?" I asked, trying to understand her reservations toward me.

"Almost. I wounded a man we pursued to arrest."

I captured a momentary flutter of her eyes. She didn't show remorse, just a pained look that said it wasn't easy to kill someone.

Staying away from alcohol in order to be alert for a long day tomorrow, we ate a simple meal of grilled shrimp on mixed greens for me, a mixed-greens salad for her, bottled water for both, and no coffee or tea. Before we left for our rooms, she learned that I was a widower. She offered her condolences with a sincerity that moved me.

∞

After my morning shower, I had an hour before we met with Quan, who would be hand-delivered to us for our drive to My Son. I logged onto to the internet with my Palm phone and checked the message board. One message appeared for me: *Puking Buzzard—Glad you arrived safely. Any sign of your friends? Love, Rex I.*

I responded to his question with a negative.

By the code word *friends*, Woodruff meant Ramsey and Loan. Ramsey stayed hidden somewhere in Hong Kong, and Loan should be picked up today—I assumed. I packed my backpack, putting in the aluminum case with the satellite phone and Palm phone. The satellite phone would be my emergency link while in the bush, and every day I ensured that the power pack had been fully charged and that the phone functioned.

∞

I started to get into the Mercedes's passenger side just as Hieu returned from another car parked in the hotel's driveway, Quan in tow behind her. "Will you drive? I will talk with Quan while you do. Follow the lead vehicle—it will lead us to Giang."

I nodded and walked around to the driver's side. Once the three of us were in and seated, a black Mercedes sedan moved in front of our vehicle and I got the signal to follow. Outside the hotel's gate, five vehicles were parked in convoy formation: two Vietnamese Army utility vehicles, similar to jeeps, and three two-and-a-half ton US Army trucks, circa 1968.

Hieu saw my questioning look. "The army will be assisting in the search. We need the manpower."

"The more the better," I said, keeping my eyes on the road. We were moving fast, seven vehicles in a tight convoy, scattering other traffic to the side. In the meantime, Hieu leaned back over her front passenger seat, asking Quan questions, trying to obtain new information as he sat in the back seat.

I remembered some information that validated our trip. "You know, Hieu, the Viet Cong headquartered in the My Son area during the war, and we had set this region as a Free Fire Zone. This resulted in massive bombings by the US, destroying some of the ancient temples. When the bombing damaged the main sanctuary, former President Nixon, pressured by the international community, halted further destruction of My Son in order to preserve the remains of these national antiquity structures."

"I know. It is the reason that Ramsey chose the spot to hide his spoils of war. Once your president stopped further bombings, Ramsey would feel secure in hiding anything here."

I raised my eyes—that made great sense. The convoy sped along recklessly, forcing me to drive faster to stay with the lead sedan; all the while, the army vehicles in the rear pressed me to drive even faster. My odometer read sixty miles per hour.

⊘⊘

We had decided to focus mainly on the Giang village because of Quan's information. Once we arrived, Hieu took charge and divided the area into search sectors, with the center being Giang. On a map spread out on the hood of our Mercedes, she marked out a circle with a ten-kilometer radius from the center of Giang, then divided the circle into six roughly equal sectors, like slices of pie. Turning to the gathered

Da Nang police agents and army officers surrounding the map, she ordered them to divide personnel equally and to search over every square kilometer by foot.

Hieu said to me, "You and I are with Quan. We will focus on the southwest sector." This became our slice of the pie.

I strapped on my backpack containing the aluminum CIA case, energy bars, bottled water, a full combat medical pack similar to the ones used in my days in the war and, thanks to Hieu, fifty rounds for my .45, as well as five full thirty-round banana clips for the AK-47. The satellite phone and case, as per Woodruff's assistant, weighed twenty-six pounds; the rest of the gear and ammunition made my carrying weight over sixty pounds, reminiscent of the loads I carried on my back in the war.

I noticed stares from the four army lieutenants and their 109 men. I felt uneasy as they tried to understand why an American in jeans and tropical shirt, armed with one of their AK-47s, stood among them. Some of these young soldiers would have had relatives who had served and died with the NVA, fighting Americans and their allies, the South Vietnamese. I assumed they knew that I had been here as a soldier during the American Indochina War, involved in killing their people. If that was the case, I understood their feelings, but was also apprehensive about being the only round eye in the group.

Hieu intervened in front of me and jabbered to them, invoking the familiar name of Colonel Tin and probably embellishing my role. I sensed no real change in their looks, but they now plunged into the job at hand. Ignoring them, I retrieved Hieu's rucksack from our SUV and put it on her back, startling her.

"Thanks for the pep talk to the troops," I said, feeling better having her with me, even without her friendliness.

"You are welcome." Her tone seemed less severe. Then taking out a compass, she said, "We go this way." She carried her AK-47 with her left hand, her nine millimeter strapped in a shoulder holster over a green police uniform shirt bearing her rank and authority. She also wore jeans and hiking boots.

I followed her with a sad and silent Quan behind me; I plodded along with my AK-47 strapped over my right shoulder and my .45 strapped into the shoulder holster over my tropical utility shirt. The troops and police agents split into their assigned teams, hustling to obey Hieu's directives, observing the New York Yankees baseball caps identifying us as the organizers of this outing. I anticipated a difficult search in the days ahead; the jungle terrain would not be a willing participant.

❧

That evening at our hotel, Major Han delivered news by phone to Hieu that didn't surprise me: Loan had escaped agents converging on him at the hotel in Phnom Penh. Our contingency of focusing on Giang and My Son defaulted as the only plan.

GIANG SEARCH SECTORS,
JANUARY 5-12, 2003

Years ago, I did psychotherapy on two Charlotte police detectives who struggled with a brutal shooting of some bad guys. One partner had been wounded while the other killed one of the perpetrators. Emotional trauma existed for both of them: One felt guilty for being wounded and unable to assist his partner, while the other blamed himself for his partner being wounded, almost killed. I learned how close these two men had grown in ten years, almost like a married couple. They shared personal thoughts, experiences, pain, and joy—often not discussed with their own wives.

After a week of humping through the Vietnamese boonies without finding anything, I realized that Hieu and I had developed a similar relationship, even though our tenure together was much shorter than that of the two former police detectives. We acted with little verbal communication, knowing what the other would do. We started arguing by the eighth day, after a long, frustrating week of nothing but dirt, heat, sweat, bugs, snakes, jungle, and more jungle, and more bugs.

Hieu glared at me. "We should have gone more to the left on this old trail, not the right!"

"Hieu, listen—we walked the left fork of the trail yesterday. How hard is that to understand?" I said, getting pissed at her, not backing down. In return, she rolled her eyes and acted as if I belonged to a subhuman species.

She raised her hands in frustration and stomped off, going right, as I had suggested. I watched her storm ahead mumbling to herself. A frightened Quan stood next to me, worried about Hieu's wrath. He had tried to help daily, racking his brains for any facts he still held, hoping to lead us to our objective. He no doubt yearned to be in Da Nang permanently, rather than being forced back here every day, only returning to Da Nang at night.

"Look, Quan, her bark is worse than her bite," I said, showing my smile, thinking he didn't understand English. "Come, my friend, we better follow her or we both will get our heads knocked off." Confused, he looked at me, trying to understand as I put my hand on his back and positioned him in front of me on the trail to begin another hard day of exploration.

By the end of another twelve-hour day, we gathered at our checkpoint in the village, Hieu instructing everyone to be back tomorrow at the same time, 0800 hours. The police agents and soldiers were glad to get back to Da Nang for cold drinks and showers. They gave questioning looks to Hieu, wondering about her mental state. I was too tired to care at the moment. Once Quan was safely tucked in a sedan with police agents for the trip back to Da Nang, Hieu took the wheel of our SUV and tore out, scattering gravel behind her. We drove for a few minutes in silence; her anger showed.

"Hieu," I said, "we're missing something."

She turned toward me, neutral, her pride preventing her from admitting that she lost her temper earlier. "That is certain. But what is it?" she said, still curt.

I shook my head slowly. "I keep racking my brain. Have we reviewed everything?"

She kept driving, glaring at the road to Hoi An. Reed's journal notes bothered me. No matter how we studied his notes, no revelation popped up to help solve our puzzle. There were only similarities to Quan's information—confirming some details but not providing the ultimate answer.

"Any word on Colonel Loan?" I asked, instinctively holding the passenger door as she sped. Her anger worried me, as it had Quan.

"No," she said.

Well, that was that, and we drove to the hotel in silence.

ତ୍ୱର

Each night after a long day of hiking through the bush, we had brief meetings, alternating between her room and mine, to review, to analyze, to study, trying to mesh her Oriental thought process with my Western thinking. Hieu, like Colonel Tin and many Vietnamese, believed in the Yin and Yang of life religiously: death versus life, darkness versus light, negative versus positive, female versus male. To the Vietnamese, one needed both to stabilize life, to ensure tranquility and harmony, each part contributing to the whole. If one was missing, then there was no balance in life. She relied on this Yin and Yang philosophy in seeking to locate the gold and entrap Ramsey and Loan. I understood her beliefs and her philosophy, but I grew up a product of American culture, heavy on pragmatism. Colonel Tin had intentionally thrown us together, hoping that our two different worlds would decipher this quandary. However, as we scurried around My Son blindly, I felt less certain than ever that this quest would succeed.

Tonight, we were in her room. Now more comfortable with each other, she sat in her sleep shorts and top, trying to relax after a hot shower, her wet hair wrapped in a bath towel like a turban. Sitting on her bed, her back resting on the pillows piled against the headboard, her caramel-colored legs stretched in front of her, she jotted ideas down on a legal pad and occasionally threw questions at me.

I had showered in my room earlier and now sat stretched out in a lounge chair by her bed scanning my notes, dressed in my khaki cargo shorts, golf shirt, flip flops, and with wet hair.

Our earlier tiff had faded but her reserved attitude remained the same since we met at the Hanoi airport. However no matter how brusque she acted toward me, and no matter how unfriendly she seemed, I welcomed her presence. It prevented my complete loneliness in this country, and I grasped at it to make our partnership tolerable, despite being mired in a mission that seemed impossible.

I understood that our only chance to capture Loan, and eventually Ramsey, would be finding the buried treasure first. That seemed to be our only hope. I also understood that the clues from Reed must matter now, and that seemed to be the other reason I had been asked to Vietnam. Everyone assumed that Reed's cryptic notes could be deciphered using Colonel Hung's and Quan's input. In all of this, I became more important since Major Han's mission to capture Loan within days of his arrival in Cambodia had failed. Frustrated, Hieu and I noted that Loan had disappeared almost two weeks ago, and still no word on his whereabouts. I also suspected that the lackadaisical attitude of Tin and the others toward Ramsey was a mere ruse. Did they want Ramsey as much as they wanted Loan? It began to seem so.

"We need to look at Marble Mountain." Hieu's softened tone reached out to me like an olive branch offering.

I grasped her overture eagerly, hating the coldness between us. "Maybe, but it just doesn't make sense. The VC held that hill. Why would Ramsey want to do anything there?" Looking at my sheets, I checked off the words that made sense for what felt like the hundredth time. "On the first sheet—My Son/Cham, Giang, Gold, Phoenix, Village—100 KIA, Ramsey. These match Quan's input as well. And we are assuming the Americans are Ramsey and Reed."

I put another question mark by Montagnards. What bearing did that tribe have? While we searched, we found no local Montagnard tribe in the area. Besides, during the war, the Montagnards hated the VC and would not have been welcome in the My Son area, which the

VC dominated. And the Da Nang/Marble Mountain reference confused me. Da Nang made sense; Loan and Ramsey met Hung there to obtain the APCs and Rome plow. But why write Marble Mountain down?

The second sheet of Reed's notes listed: Grove of Banyan Trees, My Son again, and Village elders/Giang. These words and phrases generally agreed with what Quan had told us. The word Caves seemed the only missing link, and we had assumed days ago that the gold had been placed in old caves.

"We're missing something," I said, sounding like a broken record.

"But what?" A frustrated Hieu countered, staring at me. Then she got up and padded to the bathroom, shutting the door behind her. Soon I heard a slight groan and some of her cosmetics scattering on the floor.

I stood quickly, thinking she was sick, and approached the bathroom door just as she came out, anger on her face.

"Can I help?" I said, looking at her face.

"I need aspirin for my headache and—oh, this is so frustrating."

I shook my head. *We might as well be married*, I thought. I grinned at her, which set her off glaring, yet I thought I caught a small tear on her face. She turned away, embarrassed, irritated, and almost defeated. Her barrier toward me still remained intact, however.

"OK, look, I'll go to the gift shop and buy you some stuff. Just write down the Vietnamese name for what you want so I get it right."

⚬✕⚬

Sheepishly I paid for the Bayer Aspirin, the label on the bottle in clear English. I didn't need any note. The jolly young man behind the counter talked like we were old friends for a few minutes. He eyed the package, matching what Hieu had written in Vietnamese before putting my purchase in a plastic bag printed with the hotel emblem.

"Aw, for you or your wife?" he said, curiosity on his boyish face. No doubt there were rumors as to why an older American stayed with a younger and beautiful Vietnamese woman, here at this nice resort.

"Yeah, for the wife." I frowned as I walked out of the hotel gift shop. Jim Schaeffer would love this. Maybe now there would be less gossip about us at the hotel.

Hieu opened the door, a slight grimace showed. "I am sorry that you had to do this."

"It's OK." I handed her the plastic bag.

She pulled the bottle out and unscrewed the cap, taking three aspirin with a glass of water from the nightstand. "Thank you. You are kind." She tried a weak smile. The first one I had seen since the dinner at her apartment with her family.

Looking down at her five-foot-five body, I said, "Let's get some rest. We have another long day tomorrow, and we are thinking too hard about this. Maybe some sleep will help."

She nodded. I don't know why, but I wanted to give her a hug. But I wouldn't.

When I got to my room, shutting the connecting door behind me, I stripped off my cargo shorts and fell into bed, still wearing my shirt and undershorts. I had hoped to read my notes one more time, but I fell asleep in minutes.

HOI AN, JANUARY 13, 2003

I banged on Hieu's connecting door, calling her. My watch showed five in the morning. My excitement drove me, and I stood, disheveled in my wrinkled golf shirt and cargo shorts, impatiently waiting for Hieu to unlock the door. The door opened, slightly ajar, her nine millimeter visible through the opening.

Hieu finally recognized me and let the door swing open. "What is . . . ?" Her eyes were puffy from sleeping, hair strewn over her face, right hand hanging to her side, the nine-mil pointed down. Refocusing her eyes on me, she waited for an explanation, sleep shorts and top hanging on her loosely, revealing the tops of her attractive breasts.

"I've got it!" I said. I walked into her room, pacing back and forth in front of her. "The Yin and Yang is the key, Hieu. Your philosophy held the key to the mystery." I hugged her and then pulled her sleepy body to the lounge chair and sat her down, delicately, a toy Panda doll. She sat, staring, trying to comprehend. I knew I should not have hugged her by the look she gave me, but I felt too elated to care.

"OK, just listen. The key is Da Nang and Marble Mountain, like you thought. The Yin and Yang of the war: Da Nang is held by the Americans and its South Vietnamese allies; Marble Mountain is held

215

by the VC. The Yin and Yang of opposing forces: one is good, and one is bad, depending on whose side you are on."

Hieu looked at me, slowly waking up but still eyeing me with bewilderment, as if a deranged stranger stood in her hotel room. Her mind deliberated though, as her intelligent looking black eyes absorbed my actions.

"I looked on the map and think I have the answers. Marble Mountain, say it is the Yin, is twelve kilometers west of Da Nang, the Yang, basically in a straight line. I looked at My Son on the map and plotted twelve kilometers in a straight line to the east, and it intersects a fork of two roads. The map legend shows they are basically minor roads. The key is using My Son, not Giang village, as the center of the search circle, and using twelve kilometers as a radius, not ten."

Hieu's eyes lit up. "Are you certain?"

"Not certain, Hieu, but I feel this makes more sense. We've been searching from Giang in a ten-kilometer radius and, as a result, barely touching My Son and forgetting about it since it's a bombed-out sanctuary."

"John, why not go west twelve kilometers from My Son?"

I paused. For the first time, she had used my first name. Collecting my thoughts again, I said, "I looked at that as well, but our ten-kilometer radius searches from Giang would have intersected the end of such a straight line. Thus, the only area still unsearched by us is the twelve kilometers east of My Son."

"But that would place the gold closer to Hoi An or Da Nang."

"Exactly, and I think when Ramsey buried the gold in early January 1973, he planned to move it by sea out of Hoi An harbor within a year, using his authority to access a freighter. Remember, however, the US had signed a peace agreement with the North Vietnamese on January 27, 1973, and the last US troops left in March 1973. Ramsey was stuck and couldn't risk retrieving the gold while troop withdrawals were happening. Then in October, your Central Committee decided to ignore the Peace Accord of Paris and continue military operations.

"This would have endangered Ramsey trying to come up to Da Nang and then My Son while the VC and NVA were consolidating the region. He had to wait, hoping he could sneak in later, assuming that the South Vietnamese military would stop the NVA and push them back across the DMZ. That never happened, and in April 1975, the US Embassy evacuated as your Northern brethren were on the outskirts of Saigon. Ramsey had no choice but to evacuate as well."

Hieu nodded again, fully awake now, almost convinced of my theory, but there existed a questioning look. "Why did Quan keep saying southwest of his village, Giang? And," her police mind kicking in, "was your patient, Reed, more knowledgeable than you assumed?"

"First, Quan—he was only twelve years old then, and he may have become confused about the actual direction he followed. Another idea is that he may be trying to keep the hidden items for himself— he either knows of the gold or thinks that the missing APCs are worth something."

Hieu seemed to agree. "What about Reed?"

"That's my fault. I misread the whole session with Reed. He was more depressed than I thought, and I focused on healing him without understanding his past events. And besides he wouldn't tell the complete truth. He obviously knew where the gold had been hidden. He served with Ramsey, so he must have called Ramsey after he saw him in December. His nightmare of the killings had been triggered by seeing and talking to Ramsey again. This had to overwhelm Reed, and he finally committed suicide. I think the hidden gold became secondary for him at this point."

"OK, I believe this. But Ramsey cannot take the gold out of Hoi An or Da Nang now. There is too much exposure at the harbors."

"Exactly." I pulled out an old Vietnam War map that Hieu had gotten for me. "We talked about this before. See where the old Ho Chi Minh trail starts in former North Vietnam, moves into Laos with arms branching into South Vietnam as well as Cambodia? Near the old DMZ and Khe Sanh and then west of Da Nang, there are multi-trails crossing from Laos. There is a main branch of the Ho Chi Minh trail that crosses the border from Laos toward Da Nang, merging into the minor roads that start at the Laotian border." We both looked at the map as my finger traced the route from the fork in the minor road east of My Son back to Laos in a westerly trace.

"This confirms the ideas that we proposed earlier with input from Hung—he's coming overland from Laos!" Hieu said. She stood and retrieved her jeans draped over the desk chair and struggled to pull them on over her sleep shorts.

"Hieu, slow down! Let's freshen up, have breakfast, and get to Giang as scheduled. Then when the troops are searching, you and I will go to My Son and drive overland on a straight easterly course for twelve kilometers. I think we'll find it."

She paused. "But we must hurry before Ramsey arrives!"

"Look, he can't move in daylight because if he is coming by land, he is bringing heavy vehicles and would be spotted or stopped by police. He has to cross the Laos border away from official border crossings. I also calculated that he will need heavy-duty four-wheel drive vehicles, like the Hummer H1 Alpha, as well as trailers to carry all twenty-five thousand pounds of gold."

"I do not understand."

"Each Hummer H1 Alpha has a payload carrying capacity of 3,087 pounds. Four Hummers, therefore, would allow twelve thousand pounds, or half of the gold supposedly hidden. By using four trailers, Ramsey can move the rest of the gold, giving a safety level in case a Hummer breaks down."

My assumptions made sense, but were they accurate? Had I assumed too much of what Ramsey and Loan would do?

"After retrieving the gold, they drive on the minor roads going west, avoiding Dai Lanh and Giang. They will drive through Cha Vanh and then into Laos, connecting to the old Ho Chi Minh trail, and then go further south to Attapu, located on the national road, a good, solid highway. Ramsey enters the national road there and drives west to Pakxe and the airport. A large transport aircraft takes them out of country," Hieu said. Then taking a deep breath, she raised her head from looking at the map; her uplifted eyes sought agreement.

I stared at her, amazed at her quick mind, and said, "Yes! We played with that scenario after our interrogation of Hung, which he indicated as the best plan. Also, remember, the CIA assumed Ramsey would arrive in Vietnam about January 27 to coincide with Tet."

MY SON, JANUARY 13, 2003

By ten o'clock, Hieu and I arrived at My Son in the Mercedes SUV, backtracking on the road from Giang. The soldiers and police continued to search the other sectors around Giang. On the drive to My Son, Hieu sat in the back, grilling Quan. She sent chills up my back as she interrogated with a staccato of Vietnamese, pinging Quan with a steady beat, penetrating him, wearing him down, hoping to extract the truth. Hieu finally briefed me from the back seat, with Quan sitting in abject terror, compressed in the corner to her left. Quan admitted to seeing a young American soldier with another American, but that was all he knew. His misdirection of having us focus to the southwest of Giang instead of My Son was, he argued, a mistake on his part. Hieu seemed uncertain about his explanation. We agreed to let him rest and to question him again later.

Hieu pulled rank on the My Son sanctuary gate guard and admission agent, allowing us to position our SUV as close as possible to the center of the My Son temple ruins. I pointed the vehicle due east. Hieu now sat up front using her hand-held compass. I set the trip odometer to zero, nodded to Hieu, and started driving. The key would be to maintain a straight line, and I worried that we would have to go around ruins, throwing off our direction and odometer readings. To my surprise, the due east direction headed straight and true between ruins instead of through them, which would be knowledge that Ramsey could have used when he sought a place to bury the gold. I began to feel confident that we had solved the mystery.

Hieu kept staring ahead, tense and excited, her vibes also confident that we were on the right path. She kept pointing out old vehicular trail ruts in the hard ground in front of us, obvious that years ago, even over thirty years ago, someone had steered a dozer this way, cutting a straight swath and allowing other vehicles, such as APCs, to follow. A Rome plow, with its heavy, massive, sharp blade, would have been the ideal choice. Fortunately for us, we were in the upper portion of the Central Highlands, which was more arid than the Delta around Saigon; thus, wild vegetation grew slower, helping us find an old trail possibly made by Ramsey and his conscripted crew.

Five kilometers from the center of My Son, we left the ruins, approaching foliage and trees. Our forward movement stopped, blocked by a huge pile of dirt overgrown with bushes and elephant grass. Hieu stayed with the SUV while I climbed the ten-foot-high mound. On top, I looked due east, facing the jungle. An overgrown road or trail was in front of me in the same direction. The thrill of discovering the path that might lead to the gold, and eventually Ramsey and Loan, fed me energy. Maybe the many gods of Vietnam had rewarded our tenacity. I watched Quan while Hieu confirmed what I had seen standing on the top of the mass of overgrown dirt. When she climbed down, she asked Quan if this was familiar. It certainly matched his original story about coming to the end of vehicle tracks, finding his way blocked by a large pile of dirt and debris. His concurrence seemed genuine, as did his sigh of relief.

After reconnoitering and finding the jungle on either side of the ten-foot high, twenty-foot wide dirt mound too impenetrable for the vehicle, I decided to drive the SUV up and over the dirt obstacle. I hoped to thrust the front end high enough in the air to cause the SUV's center of gravity to shift, plunging it over the mound without its undercarriage hanging up. Hieu agreed. The three of us buckled up as I backed up about one hundred feet, stopped, and then thrust into drive. I stomped on the gas pedal. The automatic transmission shifted smoothly as the SUV accelerated on the rutted trail, tires digging into the ground, gaining speed. Hieu showed little concern as trees, brush, and bushes flashed by, front tires hitting the slope, gaining traction, pulling the vehicle forward, rear tires pushing the front end up, pointing it to the sky, rising higher. I saw only blue horizon, front tires now spinning with high RPM torque, singing, clawing the air. The front end finally tipped horizontally, slowly dipping back to Earth. Suddenly gaining momentum, the SUV crashed nose first, front bumper skimming the ground, shock absorbers oscillating, stabilizing the front end. The front tires tore into earth, propelling us forward, as we drove away from the mound.

As soon as we cleared the little hill, we stopped to check the Mercedes; there seemed to be no apparent damage. Continuing, we maintained a straight course due east, crunching through bushes and small bamboo tree clusters. We ignored the constant scraping on the sides of the vehicle. Seven kilometers from My Son, we drove on, heavily concealed by the jungle canopy, its foliage surrounding us while we pushed forward on the old track ruts, overgrown with elephant grass, bushes, and occasional small saplings that easily bent under the Mercedes.

The going slowed, but by 1300 hours we had reached twelve kilometers, per the odometer. We stopped the vehicle and stared at a rocky hill structure that spread several hundred feet to our left and right; it rose over fifty feet at the highest point, overgrown with banyan trees! Hieu pulled Quan out and grabbed our AK-47s from the rear. She gave me mine as I waited in front of the scraped and dirty SUV, peering at the huge hill.

"Hieu, let's see if our theory is correct. If we go to the left, we should see a minor dirt road in the distance running east and west, intersecting another dirt road going south behind this hill."

We humped through the dense brush and trees, skirting the base of the hill, looking for openings to caves or underground bunkers. Thirty minutes later, wet with perspiration from breaking a trail, I finally came around the left end of the hill and saw the minor road in the distance, over one hundred yards away, with no traffic. The other road forked off to the right, heading south toward us but eventually bending behind our large hill. We continued walking around the prominence, which revealed that it stood bigger than initially thought. Five hundred feet long and six hundred feet wide, it dwarfed us as we looked toward its peak for signs of a cave or diggings. The tall banyan trees added more height and density to the hill, reaching to the sky and offering us some shade from the sweltering sun. By 1600 hours, we had explored the entire perimeter of the hill and stood in front of our SUV, staring at the probable spot where a buried cave might exist.

An exhausted Quan acted confused. During our forced march around the hill, I eyed him regularly, feeling that he knew more about our discovery than he had revealed. Hieu must have felt the same and kept checking on Quan as he stood silently drinking from his bottle of water.

Even though we had snacked on power bars before we trooped around the base of the large hill, our energy levels had sunk lower; we drank more water to begin rehydrating as we stood in the forest canopy's shade. Personally, I had delayed too long on drinking water and started to see little stars flashing in my eyes.

"Hieu, I think we can drive around the hill to the left and cut across the fields to the dirt road. I'd rather do that than go back along the old trail when we leave. The way we came is too slow."

She agreed, standing there in her sweat-stained blue police tunic drinking water. I admired her endurance, never stopping until I stopped. Still, the heat and the physical exertion had taken a toll on her today; she looked haggard.

I walked over and gave her one of my malaria pills, a routine to which she acquiesced when we arrived in Da Nang. Living in Hanoi, the chance of catching the disease was slim, but now that we were in the brush and jungle, I worried about her since she had no pills; it was a precaution she never even considered, being native to the country. The countryside produced infinite mosquito-breeding areas, a fact that had not changed since my days here during the war. I had taken the daily malaria pill religiously for my entire tour and still had minor chills and fevers during the first year of my return to the States, although the symptoms also stemmed from the parasites and amoebas that had infiltrated my blood. This had such serious implications that the military instructed returnees to avoid donating blood for three years.

I knew Hieu would be as vulnerable to jungle diseases as any nonnative. During the war, the NVA and VC suffered from malaria and other diseases, just as Americans did. Plodding through the forests and jungles of Vietnam spelled danger.

As she swallowed her pill, I hoped that I had not started her too late. The prescription drug required starting the daily doses two days prior to arrival in the infested area, a luxury we had not had. I counted on her slight native immunity to help initially.

"If Ramsey and Loan come from Laos along the dirt road that we observed to the left of this hill at night, he can hide his vehicles in this same spot." I pointed to our parked Mercedes and the trail behind it, which we had driven earlier.

"Yes—if this is the place." Hieu stared at me. Her sweaty, dirt-covered face peered at me from under the New York Yankees cap.

I turned around and looked at the hill rising in front of us. "Ramsey used a Rome plow to cut through this jungle area, probably followed by the two armored personnel carriers loaded with gold. Is this then the hiding place, and if so, how do we get into it?"

I walked to where the trail stopped by the mound; huge piles of dirt and debris were piled against it, covered with different vegetation and blending with the hill. There were symmetrical rock edges protruding around the placed dirt, forming what looked to be the entrance to a cave.

"This could be the entry point to a cave. I suggest we get a crew here tomorrow and start digging at this spot," I said.

Hieu now stood by me, looking with full attention to where I pointed. I heard a rustle behind me and turned. We had forgotten about

Quan. I thought I saw movement on the trail behind the SUV and I began to chase him, signaling for Hieu to get in the vehicle and follow. She scurried to the SUV as I sprinted, my exhausted body groaning as I ran down the trail. Why the hell did he run?

Even though tired, I surprised myself with my fast pace and sighted Quan some fifty feet ahead of me, struggling to outdistance me. I had sprinted over a hundred feet at a steady pace but now felt my energy waning as I gained on him. Although in good physical shape, I strained for oxygen in the thick humid air that pressed against me. The tightness of my shoulder holster with the pistol and my AK-47 and my backpack, all unnecessary weight for my dash, constricted my chest and breathing. Quan continued to run, but he too suffered from this heat and the oppressive air. We had gone another twenty feet and I had started to grab at him when he stumbled on a long vine crossing the trail and fell, sprawling to the ground, sliding on his face and hands for several feet. I slid to a stop and yanked Quan up with my left hand, holding him by his dirty, sweat-stained shirt collar. He exploded into tears, chanting in Vietnamese, covering his face with his hands.

Hieu had rapidly backed the SUV and came screeching to a halt a few feet behind me. She rushed out of the vehicle, engine running in park, and grabbed Quan, slapping him and yelling at him in Vietnamese. I released him to Hieu; dizzy, I walked to our vehicle, took my rucksack off, and shoved it in the vehicle's rear with the AK-47. I then got in the driver's side and turned the air conditioning to high, trying to cool my body temperature to normal, worrying about heatstroke.

Hieu dragged Quan to the Mercedes, shoved him onto the back seat, and handcuffed him. She slid in next to him and continued yelling at him in Vietnamese, brutally, while he winced at her harsh words, crying and falling apart. Suddenly, she switched to a softer tone, and I heard her concerned voice reach out to Quan; the efficient Hieu had matters in hand, using her own psychological techniques. Finally, the talking stopped. My head thumped with a headache behind my closed eyes, accompanied by more small starbursts. I drank from my water bottle. Nauseous and shivering, my body's temperature slowly dropped, and I faded in unconsciousness.

⚬⚭⚬

"John!" Hieu held a wet cloth on my forehead. I heard Quan snoring in the back. I turned my head to check on him; he lay curled in a fetal position, asleep, soaked in sweat and covered in dirt with bloody scabs on his face from his fall.

I returned to Hieu, sitting in the front seat leaning over me. "John, are you OK?"

I stared at her in a daze, trying to focus on her.

"Yeah . . . I think I feel better now." I looked at her concerned eyes and her attractive face. My mind wandered. "I'm some partner! Christ!" I said as I sat up from my collapsed position.

Ignoring my mumbling, Hieu held a bottle of water to my lips and forced me to slowly drink. She loosened my shoulder holster.

"Why did Quan run?" I said, the fog in my mind clearing.

"He panicked because he had lied to us about where his dad and other villagers were killed. They are buried in that hill. He knows nothing of the gold. Instead of fleeing the village with his mother and siblings that first night, he sought out his father. He followed the tracks as he said, but to here, where he came upon the villagers filling most of the entrance to a cave, just where you suggested we dig tomorrow. The dozer piled more dirt near the cave's entrance while Quan hid in the bushes and trees.

"The APCs were parked, their engines running, while the drivers awaited instructions from three men: two Americans and an ARVN colonel. As his father and the other villagers finished shoveling dirt on something in the cave, the Americans and the ARVN colonel stepped behind them in the gathering dusk and shot them using AK-47s. Quan said he was so scared that he could not cry out. He watched as the bulldozer pushed the bodies of the hundred Vietnamese villagers into the cave entrance, the blade spreading dirt over the dead. Quan remembered coming here often with his father on hikes, as this used to be a Montagnard village, deserted long before the war started with the Americans. They had found this large cave used by the Montagnards to store foods and other items." Hieu refreshed the wet rag on my forehead.

"Thanks," I said. "That explains Reed's notes referring to the Montagnards."

She nodded and said, "Yes."

Reaching over to me again, she felt my face. "Your skin feels cooler now." Hieu further explained that she radioed Captain Tho, the commander of the army unit we had been using in the search. He would arrive with equipment to excavate the site tomorrow.

The psychologist in me tried to explain. "He probably experienced a mental shock when he saw his dad die. At age twelve, that is a huge traumatic event. I believe he struggled to give us the correct information, but his mind blocked certain facts and then he compensated for the repression with inconsistent facts. I believe him. I think he is trying to remember it all. I hope he is not in trouble."

"No. I too understand his pain. Many of my relatives died in the war at the hands of the ARVNs and their secret police. He should not be punished for losing his father as well."

I looked at my watch; it was five. "We should go back before it gets dark. What about security for this place?"

Hieu thought a moment. "I am afraid of scaring Ramsey if he arrives early. Captain Tho will place a hidden observation post near the fork in the dirt road to observe this hill tonight. His position will have good line of sight to this location."

"Good, and Quan?" Feeling better, I sat up and put my seat belt on. I eased the Mercedes into drive, drove to the hill again, and turned to the left through small undergrowth, which yielded to the sure-footed SUV.

"We will place him under protective custody until this is over. The Da Nang agents are waiting for us at the hotel to take him. There is no further need for him. He has suffered enough remembering where his father is buried and how he was killed."

The normally cold Hieu showed some empathy which surprised me. Then again, my slight heatstroke may have shaken her; she probably worried that Colonel Tin would have her ass if I died. That made more sense to me. As I looked out the driver's side window, my grin at that thought reflected back to me.

Now that we had exploited Quan for information, I hoped he would recover from the trauma. Quan had paid a huge price in the war: the hardship and pain of saving his mother and siblings; the sacrifice of not pursuing his own desires for a normal life; and the huge pain of seeing his father killed by corrupt and greedy Americans and South Vietnamese, buried like trash.

After I crossed the bushy field from the hill, I drove to Hoi An on the minor road. Hieu had closed her eyes, taking a nap. We had both pushed our physical limits. Maybe this would end soon.

HOI AN, JANUARY 13, 2003

As evening arrived, I had completed four lazy laps in the cool and soothing pool. The hotel grounds resembled a tropical island engulfed with palm trees and beautiful flowering bushes. I reached the edge of the pool on my last lap and spotted Hieu leaving her bungalow. Clad in her beige bikini with the setting sun behind her, she eclipsed the sun like a goddess, slowly, enticingly walking toward me. Like a loyal subject of a queen, I made room for her as she gracefully eased down onto the pool's rim.

"Hello," she said.

"I have to say, you look stunning in that bikini." I diverted my eyes from her and looked toward the beach and the ocean waves rolling in.

She noticed my withdrawal and tapped me on my shoulder. I returned my gaze to her. "Thank you," she said.

I nodded as I pulled myself up to sit by her, letting my feet dangle in the water. Our relationship had moments of tension. Since I was American, she would have despised me during the war, and even now, because that war cost her and her country so much in terms of lives and quality of life. Just the Agent Orange defoliation of the land caused birth defects, cancers, and neurological problems for generations of Vietnamese, as the toxic chemicals seeped into the soil, the water table, and the crops. The US had sprayed twenty million gallons of the deadly herbicide, and this on top of the massive bombing of the country that exceeded all the bombs the US dropped in World War II, destroying more lives and cities and contaminating the environment. Over two million Vietnamese civilians were killed, with some 1.2 million NVA and VC soldiers killed.

Americans had forsaken the high road with our war actions, all for the sake of accomplishing an undefined mission. It seemed that the end justified any means.

Needing to redirect my thoughts, I looked at Hieu and said, "You have mosquito bites on your neck and shoulder. You need to watch that. Tomorrow before we leave for the field, you should spray with insect repellant."

She continued to look at the water, reflections glimmering across her face and sunglasses. "OK, I will spray tomorrow. You have become a worrywart. Is that correct English?"

"Yes," I said. I closed my eyes and leaned on my elbows, relaxing, recharging my body and mentally preparing for the next hot and humid excursion tomorrow.

Being near her at the pool and working together every day, I felt a closeness that I cherished now. Certainly, her attractiveness had something to do with it. But there was more: We had started to form the beginnings of a bond. I respected her marriage and her family, and I couldn't think of her as anything other than an ally on a complicated mission. Glancing at her brown body accented by her bikini, I knew we needed to stay professionals.

Changing the subject, I asked about her life as a child, guessing that she was born before the war ended when North Vietnam captured Saigon in 1975.

"As a baby, my mother cared and worried about me due to food shortages. We all suffered for lack of adequate food. People were starving after the war ended because of the destruction everywhere, and also because the Central Committee in Hanoi made serious mistakes in planning crops and other agricultural reforms. The inefficient bureau-cracy hampered the recovery until after 1986.

"I remember as a little girl, my family raised a pig in the bath-room of our Hanoi flat to ensure food for five families. It was very hard on everyone. My father served in the NVA because he believed in Ho Chi Minh and the national movement to get rid of the foreigners and unite the country into one Vietnam. Yet his family received no special allocation of food. Everyone suffered. You Americans were seen by the North Vietnamese as invaders, conquerors of Vietnam, and were thus despised and hated. The war divided our country, our people, and we are only now starting to become a progressive nation with a future. It is sad that so many Vietnamese died and so many families suffered." She looked off into the distance. I listened as she released her feelings.

"You may ask how divided the people became. The other day, you and I talked with the hotel's concierge, and he said that his uncle died fighting as a Viet Cong. His father was an ARVN officer who recently died after spending years in the reeducation camps my government ran to purge the corruptness of the South Vietnamese."

I sat up and leaned toward the pool. "War is horrible and humans never learn that. Ideology, politics, power, and religion seem to divide people everywhere. And we kill so easily."

"Yes. Also, I do not agree completely with the camps. But when we see such corruption by Colonel Loan and Hung, it is hard to not support the programs." She looked at me, almost melancholy, and continued. "Please do not think badly of me or my people."

"No, Hieu! I won't." It startled me that she even cared what this American thought.

"I worried when I was assigned to work with you. That you would be like the 'Ugly American' I read so much about. Now I think you would make a good Vietnamese." She gave slight chuckle.

I turned to look at her. She stared back, hiding behind her sunglasses. Metaphysically, we were both part of mankind and each other, just as the sun, now setting in the west, was part of the universe.

Ideally, we should all be good to each other. Realistically, the biases of man continue to counter this. The Vietnam War grew because of American political leaders' unwillingness to listen or understand that nationalism had evolved in Southeast Asia.

We sat in silence for a long time as the warm evening turned into a pleasant night. The Asian sky was full of sparkling stars, awing me with the magnitude of the universe. Spiritually, we were two people from different cultures, but we were still people, the same species, with the same desires and the same hopes for normalcy. It was a magical moment for me. All these long years after the war, I finally discovered some clarity of life. I could not describe it in words—I just felt it emotionally, a bonding of my soul with nature. I now understood the cycles of life that took my Katy physically, but she still existed in the stars, in the air, in the breeze, and in me. I didn't know if Hieu sensed my enlightenment about my wife as she sat by me. However, despite the differences in our skin color and language, I felt closer to her because of the beautiful night sky. When I turned to look at her again, she was looking at me, her sunglasses off, the stars reflecting in her dark black eyes. I smiled, silently thanking her for being there. She gave a small smile back.

MY SON, JANUARY 14, 2003

The pounding on the door that connected my room to Hieu's thrust me from my bed. Staggering to the door with my pistol, slightly woozy, I looked at the alarm clock on the nightstand: 5:12 a.m. Hieu yelled, "John, get up!"

Slowly, I opened the door, holding my .45.

"I have French baguettes and strong Vietnamese coffee," she said, sliding by me as I stood in my sleep pants and T-shirt. On the desk, she arranged a basket of crusty mini-baguettes and two Styrofoam cups of hot coffee. The wonderful aroma of coffee and fresh-baked rolls woke my stomach before my tired mind caught up.

"Why are you here? I thought we were going to meet at eight this morning?" I said as I tasted the good strong coffee and felt the caffeine start to kick in. Then I reached for a baguette, buttered it, and crunched into it, savoring the rich flavor. Not waiting for her answer, I said, "The best part of the French influence on Vietnam is this—the great bread."

Hieu nodded. "I just finished my phone call with Major Han, and he is pleased. He wished to thank you for your help! Colonel Tin also has been briefed. He still expects you at his house for Tet celebrations, but I think you should come to our home. You already know my children and husband." Less reserved today, she still orchestrated my life while enjoying coffee with me.

Thanks to the hotel laundry service, we had clean clothes available daily. Today Hieu wore khaki pants with her standard police tunic with her sewn-on badge. Her rank as a senior agent established her authority among the troops. As always, she wore her shoulder holster. She crossed her legs, showing that her soft-sided hiking boots had been cleaned. "Are you awake now?"

"Yes. First, I need a shower. What are the plans for the day? Obviously, something has changed."

"I will explain as soon as you shower and dress, and while we drive to the hill area to wait for the heavy equipment from the army. Also, there is a team of scientists coming to examine and remove the bones of the dead Vietnamese once we uncover them. It will be sad to find the dead villagers, yet the removal and proper burial of the dead is important for my people and their living relatives."

ФЮ

As I drove, Hieu talked constantly, alternating between her cell phone, the FM radio, and me. Her energy flowed through the vehicle, and I understood why. Her big moment as a professional policewoman had evolved, a chance to show her competency. She deserved any accolades for the mission.

Finally, she revealed what had gotten us going earlier than planned this morning: a phone call from Captain Tho. In the early hours, his men had observed some lights and movement in the forest area several kilometers from the hill. Although this activity could be unrelated to Ramsey or Loan, the young captain, caught up in the moment, dispatched a platoon of elite airborne troops to beef up the operation as a precaution. As a result, Hieu and I were requested to be there sooner rather than later.

ᘒᘓ

At seven, the captain briefed Hieu at the concealed observation post. I stood stoically, trying to grasp the gist of the conversation, waiting for her to explain afterwards. I estimated a platoon of thirty young soldiers, disciplined and heavily armed, had been deployed to conduct patrols around the area. So far nothing had been discovered. I watched the five-man patrols come in, brief the captain, and then rotate with another patrol while they rested. Their seriousness permeated the briefing area. Radio silence had been initiated as well.

As I looked at them with begrudging respect, I remembered how their fathers, their grandfathers, their uncles, had all stalked American units, ambushing at the first opportunity, inflicting casualties and then disappearing into the jungles or their tunnels as the smells and sounds of high explosives dispelled. NVA soldiers were dedicated professionals, hardened by many years of war. As their current descendants walked by me with camouflage-painted faces, armed with AK-47s, eager, devoted, serious, and ready for combat and killing, I perceived the tradition these young men bore from those former warriors. A few of them glanced at me, curious why I worked with them in their country and at their command post. No smiles came my way.

Hieu walked over to me. "Captain Moore—I hope you are alright with your former rank in my addressing you—there is no sign of anyone in the jungle. But I thanked Captain Tho for his prompt action, and he will continue to cover the area while concealing his men and this command post."

"I assume you are using my former rank to impress Captain Tho?" I said, catching Captain Tho looking my way. He was not the normal five-four height, but rather close to five-seven or five-eight. His upper body bulged with muscles, and his head almost seemed to merge into his torso due to his short muscular neck. He looked sharp in his crisp green fatigues, showing a command bearing. His dark hair in a military buzz cut conformed to army regulations and also made his face look thin and firm. His dark eyes showed intelligence as they probed me, trying to understand me.

Being in his thirties, Tho projected youthful arrogance and a sense of immortality. I had seen that confidence before in NVA officers leading their men to their death against the US Army's massive firepower—yet they followed, dying with their leaders. Tho had that look; he could lead men anywhere. I broke my gaze as the brief spasm of nostalgia swept through me.

Hieu nodded at me. "I used your former rank for status with Tho and his soldiers. They respect fellow military men." Then Hieu explained the preparations. The plan was simple. The airborne platoon would stay hidden, monitoring the hill around the clock with five-man patrols. When the bulldozer, the regular infantry platoon, and the anthropologists arrived at the prominent hill, we would meet them, start the excavation of the bodies first, and then hopefully find the gold.

ᘓᘔ

The work grew tedious, dirty, and hot. The high humidity prevented anyone from cooling off. By four in the afternoon, we had uncovered twenty-one bodies, represented by broken skeletons with rotted clothing still attached. The remnants of ARVN uniforms were attached to at least two bodies, validating that Ramsey and his team had also killed soldiers to cover up the operation. The anthropologists regulated the retrieval of the skeletons and loose bones, slowing the recovery process, ensuring complete skeletons were assembled, allowing for proper identification later. Watching the uncovering of so many dead Vietnamese saddened me.

It also impacted many of the soldiers who, armed with shovels, worked with little rest, disheartened by the bone piles forming around the base of the hill. The soldiers saw the remains as sympathetic peasants who were brutally murdered by Americans and South Vietnamese. I worried that my presence betrayed their dead, causing the troops to focus their hatred on me, forgetting that I had come here to help the Vietnamese government, forgetting that I personally had nothing to do with this massacre. They didn't see my own anger over this senseless killing. Their hatred extended to the two ARVN remains, as they piled those skeletons away from those of the villagers.

Hieu and I helped with the digging, working together as a team. I quickly noticed that many of the bones of each skeleton had multiple bullet holes or craters formed by the slugs ricocheting. The hapless villagers had been shot with AK-47s set on fully automatic, rounds ripping into them. The killers wanted to ensure the deaths of the peasants, and I counted at least twenty or more bullet abrasions on some completed skeletons. It was difficult for me to believe that someone shot and killed these unarmed civilians. It repulsed me, and I could not justify such brutality, not even in war. The two still alive who were responsible for this act deserved punishment. I knew now that I would do whatever it took to bring Ramsey and Loan to justice. Hung, it became more evident, had not been involved.

During a break, Hieu reclined with me against the side of our Mercedes, having noticed my foul mood. It was comforting to have her near me. She represented some sanity for me here in this jungle.

"Just can't believe anyone could do this. Especially Tom Reed— I'm shocked to find that he was a part of this!"

Hieu said nothing and stared at the working troops. I looked down at her. She truly seemed a unique creature, mysterious as the Orient but astute to deal with the modern world. She embodied the Yin and Yang philosophy.

Hieu had ordered floodlights so work could continue into the night. We decided to spend the night at the site, and I drove back to the Hoi An hotel to pack a set of clothes for each of us while she remained, supervising.

◎X◎

After I packed a clean set of my jeans, a shirt, and underwear with some toiletries, I headed over to Hieu's room with her written list. I found the clothes and toiletries she had requested, slightly embarrassed, wondering why she felt comfortable with me getting her items. I packed her items on top of my stuff in a duffle bag that Tho provided then headed to the Mercedes.

When I returned to the site, another ten complete skeletons had been recovered, bringing the total to thirty-one. If the original story remained accurate, there were about seventy more to go. Dusk had settled when Hieu dragged me back to the dig to take our turn again. Although tired, I worked hard alongside her, despite the dirt and the bugs, ever increasing in the beams of the floodlights. Hieu stopped long enough for me to spray both of us with insect repellant. It helped greatly, but I still hated the smell of Deet. It reminded me of the war here, of spraying the stuff before digging in for the night, waiting and watching for the enemy, expecting to kill or be killed.

By midnight, fifty skeletons had been retrieved. Hieu and I, along with a few soldiers, examined the tunnel still blocked with compacted dirt. We decided to call it quits for the night, allowing the military to continue digging. The captain had organized the straight leg platoon into shifts for digging, for guard duty, and for sleep. He kept the airborne platoon back at the concealed observation and command post as his reserve troops. I needed some sleep. I looked for Hieu to coordinate our sleeping arrangements and saw her by the SUV.

Hieu waved and pointed to the nest she had created in the back seat with borrowed army blankets. Both rear seats were reclined, ready for use. Hieu took the right rear seat, and I the left, after we both took off our hiking shoes, leaving our clothes on, too tired to care how dirty we were. Within minutes I descended into hard-earned sleep.

೧೧

The chilly night air woke me at two in the morning. Hieu's head had slid over and rested on my chest. She quietly breathed in rhythmic spurts; her legs were curled, her knees pressed against my ribs. I lay next to her warm body, not daring to move and wake her. The blankets were askew, but Hieu's body provided enough heat for both of us. I closed my eyes as she murmured something in her sleep.

I fell asleep again.

MY SON, JANUARY 15, 2003

The sunrays passing through the windshield warmed and woke me, as I lay spread out and alone on the rear seats, my back aching, legs cramped. I had no idea where had Hieu disappeared to. I heard the work going on at the site and glanced at my watch—it showed seven o'clock. In sixteen days, Tet would officially start; already, the volume of travelers had increased and would culminate two or three days before February 1. Hieu and I both thought that Ramsey or Loan would use the heavy traffic in the weeks ahead to make a move for the gold, if it was here.

The right rear passenger door opened and Hieu offered me a travel mug. I smelled the steaming hot coffee. "Good morning. Was sleep OK?" She studied me, handing me the mug as I sat up and answered, "Yes." Her serious eyes locked onto me for a second then she looked at the dig site.

I felt too old for this lifestyle, with my back aching and my right arm shooting jolts of pain from sleeping on it. I saw that Hieu had already changed into clean jeans and a shirt.

As if reading my mind, she said, "The rear and side windows are heavily tinted. You can change back there. I have a pan of hot water and soap for you on the hood."

Mug in hand, I got out. "Thanks for the coffee, Hieu. You constantly amaze me." But she had already turned to instruct one of the anthropologists, her ponytail swaying from the back of the baseball cap as she pointed, walking away from me with the individual, her firm and feminine body held erect, commanding every male nearby to focus on her. I went to wash up.

After a quick sponge bath with just my shirt off, I crawled into the vehicle's rear to change into clean underwear and clothes. Upon reflection, waking up last night with Hieu's head on my chest, seemed to show a degree of trust in me, an American. She was, after all, a lone woman camping out with a bunch of guys.

☙❧

Sipping coffee during my break, I watched the soldiers being directed by Hieu and Tho as they worked on the tunnel. The pleasant weather lifted our spirits as the palm fronds rattled against each other in the cool breeze that blew through the work site. The chirping birds and clear, light blue sky overhead all renewed my memory of the rare beauty that tropical Vietnam offered.

By noon, the cave, probably over hundreds of years old, once dug by Montagnards from the limestone that formed this hill, opened to us as the soldiers removed the final dirt deposits—placed there at the commands of Ramsey, Reed, and Loan. Hieu approached me with Captain Tho and several of the Da Nang policemen.

She turned toward me, translating a question from Captain Tho. "What do you think happened with the bulldozer and the APCs?"

"My guess—because of the war going on and this being VC-controlled area, Ramsey would have had the drivers of the APCs and the dozer killed, the equipment abandoned on the road or in the jungle, far from this site. Set up to look like the VC probably killed the ARVNs, hiding their bodies in the jungle. Who would argue in those days?"

Captain Tho nodded before Hieu had a chance to translate. I thought most of the military officers and senior police officials had a decent grasp of English; this confirmed it. He continued to stare at me, though. Then he finally broke the chill.

"You must know that my father died in the South, on the Ho Chi Minh Trail. He was a young soldier, recently married to my mother, deployed from Hanoi to fight you Americans and your corrupt allies, the South Vietnamese. Your B-52 bombers raided the A Shau Valley and the trail he was on. He died from massive internal bleeding from the shock of the 500-pound bombs. His eyes blew out and his brain became . . . what is word . . . ah . . . mush. I was born eight months later. It seems Agent Hieu respects you, but I have no love for the Americans. Thus I am reserved around you."

Responding to his story meant addressing the pain for all soldiers; I could only grapple with his emotions over the war and his father, whom he never met. I looked directly into Tho's eyes and said, "I commanded a unit of 110 men along the A Shau Valley and lost many in combat. We both suffered due to the war. It changed my life, as it did yours, but I bear you no ill will. It is now the past." I turned to walk away, before I allowed my anger to show.

Frustrated with Tho, Hieu grabbed my arm and stopped me. "Please, we need your recommendation."

"On what?" I turned around, trying to avoid further confrontation with Captain Tho.

"If we find the gold, how should we leave this site?" Tho asked, his dark eyes still boring into me.

Addressing both Hieu and Tho, I said, "If Ramsey and his people are coming here by vehicles, we need to deceive them by restoring the area to how we found it. And certainly refill the cave with dirt, forcing them to dig while you, Captain, deploy troops, then alert Hieu so we can participate in capturing him."

"That can be done," Tho said.

"I also suggest no troops remain here. Use your best men, preferably from the airborne platoon, camouflaged and hidden near your current observation post, away from this hill. They stay in touch with you by radio, while you coordinate the military aspect of the operation. They should have enough food and water to stay in the field, completely hidden." I thought of something to remove some tension between us and said, "As an NVA soldier, your father had these same skills. As a former American soldier, I would have respected your father for such professionalism. He would have been a formidable enemy in combat."

Tho raised his eyes. Ancestors are important in Vietnam, and the respect shown for the deceased is a key part of the culture, even under the communist regime. Tet crept toward us, and the Vietnamese would be celebrating at least three generations of family, past, present, and future. Tho wouldn't become my friend for life because I complimented his dead father, but I hoped he now understood me better. I harbored no illusions that the US could have won by bombing more or sending more troops, the standard military thinking used by our generals; Nam became a war we couldn't win. We lost when we allied ourselves with the inept, corrupt South Vietnamese regimes, taking on the war ourselves rather than developing honest allies.

The North Vietnamese worshiped Ho Chi Minh, and they knew they would win. He summarized their passion when he said, "You will kill ten of our men and we will kill one of yours, and in the end, it will be you who tire of it." He was correct.

Captain Tho talked to Hieu briefly, isolating me with his Vietnamese. Hieu, never the timid one, firmly interjected some information, pointing at him then me, emphasizing some topic while Tho diplomatically acquiesced to her. He then turned to me, did a hand salute, and walked away.

I stared at his back as he sauntered to the cave, giving orders to his troops digging in the earth. "Thank you," Hieu said as she stood staring after him with both hands on her hips, shaking her head.

"For what, Hieu?"

"For your diplomacy and your honesty—he may be more open with you now."

"OK. How about the bodies?" I asked.

"Yes, all of the hundred remains have been recovered. We are digging to find the gold now."

I wondered what had happened to Loan. How did he escape the trap set for him by the Vietnamese agents in Cambodia? Somehow, I knew the end game: Loan would contact Ramsey and plan on meeting where they had buried the treasure. There seemed to be no other option. I just hoped they were planning on coming to this location.

I said, "The CIA thinks Ramsey left Hong Kong this week. They checked all flights to Vietnam, but no luck. He has to be going to Cambodia if Loan is hiding there too." I didn't think this would be new intelligence to her, as the Vietnamese agents no doubt knew this.

Someone shouted from within the cave. Hieu grabbed my arm and dragged me after her, jogging to the entrance. Captain Tho emerged, tired. He reported to Hieu and she turned to me, disappointment showing.

"There is no gold!" she said.

℞❦℟

By six that afternoon, the four Vietnamese army trucks were loaded with the skeletal remains of the Giang villagers. Hieu reported to her home office that the gold no longer existed in the old cave. Several old wood lids and crates had been found, confirming that the gold had been buried here at one time.

I showed no emotion, as I had worried all along that the gold had been removed years ago—but by whom? Relegated to an observer role, I focused now on the final body bags holding the remains of the dead villagers. Hieu told me that they would be taken to the Da Nang morgue. The anthropologist would identify the remains before they were returned to the village of Giang and buried for final closure for any surviving relatives. These one hundred villagers would hardly make a dent in the tally of over three hundred thousand NVA and VC still missing in action versus America's missing two thousand, but the local relatives could finally stop wondering what happened to their husbands or fathers. Any closure worked for these war-weary people.

HOI AN, JANUARY 15, 2003

Captain Tho and his infantry stayed behind as the convoy departed, guarded by the police. His troops started restoring the area back to its original facade, also placing sensors and listening devices around the hill. Even the straight leg infantry soldiers were unaware of Tho's airborne troops about a kilometer away, concealed and hidden, waiting and watching. We betted on one thing: That Ramsey and Loan still thought the gold was buried here in the Montagnard cave. However, if they had moved the gold somewhere else in the last years of the war, then we had been screwed.

We followed the convoy until it split off to Da Nang, then we drove to Hoi An and our hotel. After her extreme disappointment over not finding the gold, Hieu, too exhausted to stay awake, slept peacefully on the passenger side while I drove. I wondered if Ramsey and Loan would appear after all, and what they would do once they discovered the gold missing. It would be over for them. They would try to flee the country to avoid capture, knowing that prison or possible execution waited for them both. Based on Woodruff he had forced Ramsey onto the Vietnamese in exchange for giving them Loan. Did Ramsey know?

On the other hand, if Ramsey and Loan had moved the gold years ago to another location, then we lost in our gamble on the My Son area hill. We had no other contingency to fall back on.

I struggled, trying to understand. If Ramsey and Loan hadn't moved the gold, then who did? Hung? But Hung had been incarcerated for over thirty years by the new regime. If he had the gold, why didn't he bribe his way to freedom? It just didn't fit.

Then there could be others in the corrupt ARVN military who may have learned of the buried treasure. Had some soldier or junior officer learned of the cave and then stole the treasure?

And then we had Quan. Could he have gone back later and discovered the gold, and taken the treasure to share with the remaining villagers, who had lost the hundred male adults, by execution? The possibilities seemed endless.

I tried to get into Ramsey's head, thinking like him. He had served in Nam longer than me, possibly five years, exploiting the country, learning about its politics, its ways, and its internal dissension. He could take advantage of this knowledge to bribe individuals for additional manpower. Having Loan with him would also be essential. Graft was common in present-day Vietnam, fueled by current laws that made it impossible for former South Vietnamese who didn't support communism during the war to obtain a job in the government, military, or police—at least for three generations. For the Northern victors, it was their payback to anyone in the South who opposed Ho Chi Minh and the reunification. Loan could leverage the dissent by some of the former South Vietnamese to aid him and Ramsey.

However, instead of hiring Vietnamese, I sensed he would assemble his manpower in Cambodia, thus avoiding any information leaks or loose talk by Vietnamese personnel. They could buy their way across all three borders to haul the gold using trails or dirt roads, staying away from major highways. I still believed that my calculations were correct and that four Hummers with trailers would be needed to haul the supplies, hired personnel, and weapons. No, I began to feel certain that they were coming here to the cave near My Son for the gold. Once they discovered the gold missing, they would try to escape—and we couldn't let them. That Sally's father was killed by mistake because of me—orchestrated by Ramsey and Loan—drove me to finish this. For

Sally, for her father, I had to help capture these two and leave them to rot in Vietnamese prisons, ensuring her safety and that of her family.

As I turned into the hotel driveway, coming to a stop, Hieu woke up. "We are here?"

"Yes, safe and sound," I said.

"Thank you for letting me rest."

"Hieu, we should remain extra cautious since Ramsey will be coming to this area."

"Yes, Ramsey is a threat, and we need to watch over each other." Her serious tone summed it up. "I have talked to Colonel Tin."

She didn't explain further.

ೋ

That evening, while I watched BBC news on the room's TV, I could hear Hieu talking to her family on her cell phone through the open connecting doorway. Every so often I could see her as she walked by in her sleep shorts and top, comfortable and uninhibited. She actually giggled as her husband talked and then laughed raucously when her boys came on the phone. Then I heard her voice become stern as she directed some motherly tough love to them.

I wore my long sleep pants and T-shirt and sat in my room's rattan lounge chair, catching up on US and international news. With my Palm phone, I had also checked the message board: no news from Woodruff. I heard Hieu hang up and watched her enter my room, swinging her arms joyfully. She came over and plopped down in the other rattan chair next to me.

"My sons were devils this week, and my husband is too soft—he is such a typical professor and will not discipline them as he should. It is always up to me." She started laughing again.

I watched her, bemused by her mood. "What did your boys do?" I asked.

"They were in the science fair this week, and students from all grades could combine for a joint endeavor. My older boy led my younger ones down the path of 'no glory,' and they created a volcano model with too much sulfur, intentionally so, and the school building had to evacuate from the stink."

We laughed. Then her cell phone rang; as she answered it, I couldn't help looking at her shapely legs as she stretched them while talking. When she hung up, I think she noticed me looking.

Reverting to her professionalism, she stood and said, "Captain Tho reported that all is quiet and there are no observations of activity near the hill. He will personally monitor his outpost from the Da Nang army base tonight. He placed a good lieutenant in charge at the observation post. So now we wait."

"Yeah. Now we wait. Do you think we need to question Quan again?"

She turned toward me and said, "I have the Da Nang police interrogating him now. Hopefully we will know soon if more is revealed." She continued to look at me. "Do you have a girlfriend, after your wife died?" she asked, catching me off guard.

"Well . . . basically, when my wife died, I withdrew from dating women. Recently I had someone, but . . . that too failed."

She frowned. Sitting back down and studying me, she added, "In Vietnam, marriages are not necessarily a romantic involvement. They are practical unions for financial security, safety, and a better life—especially for peasants in the villages, where life is very harsh. Marriages are a necessity for survival—large families are needed to help till the land for food and money."

"Is that how you view your marriage?" I glanced at my Palm phone for any emails, suddenly feeling guilty for my remark.

Hieu paused a moment. "I have learned to love my husband. He is loyal and he gave me three sons. I must be a good wife." Without further discussion, she stood up. "I think I need some sleep. Good night, John."

"Good night, Hieu," I said and put my Palm phone down.

I thought of how she described marriage in Vietnam as she walked to her room, closing the door behind her. She remained unaffected by the close proximity of the rooms we shared, uninhibited like a young girl, yet strong-willed and confident like a professional senior agent. She showed no weakness, and I sensed she could kill if confronted. She had every right to dislike me, an American. The war had impacted her more than the average American would ever understand. Yet recently her cool attitude toward me had slightly dissipated. Was it because she finally accepted me as a partner in this crazy endeavor? Even as partners though, she had more loyalty to her government and shared only what she had been authorized. I had to trust her and hoped she would not let me down when danger came into play. Deep down I knew that we were close to peril, and death.

HOI AN, JANUARY 26, 2003

Eleven days passed, and we had a steady diet of working out in the hotel gym, swimming in the pool, talking, eating, and planning, while waiting for word from Captain Tho. Hieu checked with him two or three times a day, receiving no new updates. Living so close to each other didn't help with the growing frustration over waiting for Ramsey and Loan. Again doubts had crept into our minds: Ramsey and Loan had the gold hidden elsewhere and had taken it all and fled. And as the days progressed, I grew fonder of her, which I knew would never go any further than being friends. This didn't help the tension, though.

The Tet holiday, or Tet Nguyen Dan, started in a week. Hieu reminded me that this was the year of the goat, and I laughed, telling her I felt like a goat, being played by Ramsey and by Loan. She didn't understand my humor.

Anxious, I worked the Palm phone for messages several times a day. Woodruff hadn't had news since the day he informed me of Ramsey leaving Hong Kong. The waiting game had me second-guessing myself: Ramsey was not coming; Ramsey was coming. The uncertainty weighed on me.

❧

That afternoon in the fitness center, I held a heavy rubber pad in front of me while Hieu did a vigorous kickboxing workout, repeatedly jamming her right foot and then her left into it. Her legs sliced at me in strong but graceful arcs, jarring me backward as I absorbed her kicks. Her legs were like steel, and I felt every thrust pummel my arms and body for a solid thirty minutes. Sore, sweating profusely, my gym shorts and top drenched, I gutted it out. Hieu, also soaked, kept the furious pace. Again and again, I looked at her graceful and lithe body, drawn to her. She didn't fail to notice and gave me a dark-eyed look in return while continuing her workout. I wondered if we could ever be good friends, but I pushed myself back to reality as she stopped her exercise. She bent over to pick up her towel and stood up, graceful still, drawing my eyes to her face.

"I am going to shower now," Hieu said and headed for the exit door.

"I think I'll do some weights," I said, deflated.

She turned toward me, weakly smiled, and then left. Any smile was better than none. I worked another forty minutes on the weight machine, honing on my triceps, biceps, and quads, wearing away my thoughts about Hieu. When I finished, I walked back to my room and saw that she sat by the pool in her bikini. She saw me and waved, apparently in a better mood.

"Go shower and join me," she yelled in a friendlier tone.

I waved and headed for my room. The connecting door had been left open, and I glanced into her room for security reasons. Hieu remained very neat, almost tidy to a fault, and her bathroom was always painstakingly picked up. I shut her door, after ensuring her room was empty. Then I went to my bathroom and started my shower. The hot water cascaded over my back and shoulders, relaxing the tight muscles, releasing the aches from the bruises of her kicking routine. Her strength and reflexes amazed me. Suddenly, the bathroom door burst open and

Hieu, fully dressed in her field outfit, yelled at me as she held her cell phone to her ear. Startled, I thought only of my nudity while she busily responded to her cell phone and tried to tell me something, jabbering Vietnamese into her phone and to me, forgetting her English. She grabbed a towel and handed it to me around the glass shower door, all the while staring at me.

With flushed cheeks, she at last said in English, "Tho has confirmed contact with one large vehicle at the hill site and four or five individuals—mostly Cambodians. He awaits us. Get dressed, please."

I grabbed the towel she held out and wrapped it around me. She just stood there in the bathroom watching me.

"Hieu, I need to dry . . . "

"Hurry." She rushed out, shutting the door behind her.

I dried as fast as I could and had just hung up the towel when she rushed into the bathroom again, holding my clean jeans, shirts, socks, and underwear. "Quickly get dressed," she said.

I took my clothes and started to put on my underwear and saw that she hadn't left. "Hieu please, I need some privacy," I begged.

"I have seen a naked man before."

"Go, please," I said, struggling to respond. With one leg in my undershorts, I gently grabbed her by her shoulders, turned her around, and pushed her out the bathroom, shutting and locking the door behind her. I shook my head.

"Hieu, pack our equipment, I'll be right out," I yelled through the closed door.

Minutes later I walked out of the bathroom fully dressed, my wet hair combed with my fingers. Hieu waited for me in my living area with our backpacks and the case that held our AK-47s. Standing up from a chair she headed toward the door.

She stopped before opening it, turned and smiled deeply to me for the first time. "You are shy?"

"Hieu, you know . . . it is difficult . . . "

"Difficult?" she asked.

"Yes . . ."

She stared at me trying to understand. Then, as if a light flicked on in her head, she said, "Oh, I see—but we are professional partners. Come, let's go. It is 1730 hours."

Shaking my head, I followed her out the door and then to our Mercedes, watching her sway in her jeans while she carried both our backpacks. I lugged the gun case with the AK-47s and ammo. We had our pistols in the backpacks to avoid frightening hotel guests.

DAI LOC, JANUARY 26, 2003

Our drive to meet Captain Tho took close to an hour. I drove while Hieu checked the map, not saying much. I couldn't decipher if we were more like an old married couple or partners on a case. As usual, she did a great job of concealing her emotions.

We had been instructed to meet Captain Tho at the village of Dai Loc on the main highway from Hoi An. Dai Loc sat a mile north of the dirt road and the fork where the observation post overlooking the Montagnard hill had been located. Per Hieu, after meeting with Tho, we would drive cross-country as close as we could and then hike to the hidden observation post, joining his team. Imposed radio silence dictated that we wait for a further update on the activity at the site until we met with Tho.

I drove fast, despite the increased traffic of people returning to their home villages to prepare for Tet. Over the next five days, the roads would be snarled with more cars, bikes, buses, and motorbikes as sons, daughters, uncles, aunts, and other relatives traveled to parents or grandparents in tiny villages everywhere for the sacred duty of celebrating their past ancestors, as well as feting with the present generations to ensure the future brought happiness, health, and harmony to the family. Ramsey had picked the perfect period to travel, and his group would mesh with the steady stream of humanity making its exodus into the countryside.

We arrived at Dai Loc at eight. Tho stood waiting for us by his Russian-made military utility vehicle at the turnoff to the village. He waved for us to pull over next to his vehicle. Dusk had turned into evening, but lights from the village and the flow of vehicles edged some of the darkness.

He greeted us with a slight bow and shook our hands as we stepped out of our vehicle. The captain was less surly toward me.

"Captain Moore, please, my English is not as . . . good . . . As is Agent Hieu's, so I will talk to her first."

I leaned against the front of the Mercedes and watched them proceed in Vietnamese, animatedly pointing with their fingers to the south and referring to a map that Tho had unfolded and spread out on the hood of his vehicle. The flashlight in his hand outlined information for Hieu. His driver sat inside staring at me. I still felt out of place, and the steady flow of Vietnamese passing me on their Tet pilgrimage increased the feeling. Finally, Tho saluted Hieu and got into his vehicle, motioning for us to follow.

Hieu climbed into the Mercedes as I got behind the steering wheel and drove slowly behind Tho. "We will drive along old rice paddies on an access trail going south from here until we meet with Tho's men." She pulled her pistol from her shoulder holster, checked the magazine, and returned it.

"What did he say about Ramsey's men?" I asked, my armpits getting damp from the humidity and tension.

"They are now digging at the hill and the cave that we uncovered and reburied. There are four Cambodians and one Caucasian, possibly American. Tho's planted listening devices, and sensors are allowing his men to monitor the discussions, which have been only in Cambodian. The white man speaks the language, but his accent is English or American."

I wondered if that Caucasian could be Ramsey. Certainly, the timing would be correct. But then what happened to Loan? This whole mission had holes in it, and we were reacting rather than taking bold steps forward. I hoped Tin understood the tenuous situation we had jumped into. My chest felt tight as I drove.

"How many vehicles are there now?" I asked, breaking the heavy silence that had taken over.

"There is one and with a trailer. What do you think that means?" Hieu faced me, waiting and unsmiling.

"If I was Ramsey, I would send a trusted person to verify the gold is still buried. On the other hand the Caucasian is Ramsey, or he is nearby. If the American at the scene is not Ramsey, then he is probably a trusted man. Ramsey probably has the other vehicles hidden, ready to arrive as soon as the gold is uncovered. Loan could be with Ramsey as well. Again, we're assuming that they will load up and head back to the west and the Laos border, catching a chartered freight aircraft at Pakxe or another airstrip." My repetition of our favored scenario sounded more and more like an attempt to validate the decisions we had made.

Hieu nodded as I drove behind Tho's vehicle along an old route bordering pungent rice paddies. The smell of water buffalo dung and centuries-old soil wafted through our nostrils. The night insects outside our SUV serenaded us, a chorus for our little convoy of two vehicles bumping and grinding along a path that I would never have driven in daytime. Yet here I strained with the steering wheel in the night. I had the vehicle in four-wheel drive, and we churned the trail into more mud, duplicating Tho's action ahead, a slow and tiring quest. We were surrounded by water on both sides, and the darkness countered by the two vehicles' headlights and taillights set on military blackout mode—just functional enough to use on the rutted trail. The village lights and its road traffic over a half mile behind us provided no additional illumination now, only a far silhouette in the night. The eerie darkness grew like an abyss as we drove, splashing mud, seeking our unseen destination. A mosquito buzzed by my left ear, having slipped through our vehicle's metal and glass defenses. It landed on my cheek, probing for my blood. I slapped at it, hitting my cheek, smearing the ooze of my blood and the carcass of the dead mosquito.

Sweat covered my forehead and perspiration continued to pool in my armpits, gradually seeping along my sides. My heartbeat escalated as I strived to stay on the narrow trail meant for water buffalos and farm carts. My arms and hands were stiff and strained, battling the muck, the deep ruts, steering the vehicle forward.

I sensed it on my skin, in the pit of my stomach, in my almost sightless eyes, and in my nostrils. I returned to the war jungles of Nam as the itching spread on my moist skin, exacerbated by the sticky, humid air, overcoming the air-conditioned cab.

In the war, my skin felt the same: exposed to mosquitoes, large cockroaches, ants, and the leeches, all wanting me and my ten men on ambush patrol near Mai Loc. We waited in the dense brush and bamboo trees as the NVA sappers crawled toward my company. Seven small, wiry, and dedicated warriors out to destroy and kill Americans, carrying satchel charges on their backs, dragging poles along their sides to push the explosives through the defensive concertina wire stretched around my unit.

Hidden in the jungle since early evening, tied to each other by nylon cord for communication purposes, we watched and waited until, at two in the morning, the two soldiers on guard duty, one on each end of my patrol, jarred the rest of us to consciousness, tugging on the ropes in both directions, readying us to kill. We had formed a simple linear ambush, occupying the upper side of the dried streambed, a natural route for night movement by the enemy. My ten men waited for me to initiate the ambush once I knew the NVA were completely in the "kill zone." I opened the slaughter with a burst from my M16. The soldier to my left clicked the claymore mines set at both ends of the kill zone, ripping apart the trailing and lead NVA soldiers. My M60 machine gunner sprayed the area below us from his right to his left, while the rest of my men emptied their initial magazines into the gulley below.

I often hear those dying NVA soldiers screaming, mortally wounded, their torn bodies writhing in front of me in the dirt and on rocks of the dry gulley. No one said a word as I signaled my men to withdraw, following me, tense and fearful that more enemies approached. We quietly sneaked back to the company area to await the pending attack by the NVA regiment formed somewhere in the jungle. We had survived another day of war but felt no satisfaction, no relief; we had just killed seven men.

Hieu grasped my right forearm and shouted, "John!" I slammed on the brakes, the Mercedes sliding to a halt a foot from the rear bumper of Tho's stopped vehicle. Tho was walking toward us on Hieu's side of our SUV.

"Sorry, Hieu, I...." I looked at her shaking head, feeling haggard and queasy, like I had just returned from that night ambush.

Hieu stared at me, concern on her own tense face. She watched me as she exited the Mercedes to talk with Tho. After a few minutes, she sat back in the front passenger seat. "Captain Tho said we are almost there. You will need to drive slowly and follow the soldier he posted now in front of our vehicle. He will guide us to the hidden parking area. We will have to walk after we park." I didn't look at her, still struggling over my flashback.

I watched Tho get in his vehicle and drive into the dark. The young soldier had luminous strips sewn to the back of his dark green fatigue uniform reflecting toward me. He motioned for me to follow. Our vehicle crept after him while my mind still thought of that war and the death I caused; its sadness weighed heavily.

Before we left the village of Dai Loc, Hieu had us strap on our shoulder holsters. Now she stretched between our front bucket seats to open the rifle case with the two AK-47s and the ammunition magazines. She pulled the AK-47s to the front and then returned to the rear seats and retrieved our backpacks. "Now we are ready!" she said, forcing a worried smile.

Too intent on the dark trail and my guide in front, I avoided looking at her. "Hieu, back there, I sort of went back in time. I'm sorry, I..."

"I know what you are experiencing in the night." She returned to her AK-47, chambering a round with the sliding bolt, placing it on safety. She did the same for my rifle.

I glanced at her quickly and saw this city girl, this attractive woman, now looking like a killer, as the eerie green light from the SUV's instrument panel highlighted her face. I shuddered. I had returned to war.

MY SON AREA, JANUARY 26, 2003

By midnight we arrived at the concealed outpost manned by Tho's airborne troopers, camouflaged with fresh leaves and grasses of the jungle they occupied. The troops resembled ghosts, their faces streaked in dark greens and browns from grease pencils. In the small command post, I used a headset to listen to the voices being monitored while Tho's radiotelephone operator adjusted knobs to improve reception and volume. The wireless devices hidden in the trees around the site confirmed everything that Tho had told us earlier: four Cambodians and one Caucasian who spoke adequate Cambodian. I knew immediately that the white guy had to be an American, specifically a Texan; the Southern twang overpowered his speech. Ramsey wouldn't have such a twang.

Until now, they had been digging while the American gave orders. Something changed as the American switched to English: "We just found the bones. We should be ready by early morning." Hieu and Tho looked at me, their headsets on as well. Did he just communicate to Ramsey and Loan on the other end of the short wave?

"I'm guessing that the others must be hidden on the border with more vehicles. Maybe in Laos along the old Ho Chi Minh Trail," I said.

Hieu and Tho pondered all this as our headsets transmitted more dialogue from the American. "Yeah, leave now. Since it's midnight, that will give you six hours of darkness to get here." There was a pause. "OK, see you around six." The work team returned to their chatter as the digging continued.

I turned to Tho. "Did you plant bones?"

"They were farm animal bones we secured from the villages. Also, monkey bones and skulls were placed."

"Nicely done," I said, impressed by Tho's foresight.

"What do you recommend we do?" Hieu asked me.

"I suggest that we move in around 0200 hours. Capture this group to ensure we have the edge in numbers. We don't know how many men are with Ramsey or Loan, and this will help reduce their force. Also we must get to the American first before he can use the radio to alert Ramsey."

Captain Tho's eyes stirred. He seemed ready for action, bored with just monitoring. He said something to Hieu, who turned to me with a frown. "He agrees with you and will plan the attack. I think we should wait until Loan and Ramsey arrive."

"You're the boss, Hieu, but I think we have the element of surprise. We capture these five and then sit and wait for the rest of them to walk into our trap."

She thought a minute, looking at the radio set. Tho and I waited for her decision. She finally turned to us and said, "Yes." Captain Tho nodded and headed out of the command post.

As he exited, he said in English, "We will depart at 0130 hours. You rest, as we will do a fast march over one kilometer." His look told me he had already prepared, and he seemed agreeable to include me in the military operation.

I sprayed Hieu with insect repellant, and she reciprocated. Now a firm user of my malaria pills, she reminded me to take my daily dosage as she swallowed her pill, not knowing when we would have the next opportunity. We both sat quietly on the ground, drinking bottled water for hydration, checking our weapons and backpack gear. We said little at that point. I knew that Ramsey and Loan and his men would be armed, and there would probably be casualties in the next twenty-four hours. Before I closed my eyes and tried to rest, I looked over to Hieu. She sat in a familiar yoga pose, legs crossed, hands in her laps, eyes closed, quietly meditating, escaping from the physical world around us.

We still sat on the ground when one of Tho's soldiers approached us in the tent. He first draped me with a camouflage net that covered me from my baseball cap to below my waist. Then he quickly marked my face with the camouflage pencils, deftly doing the job in less than a minute. He finally covered my face with the netting. Once satisfied that my white face didn't reflect, he turned to Hieu and did the same.

Adrenalin increasing in anticipation of the military operation, I ironically thought of my changed role: I now worked with the Socialist Republic of Vietnam Army, the successor of the NVA, the enemy that I had fought against for a year with my eighteen- and nineteen-year-old draftees. But now I prepared for combat allied with the offspring of my former enemies. I wondered about what mental price I would pay for returning to the killing fields of Nam.

Tho burst into the tent, startling me from my reverie. "We are ready." He grinned. "Agent Hieu and you, Captain Moore, will be in the center of our column. Stay together and move fast. My men are swift. Do not stop unless the unit does. Carry the rifles at port arms. Keep your weapons on safety. Let us move out."

Hieu and I followed him out of the tent. He took the head of the column, with a point man twenty feet ahead of him. As we formed, he explained the simple plan to Hieu, who relayed it to me. "We will do a forced march to the hill, surround it, secure it, ensure no other personnel are around, and then, upon Tho's orders, we will sweep in and disarm the five men, preventing them from alerting Ramsey with the field radio."

"OK, we're as ready as we ever will be," I said. "And please be careful. I would miss you if anything should happen."

Her dark eyes studied me, trying to understand. Then the column began moving and I followed Hieu, protecting her back. The pace was alarmingly fast for the pitch-black night, but the troops moved stealthily. I sensed that I made the only noise as we glided through the dense growth, following stakes with reflectors facing us, placed by Tho's pioneers, who had preceded us several minutes earlier, reminiscent of the NVA tactics used to attack American units at night. The efficiency of the preplanned route, physically marked, ensured speed of movement. We marched silently, as phantoms in the night, a blur with the darkened jungle. The column had twenty of us: eighteen military, plus Hieu and me. No one talked. Grim and dedicated, I now knew how the NVA felt as they moved into attack positions on American or ARVN units. The covertness, the rapidity, and the focus of this column impressed me. They had little time for fear, just the mission. The unit pushed on, encouraging the troops to succeed. The cumulative adrenalin surged us forward, our legs in sync: swish, swish, swish, and swish. . . . I became one of them.

✆

By 0200 hours, we had surrounded the site and were observing the four Cambodians taking a rest from digging in the tunnel, illuminated by the headlights of the lone Hummer with an attached trailer. We didn't see the American, and Hieu guessed he was in the cave, checking the progress of the work. Hieu and I lay next to Tho, watching him take a confirming report from his point men, who had swept the entire perimeter surrounding the hill. They found no others. He sent some men out to secure our flanks. Then Tho used a toy cricket clicker, clicking it four times to signal the ready for the attack, waiting for confirmation clicks from his three fire teams, numbered one through three: one, two, and three clicks respectively. Satisfied, he waited the full two minutes as planned per synchronized watches, then stood up and charged into the site with Hieu and me at his side. The four Cambodians, who had just started sharing a bottle of water, were shocked as the Vietnamese soldiers thrust AK-47s into their faces. Fear on the four faces summed up Tho's success so far. His men gagged, blindfolded, and tied the four men, connecting all four with a single rope. The enemy had been neutralized in minutes, with stark efficiency and no shots fired.

I rushed to the cave entrance, but the headlights from the Hummer showed it empty. The American had disappeared! I turned and stared past Tho and Hieu, who also scanned the area, and looked down the trail, the one that Hieu and I had used driving from the My Son ruins to find this hill in the first place. Coming toward us with a roll of toilet paper in his hand, the American strode calmly, looking at the ground to avoid entangling vines. Suddenly, fifty feet away, he stopped, staring at us in confusion. In seconds, he turned and ran back up the trail. I handed my AK-47 to one of Tho's grunts, slipped off my backpack, dropped it to the ground, and sprinted after him. The American had to be stopped from warning Ramsey or Loan by radio.

His huge weight-lifter's body, two-hundred-and-fifty pounds of muscle on a six-foot frame, thumped down the trail like a huge elephant. He had fifty feet of distance on me, but he was no runner; that was my strength. I gained ten feet, but seeing the gap close between us, he reached behind him to pull out his field phone. He planned to warn the others! I felt Hieu behind me, breathing steadily, loping, closing the distance between us. The American struggled to pull out the radio on his hip. Suddenly, he turned and dropped to his knees; he had a Glock in his hand, not his radio! Two quick shots whizzed over my head as I dropped to the ground, pulling out my .45. I heard Hieu slide to the ground somewhere behind me.

I estimated the distance to him equaled less than thirty feet, well within my accuracy. Holding my pistol in both hands, I fired one shot, aiming at his right shoulder. He screamed and dropped his Glock as my slug tore into him, spinning him to his right and onto the ground with a thud. The .45 caliber is devastating to the body, even with a grazing shot. He would be hurting. I pushed up and rushed him, pistol pointed at him, looking for his radio, which I now saw was still on his belt near the empty Glock holster. Hieu ran up beside me, her nine millimeter at the ready, held in both hands, pointed toward the downed American. I kicked his Glock away and watched as he struggled in shock from the wound. The guy had to be about thirty years old.

As Hieu kept her gun aimed at him, I bent down and yanked his shortwave from the holder. It was still turned off. Sticking the phone inside my shirt, I leaned over him and checked his wound. My shot had done more damage than I thought; he bled heavily, the bloody froth on his lips indicated a hit artery and collapsed lung. I felt no remorse, which shocked me. He was the enemy and I was once again at war.

He opened his eyes, confused, recognizing a fellow American. Tho and one of his medics rushed to us. The medic dropped to his knees and started to administer first aid, all the while shaking his head; the American would die. With dying eyes, he muttered in his Texan drawl, "Who are you?"

"No one you know," I answered. "Where's Ramsey? And Loan?"

He stopped muttering. I knew he would fade fast; I had to pull the information from him now.

"Tell me—where are they located?" I yelled at him.

"Don't let me die," he mumbled.

"Look, before the morphine kicks in while the medic saves your life, tell me. Who are you? Where's Ramsey?" I said. The lie ate at me. The medic had given up. He said something to Captain Tho, who shook his head toward me: the American had little time left.

". . . Ramsey hired me with the Cambodians. All by phone . . . no idea . . . him or this other guy . . . located." He closed his eyes thinking he would live. A few minutes later he died.

Captain Tho came up to me as I stood, twitching slightly and depressed. My hanging right arm held my .45 pointed to the ground. Tho put his hand on my back. "You did the only action possible. We focus on Ramsey and Loan then."

I stared at him and nodded. I had killed in self-defense, but it didn't make it easier. Tho knew what I felt and tried, as any other soldier would for a fellow comrade in arms, to help ease the pain, the hurt. I looked down at the body once more, hit with flashbacks of the war, images in short bursts, repeating the long line of downed soldiers I had seen. Both Americans and North Vietnamese bleeding, begging for life, and then begging for death as the pain became a living hell, and finally dying, sometimes with help from a pistol shot from his comrade or the enemy.

I holstered my pistol, acknowledged Tho, and kneeled to look through the pockets of the dead man. His Texas driver's license in his wallet and the US passport identified the body as Bill Carolton from Dallas. I handed the wallet and the rest of the items to Tho for safe keeping. Turning I started to return to the hill when Hieu grabbed me from behind, put her left arm through my right, and walked with me, saying nothing. I needed her human touch, that understanding. She felt my body shudder and patted my arm with her free hand. I looked into her eyes; those dark pools reflecting back to me, knowing what I did. We continued to walk as Tho's troops finished securing the area and removed the corpse.

"Don't worry, we will find Ramsey and Loan," Hieu said.

MY SON, JANUARY 27, 2003

Captain Tho gently shook my shoulder, waking me from a deep sleep. He smiled and said quietly, "Come. I have hot tea for you." Then he added with a grin, "Agent Hieu must have been cold." He glanced past me to my left. My head, in a fugue, turned to follow his eyes to Hieu. I felt her warm body, her back shoved against my left side, her head on her outstretched arm, the mosquito netting wrapped around us. Not wanting to wake her, I slowly slipped away from her body. Pulling myself through the netting, I followed Tho to his concealed camp spot where his gear was stowed. My clothes, musty, moldy, splattered with mud, stained with sweat, wrinkled from sleep, served to remind me of the war days; I yearned for a hot shower. Earlier this morning, Hieu and I had spread out the blankets that Tho provided under the only extra mosquito netting available. We started sleeping about a foot apart. She at least trusted me to behave. More importantly, her presence had helped soothe my mental anguish over killing the American.

Captain Tho pulled out a huge thermos from his backpack and poured hot tea into two metal military canteen cups. Sipping the strong brew quickly erased my grogginess. I glanced at my watch: 5:00 a.m. Scanning the site, I saw that very few of Tho's grunts were visible; most were hidden, prepared for their next confrontation. The Hummer stayed in its original place, pointed to the partially dug tunnel, bait for Ramsey.

"I have placed my men in concealed spots around the hill. We will ambush Ramsey and Loan when they arrive. The four Cambodians are in Da Nang jail."

"What about the dead American?" I asked, still conflicted over the killing.

"We buried him in the jungle. I assumed you did not wish to take him back to America." Tho grinned as he handed me the American's billfold and passport.

Taking the personal effects, I searched through them to see if I could get any information on Loan or Ramsey. None existed, so I tossed both items into my backpack. I assumed that Ramsey had hired Carolton as a gun for hire. Ramsey or Loan probably briefed him only as needed. The Vietnamese government would not want to be involved in killing him, but they certainly had an out, since an American citizen did the shooting. My mood darkened as I realized that if the Socialist Republic of Vietnam needed a patsy for political gain, then I would be used.

In the meantime, just like the bodies from the war still buried in the jungles of Nam, the dead American had been added to the earth, to rot, to disappear forever.

Tho said, "I will give Agent Hieu tea when she wakes up. By the way your SUV is hidden thirty meters in the jungle from us. I took the liberty of transporting it here from the command post." He pointed southwest from our spot.

Instead I looked toward the west, as if I could see Laos and the border, and said, "Now we wait for Ramsey."

Captain Tho looked westward as well. Nodding, he said, "We wait."

ल्ॐ

Dawn broke and my watch showed 6:10 a.m. We were hidden in our camouflage nets, observing the hill site; all the avenues of approach were covered by Tho's men. The morning breeze blew through the trees, rustling the leaves, covering any minor noises that we made from bodies shifting on the ground. Tho, barely visible to me, lay about twenty feet to my left, while Hieu stayed five feet to my right, covering me. My AK-47 was on the ground beside me on my right; Hieu had hers in front, safety off.

The breeze helped thwart the flying insects, so lying in wait for Ramsey wasn't totally unpleasant. Hieu looked tired, her eyes puffy; she had to be anxious to end this mission and return to Hanoi. When she woke up, about thirty minutes after me, she searched for me, carrying my baseball cap. Over her cup of hot tea, she explained the importance of my wearing the cap so that we could recognize each other during the confusion in battle. I grinned again over our physical differences from the rest of our companions, but I accepted the cap, placing it back on my head, respecting her authority. Standing next to us, Captain Tho grinned over the cap issue.

At seven, I worried that Ramsey wouldn't show. From my prone position with the hill to my right, I could observe the minor dirt road running west and east, which Ramsey would probably use, as well as the rutted trail from My Son running from the west, where I had already chased two men, one being the dead American and the other being Quan.

We waited. No Hummers. No Ramsey.

Suddenly, the strain of a vehicle approaching in low gear reverberated on the trail from My Son. They were coming over the old trail again. Already in a firing position, Hieu sighted her AK-47. I pulled my rifle into position, releasing the safety. Strangely, I felt some relief, sensing that this could all end today, ensuring anyone associated with me would be safe from Ramsey and Loan. Did Ramsey's life have to end? I hoped that he would surrender; I had no stomach for more killing.

A lone Hummer with attached trailer appeared in the clearing, stopping behind the first trailer and Hummer. Leaving the engine running, the driver and his passenger, both looked like Cambodians, cautiously opened their doors and stepped out, AK-47s at the ready, eyes sweeping the terrain around them. One of them yelled a name, seeking one of the four missing companions. I double-checked but couldn't see anyone else in the cab. Neither Ramsey nor Loan were there, and I now realized that he had sent these two to check on the first group. There had to be a final communication check between Ramsey and the American I had killed before Ramsey would continue to the site.

While the driver walked to the tunnel, the other Cambodian chattered nervously and paced behind his Hummer, constantly searching the jungle and elephant grass. He jerked to a stop and raised his AK-47 to waist level, firing a burst along the trail. He sealed his death as two of Tho's soldiers, hidden in the brush near the trail, fired short bursts into him, all bullets impacting his body. The Cambodian collapsed to the ground with no sound. The driver came running from the tunnel to his Hummer, trying to jump into the cab. Tho's men hidden near the hill now emerged and cut him down with short, efficient bursts.

I groaned. We needed one of them alive to help find Ramsey's.

I pushed myself up, rushed to the dead men's Hummer, and jumped onto the hood to gain a better view of the dirt road directly north of us. Tho had followed and handed me his binoculars. I focused and swept the dirt road from my right to my left. They had to be near, and I ruled out the old My Son trail that we had used as too dangerous for them to traverse. Ramsey would know to avoid using the same route, and he would be waiting for a go-ahead signal before driving across the grassy field from the dirt road to this hill.

I saw them! Two hummers, maybe a mile away, parked off the road, almost hidden by banyan trees. A white man stood on the hood of the first Hummer, staring in my direction with his binoculars. I doubted he could see me, but he must have had heard the pops of the AK-47s and now knew of the trap.

"What do you see, John?" Hieu asked, standing below me on the ground. Her frown reflect how I felt.

"It has to be Ramsey, with another Asian standing next to him, maybe Loan, and two others, probably Cambodians—shit, neither Hummer has a trailer. Ramsey must have parked them to ensure a fast escape. Probably knew something was wrong." It was now obvious that the lone American that I killed had to give Ramsey a final all-clear signal. He sent another team to verify this. We should have known.

I saw Ramsey talking to the Asian, pointing in our direction, then he jumped off the hood, rushed to the passenger side, and got in. His partner followed, getting into the driver side. This had to be Loan. The two Cambodians ran to the second Hummer, parked behind Ramsey's vehicle. The lead Hummer swung onto the road in a sharp U-turn, followed by the second vehicle. They were returning west, fleeing toward Laos!

"Shit," I yelled and jumped off the hood. Running to our parked vehicle, I yelled at Hieu to join me.

Tho ran alongside and said, "I will call in for vehicles to chase them. You will wait."

"Tho, we have no time. Send help as soon as you can. Hieu and I will chase them and try to stop them before they cross the Laos border. Once they get into jungle on the Laos side, we've lost them."

He didn't like it and slowed me down, finally stopping me. Hieu ignored us and ran past. I knew why she headed into the jungle. Tho wouldn't budge, standing in front of me.

"Captain Moore, you are our guest, and you will comply with my orders. We will pursue them together!"

"You're wasting time, Captain." I didn't want to chase Ramsey alone with Hieu, but we couldn't wait for his troops and trucks from the military installation in Da Nang or his lone utility vehicle at the hidden observation post. "We will follow them and relay their location back by radio. Tho, you know this is the right move!" Tho stood firm, not budging, as I grew angrier.

Suddenly, the Mercedes came bumping through the brush and tall grass sliding to a stop next to me, whining in low gear. The passenger door swung open as Hieu shouted orders in Vietnamese to Tho. The captain stepped back mad but acquiesced to Hieu's commands. I jumped in as Hieu accelerated the SUV past the two parked Hummers, going north through the brushy flat field that bordered the dirt road. The chase had begun. Halfway across the rugged field, Hieu slammed on the brakes.

"You drive, John. I will operate the radio," she yelled, her energy flooding over me.

She slid over me while I pulled myself to the steering wheel and quickly put on my seat belt while Hieu did the same. Slamming into drive, I accelerated toward the road, trying to regain lost time. Our only help would be the Tet traffic, swollen with travelers. It should slow Ramsey with his wide-body Hummers. We would be impacted as well, but we had more clout on the road. Hieu, reading my mind, turned on the flashing blue police light mounted in the grill. We were in hot pursuit and the Vietnamese would move over for us, the National Police. I reached the dirt road, careening over the low berm of the dry ditch and onto the road, never letting up on the gas; the vehicle slid, sharply tipping toward Hieu's side. I finally gained control of the SUV and accelerated some more, following Ramsey somewhere ahead. We would reach the paved road and heavy Tet traffic in a few minutes.

"Hieu, pull out the map of the Ho Chi Minh trails that branch from Laos into Vietnam, especially by Cha Vanh village in Vietnam. It's near the Laos border."

Hieu grabbed other maps from the back seat and studied them. She pulled the hand mic from the mounted FM field radio and began transmitting calmly. My heart pumped. Hieu gave instructions into the handset, referencing the old map and the village of Cha Vanh, and then she shouted at me to go faster, her excitement boiling now. The

Mercedes gained more speed while Hieu gave firm orders into the handset, first in Vietnamese and then repeated in English for me.

"I have alerted the police in Da Nang and have talked to Tho as well. He is following us in the two captured Hummers with four men in each vehicle, plus himself. He will be in the first Hummer. The rest of the men will wait for the trucks from Da Nang and, of course, they have to bury the bodies first."

"Christ, why didn't we think of that in the first place? Tho will not be that far behind us then. That makes a difference for us in numbers."

"I told him to use the Hummers when I stopped to pick you up. Maybe a woman is more rational than men in an argument—angry like two roosters fighting over the hen."

I laughed with relief. "Yeah, I guess we were all a little mad."

She reached over for my .45, pulled it out of my holster, ejected the magazine, and looked at it. "One round fired. I will reload it so that you have a full load of eight rounds."

"Thanks. That will give me seven in the magazine and one round chambered." The explanation was not necessary for her, but it distracted me from the tension as we sped along.

Hieu then arranged our two AK-47s, barrels up, against the car dash, her legs holding them in place. We were ready.

We reached the paved highway and barreled onto it going over sixty miles an hour, almost spinning out of control as I overcompensated for the rear end sliding away from me. Hieu stayed calm, focused on the road and the radio.

People scattered to the side as they saw our flashing blue lights and the official police license tags. Motorbikes and bicycles yielded as best as they could. One old man riding his bike stopped to pull over, lost his balance, and fell, the bike crashing on top of him. I drove recklessly now and worried about killing an innocent pedestrian. I slowed down to forty miles per hour in this stretch of traffic. Hieu didn't seem to notice and continued talking on the radio.

She pulled out the regular highway map and studied it. She raised her voice over the noise of the SUV. "We are approaching Dai Lanh village. It will be seventy-five kilometers from there to the border."

I nodded. That meant forty-seven miles, over an hour if we stay at forty. The Hummers could easily go over sixty on these roads, but I counted on the heavy Tet traffic to impede their movement as well. Where possible, I would increase my speed, but they would do the same. As we flashed by the village of Dai Lanh, a clear stretch of road with little traffic opened before us. I pushed down on the accelerator and we flew to seventy-five miles per hour. Again, Hieu urged me to go faster; she had the intent to capture Loan and Ramsey. I glanced at her and saw her eagerness for battle, her mood cold and dark. She had turned into a predator, and there would be no escape for her prey.

We cruised between fifty-five and seventy miles per hour when open stretches of road allowed. We had driven for over thirty minutes when I began to worry; we hadn't seen the Hummers. Hieu and I looked at each other, our minds melding. She picked up her handset to contact Tho and discovered that he had just arrived at Dai Lanh. She instructed him to do a quick drive through the village, to look for the Hummers and to query the villagers.

About one mile from Giang, we had to slow for three wrecked cars scattered on both sides of the highway. Traffic moved at a crawl as onlookers and victims milled around the damaged vehicles. Some bystanders saw our flashing lights and rushed to us, all talking at once, pointing down the road. Those who approached my side were confused to see my Caucasian face stare back at them and gladly moved around the car to Hieu's side. She asked questions, yelling at them as well. She discovered that no serious injuries or deaths had occurred, and that two big, speeding trucks—the Hummers—had sideswiped the cars, causing the accident and departing the scene. It had happened ten minutes ago. We were still fresh on their track.

"I am sure they caused the accidents to slow us down," she said.

"Yes. But we're still gaining on them!"

Hieu told me to drive on while she called for medical and police support on her radio. I left the confused Vietnamese standing on the road arguing and pointing at our departing vehicle. At Ben Giang, some five miles further, we had to slow down again and go through the village, leaving Highway 14 and moving onto the road to Cha Vanh. We assumed that Ramsey headed to the Laos border at this juncture. Hieu and I agreed to stay the course. I pressed on through the small village then onto the dirt road headed to Laos. We would know soon.

Once we cleared the village, I saw the dirt road with some asphalt patches, unencumbered with traffic. Instinctively, I geared the Mercedes up to a solid sixty-five miles per hour. Within five minutes I saw the first sign of vehicles ahead: dust clouds. Hieu and I looked at each other, nodding; we knew that we were on the right road. She radioed the information to Tho, who had just finished his search in the village of Dai Lanh. The villagers' lack of any sighting of the Hummers verified our course of action. Tho's detour to Dai Lanh helped to confirm our direction of pursuit. However, it slowed him down and meant Hieu and I would have to act alone until Tho, and his troops caught up.

As I turned along a sharp, winding curve, I had to swerve left, slamming on my brakes to a hard stop, nearly running off the road to avoid hitting a small herd of water buffalo being driven by two young Vietnamese boys. The kids were terrified, thinking they had caused an accident—their frightened faces frozen.

Hieu shouted to me. "Wait. I will ask the boys what they saw on this road."

"Hurry, we're losing time," I said.

She jumped out of the Mercedes and jogged back to the boys sitting on their water buffalo. The buffalo studied the new human intruders to their domain, chewing grass along the roadside.

I watched through my rearview mirror as the boys emphatically pointed west, chattering continuously. Hieu showed her smile as she left the relieved boys, who waved at her as if she were an old friend.

"It was good stop. One of the Hummers almost hit the water buffalo at the last bend and took a sharp turn into the ditch to avoid them. The Hummer damage would have been extensive if they hit one of the buffalo. When it left, white smoke was coming from the front."

"They must have damaged the radiator in the ditch and are leaking water, or maybe they damaged the oil pan. They'll not get far without repairs." I jammed the gas pedal down and we accelerated on the road, kicking up gravel and dust behind us. A small river flowed to our right and well below us. We were gaining elevation as the mountain range formed on the horizon. Somewhere ahead, once we reached Cha Vanh, we would find a branch of the Ho Chi Minh Trail leading into Laos and, I hoped, to Ramsey.

On both sides of the road were terraced rice paddies and farm fields with various crops growing among the plateaus that formed before us. Finally, the road ended, and we arrived in Cha Vanh. Ahead toward Laos, various trails climbed and meandered into the hills, mountains, and the surrounding jungle. I slid to a stop as Hieu rushed out of the SUV and started questioning some villagers walking along the road. I had Tho's binoculars and scanned forward, sweeping back and forth—nothing.

Hieu jumped into the Mercedes and a teenager hoped into the back. "John, this is Tram. He knows the trail the Hummers took," she said, her pride visible.

I waved to Tram and said, "*Xin chao*." The boy, shocked by a foreigner saying hello to him in weak Vietnamese, responded with a stare, surprised to see an American so far inland in his tiny village.

"We will take him only as far as the trail he points out. There are many used today by the farmers and rural tribes, most of which are part of the old war trails my countrymen used in the war," Hieu said.

She leaned back and handed Tram 9,000 dong. He grabbed the money, stuffing it in his shirt pocket and returning a grin, minus a few teeth. I estimated that equaled fifty cents in US currency. Hieu explained that for this sixteen-year-old village kid, any money was valuable. His daily existence was dedicated to farming the family's rice paddies and tending the pigs, water buffalo, and the small vegetable gardens. He had received his free, mandatory education from six to eleven years of age, and since his family could not afford to pay for further education, like his older brothers and sisters, he would live at home, farming the land.

Hieu also reaffirmed that but being related to former Viet Cong relatives—his father and grandfather—he could join the army and maybe progress into a different life. I imagined that the village of Cha Vanh existed as a VC and NVA haven during the war, since it so closely bordered the Ho Chi Minh Trail branching from Laos through this area.

Tram babbled joyfully to Hieu, feeling important in helping such an attractive woman, and a high official of the government and a member of the Communist Party. I sensed he knew this could help him to explore another life, another job. I admired the Vietnamese's stoicism and realism. They had seen so much war over their two-thousand-year history that they were realistic about their future. The Yin and Yang of life had been instilled in all of the villagers, almost to a superstitious fault. They prayed to their Buddha or the water, heaven, and forest goddess in the small spiritual houses hanging like bird cages in the banyan trees near their village huts. When Hieu told me that 75 percent of Vietnam's eighty-four million inhabitants were rural, toiling on the land, I better understood how the complex religions and superstitions were part of their makeup.

"We take that right trail that heads north to the river. There is a ford for us to cross. We will drop off Tram there. He says that is the trail the Hummers took just a short time ago. He also saw them drive from the jungle on that same trail up to the village very early this morning when he herded his water buffalo."

Reflecting the sun, gleaming and sparkling above and below us, were more terraced rice paddies. The trails used to access the various garden plots and the forested areas formed and spread out in multiple directions to our front and left. In place since the war ended, no longer camouflaged from American aircraft, the trails were used daily to harvest the land, a peaceful use by the villagers. As we descended down to the shallow river ford, I could see wide, wet, and muddy tracks on the other side; the Hummers had just crossed!

We stopped and let Tram out. He begged Hieu to stay with us. Hieu laughed but ordered him home in crisp phrases. As we drove across the narrow, shallow river, bumping against river rock, I glanced back at Tram standing in his black silk pajamas, waving at us and grinning, a good kid learning to deal with life's harshness. He still stood there when we drove out of the water and proceeded up the inclining trail into the jungle and, we hoped, a passage through the upcoming hills and mountains into Laos.

Hieu, studying her map, continued to instruct me. "That mountain to your left is 2,193 meters high, and the mountain further north, called Mount Atouat, is 2,500 meters high. Both are in Laos, and this old war trail goes between the two."

I converted the meters quickly: Mount Atouat to the north of us scaled over 8,000 feet, and the unnamed mountain to our left, west of us, had to be about 7,100 feet. But now I focused on the trail ahead as it entered jungle canopy, the branches of various bushes scraping the SUV. The Hummers had widened the trail through the dense growth, making it easier for our narrower Mercedes. As the SUV bumped and strained for about a mile, I scanned the surrounding jungle. This trail made an ideal ambush site. My recall of the war didn't help, as the canopy formed by trees filtered out the sunlight, creating shadows and spooks, as if the VC or NVA were watching, lying in wait.

My concern materialized just as I turned left along the bend of the trail and sighted the sandy-colored Hummer; it blocked our route, the hood up. I slammed on the brakes, fishtailing to a stop a hundred feet from the vehicle. Hieu and I stared, frozen in place. We couldn't see any sign of life. It felt wrong! Cursing my slow reaction, I quickly unbuckled my seat belt and pushed Hieu down on her seat, stretching across her, protecting her while I struggled to open her door. I felt her unbuckling her seat belt; she had reacted intuitively, uncomplaining about my weight on top of her.

"Hieu, get out now!" I whispered. I grabbed our backpacks. The door swung open, and we tumbled out together from her passenger side as the first rounds from AK-47s slammed into the front of our Mercedes, shattering parts of the windshield, impacting the front grill. Steam erupted from the radiator and the front tires burst, slamming the front of our SUV hard to the ground. We quickly crawled from our vehicle to the bamboo and elephant grass ten feet from the open passenger door. Hidden in the jungle growth, holding onto our AK-47s we donned our backpacks. Hieu had the foresight to grab the hand mic, stretching its bungee-like cord and contacted Tho about the ambush, whispering into the handset the whole time, she told him that we had met the enemy! Another burst of bullets hit the SUV and sprayed more windshield glass around us. We quickly crawled to the rear and away from the damaged vehicle, its steam and smoke helping to conceal us.

The ambushers were somewhere to our left, firing from the slope above the trail. Hieu and I continued to crawl from our vehicle. Hidden from the shooters by the trees and the curve of the trail, we entered the jungle to the left of our SUV and ascended up the slight slope, while looking for the flashes and listening for the familiar pop, pop, pop of the AK-47s. We had been able to move perpendicular to our ruined Mercedes, looking down at it now and seeing the Hummer as well. Another burst of rounds slammed into our Mercedes, this time igniting something. Dark, oily smoke curled upward as a small fire erupted underneath it. I thought I spotted where the rounds came from and touched Hieu's left arm, signaling her to follow me further up the slope and away from the burning Mercedes. We crab-walked some fifty feet, amazingly making little noise. I once again felt at home in this ungodly dense jungle, like the insects and monkeys that were chirping and chattering, spooked by the noise and smell of battle that their relatives had experienced so many years ago.

I whispered, "Hieu, stay here and cover me while I climb the slope another twenty feet. I think there are two of them and they might think we're dead. Let's catch them in our sights as they attempt to return to the road."

She nodded, released the safety on her AK-47, got into a prone firing position and pointed her rifle in the general direction of the last fired rounds. Her dark eyes showed no emotion; her face turned deadly serious. I quietly moved further up the slope, well hidden by the jungle. In a few minutes I had reached an even higher position that overlooked both the Hummer and our damaged SUV. I released the safety on the AK-47, sat down into a firing position, and waited. They had to make their move soon.

Another burst by two AK-47s sprayed bullets around our burning vehicle. Those had to be their insurance shots. They must have assumed that they had killed or wounded us, and plus, without our Mercedes they had stopped us from pursuing them.

A twig snapped, and then I saw him as he walked in a slouch from the vegetation down to the Hummer. The Cambodian looked around, staring intently in all directions, then finally stood erect and yelled back up the slope. Standing, cocksure of himself, he went over to the Hummer and slammed its hood down, locking it in place with the hood straps. Leaving the door open, he started the Hummer, its engine running rough but still functioning. He got out, stood by the driver door looking up the incline, and again yelled to his friend. Then I saw the second guy, barely forty feet away from me. He stood up and began a noisy descent through the trees and bushes, branches swinging, brushing him as he rushed to the trail.

I looked to Hieu, who stared at me, waiting, and gave her a hand signal to shoot the driver. She turned from me, pointing her rifle just as the driver looked back at our burning Mercedes. A short burst of five or six rounds emitted from her AK-47, and I watched the driver collapse facedown onto the trail; all bullets hit him chest high.

I swung my AK-47 toward the other man, who stopped, frozen in place. Confused, he started to crouch down; I shot him with a burst of rounds, pointed lower than normal, trying to avoid overshooting on this slope. The Cambodian, his face expressing disbelief, dropped his weapon but still stood, now a few feet from his dead or dying partner on the trail. I emptied the rest of my magazine into him—another twenty rounds. I knew I hit him the first time, but with the trees and bushes deflecting rounds, I had no read on how much damage I had done to him. He jerked forward toward the Hummer, falling facedown, head slamming onto the exposed part of the trail.

Hieu and I rushed from our hiding places in staggered moves, constantly checking the terrain for anyone else, covering each other. When I reached the man that I shot, I turned him over. His stomach and groin areas were pulverized. I had over-killed. Hieu stepped past me and looked down at her kill, who was barely breathing. Turning him onto his back, she saw that her rounds had hit the driver in a tight circle on his chest. He murmured, wanting to live, fighting death. But from my combat days, I knew the battle had ended for him. Still, the guilt nagged at me, and I thought of pulling out my first-aid pouch. Hieu acted before I did. She withdrew her nine millimeter and in one fluid motion pointed and shot the dying man in the head. Flashes of NVA soldiers who finished the kill on dying Americans after an ambush flooded over me.

Hieu shouldered her pistol and waited for me to say something, looking at me intently. It was a mercy killing, but that didn't make it any easier. I searched her tired face and saw the sad expression; it would have been her first kill. I ached for her. Her life had changed today, forever. I hoped she wouldn't have nightmares over this, as I did over my war kills. It now became my turn to act human, and I put my arm around her. I felt her slight shudder. She didn't resist; her hurt was real. The insanity of this operation had reached its peak here in the Laotian jungle. Slowly, I released her.

"Ramsey and Loan must be further ahead. I'm assuming they are the only ones left," I said, hoping to bring her back to focus on catching the two.

She nodded, glancing one more time at the two dead men near our feet. I collected the remaining magazines of ammunition and the AK-47s from the dead men, throwing them into the Hummer. Hieu reloaded my AK-47 first, then hers, and climbed into the Hummer's passenger side. The acrid smoke from the smoldering oil, plastic, and electric wiring of our damaged Mercedes stung my eyes. Larger flames erupted. I jumped into the driver seat, with my backpack on and shifted the transmission into low gear. Wary and uncertain of what faced us ahead, our confiscated Hummer crawled down the trail toward what I knew would be the final phase of our manhunt. The end had to be near.

LAOS, JANUARY 27, 2003

Fifteen minutes later, we had driven three miles when we passed another branch of the Ho Chi Minh Trail headed north, further into Northern Laos and eventually Northern Vietnam and then China. I made a mental note of it since it showed a prominent trail, which could be used as an escape route for us—my own military contingency planning. Hieu, looking at the old war maps, explained that the trail we were following would angle south, and by the fresh tire tracks, we knew Ramsey had taken it. The broken tree branches and torn brush that we passed provided further confirmation. By all indications, they headed toward the main highway in Southern Laos that would lead them to Pakxe and eventual escape.

We ate power bars and drank from our bottles of water as we cautiously followed the trail; we still had reserves for each of us in the backpacks we wore, ready for quick exit from the Hummer. By noon, I felt the physical and mental exertion from doing battle with the Cambodians and chasing Ramsey. Hieu and I agreed that the next confrontation would be as deadly as the last one. Our only hope of surprise depended on using the captured Hummer to fool Ramsey into thinking we were his men returning from ambushing the pursuing Vietnamese police.

Ramsey placed those two men to gain more time and distance for himself and Loan. Since we didn't hear or see the Hummer as we chugged along on the trail, I worried that the delay had allowed Ramsey to escape. The Hummer's engine rumbled sluggishly, and I saw the temperature gauge steadily move from the green zone toward red. The coolant had leaked to a dangerous level, and we would have to stop at the first stream or pool of water. As if on cue, I heard a small stream ahead, and then Hieu pointed out the water cascading over boulders and rocks. On the map, her fingers showed me a large open area with a stream in the middle: an old NVA staging area on the Ho Chi Minh Trail.

"We are definitely in Laos, John," Hieu said. She didn't hide her nervousness.

"Are we in trouble with the Laotian government?"

"Possibly—but there are few border patrols here," Hieu said, now an accomplice in an international border violation.

"I don't have a visa for Laos," I chuckled.

Hieu stared at me, not saying anything, but her face had softened.

The stream flowed ahead and to the right; sunlight emitted from the large open space as the jungle canopy over our trail ended abruptly and we entered the clearing's edge. I stopped the vehicle, mesmerized by the vast area ahead of us, about three hundred feet long and two hundred feet wide, with destroyed fighting bunkers made of logs and sandbags scattered along the cliff to our left. Overhead, nothing but blue sky welcomed us to this former NVA refuge. Ahead old log poles protruded from the ground at skewed angles, remnants of torn, rotten camouflage nets flapping in the slight breeze, deteriorating since the war's end. B-52 bomb craters pockmarked the ground and the cliff, reminding me of that old war.

Then I saw the fourth and final Hummer parked at the far end of the clearing, enclosed in the shade of bamboo and banyan trees where the trail continued south through the dense jungle. I braked the hummer to a stop and continued to stare through the windshield. Two trailers were parked side by side, behind the Hummer.

"Ramsey used this location as his staging area," I said.

Hieu didn't respond; she focused on the scene in front of us.

At the far edge of this clearing, about three hundred feet from us, an Asian sat on the Hummer's bumper, with an American standing on the hood above him. Both looked in our direction with binoculars. They saw us!

I grabbed my binoculars and scanned the standing man; Ramsey! He jumped off the hood and yelled to the other man, who stood up and ran back to the rear of their Hummer.

"Hieu, they know we're not their men. Get out of the Hummer."

An RPG, smoke streaming behind it, wobbled toward us. Hieu had barley opened her door as I pushed myself out the driver side when the rocket slammed into the ground short of the Hummer's grill, exploding, lifting the front end of the vehicle into the air. Smoke engulfed me, noise rang in my ears, lights flashed in my eyes. I hit the ground hard, rolling on my left side while the front of the Hummer finally dropped, hitting the ground with a screeching metallic thud. The dying beast settled on its four tires, groaning. A direct hit would have killed us. I scurried away.

"Hieu," I shouted. She moaned. I crawled madly around the back of the smoking vehicle to the passenger side. She hung upside down from the cab, a limp rag doll, her left foot jammed under the seat and her head barely touching the ground.

Her ashen face told me she was in shock. I touched her left leg and she moaned. Regaining consciousness, she shook her head. "I think . . . is broken," she said, breathing heavily. I raised my head, looking through the dissipating smoke, and saw both Ramsey and Loan, older now than in Nam, but it was them. They approached, walking spaced apart from each other, Uzis at the ready. They hadn't crossed the small stream, which flowed about two hundred feet from us. I took my AK-47 and shot one short burst at them, missing them but forcing them to scatter and hit the ground. Taking a deep breath to counter my adrenalin, then releasing it slowly, I pointed my AK-47 at their parked Hummer and squeezed a burst at the front tires. After pausing for a second, I fired another volley. I heard both tires pop and saw the heavy front end sink to the ground, resting on its wheels, tires flat. For good measure, I shot a longer burst at the front grill. At this distance I had no clue as to the real damage I inflicted to their Hummer, but Ramsey and company would not be driving it any time soon due to the flats. Bullets from their Uzis started to clink against our immobilized Hummer.

Ducking lower, I focused on Hieu and said, "Hold your breath— this will hurt."

I reached under the cushion and found that her left leg had wedged under the metal frame of her seat. It was broken, but thankfully I didn't find protruding bone from a compound fracture. I firmly held her leg and pulled it out in one motion. She screamed.

"I'm sorry, Hieu." I looked down at her crumpled body; she had passed out.

Hearing Hieu scream, Ramsey and Loan paused in their flanking attempt. They must have thought they had hit someone with their Uzis, and it had to be obvious to them the RPG explosion made the Hummer inoperable.

I had only one choice—retreat on foot using the smoke around our Hummer to conceal our escape. I slung both our rifles over my back, straps diagonally crossing the chest, lifted Hieu into my arms, and hustled down the trail we had just driven, following it, hoping to reach the northern branch of the Ho Chi Minh Trail that we had passed minutes ago.

Hieu remained unconscious. She weighed slightly over a hundred pounds, and I had to carry her to the other trail before Ramsey discovered we had escaped. My legs moved in a steady jog paced for our combined weight, years of exercise paying off. I needed to find cover and concealment in order to check Hieu's wound before I could plan my next move. The heat and humidity began to wear on me, but I kept at my pace; it meant life and death now, and I had to save Hieu. The minutes seemed like hours, but I pushed on. I didn't risk stopping. Then I saw the opening of the northern trail and turned left onto it, jogging for another five minutes, soaked in my sweat. I scanned both sides of the trail and finally found what I needed, barely visible, about thirty feet off the trail: an old NVA bunker cave. I pounded up the slight slope and entered the cave. I set Hieu down and covered the entrance with dead branches I found on the slope. It would have to do for now.

Back in the cave I laid Hieu on her back, pulled my knife from the backpack, and cut the left leg of her jeans along the seams. Her entire leg below the kneecap looked terrible—black and blue and severely swollen. The shin looked deformed; she moaned with pain. I had to get splints in place to support her leg. I worked feverishly. Pulling my extra white T-shirt from my backpack, I ripped it into strips and then set her left leg as straight as possible. Barely conscious, Hieu whimpered in pain as I wrapped the large-sized cotton dressing from the medical kit for additional support. Then quickly I placed several small bamboo stems that I gathered in the cave on top of the dressing and wrapped these splints tightly with the cotton T-shirt strips. The improvised cast would work temporarily.

"Hieu, can you hear me?" I said, coaxing her, lightly shaking her.

She opened her eyes, still wincing from the pain, having endured a lot while I administered my limited first aid. I looked in the medical kit and found morphine syrettes, like we used in the war, and injected one into her left thigh. She glared at me, feeling the prick of the needle. I smiled at her, glad to have her conscious.

"I hate needles—where are . . . ?" She asked, scowling.

I explained our bunker. She shook her head, telling me to leave her and get help.

"Not leaving you, dear. I don't want those jerks to capture you."

"I can fight . . . "

"With one good leg and drugged—forget it."

Nonsensical chatter emitted from her as the morphine kicked in. I searched in the medical kit, pulled out a packet of penicillin tablets, and had her take one, forcing her to drink slowly from a bottle of water.

"They probably are escaping anyway . . . " she said incoherently.

"No—I ruined that for them. I shot out their tires," I said, covering her with the space blanket I found in her backpack. "Now I forced them to fight us."

Hieu gave a drugged smile, staring off somewhere. Then she faded into sleep. Outside, afternoon monsoon clouds darkened the sky. Rain now hit the ground and jungle growth, savagely pelting the leaves, a cacophony outside, while Hieu shuddered in her stupor as I held her tight, trying to warm her.

They would be seeking shelter as well, so I had time to let Hieu rest. Ramsey had two choices: repair his Hummer and flee out of Laos or seek and kill us.

The gold no longer existed; his crew had been eliminated; he and Loan were alone. A rational man would try to escape. Could Ramsey be rational? I couldn't take that chance, not with Hieu wounded. I had to protect her. In order to do that, I knew I had to get to Ramsey and Loan first.

I didn't like this decision but letting Ramsey bolt would also negate my revenge for Sally's father. I couldn't allow that either. My plan counted on him believing that we had retreated, lulling him into a false sense of security to repair his Hummer and then escape the clearing.

The monsoon rain continued to pour outside, the noise growing, a crescendo, echoing in our cave. I dug out the aluminum case from my backpack and retrieved the satellite phone. Thankful that I kept it fully charged, I positioned the case's lid with the built-in antenna toward the cave's entrance and dialed Woodruff's number as I checked on Hieu's sleeping. It was 2:16 p.m. in Nam, and it would be 2:16 a.m. in Washington, DC; I hoped he would answer quickly. The phone rang several times before his groggy voice came through.

"John, is everything OK?" Woodruff sounded genuinely concerned.

"No! Can you GPS this phone and pass on the location to our friend Colonel Zang so that he can guide a Captain Tho to me and my wounded partner?"

"Shit, John, yes, hell . . . yes, but what is happening? Who is wounded?"

"No time to explain. My partner and I are in danger. Just get the grid location to the Vietnamese ASAP! Also, there is a Major Han who will know how to contact Captain Tho. Zang should know all this. But for god's sake, hurry!"

"OK. Leave the phone on. I'll get the ball rolling. Is Ramsey nearby? How about Loan?"

"Yes to both, but I'm going after them now." I heard the rain stop—a momentary break. "My partner is at this grid location. Leaving the phone on for her, but she is in a bad way. Had to drug her with morphine, so be patient with her." Finally, I said, "One more thing, James, just two of them are left—Ramsey and Loan. If I don't make it, please get them. Have to move out now."

I heard the tension as he said, "John . . ." Ignoring him I carefully put the phone into its case, the line still open. Hieu stirred, trying to come out of sleep.

"John?" she asked, trying to focus, leaning toward me.

"Wake up, Hieu." I shook her lightly. With her eyes wide open now, she nodded. "Stay in the cave and out of the rain. You should be safe and dry in here. Keep your weapons near you. There is a James Woodruff on the satellite phone, and he will get ahold of Captain Tho. When you are able talk to him."

"Where are you going?" She said. I could see the worried look.

"Hunting," I said.

She understood and tried to get up. "John, no—wait until Tho arrives, then we can go together."

"No time. Tho has a rough drive on the muddy trail in this monsoon, and our damaged Mercedes is blocking the trail, which will delay him further. But I will be back. Stay alert and watch for me. And stay still. Your leg is broken."

She tried to smile but touched my arm instead. "Please be careful."

"Oh, yes, watch over my baseball cap. I will need it when I get back so that Captain Tho will recognize me," I said, a wide grin spread on my face. I handed her the cap as she tried to smile, despite her pain.

Leaving both backpacks with her, carrying three extra thirty-round magazines for my AK-47 in my big shirt pockets, as well as extra magazines for my .45, I slipped out of the cave as the rain returned, a typical monsoon, steadily drenching the jungle. I checked the trail and the jungle surrounding it. There were no signs of anyone. I moved into the jungle, paralleling the trail, stopping regularly to listen for the enemy. I headed toward the southern trail we had driven with the Hummer earlier, watching for Ramsey and his partner. I ensured that my holstered pistol had a round chambered. Checking my AK-47, a full thirty-round magazine inserted, round in the chamber and safety off, I proceeded further into the dripping jungle.

ༀ

Seeing the southern trail through the palm fronds about eighty feet from me, I turned right, staying concealed in the jungle, moving unseen and parallel to the path, creeping toward the large clearing ahead that I hoped Ramsey still occupied. Now soaking wet, I stumbled through the dense growth, the rain-plastered leaves pouring more water on me as I pushed on. The stench of the moldering jungle floor, many years in the making, swallowed me. I stumbled through the vines, creepers, and palm fronds entangling me as cicadas sang, disturbed by this alien in their domain. The tall bamboo shoots, almost tiny forests, detoured me, costing me precious time. Breathing became harder, but the exertion gave me some warmth against the damp cold.

Hurrying to make up time, I blindly stepped over a fallen dead tree and sank to my armpits into a stagnant pond camouflaged with dead leaves, hanging vines, debris, and bamboo; I gasped as the cold water surged around me while the bottom, with its gripping mud, sucked me down. Defenseless against Ramsey if he found me now, I panicked and fought the muck, stirring the water, strengthening the mud's grip on me. Exhausted within minutes, barely able to stand neck deep in the brackish water, I stopped. Shuddering from the wet, growing cold, I took deep breathes, allowing a calmer me to regain control, returning to my past jungle instincts and experiences honed by war.

Looking above, I saw tree vines dangling over my head and lurched for them. The first ones I grasped broke, and I sunk back into the water, the ooze covering my head. Surfacing, I took a deep breath, looking for more vines. Recognizing a live one, I reached up and grasped it. It held firm, supporting my weight as I slowly pulled myself out of the water. Checking my watch, I saw that it had been over thirty minutes since I left Hieu in the bunker. I finally crawled out of the torpid water, reaching the other side of the small swamp. On more solid ground, soaked and exhausted, I stayed facedown for several minutes, ignoring the few insects that discovered me, impervious to their bites. I felt colder on my right side and finally noticed that I had toppled onto a tiny feeder stream that flowed to the swamp. I shivered, forcing circulation in my tired body, as the water I dammed with my prone body flowed around and over me. I loosened my grip on the AK-47, still by my side but covered with mud—a weapon that would fire despite this condition. I grunted with satisfaction that my military training never let me lose my rifle. It was a good sign that I had not totally lost it. I stayed prone, breathing deeply, my lungs screaming for more oxygen; my leg and arm muscles felt like mush. Slowly, I rolled onto my back.

I tried brushing off the tenacious insects stuck to my face; my fingers mingled with soft, fleshy creatures stuck to my dirty, wet face. Christ! Leaches! They were gorging on my blood, enjoying their feast as I slowly and carefully pulled several from my face and neck; they disgusted me. Then I reached into my pants and pulled one sucking on my thigh. My aversion to leeches, like childhood nightmares, hadn't changed since my time in the jungles of the Vietnam War where I first encountered them.

Finally, I stood on wobbly legs and scanned the drenched forest, listening through the thunder of approaching monsoon clouds; no sign of my enemy appeared. But the howling monkeys sounded their approval of me getting up.

Exhaustion had taken over, physically and mentally. The wetness and accompanying cold temperature deteriorated my condition, but I had no choice—I had to press on. Hunching down, I pushed and battled through the dense underbrush for another twenty minutes until I spied the RPG-damaged Hummer through the trees to my left. Dropping into a crawl, I eased forward through the slimy muck of dead plants and the mud of the jungle floor, regularly scanning to my sides, front, and rear. Slithering to within forty feet of the Hummer, I discovered the shadow of someone in it, staying dry despite the damaged windshield and front end, his bundled face pointed to the rear of the vehicle, waiting, probably armed with his Uzi. I couldn't recognize his face—but assumed it was Loan. A small garter snake slithered over my hand and I jerked up. And just as quickly, I hugged the ground, hoping the incoming thunder and lightning covered my stupid reaction to the snake.

I crawled to my right and found a small opening through the underground brush, an opportunity to observe the other Hummer at the far end of the large, open clearing. Ramsey worked in the mud with the right front tire jacked up, bolting on lug nuts. I mused that they could replace the front tires with the spares from my damaged Hummer as well as Ramsey's Hummer. I had bought time by shooting the tires earlier. I now knew that he prepared to escape. And I had to stop him.

Ramsey still had to replace the left front tire and wheel, and its replacement leaned against the front bumper of his Hummer. Making my decision, I crawled back toward the Hummer with Loan in it. He still did not know of my presence, calmly sitting in the cab looking back toward the trail. With the sun blocked by the growing monsoon clouds, it had gotten cooler, and my energy continued to drop; it had to be now. I slowly progressed toward Loan, taking another ten minutes to crawl closer, quietly. Barely twenty feet away, I stopped, laid down my AK-47, and pulled my .45 from its holster. Holding it with both hands, I aimed it at Loan's head.

The rain had settled into a steady drizzle; water combined with the mud on my face and oozed into my eyes, stinging and clouding them. Losing more of my humanity, I pulled the trigger. Loan slumped as his head dropped forward. The side windows, clouded from all the moisture, blocked me from seeing any blood or brain matter exploding in the cab.

Holstering my pistol, I grabbed my AK-47 and jumped up. I ran into the large opening, passing the damaged vehicle, ignoring my kill. The war's nightmare returned: *Charging with my men to retake the battered landing zone, stumbling over dead bodies of both sides as the monsoon wind and rain slashed through our ranks, slowing our progress, limiting both sides from seeing, allowing only blind killing.* I forced myself to sprint toward the area where Ramsey struggled to repair his Hummer, my AK-47 set on fully automatic. The element of surprise had disappeared when I fired my pistol, killing Loan. Ramsey seemed confused, trying to locate the direction of the gunfire, muffled by the thundering monsoon and the jungle vegetation. The heavy rain roiled with a vengeance, following me, immersing me, racing ahead, as we both sped toward Ramsey.

Ramsey finally spotted me, but his Uzi must have been in the cab, kept dry from the rains. He dropped the lug nut wrench and rushed to the cab. I ran toward him with my AK-47 at hip level, squeezing off short bursts. The slugs hit the Hummer, blew out the tire Ramsey had replaced, and clipped him in his legs. He dropped short of reaching the open door, but he was not done yet. He pulled himself to the right front fender, and his hand reached for the Glock holstered on his hip, pulled it out taking aim at me.

Shots rang out. I ran a zigzag pattern, shooting short bursts, closing to less than a hundred feet from him. My breathing labored. My adrenalin waned as my legs churned in the mud, its grip trying to hold me. The monsoon's growing wind and rain buffeted me in all directions, keeping clothes wet and saturated, adding more weight for my burning muscles to support. My pace slowed to a stutter step. I kept mumbling to myself, "Move it. Move it . . . " I lost momentum. I saw lightning flashes; the hard thunder echoed around me. I struggled forward until the burning pain in my left shoulder surprised me. The bullet imploded, jerking me to the left with searing pain, shoving me to my knees.

I looked toward Ramsey, who held his Glock in his right hand; the surprised look on his face confused me. He lowered his pistol as I fell face forward into the mud. I knew this would be my epitaph: "I returned to Nam to die." It was my destiny, with all my nightmares, all the emotional pain.

I screamed as I felt the boot, crunching into the wound, rolling me over. The rain cleared some of the mud from my eyes as I stared into the face of Colonel Loan!

Numb, I pushed up from the mud, leaving my rifle to settle into the muck. He kicked me back down onto my back. I screamed from the pain.

"Ah, our Captain Moore. So long since our days in Saigon, where my men failed to end your life. You are hard to kill. Now, obviously I failed in North Carolina." Standing over me with his ugly smirk, he raised his Glock, pointing to my head. "Age has impacted my shooting skills. If I were younger, my first bullet would have found a more critical spot. I would love to chat, but as you can see, we are in much hurry."

I closed my eyes, knowing I would die. I heard the shot, but still only felt my left shoulder throbbing. Then my shoulder burst into fresh excruciating pain as weight collapsed on me and my left side. I opened my eyes and stared into Loan's bloody face, inches from my face, a bullet hole centered in his forehead.

With my waning strength, I pushed him off of me and leaned on my right elbow, pushing myself up, turning my head toward Ramsey. Wiping Loan's blood off my face, I drew out my .45 and slogged toward Ramsey, shuddering, bleeding. I stopped ten feet from him. He held his pistol as he looked at me. Then he threw it forward into the mud. "That was my last round, Moore," he said, breathing heavily, bloody froth on his lips.

Mechanically, I released the safety on my .45. I looked down at him, pointing my weapon to the ground. In front of him his empty Glock sank in the mud, acknowledging his defeat. He placed his hands on his abdomen in submission. Approaching closer, I saw his wounds; both his ankles were bloody from my AK-47 rounds, mostly grazing shots, but the killing shot impacted his lower abdomen, where more blood flowed.

Rasping, he said, "I always did hate Loan." A slight smile came up. He moaned and looked confused.

"Why did you save me?" I asked.

"Why? You didn't deserve to die by that piece of shit," he gasped. His moans reached a new level, the cold rain and mud not helping his wounds. "That crazy fuck, Loan. I never ordered . . . hit on you."

"Where's your first-aid pack? I'll inject some morphine until I get medical help." I lowered myself to my knees beside him, holstering my pistol.

"Too late for me . . . " he said. A bolt of lightning hit a banyan tree several hundred feet up the slope. The smell of smoke and acrid ozone filtered through the rain to us. "I had no goddamn beef with you. Loan . . . the crazy bastard. Got Reed drunk and helped him commit suicide. Against my orders." Ramsey groaned. He grunted, and his eyes took on lost look, the same thousand-mile stare that my grunts had worn after combat, bloodied from battle.

Ignoring him, I made my way to the Hummer's cab and dug through the glove compartment, finding the first-aid kit. Back with Ramsey, I wrapped the abdominal bandage around his gut wound, which oozed blood mixed with mud. I stuck the only morphine syrette from the kit into his stomach muscles, hoping to reduce his horrendous pain.

"You're dying . . ." I said, bewildered. Then I had to ask. "Woodruff had said that you ordered the hit on me?"

"No. There's no reason. God, I'm going to die . . ." The morphine started to quell his pain.

During Nam, I saw my share of young Americans dying from severe gut wounds, knowing they had little time to live, begging for relief from their agony. Sometimes the medic would administer excess morphine to ease the dying. The "dust-off" helicopter could not save them.

Ramsey moaned irregularly as the pain pulsated. I felt sad. The killings he had committed in the war earned him no leniency, but he had saved my life today. I had no hate left for him.

"This gold . . . should have known Hung had found it after Loan and I abandoned him in 1975. The fucker got his revenge." He took a deep breath. "Motherfucker is smart—lured us back for revenge because we abandoned him . . . but I never shared where we had it buried."

"Thanks for saving my life," I said as I plopped down next to him. I shuddered from my wound and knew I needed help too. We both were pathetic, talking like comrades in arms.

He gave a curt nod. "I won't kill myself. Don't believe in that suicide shit . . . You need to do this. The morphine will wear off soon," he said as a sob broke out.

"I . . ."

He ignored my concerns. "Look, you have to know this. Woodruff has it in for me. Wants me dead to tidy things up at the agency. I know shit that will end his fucking career . . . Political asshole . . ."

"What is. . ."

"You'll find files in my briefcase in the Hummer. Don't let Woodruff get them . . . they are the only copies left, and the proof," he said, whining as I eased him to a prone position. Sitting was now unbearable for him.

"Look, Moore," he said, breathing harder, "there's one more thing. Tin wanted to kill me during the war because I lost control, lost my morals when I killed his mother during an interrogation. I have always regretted that deeply . . . but we were after him, a very high-ranking officer in the NVA . . . "

"Shit, that helicopter episode—you wanted to kill Tin before he killed you?"

He nodded. "You fucked it all up by being fucking ethical. The cowboy in the white hat."

"You could have had him killed in the POW camp at Camh Ranh Bay," I said.

"I planned on doing it that week. But . . . the next fucking night, an NVA commando unit sneaked into Cam Ranh Bay . . . they shelled with mortars and rockets to cover them and freed Tin and his lieutenant. The fucking ARVN soldiers were probably bribed to help them."

I pushed myself up. "I need to get help for you. I'll get medics." My own mind started to lose the battle to stay rational.

"Moore quit fooling yourself. I will die, and the pain is growing . . . won't be able to stand it. Please just do it, goddamn it. I deserve to die. Saving your life earns me that. We have a history . . . and I can't die by Vietnamese hands. They will make me suffer . . . "

He closed his eyes. I drew my pistol out as I stood, trying to keep it dry, knowing it was futile. The rain pelted us in horizontal sheets as the monsoon continued to gather strength, forcing me to dig my spread feet into the mud and lock my knees. Shivers ran through my left arm, the wound burning as I leaned into the buffeting, twirling wind. Ramsey opened his eyes, and for a moment I sensed he felt relieved. I pointed my pistol at him.

"This war fucked us both, Moore. Do you have nightmares of the dead, of those you killed?" He looked at me, waiting. His eyes needed confirmation.

"Yes . . . " I said, shuddering.

"Well, I dream everyday of those Vietnamese I killed, kids, even babies. I . . . " he paused. "Glad you are here to end it. You know my PTSD. You were there with me. You have the same shit as I do. We're going to hell . . . "

I stood confused, holding the pistol, waiting. The relentless monsoon continued to beat us as I stared at Ramsey. His eyes fluttered, his pain excruciating. Our physical and mental misery bonded us in the land where it all started over thirty years ago. Somehow, I wanted him to live. Damaged from serving in Nam, I understood him now. I believed him. He never ordered the hit on me. Loan did the shooting on his own, and yet the CIA led me along—but for what reason? Why did Zang, Tin, and Woodruff so desperately want me in Vietnam?

Ramsey nodded to me, moaning more; his eyes closed once again, the pain horrible on his contorted face. I steadied my pistol.

"Look, maybe we can save you," I said, my mind confusing me again.

"Too late, Moore. Pull the damn trigger. It's the only way."

I squeezed the trigger. The boom rang loudly in the clearing. The harsh rain pummeled my back, and I shivered violently. I bent over and checked his pulse: dead. I thought I noticed a thin smile on his face, maybe contentment or relief. Standing over his body splayed in the mud, my body shook, wounded, cold, wet, exhausted. I had remorse for killing him, even if it had been a mercy killing. The NVA also killed their dying to ease the suffering—their medical support rudimentary compared to the American's. He would have died anyway, but I hated to see him suffer any more. I wasn't any different than an NVA officer putting his critically wounded personnel out of their misery.

And in the back of my mind, I felt betrayed by Woodruff and Tin. I turned and walked over to Loan's body, bent down, and checked his pulse. Ramsey's shot definitely killed him. As I stood again, I looked down at Loan, the blood on his head still being washed away by the rain. He looked as evil as he acted in life. His rodent features caused me to shiver. I turned to look at Ramsey's body. Vietnam had cost me mentally, had cost us all.

I needed medical attention now more than ever, or I would join Ramsey and Loan. The depleted first-aid pack that I found for Ramsey could not help me. Our first-aid kits were back in the cave with Hieu, so I ripped a section of my shirt and tied it around my wound. The bleeding had slowed, but exposure to the elements, especially the mud seeping down my arm, worried me. I would need help soon, before I went into shock from infection. If the bullet had lodged in my shoulder, against the bone, I would be in more trouble. If I could get back to Hieu, she could help tend to my wound. Stopping first to pick up my muddy AK-47, I turned and slowly forced my legs to walk out of the clearing. "A soldier never leaves his rifle," I mumbled to myself, sloshing toward the trail, past the Hummer with piled clothing that deceived me into believing Loan sat there. The fork of the trail that headed north to our little cave seemed an eternity away; my mind kept pushing my body despite its wretched condition. The darkness increased. My watch showed after five; I had been away from the cave and in the cold, soaking rain for three hours.

The settling dusk cut my visibility, and I had to stay focused or I would miss my trail. What Ramsey had said made sense and made me feel used. I forced myself forward, shuffling, my energy waning. It seemed I'd been walking forever when I finally reached the correct path. Feverish, aching, I pushed on until I found the slope to the bunker's opening. The monsoon downpour drowned my weak call to Hieu.

"Hieu, it's John," I shouted once more as I cautiously crept to the opening. Slowly sticking my head into the darkness, I spied a smiling Hieu as she put down her nine millimeter.

Her condition looked bad as well. Shivering, she said, "I am sleepy and so cold." But when she saw me, completely mud streaked, wet, bleeding from my makeshift bandage, she reacted. "Turn your left side to me." She opened the first-aid kit and began work on the bullet wound.

"We need to get warm." I sat down by her catching my breath, shaking badly, my left arm shooting bolts of pain that added to my misery, my body sinking fast.

Hieu discovered that the Glock slug had gone through my shoulder muscle, but it had done a job on the tissue. She cleaned the wound and wrapped a bandage around the shoulder. I took a penicillin pill and then checked on her broken left leg, ensuring the makeshift cast still held in place.

As we tended to each other, I gave her the details of what had happened in the clearing; neither one of us seemed elated over our survival. We had reached our limits.

I listened to Hieu explain using the satellite phone after I had departed to battle with Ramsey and Loan. How Woodruff had relayed between Tho and Colonel Zang. With the heavy monsoon rains flooding the streams and the trails, plus the darkness of night approaching, Tho and his team were stuck at the village of Cha Vanh. Colonel Zang had sent the cave's GPS coordinates to Tho; we just had to wait out the night since the storm prevented further help.

After I gathered some dry palm and banyan leaves close to the cave's entrance, we were able to make a decent covering of layered leaves over the dirt floor. In my weak condition, I still managed to move Hieu onto the cushioned pile of leaves, then I settled next her. To warm us, she embraced me with her arms, and I placed my head on her chest, becoming sleepy, wrapped in the only space blanket we had. I tried to stay awake with my right arm around her as she trembled from the cold and pain of her broken leg; my left arm was held tightly to my chest but pressed against her. Those were my last thoughts as my devastated body surrendered to sleep in the cold night.

DA NANG, JANUARY 28–31, 2003

Before dawn on the twenty-eighth, I heard the loud engines of two Hummers approaching, scraping tree branches on the trail to our old NVA bunker. Hieu still lay next to me; her warmth felt comfortable. I knew it had to be Captain Tho and woke her up.

The vehicles stopped by the cave's opening. Tho shouted, "Captain Moore! Agent Hieu? Are you in there?"

I yelled, "We're here."

I accepted Tho's use of Captain Moore for me, although it meant little anymore. On the other hand Hieu had started calling me John and that felt good.

I crawled out as Tho reached me and helped me out. The medic examined my left shoulder and arm, approving of Hieu's temporary fix. But as he felt my brow, he shook his head. My fever had grown, and I barely could stand. I briefed Tho on Hieu's condition and went back into the cave to help retrieve her and our stuff. The medic set a stretcher out for her, then did the heavy lifting of her out of the cave. Then some soldiers helped the medic put her on the stretcher. In the morning light filtering through the canopy, she radiated a simple beauty even with the facial cuts from the Hummer's exploding windshield. My wounded shoulder prevented me helping to load her into the closer parked Hummer. I crawled into the vehicle after her, tossing our back-packs into the rear of the truck. Tho sent us back to Cha Vanh with the driver and the medic, where a helicopter waited to airlift us to Da Nang. This time the Vietnamese respected the Laotian territorial border. I glanced at our destroyed Mercedes shoved off the trail as we churned by it; the freshly dug graves of the two dead Cambodians near the wreckage reminded me how close to death Hieu and I had come.

Captain Tho remained with his men to sanitize the area. I showed him on Hieu's map where to find Ramsey and Loan's bodies. Later I would learn they took Loan's body back to Vietnam. Proof that the war criminal had been killed. They buried Ramsey in the jungle, conceal-ing his grave, thus inhibiting any questions about the dead American.

Hieu stayed quiet on the flight, falling in and out of sleep, while I stayed awake from my shoulder surging with pain. Seeing my wound bleeding again since it had opened, I knew that an infection had taken hold. The Vietnamese doctors in Da Nang stood at the helicopter pad, rushing to treat us as soon as we unloaded from the helicopter. When they wheeled us into the hospital, we were side by side on the two gurneys, incoherent and unable to focus on our surroundings.

Since the infection got worse, the doctors had to operate on the shoulder to clean it out, stuffing me with antibiotics. All the while, I stayed on a morphine drip that kept me in a dream world. My weak-ened body had surrendered to the doctors. I thought Hieu sat by me late that night, holding my hand. I tried to smile, but the narcotics spaced me out. In my delusion, she seemed real, her smile and her tears. It left me hoping that she had been there. However realistic the vision, it all became a dream as I lay in my stupor.

The next morning, the doctors worked on me again; my fever had scared them. I intermittently heard Hieu's voice in the room, her authority resounded as the nurses and doctors scurried, arguing with her. I passed into euphoria from the morphine and slept through the morning, leaving the pain behind.

When I woke, Tho stood by my bed. My dry mouth said some-thing to him.

"It is January 29, and close to 1500 hours. How do you feel, Mr. Moore?" Tho said.

"Like a drug user . . . a bad headache . . . "

He nodded and then briefed me. "Hieu's leg is set and will heal with no limp. She flew back to Hanoi this morning with Major Han." Tho laughed as he described Hieu's anger; she grew upset that she had to leave me behind. But Major Han wouldn't budge.

I smiled at Hieu's stubbornness, but she needed to return to Hanoi and brief the top brass. Her career had been given a boost; the mission had been completed, and she needed to receive the accolades for it. Yet she wanted me there as well.

"You two were very close. One took care of the other," Tho said, standing by the hospital bed, watching me, showing friendliness and respect.

I just nodded. My growing feelings for her would have to stay with me.

Tho and the Da Nang Police had been assigned to ensure my security while in the hospital. I glanced past him and recognized one of Tho's airborne soldiers in the hallway, dressed in clean fatigues and armed with his rifle, glaring at the nurses until he looked into the room and at me. He smiled and gave me a polite bow, respecting a fellow comrade in arms. That boosted my morale. He had been the one who did my camouflage that early morning at the observation post. I smiled back. A doctor came in and told Tho to leave; I needed more rest. Before Tho left, he placed my cleaned baseball cap on my chest. "Agent Hieu insisted that you wear this at all times," he said. We stared at each other and then broke into a laugh.

As he departed, I pulled it to me and thought of Hieu before sleep grabbed me.

On the morning of the thirty-first, they released me from the hospital. Tho drove me to the Hoi An Resort to pack my stuff. I would catch a flight to Hanoi that afternoon by orders of Colonel Tin. The doctors had given permission for me to be released to travel back to Hanoi.

Tho waited in the hotel lobby while I walked through the beautiful gardens to my room, passing the pool that Hieu and I had enjoyed all those afternoons. When I walked into my room, I thought I could smell Hieu's delicate perfume lingering in the air. I missed her! She had already taken her stuff but left a note on the nightstand. In English, she wrote:

Dear John:

I must report to Hanoi, and as you know, I wished to have you return with me. But my duty and family called me back. This is not goodbye—you promised to celebrate Tet with my family, and I expect you. Thank you with all my heart for protecting me and taking care of me. I will call you to arrange the Tet celebration.

My deepest respect and as your friend, my love to you,

Your devoted partner,

Hieu (we are partners, are we not?)

I felt a twinge of pain. She would never know how I felt about her, or maybe she did, and she was doing the correct thing here, letting me drift away.

☙❧

On the way to the airport, I learned that Hieu took my .45 with her, making it easier for me to get through security and that it would be sent to Colonel Zang in the diplomatic pouch. Captain Tho returned both AK-47s to the national police in Da Nang. I had only my one duffel bag and the cleaned backpack, which Hieu had left with my CIA aluminum briefcase in it.

With time to kill before my afternoon flight, I turned to Captain Tho.

"Could we stop at the Cham Museum?"

Deep in thought he slowly nodded. "We can spare an hour."

"Thank you," I said. I hoped that Quan could still enlighten me about My Son and the gold.

Ten minutes later, we pulled into the museum's parking lot, and accompanied by Tho, I headed for the front door. In minutes I found Quan among his artifacts, updating some of the displays. I asked Tho to wait in the lobby entrance.

I smiled at a startled Quan and said, "Tôi biết bạn có thể nói tiếng anh." *I know you speak English.* I had prepped with my Vietnamese dictionary while in the hospital, contemplating this moment.

His frightened reaction confirmed it. He gave a bewildered look at Tho standing in the entrance way.

"I am not here to repeat anything you say or have you arrested. You will have to trust me. I promise. And just to ease your mind, I don't care about the misssing gold."

"Why do you . . . ?" he said. His confusion grew.

"OK, what if I start it off? You knew where the gold was hidden all along. And I am assuming you removed it years ago. All of your actions were a deception to divert us. Am I correct?"

We stood in a time warp, Quan nervously eyeing the lobby, where Tho examined some literature at the front desk.

"You tell no one?" Quan finally whispered.

"I promise."

"Yes, I knew gold was buried the night that I observed my father and other adults killed."

"So you came back later to remove the gold?" I said. I was too tired to get over involved, but I needed to know.

"Yes, years later in 1976, when I felt it would be safe. You must know that before my father was killed that terrible night, he and I had explored that hill. We had looked for ancient Montagnard artifacts and discovered several hidden entrances to the main cave. The same cave that was used to hide the bodies and gold."

"You used the hidden entrances to remove the gold?"

Quan nodded. His anxiety hadn't dissipated.

"What did you do with the gold?" I asked, certain I knew the answer.

"We shared with all the families of the village. All were told to hide and only use in small amounts as needed to live. Vietnamese are very . . . you say, frugal? Not showy." He pointed to the various stone statues near us. "With the gold were these statues. I retrieved for this museum. It is a work of love for me. Saving these items meant more than the gold."

"I see."

"The families deserved the gold." Quan, arms akimbo, leaned against a display table that held several stone Cham pots. "You now take back the gold—what is left—and punish us?"

"No, Quan. What you did is your decision. I don't care." I thought some more and then asked, "Did you influence Colonel Hung to contact Loan, warning him of possibly losing the gold?"

His startled look confirmed it. "Yes . . . " he said. "Several of us, the sons who survived, wanted revenge. We hoped that we could draw Colonel Loan back to Vietnam. To have him arrested and executed. Our way of life had been destroyed by his greed."

"One more question then. Hung didn't know you had removed the gold or where it was hidden in the first place?"

He shock his head. "No. By then he must know that gold had been taken by others."

"Thank you, Quan. No one will know what you told me, I promise. I wish you peace in the future and a happy Tet," I said and shook his hand.

He bowed, showing respect, but still wary. I walked out to catch the flight to Hanoi.

෨൪෪

At the drop-off by the airport entrance, Tho got out of the parked jeep, followed by the driver carrying my duffle bag. I carried the backpack in my right hand. In the terminal entrance, a young NCO hand saluted us and then gave Tho a large manila envelope and an attaché case. Tho gave my tickets to the NCO, who proceeded with the driver to check me and the luggage in at the counter. Captain Tho then handed me the bulky package and the attaché case.

"I took the liberty of retrieving Carolton's IDs and wallet from your backpack before we cleaned it. They are in the package with Ramsey's items," Tho said.

The packet held the wallets, money, and passports of two dead Americans: Ramsey and Carolton. The attaché case had belonged to Ramsey. Being out of it with my wound, I had forgotten Ramsey's final words about taking his files on Woodruff. I didn't feel eager to look inside, certainly not now.

Tho stood for a moment composing his words before he said, "It was an honor to have worked with you. I know if my father lived, he would honor you as well."

Slightly embarrassed, I thanked him, then saluted him, an army officer doing his duty for his country, proudly wearing the uniform. He mirrored my salute. The NCO returned and gave me my boarding pass.

"You have the entire row to yourself so that you can take care of your wounded shoulder," Tho said.

"Thank you, Captain Tho," I said.

"Goodbye, Captain Moore," Tho said. He smiled, looking at my head, and finally said, "Hieu would appreciate you wearing the cap."

He turned and walked to the exits followed by the NCO and driver, who both glanced back at me several times while talking to each other. I was proud to have known Tho and his soldiers. It saddened me that I would probably never see him again.

ঙ৹৩

Major Han met me at the Hanoi airport with his driver and car. As
we drove to the Nikko Hanoi Hotel, Han and I chatted in the back seat.
He complimented me on the success of the operation. I intentionally
placed all the praise back on him, his Agent Hieu, and of course Captain
Tho. Authority being crucial in Vietnam, I knew that Han had to be
acknowledged as Hieu's boss and a key part of the operation, giving
Hieu freedom to make decisions. He acted modest at the praise I piled
on him. I sensed that he no longer viewed me as the pushy American or
as a former enemy. Soon we arrived at the hotel, and as I exited the car,
I wished him a happy Tet Nguyen Dan. He smiled back at me, waving
from the back seat as the car pulled away.

In my room I listened to the voice mail message from Hieu: "John,
be ready tomorrow at 1000 hours. Suit is cleaned and hanging with
clean shirt and tie in closet. Shoes are polished also. Look for my driver
to bring you to celebrate Tet. Missed you, Hieu."

I forgot about leaving my suit and accessories at the hotel when I
left for Da Nang almost a month ago. Obviously Hieu did not. Again,
warm thoughts about her slipped into my weary mind.

I had hoped to skip the new year celebrations, Tet, and convince
someone to let me fly back to the US, but technically I still worked for
the Vietnamese, on loan from my government. I had killed three men
and it weighed on me, heavily, struggling with remorse, worrying how
this would impact me going forward.

I picked up my CIA Palm phone and dialed Woodruff. At 4:00
p.m. in Hanoi, Woodruff would be awakened at 4:00 a.m. in DC. I didn't
care; he had the easy part of this assignment. Besides, I now knew he
took my calls no matter what time, and I needed to find closure about
why I had been sent here. He also obviously needed something that I
alone could provide.

He finally answered, "John! Glad you're recovering from the
wound. You're some kind of hero. Maybe I will use you on future

missions. It seems a psychologist can do a field operation and succeed. Seriously, I'm proud of you—no words can say how I feel."

It all sounded like fluff. He wanted to talk through the situation and make me feel warm about my actions, avoiding the complete truth. I didn't ask him what to do with the IDs and wallets of the two dead Americans. I knew he would hedge on that anyway. It would be my decision, my burden now, and I would use the shredder in the hotel's business office to destroy all documents. Any cash would be donated to the hospitals in Hanoi to help children born with defects from Agent Orange contamination. It would be a fitting end to their lives.

Woodruff startled me with his directness. "Did Ramsey have any files?"

"Not that I know of. Certainly, after killing him, I needed to get medical aid for myself." I was surprised the lie came so easily.

Woodruff's pause worried me. Did he catch the untruth?

"OK. Just ensuring we have everything cleaned up. Again, great job, John."

"Thank you," I said, refraining from calling out his deviousness. I glanced at the attaché case on the hotel desk and pulled it me.

"Jim is up to speed also. Look, take a long vacation there. Of course, Tin and other key Vietnamese officials want you around for a while, so I have to honor their formal request. Just let me know when you can leave, and you'll have first-class return all the way to Charlotte. It's on the company—you deserve it."

"Thanks again. Tell Jim hi for me." I waited.

"OK, take care . . . "

"How is Sally?" I asked, not giving him an escape.

"OK. Aww . . . Why do you ask? I haven't talked to her since I gave her your lists of things for her do with your firm."

"No idea what she is doing?"

"No, say look, when you get back from Vietnam, talk to her. I don't think she likes us CIA guys."

It hurt. I helped destroy her life and any words from me could never make it right.

"Tell me again why I had to help catch Ramsey?" I said.

The pause seemed to last forever. "Well . . . John, he did try to kill you. He also orchestrated Reed's death."

I wanted to yell, to scream at him. Call him a damn liar. I believed Ramsey's dying words: He had nothing to do with Loan trying to kill me and mistakenly killing DuPee Catton instead, nor with Loan manipulating Reed's suicide.

I could hear Woodruff's breathing.

"I feel somewhat used," I said, avoiding the ugly confrontation that could ensue. After all, Ramsey could have lied to me as he lay dying. But I doubted that. Ramsey had sought death by my hands for redemption of his sins, his evil actions. His PTSD had conquered him in the end.

"Now, John, can you see the big picture? We got rid of two bad guys. You did it for the good of the US and our relations with Vietnam."

"For god and country, right?" I asked, egging him.

"Well, obviously that. You did a superb job for your country. You are a true patriot."

"You know, I could have gotten killed. You could've told me all the truth."

"Would you have gone if I did?" he said.

He had shown a chink in his facade. "To protect Sally . . . but what is the complete truth?" I pressed.

"John, get some rest. We'll talk when you return." The phone's silence took over. I didn't expect much more from him anyway. Maybe I would confront Woodruff on his turf after I returned to the States. But then doubt creeped in: *Or would I?*

I flipped Ramsey's attaché case open; the locks sounded gravelly from being in the dirt and mud of that clearing where I killed Ramsey. Strewn throughout its interior I found maps, checklists, and an airline ticket for return to Hong Kong. I ignored the handwritten notes detailing Ramsey's plans for this excursion. Finally in the bottom of the case I discovered a thick, light brown folder. The file tab imprinted simply, in all caps: WOODRUFF.

I paused. If I opened the file, I would know more than I probably wanted. I sat there staring at the brown folder. Woodruff obviously wanted this file, to protect himself. He did something that could destroy him, and Ramsey kept it for protection while in the States. But he was dead now. If I opened the file, I would know something dark about Woodruff, placing me in the middle of all this deceit. Woodruff didn't know for certain if I had the file. I returned the folder to the case, shut it, and put it on the floor by the desk. I needed time to think on this.

HANOI, FEBRUARY 1, 2003

February 1 and the first day of Tet found me waiting for my ride in the hotel lobby, dressed in my only but freshly dry-cleaned suit, the same one I'd worn from LAX to Hanoi a month ago. My tie and the cleaned and starched shirt completed my look. As I stood in the lobby, I tried to rationalize the last thirty days. I was used, and I wanted more answers to justify the three killings. Those killings cost me psychologically. Being close to death again did not differ much from my yearlong tour during the Vietnam War, but this time it had been very personal, and I hoped that I could cope mentally. Time would tell.

Because everyone celebrates their birthday during Tet, as opposed to on their actual birth date, I had bought gifts for Hieu, her husband, and their three boys: a gold chain with a Taoism pendant with the black-and-white, S-shaped design, representing the Yin and Yang that Hieu so fervently believed and loved; a bottle of Johnny Walker Black Label Whiskey for hubby, his favorite, as I had learned from dinner at their apartment; and plastic airplane model kits for each boy—one Vietnam Airlines jet, one Laotian Airlines jet, and one Cambodian Airlines jet. I figured the boys could pick and choose their own favorites or, as would probably be the case, they would fight over them, forcing Hieu to decide for them.

I recognized the black Mercedes sedan as it pulled up by the hotel doors, and I walked out toward it, its tinted glass not revealing any of the occupants. Hieu's driver got out and rushed to open the right-side back door. All smiles and politeness, as only Vietnamese seem to exude, he shut the door behind me. Climbing back into the driver's seat, he slowly pulled away from the hotel. I had hoped that Hieu would be in the car.

Hieu's apartment being only four blocks from the hotel meant a short ride. The driver parked the car and scurried to my door. As he held my door open, he asked, "You need me . . . show way?"

"No, thank you. I can find the apartment."

"I no stay. I go home now for Tet."

"OK then, my man, have a good Tet," I said as he closed my door and walked to the driver's side.

"Tet Nguyen Dan," he said.

"Yes, Tet Nguyen Dan," I said.

He accepted my meager spoken Vietnamese with a big grin, and I waved to him. Carrying my bag of presents, I entered the apartment building. Because I still was weak due to my wound, Hieu's fourth floor apartment meant that I had to take my time going up the stairs. The exercise felt good after days in the Da Nang hospital. But nevertheless, my shoulder hurt a little more when I reached her apartment door. Its complete healing would take time.

I heard many voices behind Hieu's apartment door as I knocked. Moments later, it swung open and there stood Hieu's husband. He grabbed my arms and pulled me inside. I winced as the tender muscles in my left arm reacted to the sudden pressure from his hands. He yelled to the crowd in the room and they stopped talking suddenly, all turning to face me.

"John, you are the first-footing and bring much dignity and honor to our family." He bowed and took my gift of Johnny Walker Black Label, gleefully showing the bottle to his relatives, who murmured their approvals. It seemed all the Vietnamese in the room moved toward

314

me, congregating around me, talking to me, touching my suit, bowing, and smiling. Some were toasting me with their wine, others with beer.

The volume grew boisterous as the laughter and happiness grew, overwhelming me. I had to move from the crowd in search of a quiet nook. A delicate touch on my right sleeve made me turn. Hieu stood next to me, smiling, balancing herself with a cane, her left leg in a cast. She looked stunning in her *ao dai*, an ivory white tunic and light blue pants. Her black hair was combed out to a bright sheen, cascading around her delicate, beautiful face. She reached up and pulled me down, placing a kiss on my cheek, intoxicating me with her delicate perfume. I blushed, worrying that my feelings for her would show. Quickly, I reached into my bag and gave her the wrapped box containing the gold chain. She laughed with delight and I got another kiss on my cheek. She told me she would open it later, whispering her thanks and leaning into me momentarily. I gave her the bag with the presents for her boys. "Please give these to your sons," I said. Taking the bag, she pulled my head down again to hear her above the noisy room.

"You should feel honored, John. Remember, I told you earlier that a first-footing is the first invited guest to the family's Tet celebration, and he or she must be honorable, successful, and professional. You now bring good fortune to my family. My husband is very proud having you here, as you can see from the attentiveness by all the relatives."

"Thanks for the honor."

"I wanted to say thank you again for protecting me," Hieu said, stifling a tear.

Ignoring her emotions, I said, "How are you feeling? Your leg . . ."

"Oh—I will be doing light work for weeks, but then my new job is special director to Colonel Tin. Very huge promotion, and I have my partner to thank." She squeezed my right arm. "Come with me for drinks. You will enjoy tonight, and do not worry; I will be near you. I do not want you to forget me." She laughed, winking at me.

I grinned as she dragged me along, holding the cane and my presents in her right hand, her left arm threaded through my right, squeezing me tightly. In seconds, her three boys confiscated their gifts, running to their rooms. She looked happy, and I was happy for her.

The enormous amount of food and alcohol sitting on the serving tables, kids shouting, and adults laughing and talking overwhelmed me as the day progressed into night. I finally found an empty chair to sit in. My wound ached, taking its toll on my body, and with the sticky rice wine, *ruou nep*, that Hieu's husband kept pouring into my glass, I became mildly dizzy. Hieu was a great hostess, and she worked the room, often swinging by, checking on me, a lively glint in her eyes that I took to mean for me alone. By midnight, many of the celebrators had departed to return again tomorrow and the following day, while some remained as houseguests in the crowded apartment.

Slight twinges of pain continued from my wound when Hieu sat down again to my right, avoiding my left side. "John, tomorrow Colonel Tin is expecting you at his home. I believe the president of our country will be there for a short visit. You must go at ten tomorrow. Tin will send a car to pick you up at the hotel. Here is my present to you." She gave me a wrapped, shirt-sized box.

"What is it?"

"Open it, but I am afraid it is too practical of a gift."

As I unwrapped it, I found two white, folded shirts in my size. "So that I can finish the last two days of Tet properly dressed?" I looked at her, appreciating that she watched over me.

"Yes. I take care of my partner, as he takes care of me."

I trusted her, but the empty feeling I'd had since talking to Woodruff forced me to be direct with her. "Hieu, I have to ask something about our completed task." I looked into her eyes.

She grinned. "What is it, John?"

"Do you know why Tin wanted me to pursue Ramsey and Loan?" I asked, still studying her mannerism.

"Colonel Tin told me you were an honorable man who agreed to help bring Loan and Ramsey to justice. That is correct, is it not?" she said.

I nodded. It would be better to not taint her view of the operation. We sat silently for a while, and then I said, "Hieu, it is late, and I need to take some more antibiotics and pain pills at the hotel room—I should go."

"Wait a moment." She stood up and hobbled to another room. Even temporarily handicapped, she walked gracefully, broadcasting her beauty, so delicate and sensuous.

In the center of the apartment, Hieu's husband teetered, slightly drunk, having indulged beyond rice wine and into the Black Label. His visiting relatives were parading around patting him on the back, building up his esteem.

Earlier, I'd heard from the various relatives the story of my saving Hieu, as told by her three sons. It seemed the boys found the real event a little mundane and in need of embellishment. They told everyone how I had pulled a wounded Hieu out of the Hummer while dodging a hail of bullets from a hundred Cambodian bandits who wanted to capture Hieu and sell her into slavery. It made me smile.

Suddenly, Hieu's husband stood in front of me and shook my hand. "I know I am happy . . . with drink . . . but I owe you . . . forever for saving my wife." Even though his drinking had claimed his common sense, his seriousness hit home. I noticed his misty eyes and felt a twinge of guilt for thinking of his wife as anything other than my working partner.

I stood up and bent down to him. "Hieu is a good partner. She protected me. You are a lucky man, and now I must go. Thank you for sharing Tet with an American."

He sniffed and then hugged me, emotion flowing from him. And just as quickly, he disappeared into a cloud of relatives happily shouting something. As I neared the door, Hieu intercepted me.

"Look at me." She pointed to the gold chain around her neck. "It is so beautiful, and you remembered my belief in Yin and Yang. Thank you, John. You know this represents us—the Yin and Yang complete us. Forever!"

I nodded, absorbing her perfume, saddened, feeling empty. Her dark black eyes bore into my soul—I understood now whose black eyes I saw in my dream so many weeks ago in Charlotte. I had been destined to meet Hieu!

Hieu's eyes continued to penetrate me. I couldn't explain my feelings, the déjà vu, but I hoped Hieu knew. She understood me, every inch of me, my flaws, my strengths. She had entered my life before I landed in Hanoi. I blinked back to the real world. "Hieu, I have to go . . . "

"Let me escort you."

"No, you have guests and should also rest your mending leg. But thank you, Hieu, for being my friend and my partner." She stretched up on her good leg and kissed my cheek.

"Good night, John. I will call you after your trip to Colonel Tin."

"Good night, Hieu. Tell your husband and boys goodbye for me." I walked out the door as she stood staring at my back until I disappeared down the stairs. Then I heard the door closing like a coffin lid.

The walk to the hotel was as the last time, quick and pleasant. At midnight, the Tet celebrations were still in full swing throughout Hanoi. I tried not to think about Hieu romantically; it would be the wrong course for both of us. When I entered my room, I looked at it with disdain. Alone again in this world. Three years ago, my wife died, leaving a despondent man who couldn't get it together. I didn't know if I could suffer the loneliness and the void from Katy's death any longer. The emotional roller-coaster ride with Sally left me empty as well. Death joined me as my true companion.

My mysterious Hieu filled me spiritually with a completeness that I had known only once before, with my wife Katy. Hieu made me feel alive again. We had developed an intuitive and intimate bond unlike any other since my wife died. I sat down on the bed, rubbed my eyes, and stared at the wall. Hours passed before I undressed and fell asleep.

OUTSIDE HANOI, FEBRUARY 2, 2003

I walked through Colonel Tin's doorway, held wide open by Tin himself, who shook my right hand while I absorbed the hundreds of eyes staring at me from the doorway to the living room area.

"I have many relatives and special guests, John, as you can see. Please, I wish to talk to you in private before I introduce you. Come, please."

I followed him as many of his guests bowed to him and me on our way to his private office where I had met him a month ago, accompanied by Hieu.

"Please sit." He directed me to a seat opposite the desk chair that he eased himself into. Despite his age, his eyes exuded vibrancy and life, full of historical implications for his country. Ho Chi Minh succeeded because of such believers. His field generals took the war to the greatest powers in the world and won. I remember reading that when diplomatic relations were re-established in the 1990s, a US Army colonel sitting with his Vietnamese counterpart stated that the NVA never beat the Americans in any battle during the war. "True," said the Vietnamese officer, "but we won the war."

"How is your shoulder, John?" Tin asked, sincerely studying my left side.

"It is healing, Colonel Tin."

"Good—very good. We were very worried for you." He paused and then said, "I was hoping that our president would be here, but he is delayed. He wished to personally thank you for your honorable performance."

I nodded.

"So Ramsey is dead by your hand. As well as this other American, the Texan. There will be no record of them?"

"No. They disappeared into the Southeast Asia jungles, as did the Cambodian I killed." A dark shadow descended on my mood like a monsoon cloud. I felt Ramsey's death had some other meaning.

"Good. I am avenged with Ramsey's death. I know Colonel Zang breathes easier." He paused and probably saw my concerned look. "You have a question, yes?"

"I don't wish to be unkind, but I feel there is something missing about Ramsey. Loan's capture or death for war crimes as a Vietnamese makes sense. But why not let the US prosecute Ramsey, an American citizen, in legal channels? Why did you lure Ramsey back to Nam? I don't believe that capturing Ramsey represented your obligation to the CIA to get Loan here. You undoubtedly played the CIA, acting as if Ramsey would be your payment to get Loan."

"You are shrewd, John. Forgive me for my deceit. Old oriental habits are difficult to break, I am afraid. It is about face here in the Orient."

"And revenge." I sat and waited. I felt like a pawn piece used by the chess master.

Tin was visibly shaken. "You see, Ramsey killed many noncombatants, but he also killed my mother in Saigon when trying to capture me." He stopped, and I saw the sadness pool in his eyes. He turned and looked out the window. "We used you, I regret, for my personal revenge. As in your culture, an eye for an eye."

I stared at the brutal truth. It all made sense now. Luring Colonel Loan to return for the uncertain hidden gold also would bring Ramsey. The Vietnamese had no doubt that they could capture or kill Loan anytime. But getting Ramsey, a US citizen, would be very difficult. They could not assassinate him in the States nor capture him alive in Vietnam because their treaty with the US required rule of law, and any charges against Americans would need the US legal system. The Vietnamese would not endanger the trade agreements or the financial aid. Colonel Tin's solution had to be me. Get Ramsey to Vietnam and use me to be judge, jury, and executioner. They got a double win when Ramsey, in saving my life, killed Loan. As for the American hired hand that I killed in self-defense, well that could be viewed as fallout, and he too had been buried in the Vietnamese jungles. Both Americans were gone forever, and I couldn't tell anyone without implicating myself in a convoluted international intrigue.

What angered me the most was the duplicity from CIA Agent Woodruff, a fellow American. Still, I had been used by both the CIA and the Socialist Republic of Vietnam.

"John, please do not harbor ill will toward me or my country. These debts had to be paid without harming our new relation with the US."

I continued to stare at Tin, not knowing what to say.

Tin continued as if nothing had happened: "Colonel Zang wishes again to convey his deepest respect and his thanks. We can never repay you for your bravery. You are an honorable man, like our revered legendary warrior Tran Hung Dao, who helped defeat the invading Mongols by unifying the Vietnamese. What you did these last few days helped strengthen our new government and solve the war deaths of the hundred Vietnamese from the village of Giang."

"Colonel Tin, I—"

"Please humor an old man. I am steeped in the ancient history of the Vietnamese and find many parallels with modern history and wars. You must understand that four million Vietnamese civilians died in the American Indochina War. Such sorrow follows many generations to come. And Captain Tho and Agent Hieu are descendants of brave NVA soldiers, who are dead now."

A young Vietnamese woman came into the room carrying a tray with cups and a pot of hot tea, its herbal fragrance permeating Tin's office. After her words with Tin, she departed with a polite bow and a smile for me, eyeing the American so honored by her grandfather.

"I talk too much of history and death. How did the assignment work with Hieu as your partner?"

"Agent Hieu was remarkable. I could not have asked for a better partner—intelligent, brave, and professional. The success of the mission is due to her and to Captain Tho. You planned well."

"Such loyalty and humility, John. I am impressed. I found most Americans in the war maybe too arrogant, as if they were on a sacred crusade and could do no wrong. You are refreshing to talk to." He took the teapot and poured for both of us.

"Wars are often fought for the wrong reasons, and the people are often manipulated by their leaders with religious and ideological fantasies," he said, taking a sip of tea. "You may not know, but I personally selected Hieu once I read your dossier."

My face must have shown surprise.

"Yes, John, when I first met you on that helicopter as a prisoner of war, I knew by your actions to save Zang and me from Ramsey that you were an honest man, a noble warrior. Ramsey told me before we boarded the helicopter that he was responsible for the death of my mother, almost gleefully, trying to break me down for interrogation. I swore at that moment to avenge her with his death. My war experience, with so many of my soldiers killed, devastated me. I became severely depressed. After the war ended, a friend, a Buddhist, talked me into going to the temple at Da Lat. The months there saved my soul, but I could no longer kill. My plan to use you to avenge my mother's death came to me at that time."

I sat there stunned, hoping to better understand. Had fate drawn us together?

"Oh, it is out of respect for you that I gave you such a heavy burden. Anyway, when I knew you had accepted my request to come to help us, I needed to assign an agent to you who would complement you mentally and spiritually—with the Yin and Yang that Hieu believes. You two were ideal for this operation. In fact, I feel that you two were destined to be partners in this mission. When I heard how you carried her wounded body to protect her from Loan and Ramsey, I was proud of you, as if you were one of my own sons. And I will say it validated my decision to request you."

I looked at the old man, his convictions immersed in oriental beliefs.

"But she is married?" Tin added.

"Yes, and I respect her marriage."

Tin looked at me. His silence expressed his understanding. Then he said, "And understand that Hieu knew nothing of my personal revenge against Ramsey or about using you for the killing. I knew that Hieu would not hesitate to kill Ramsey if needed."

"Your plan worked, but I don't understand how it did," I said. "There were so many variables that had to come together. CIA Director Woodruff obviously worked with you to convince me to come to Vietnam. But once here in Nam—well, so many things had to fall into place. And what made you think I would kill again?"

"John, you forget the most important belief I have: Taoism and its Yin and Yang of life, of events."

"Yes . . ." I paused.

"Before I forget, I wish for you to stay longer to relax and enjoy the beauty of this land before we release you of your duty." He smiled, knowing his request had been honored by Woodruff. "You need the rest, and I can ensure you, you will be given the highest courtesy at the place I have selected for you. There are already stories spreading about the avenging American with his Vietnamese woman partner." He gave me a sad look.

"I will stay as you wish, but hopefully not too long, as I need to return to my normal life."

Tin pulled a business card from the top of his desk. "Please, if you need something, call me. I am indebted to you, forever. I hope you will consider me a friend and not one who used you. You will see me differently when you stay a few months at the special area I have reserved. It will make you whole again. And to answer the question why I thought you could kill again: John, you are controlled by demons of war, a harsh legacy for you and me. We will go to our graves bearing those scars."

"Legacy?" I asked.

"Aw, you don't know, do you? I knew your father, a former colonel in the French Foreign Legion."

I sat up, placing my cup of tea on the table.

"I worked for him, then Captain Roger Mongin, as his administrator when he was assigned to French HQ in Saigon in 1950. He fought against me eventually when I joined Ho Chi Minh. We met as combatants at Dien Ben Phu, where the French were defeated in 1954. He was the last one to survive from his company on a lonely hilltop. He was badly wounded, and I ensured his safety and medical treatment on his trip to the POW camps."

He eyed me, enjoying my shock. Turning around to a small bookcase behind him, he pulled out a book, Jacques de Mont's *La Mort de Indochina Française*.

He pulled out a letter from the inside cover.

"Do you read French?" he asked.

"Very poorly," I said.

"Then with your permission, let me read something to you." He unfolded the stationary and began:

December 1, 1976

Dear Colonel Tin,

Again, I thank you for saving my life at the battle of Dien Ben Phu. My months in the POW camp were harsh, but I survived in part due to your concern over me. I send the enclosed book about the French Indochina War and my participation, written by reporter Jacques de Mont. The author stressed to me more than once that he met my son in Saigon, a young US Army captain, in 1969. I denied it for all these years until I saw him in my town, Troyes, earlier this year.

I do not want to die until I tell someone I trust—you, my friend. From de Mont's information, my illegitimate son's name is Captain John Moore. He came looking for me at my favorite café and was about to cross the street to introduce himself. I waited and saluted him, but he turned and walked out of my life. I deserved that...

"Thus, you see you and I are connected through your father. That is why I mentioned our common legacies with Vietnam." Tin smiled.

"You do know he abandoned my mother after World War II?"

"Yes. Roger had terrible issues with women, I am afraid. But I thought you should know that you coming to Vietnam was not a random event. The history, the legacy, fit well with my plan. I believe it was destined. By the way you look like him, especially back then on the helicopter, when you saved us. That is why I stared so hard at you; I thought Roger Mongin had returned to the war."

I said nothing. I had already dealt with the pain of being abandoned by Mongin, my father that I never knew.

"You and I are soldiers who have killed, and you could do so again. Believe me. That is why I am sending you to this resort. You will understand why afterward. For me, I have found redemption through you and my monk. I can die in peace. It is your turn to redeem your soul, to find peace." He stood up, signaling the end of our meeting.

I shook his offered hand. *My biological French father fought Tin and his comrades in the French Indochina War. I too ended up here, fighting the same enemy in the American Indochina War many years later. A legacy of war for all of us,* I thought.

Forgetting my father, I asked, "Did Colonel Hung get his freedom?"

"Yes, but the doctors feel he has only months to live due to cancer spreading so rapidly."

Saddened, I couldn't say anything. *How death brings us together.*

Without missing a beat, he said, "Finally, for Agent Hieu, she will be rewarded by the state with her promotion. Now come and meet my relatives and guests—many have already heard much about the avenging American. Maybe you will become part of the Vietnamese folklore?" He smiled. "We Vietnamese are very pragmatic about our religion and heroes. Certainly, we can have an American in our legends, don't you think?"

Grasping to understand, I asked, "Colonel Hung didn't know where the gold was hidden?"

"No. But, John, he knew about the killing of villagers. And he knew he would share in the gold with Loan and Ramsey. Just because he had no knowledge of where any gold had been hidden does not excuse him from his crimes. But I honored his request for freedom because he did help me get Ramsey and Loan back here. And he shrewdly asked for you. That's why I decided to ultimately free him. You see, I respect you a great deal, more than you can imagine."

Surprised, I looked at him.

"And furthermore, I care little about the gold. We all assumed it had been recovered by other ARVNs years ago. The knowledge of the gold was used to lure all these criminals to be punished. Yes, I used you, John—an American to execute another American. My soul is cleansed because of you. We did the correct thing. You will learn more from the place I am sending you. Just keep your mind open when you are there. Then you will know firsthand why I had to use you to kill Ramsey, to get revenge for my mother."

I slightly bowed to him, this Vietnamese man who shrewdly avenged his mother's death through me. A saddened Colonel Tin turned, and I followed him out of his office into the crowed living room; a semi-circle of people had formed in front of the office door. Tin started the clapping as he turned to me, smiling now with pride, one ex-warrior to another. Both of us had finally achieved a little peace; an exorcism of our past war demons and the recent enemies who chose to return to this beautiful land in an attempt to violate it, to rape it, only to be flung back and killed like the Mongols of old by Colonel Tin's favorite ancient warrior, the legendary Tran Hung Dao. I bowed slightly to the applause with mixed emotions. I could not change recent events. Instead, I focused on Hieu, thankful for knowing her.

NOI BAI AIRPORT, MAY 1, 2003

I stood in the departure lounge at the Hanoi airport, waiting for my return flight to the States after many relaxing and therapeutic days at the mountain resort of Da Lat, courtesy of the Socialist Republic of Vietnam. The former French hill station, situated at five thousand feet elevation in the Central Highlands, had served me well: I needed the trip to fully recover from the gunshot wound and to cleanse my mind of killing three men. I must have seen every pagoda and temple in the area trying to understand the mystery of life in general and the mystery of my life in particular. I befriended one of the Buddhist monks, the same one Tin had mentioned, and we spent a part of every day together in his temple, meditating and discussing my emotional pain. Like a psychologist, he provided me with necessary therapy. I felt better about myself even as I struggled with inner confusion about why I had been dealt this hand in this country and in my life, both during the war and now, thirty years later. I kept thinking about Hieu and her Yin and Yang. She became a part of me as Vietnam had; both were mysterious entities that would linger with me forever.

On our last day together, the monk told me how Colonel Tin had been here many years ago to recover from killing in the war. He knew that Tin had taken the enlightened path and would never harm anyone else again. He gave me a written note in a sealed envelope from

Tin and instructed me to read it only at the airport upon my departure for the US.

I now pulled it out of my suit pocket, tore open the envelope, unfolded the note, and read:

Dear John,

Again forgive me, John, for using you to avenge the death of my mother. I took personal vows with the same monk you have been learning from these last few months. Those vows mean that I can never harm anyone again. I am better for it, but you see, I passed my awful burden on to you. You killed for me, but I believe you were destined from the day we were thrown together on that helicopter to help me. It is the Yin and Yang of life. This was meant to be, and I thank you for helping an old man. I now hope I helped you through my Buddhist monk friend to regain your sanity and enlightenment. You and I paid dearly for serving our countries. It is time to move on. You have cleansed the Earth of the evil related to you and me. Please move forward to bring peace and harmony to your life. I will always be indebted to you for doing what I had sworn to never do again—to kill. And you too will follow the same path. That, I believe, is both our destinies, and the legacy of our wars.

Your friend,

Tin

I folded the note back in its envelope and nodded, glancing around the room. No one paid any attention.

On that last day with the monk, I gave him Ramsey's locked briefcase, containing only the folder, which I still hadn't read. He swore to hide it and safeguard it. I didn't know if I ever would retrieve the file and read it, but I'd had enough of intrigue and wanted some normalcy in my life. Deep down, my mistrust in Woodruff drove me to this: I knew he would have US custom agents thoroughly search every item of my duffle bag and my CIA case. Whatever that folder had on him would be safely stored and hidden from him in Vietnam.

My flight's early boarding announcement for first class came over the lounge speaker. I finished the last of my Perrier and had just picked up my case, no longer stored in the backpack that I had returned to the Vietnamese government, when her voice startled me.

"John, you leave without saying goodbye?" Hieu stood in her *ao dai,* both tunic and pants matching in light blue, her favorite colors—mine as well. Her broken leg had healed, and she no longer needed her cane. She beamed radiantly. The gold chain with the Taoism pendant hung around her neck, brightly reflecting in the room's fluorescent lights. She had combed her hair out, instinctively knowing how I liked that look.

Hieu had telephoned me often while I rested in Da Lat. We continued to bond through words, never stepping over to the romantic side. I think we both recognized our deep need for each other, and her calls were part of that—the concern she had for my emotional health and my need for her.

"I . . . wanted to say goodbye, but I think you know. . . " I said, lost for words.

"I know. I will always think of you." She forced a smile. She reached into her purse and gave me a little jewelry box.

I flipped the lid open; inside was a man's silver money clip with the circular Taoism emblem. "Hieu . . . thank you." I paused, looking at her, then said what came from my heart, "We do complement each other—a true harmony of life."

She smiled. "I am your Yin, and you are my Yang. Maybe we will meet in another life." Hesitating, Hieu wanted to say something. Instead, she surged toward me and kissed my cheek, then turned and walked away, her beauty accenting the room. When she reached the security door, she turned and smiled at me, a radiating smile that belonged to me alone. Her moist eyes reflected the harsh light of the room. She stepped through the doorway, shutting it behind her. Gone!

Frozen like a statue, staring at the closed door, I stood, my own eyes misting. Hieu represented the good of Vietnam that ultimately saved me mentally, that pulled me from the abyss that my depression had hurled me into. Her honesty, her beauty, and her caring merged into a goddess for me. I would eternally think of her, metaphysically, and what could have been, the Yin and Yang of Taoism, ultimately reflecting on how she had brought back my humanity, lost all those years in the Vietnam War and compounded by my wife's death.

I turned and moved toward the departing gate, following the attendant's voice dictating the boarding process over the intercom. *Goodbye, Hieu!*